SUDDENLY

Also by Bonnie Burnard

A Good House
Casino & Other Stories
Women of Influence

SUDDENLY

BONNIE BURNARD

virago

VIRAGO

First published in Great Britain as a paperback original in 2010 by Virago Press

A CIP catalogue record for this book is available from the British Library.

ISBN 978-1-84408-640-5

Printed and bound in Great Britain by
Clays Ltd, St Ives plc

Papers used by Virago are natural, renewable and recyclable products sourced from well-managed forests and certified in accordance with the rules of the Forest Stewardship Council.

FSC
Mixed Sources
Product group from well-managed forests and other controlled sources
www.fsc.org Cert no. SGS-COC-004081
© 1996 Forest Stewardship Council

Virago Press
An imprint of
Little, Brown Book Group
100 Victoria Embankment
London EC4Y 0DY

An Hachette UK Company
www.hachette.co.uk

www.virago.co.uk

For Friends
Here and there, now and then.

2004

The Sanctuary

It's been here, in this bedroom, with Jack and without him, that she has found her only privacy. But now she's surrounded, day and night, by care. Her son Paul and his wife Kelly come to her here, as do her brother Richard and his wife, her friend Colleen. And their friend Jude comes too, and sometimes even her husband, Gus. They are all staying close, to help her. And to help Jack. A week ago she heard them at the bottom of the stairs, drawing up their workable schedule. Which is exactly what she would have done. Like many grown children Michael and Jan and April are all at a distance now, but they have been coming home when they can, and when Jack calls to tell them to come.

And there are all the variously interested parties, old neighbours and acquaintances, women from her fundraising committees, who send their selected cards and short letters and e-mails, who make their phone calls and leave their hesitant messages. Although she does like the idea of people giving her a thought and is thankful for their trouble, because where would she be without it, she often catches herself wondering if they might be more disciplined. Right from the start, every time she saw that look and heard, I can imagine, she wanted to say, Oh, no. You can only imagine. *Only.* Precision mattering more now, with all this waiting. With time this empty. Sometimes she wants to tell Jack to just cut to the chase, to be done with it, to set up his own recorded message advising people that, yes, it is definitely on its way. But thanks.

Since the move home from the hospital and then the adjustment to more potent pain management, because pain can move like water, it can find a path, she has been working hard to live with whatever comes her way. One of the things she's living with is this stainless steel bed, which is high off the floor so she can be helped more easily, so the nurses won't strain their backs lifting her, easing her from one position to another or getting her up to walk the hall or to sit for a while in the chair. Although it would be a significant drop to the floor, she argues every day against the locking side rails and sometimes, though not through the night, and not now, they let her win. The bed also has a crank for the readjustment of dead weight, to relieve her hips or her bum or her back.

The one good thing about the bed is that it offers a new perspective through the big front window. Now she can see not just her neighbours' chimneys and their sharply pitched, snowy rooftops but their locked, heavy front doors and their lit-up living room windows, one with its drapes drawn every night sharp at nine, without fail. Drapes on a timer? More likely a wife on a timer, or a husband.

And in the darkest night, having been set up in this different part of the bedroom, having had her sightline altered, she can see the city's stolid black light standard out on the boulevard, with its cone of light. At night the falling snow is backlit, theatrical, a show against the dark, and the branches of the big front yard maple, heavy with a crust of ice, catch some of the light. Before, lying in the marriage bed, she could see only the glow the standard threw. And never the stars beyond it.

Sometimes, waiting for the discomfort to break down into its smaller parts, she leaves the street and the rooftops and the pulled drapes behind and like some big-winged bird with the head of a woman, her head, she flies around the city. She climbs high on the

December wind and with her bird's-eye view she tracks the city's old grid of streets. She can go south to the once-imposing downtown or she can bank and drift over to the other, unknown side of the city, where she has never lived. She can fly above the earliest and now very modest suburbs, where the burst of post-war prosperity first established itself and where she and Jack lived for a few years with their first, terrifying mortgage. Or out to the malls that almost killed the downtown and beyond them to the newest suburbs, which she and Jack agree are evidence of something far beyond prosperity. And then out to the big-box American stores, each of them, by their thousands, identical in every city on the continent. Like churches. And here and there across the city, infill it's called, the nests of condos built for forward-thinking older couples, not unlike themselves, who, given the cost of heat and the headache of upkeep, think they might take their equity and travel. Get away. Or help their kids.

Along with the locking bed rails and the discomfort and the distracting backlit drama of falling snow, another thing she's been living with is a near pleasurable sadness. Depression's better sister. Although the sadness does have its sweet contradiction now, which is a near-greedy anticipation of decency, of generosity. She watches for these gifts, keeps track of them. Lives them again later, on rewind, when she's alone. Yesterday she told Colleen and Jude that her dying has changed people more than anything else she can think of, and she watched their fixed smiles as it dawned on them that this is what she wants. She wants them to keep up with her. Although just how, she's not prepared to say.

But she has also been living with the most nonchalant stupidity. Such as a Calgary cousin's hope, expressed in green ink on an already iffy greeting card, that she might go quickly. Go? Jack asked, letting the card drop from his hands to the floor. Such as a devout and not very close neighbour's confidential singsong at her bedside about the life to come, the detailed and appealing description of paradise, as if it were a destination the woman could recommend, a city she'd meandered through on a spring tour, like St. Petersburg, or Bath.

And there was that supportive friend of a friend who tagged along when she was still on the couch downstairs, who surely had been forewarned that it was no Atkins diet. But, to be fair, that was when her body had briefly realized its old ideal weight, the flatter stomach, the thinner thighs, the leaner, sharper face. That previous, better look. And she was still wearing the lipstick and blush and mascara and shadow that Colleen brought to her on a tray. So the tagalong visitor had complimented her, extravagantly. You look terrific, he said. But so what. Maybe, for that afternoon, he was right.

Now she is both thin and puffy. Looking nothing like herself. The word for this is *wasting.* Or *slipping.* Or *failing.* Any and all of them correct.

Four years ago, that late August when they put a name to the first of her hard little bastard bullets, she'd grown old in three days. She and Jack had invited Paul's three boys out for a weekend at the cottage and even knowing what she believed she knew, she had not wanted to cancel, to disappoint her young grandsons. But then on the Sunday afternoon she'd sent Jack back to the city with them, insisting. Convincing herself that he would be fine driving into London with his car full. He'd never done this with their own kids because he was a different man then, an eager, preoccupied young accountant, but women did it routinely, even before seat belts. And anyway the kids had been so deliriously pooped, so played out, they would have been asleep by Parkhill, every blessed one of them. Zonked.

She'd called Alice's office on the sly and her appointment was booked for Thursday afternoon. So she'd asked Jack please to come back for her Thursday morning, repeating herself, Thursday morning, not Wednesday night. She had cut these days and nights out deliberately and she'd watched Jack wonder what she wanted from them, but he didn't ask. She knew the drill. Alice would be strict. A new mammogram, a needle biopsy, which sounded god awful but, according to Jude, who had been through it, required only that she stay absolutely still, as for a portrait, which she could do. Then maybe an ultrasound and no discomfort there either, then waiting, and maybe surgery, maybe the scooping out of breast tissue and lymph nodes, and after the surgery the thick grey drainage tube that Jude had wanted to show her, that emerged not through some natural orifice but through a hole in the flesh, like a parasite on a lake trout. Then more waiting and maybe radiation, and, if it had to come, as it did, chemo. And, finally, the new pill, a different new pill. One that gave you not your defence against pregnancy but a chance to live, with, guess what, mood swings.

You didn't have to be the friend of someone who'd had it. Like many women, she had paid attention to the news reports and magazine pieces and to all the documentaries about the prevalence, about the treatments and drugs. The progress. Jack would never sit still for any of the documentaries. When he was going through his own business with his heart, with his compromised arteries, his approach had been determined in the extreme, but limited. And after his surgery, believing the threat to be behind him, he didn't even like to hear the word health. Standing beside Jude's hospital bed after her episode, standing tall as a prime example of survival, Jack had told her, "You are going to be better than new. Trust me."

And he'd been right. Jude was fine. And is still. Jude had survived the invasion because her body fought it.

And what had she done to help Jude? Had she said the right words in the right way, at some right time? No, she had not. And had her tongue-tied, graceless attempts excused her, so that nothing really needed to be said? No, they had not.

Jack would not be leaving her, she'd known that. Still, how much ruin could a man be expected to embrace? A tenderness? A scar? An amputation? And if he couldn't be tempted by disfigured flesh, how were you supposed to get by without the friendly release of middle-aged lust? The occasionally robust, late-night throws of it, as if in remembrance, and just as desired, its uneventful, Sunday morning peace.

After Jack had left with the boys she'd decided to take her tartan blanket and a mystery novel and a glass of Scotch down to the beach. The shallow shoreline waves were down to almost nothing, a thin sheen on the sand, and taking a long drink, she reached up under her frayed red sweatshirt for her breast. The unrestrained, summer free breast was sweaty and warm. In just those few days her fingers had become practised instruments. They pushed deep. Dug in. "Come to me," she coaxed. "You little black hearted misery." The sun was inching down to the far edge of the lake. She dropped flat on the blanket. Lying flat allowed the legitimate flesh of her breasts to sink into her body, to expose the small, solid core. The hard little bastard bullet had not yet been touched by any other hand and it had not yet been given any official name. She sat up again. Staying upright gave her more perfect flesh a chance to surround the thing, to overcome it, suffocate it, bury it.

She wondered about the mammogram, if an invaded breast might resist flattened inspection. For years she had followed the advice of the technician who recommended a Tylenol beforehand, or two, one for each, to soften the quick but brutal annual pinch, but she knew that the next session could be, as Jude described it, a completely new experience. She wondered too if squashing it like that, or even touching it, finding it over again and over again and worrying it with her fingers might cause some cocky, minuscule bit to break off and float away, to go looking for a more secluded home in her lung or her liver or her bones.

Shit, she'd thought. And said, too loudly. Oh, buckets of shit.

What she needed was a swim. A good long swim.

She stood up dizzy and started to climb the low grassy dunes to the cottage. They'd bought the cottage when the kids were small, when such places were affordable. It's white frame, with all the original pine inside, and wide plank floors and an old sofa and big, miscellaneous easy chairs, and it's mostly wide open, with the kitchen and the bathroom and the bedroom at the back. Jack had hired one of Gus's construction guys to rebuild the staircase up to the kids' loft because it had got wobbly, and there's a new screened porch at the front, with the deck coming out from that. And high on the front gable the name the place was given when it was built, in the forties, ThistleDoMe. The letters of the name, which are big enough to be seen from a boat not too far out on the lake, are always painted black.

Halfway up the dunes she remembered the novel and her empty glass and went back down for them scolding herself, annoyed at the forgetfulness. Only fifty-five and forgetfulness stumbling around in her brain like some drunk who wants to stay the night.

She stripped standing on the rag mat at the foot of the bed and pulled on her black bathing suit, which would have been still clammy from her afternoon swim with the grandkids. The last bathing suit she'd had that wasn't black, a dark red and the last two piece, she'd bought but didn't wear in Mexico. She had more or less stopped swimming in the daytime by then because her skin had become not just mottled but noticeably and delicately thinner, and looser, as though, if she did live long enough, it might simply fall away one morning, a second caul. Although somewhat shifted, her measurements, the numbers that had determined her worth as a young woman, had stayed close to what her mother called normal-so-forget-it when she was a compliment-starved girl. But such numbers had long since lost most of their power, or they had new significance. As markers for health, for life expectancy. She pulled the sweatshirt back on and grabbed a towel, stopping on her way through the kitchen to fill her glass.

Down on the beach again she bent to set the glass on the blanket, tossed off the sweatshirt and walked across the warmed sand toward the water as she had since she was a young competitive swimmer, with the towel slung round her neck like an athlete's towel. The thin waves breaking on the sand refreshed and consoled her, which was their job. Although the morning's castles had not been obliterated by the waves' action on the sand, they had been breached and this certainly would have caused heartbreak if the boys had stayed to see it. The blue red sun had inched closer to the water. Blue red at night, sailors' delight. So no warning needed.

She dropped her towel on the last dry sand. The Warren teenagers from two cottages down were diving off their raft and she assumed they could see her walking in. If she went under, which was not probable, she hoped that one of them might take the trouble to pause from his horseplay to notice.

Lining up her approach with the sun's reflection, which had laid itself down in a broad, fiery path across the easy rolling surface of the lake, water like that always for her a large and deceptively relaxed muscle, she wondered why she had never once shopped for the colour of a summer evening sun, the one colour she likes more than any other. She has picked sweaters trying to catch the colour of a sedum from her fall garden, chosen shoes to match a boulder. Why has she never looked for the sun low on the water?

The clean chill of the lake bolted up through her legs and she reached down to cup the cold water, to splash her arms and shoulders. She tried again. She spoke again to her black hearted misery. "You and I are going down under this water," she told it. "It will feel shockingly cold and you won't like it. You will discover that I do a lot of things you won't like."

She swam out past the third sandbar and then parallel to the shoreline away from the Warrens' raft and then back and in again to the shallower depth, where she could get her footing and catch her breath. Then she bounced up and off the smooth ridges of the lake bottom and dove straight down to stand on her hands, as she had that afternoon to entertain the boys. It was her specialty. She was the expert Grandmother who could stand on her hands in the lake, who could hold her legs dead straight above the water with her calves tight together and her painted toenails pointed skyward while everyone shouted and shrieked and counted to ten. And that wasn't all she could do. On a dreary, rainy morning she could find an invisible needle and a length of invisible thread and, one by one, sew her fingers together while children clung to her, their wide eyes hypnotized by her courage, excited by all that imagined pain. And then they could laugh at her, knowing.

She came up out of the handstand to float for a few peaceful minutes on her back, the loud raft horseplay deadened to watery silence and the lake a softly lapping ring around her face. Her exposed skin was cold because the sun was going fast, and her arm was sore, but then she'd been carrying heavy things, hadn't she? Two year old Jackson, because he liked to run away, to be chased. And the cooler packed with boy food, the hotdogs and ketchup and peanut butter and jelly.

Standing and turning to come in, pushing to shore against the strength of the water, she believed she was content to be alone. She believed she had been right to make Jack leave her behind, that it was a reasonable thing to do under the circumstances.

And now no more swimming. Not in water. She has had no right to complain, of course, because Richard got her a friend of his, the best surgeon in the city, and the thing was pounced on and cut out fast, like a scoop of custard. As she waited in the chilled operating room for the anaesthetist to show up to put her under, the surgeon, who was an old hand, covered her with a heated flannel sheet and held her shaking arm. A good time to be alive, she thought, liking his grip. Then, at her follow-up appointment, after she and Jack were reminded that nothing is certain, they were told that the lymph nodes seemed to be uninvolved, and that the margins appeared to be clean. Margin being,

Richard explained, the name they give to the place where healthy tissue takes a stand. And after the round-table team meeting where all of her professionals together determined her optimum treatment, and how glad she was to discover that she had herself a team, her skin had knit into that narrow, rubbery scar, very much like Jude's own companionable scar, and she was signed up for radiation.

To prepare her for radiation, a technician with calipers marked her with four small, permanent tattoos, the four corners like the guiding crosshairs on the scope of a gun, or like stars hanging high in a sky watching over a ship. The tattoos were the coordinates for the younger technicians down another hall, who laid her out beneath their monster machine and lined her up with beams of laser light to aim the rays down through the wall of her chest. To kill off everything, good and bad, that thought it might like to reproduce itself there. Always leaving the room, politely excusing themselves before they threw the switch, before the buzz, the hum.

Then after the healing flesh was thoroughly cooked there came a soviet plan, a five-year plan, a daily dose of tamoxifen, the estrogen killer. And curled in bed with Jack curled warm behind her, running his finger along the narrow ridge of her sewn-up skin and both of them exhausted with relief, she decided to sink her trust in modern medicine. Jude was holding steady, Jude was strong again, so why not her?

For a while, to someone not in the know, her breasts under a sweatshirt still looked more or less authentic. Certainly they had never been anything to write home about, but she had reason to admire and enjoy them. And because they'd been relatively modest breasts, they had held their own against middle-aged gravity longer than others she'd noticed. But now they are gone and she misses them, wherever they are. Every woman has, or should have, some near-perfect thing. Colleen has her perfect legs, which, even veiny, are still something to envy, to bitch about, to want for yourself. And Jude has her bank of barely manageable sweater-girl breasts, riding lower to the ground now and with that scar she insisted they see, but at least a reminder.

Her hair is back now, for good. The same faded colour, nearly, but undeniably different hair. "Awful hair," she tells the room, reaching up to pull hard, to check that it stays rooted.

She could reach to wake Jack, of course, to complain about her hair. But she doesn't.

Later, Colleen and Jude will come for lunch again and then one of her travelling health care workers will arrive with another injection for the pain. Or as some of them like to call it, the discomfort. Most of the nurses are less formal now than old nurses, and they are often casually kind, which is sometimes all right. Nevertheless there are days when she longs for that colder, lost authority, when she would be grateful for a more disengaged, practised personality, for the quick and honest hands of a take-charge woman in a dark cape, in a white starched cap and ugly shoes. Because there are times when the kindness can do nothing for her. When she wants to say, No, kid, in spite of that smile of yours and that good-hearted empathy, we are not in this, or in anything else, together. She does give the nurses full credit for the discipline of their punctuality, their rushing around the city trying to show up before the discomfort gets ahead of anyone.

What is threatening to get ahead of her are random cramps and suspiciously everyday aches and the points of knives, all manner of knives. Pain that can announce itself like a frantic child and then, miraculously, settle down, to rest. Or best of all, die, suffocated three times a day by her new best friend, morphine. Although not dependably and not perfectly, morphine can blunt not just the pain but the shards of dread. The abrupt and pure and foreign dread. A month ago they had her on a liquid morphine, which she swallowed with grape juice, to kill the taste. Communion, Jack called it, mixing her cocktail. *Communion.*

God will be what God will be. That's what she believes. So there is nothing to comprehend, nothing to decide to do. She'd lost all desire for her mother's God years ago, and in losing the desire had lost the dogma, too, so it isn't the terrifying, paralyzing, childhood-promised afterlife she dreads. It's the leaving. That maudlin folk song from the sixties had it wrong because, yes, it *is* the leaving of Liverpool that grieves you. Not your poor sore body but all your known life, gone, stopped. Taken. As if you haven't loved it, or earned it. And your own loss doubled and doubled and doubled. In Jack and in the four kids, who are going to have to live through it, this hard first lesson, without her. And in Colleen and Richard and Jude and Gus, who are, it has to be remembered, every one of them, losing her.

"Think other thoughts," she says, wanting to start over. She doesn't talk to her tumours any more, not since the last surgery when even the most rational begging had to stop.

Throughout all of it, to deal with the concern and distress that have rushed her from every direction, she has wanted to stay calm. Where Jack's stance with his heart attack was the hard-nosed, bruising fight, and Jude's with her cancer was forthright and pragmatic, she has chosen calm. Colleen and Jude helped Jack see her in and out of hospital that first time four years ago, but after she was home with the incision healed, she wouldn't let them drive her to her radiation treatments, and she wouldn't let Paul or Kelly either, because, like Jack, they were all supposed to be busy with their own lives. I'm fit, she told them. I've got my car. This is almost behind me.

But those were the months when she could take refuge in hopefulness, when she could use her little scraps of cleverness to encourage the people who loved her, or liked her, or thought about her. The brave hearts who believed, as did she, that she stood a good chance. As good a chance as anyone, that was the hope. The people who wanted to look back one fine day and discover solace in the attention they'd given her, or maybe recall the superhuman energy that the sick, the beloved sick, can create.

A few of them would have been ready to repeat all the best lines verbatim, to tell you exactly who said exactly what, because after any extraordinary situation has passed there are people who can do this. And others would have wanted to remember, remember fondly, the good times, and in those good times, all that contained, distilled laughter. But too many of her visitors have used their laughter as proof of their stiff-necked southern Ontario courage, and she's been as bad as the worst of them. And now that she's had enough of that laughing grace under pressure, she wonders what it might be like to die in another place.

The good months ended in September of 2001, the same morning the towers in New York came down, when her surgeon, who had neither seen nor heard about the first plane, called with the results of her further tests, with the news that the margins had not, in fact, held. He wanted to go back in, he said, disappointed. It's such an unknown, he said. Jack had to take the phone to tell the guy to get to a television, and then he bent down and lifted her off the chair up into his arms to tell her that it was still, Jesus God, it was still nothing. Michael and Jan and April came right home again, braced for the bigger fight, but the surgeon had to take both breasts and then it was new tattoos and more radiation and chemo cocktails and a couple of classy silk scarves until her hair decided to come back.

After that second surgery, with everything gone and the bras all garbaged, she told anyone who would listen, No garden, no weeds.

But when they found it in her stomach, she had her well-rehearsed talk with each of the kids and then made Jack stop answering the phone. And he did stop, for as long as he could stand it. Explaining to her that if he didn't take the calls, people would just arrive at the door. Or some would.

And he was right. Up until a couple of weeks ago, some of her most determined visitors did come to her unannounced, and perfectly ready for straight talk. But she'd held her own against their straight talk because why should all the best choices, the tone of voice, the arrangement of words, the very point of the words, be taken away from her. Why the hell should I have to change, she'd asked Jack. And she'd put the question to her fleeting oncologist too, the man whose back she came to know better than his face: Why would anyone want to mess with such a perfectly tuned personality? But really, the oncologist's only job was to prod her with his educated fingers. Prod her and then lean in close with his quiet breath on her skin as if to listen to the corrupted cells. He had neither the inclination nor the time that morning to pick up on nuance, to understand that what she needed lying on his table was just a little play.

Colleen and Jude play with her. Now, like designated angels, they are letting her get away with things, protecting her. Now it's all, *yes,* and *if you like,* and *if you want,* and *sure, no reason why not.* Watching them think and think again, watching them bite the tongues they've become afraid of, she sees that she has never paid adequate attention to groups of friendly women, to the clusters of them everywhere you look, like hunting parties safe in their number. What she is finally beginning to understand is that all those years of talk, the pleasure of idiocy, the bouts of worry, the complaints, the humouring of memory, even the offhand, underdone affection, these are the least of it. The best of it is being known. Known over time.

So until the rest of her kids get home, these two useful friends are, with Jack and Richard and with Paul and his wife Kelly, in charge of her. Although she does know that there might be a time, a short time, she hopes, when no one but the lady morphine will be in charge.

Jack is actually swaying on the chair now so maybe she should reach over to rouse him? To save him? No, not yet.

She has been saving Jack forever, and he has saved her, too, taking his turns. Although he was already a lapsed Catholic when she met him, pretty generally lapsed actually, he agreed to be married in her mother's church, for the sake of peace on earth, he said. But even now he holds to some of his Catholic habits, one of them a friendship with a priest, Father Tony. Father Tony golfs with Jack and Richard and Gus, and when they go up north to that fishing camp, he sometimes goes along because he likes to gut and cook fish. And he has come to sit beside her bed, several times, to talk about her life on earth.

One of the best things about marrying Jack was that she could stop imagining a life bereft of a man. But then with his heart business she imagined it again, right through to her most selfish, left-behind self. If it had been him, if Jack had, as he'd threatened to, died, his acquaintances would no doubt have surrounded her with sincere but vague support, with murmurs of concern laced with confidence in her strength, as if they had always seen it. And this might have helped, as long as it lasted. She would still have had the younger men, certainly, her sons' and her daughters' partners, and Jude's son Liam, men who were separated from her by a generation and what that brought with it. And Richard would have stayed as he was, with his brotherly solidarity and his being Colleen's husband. Jude's Gus would have remained Jude's very solid Gus. Many things about him might have made her want a man again. Never him, but a close copy.

Horribly, she'd even imagined placing an ad in the *Free Press* personals. Mature woman, once firm and fit and with pictures for verification, seeks romantic partnership. Fun for all but nothing long term. Just until the end. She would have made Colleen and Jude help with the wording, called on Jude's vast experience with her untold seductions, and on Colleen's more measured guidance.

But Jack didn't die.

And now it's going to be her, and what is he, at his most left-behind, imagining for himself? Nothing. That's what she would say, knowing him.

"It's up to you, isn't it?" she says. "To tell him that he's going to need someone."

Jack had not got to her first because the sixties had begun to change things, and young women like her no longer had to twiddle their thumbs waiting. But how witless she'd been, before she met him, before he convinced her to trust herself. Wanting love without loving instinct. And those other eager young men and all their brave suggestions, their gratitude, and their well-mannered disappointment. Young women are luckier today, she thinks, with attitudes shifted beyond recognition and the pill a given. And with so many different species of women to watch, to imitate or to ignore. But Jack didn't care about what other kind of woman she could be. And so she signed on to this life with him, church vows and all. Although she didn't mind giving up her maiden name, McKellar, she refused to speak the word *obey,* asking for *cherish* instead, or maybe it was *esteem.* Something more likely, she'd told her mother.

"Hey," she says. She reaches over the bed rail to take his arm. "Hey, my good man." He comes to with a start, groaning one of his stiff groans. His glasses, hanging from their cord against his chest, make him look like some stuffy old man in a play.

"Part of me wanted to see you fall off that chair," she says. "For the uproar."

"Did you?" he says. He stretches his arms and leans down to kiss her.

"Sorry," he says. "I'm sorry."

But Jack her good man, her good and cherished man, is a lot more than sorry. He is ashamed. Because he should have been awake. If he could just get a few solid hours. If he could just get caught up.

He drops her bed rails and goes into the bathroom to pee and to wash his face awake. Then leaning over the sink, watching his scowling reflection in the pocked mirror, he sees that sleep isn't what his body wants. His jaw is heavy with yesterday's growth and he has a touch of pink-eye, so he finds the tube of ointment in the medicine cabinet and then washes his hands again, scrubbing his nails with the brush. Finished, he turns to look out the narrow window on the snowy backyard. In the dark of night the moon will bounce off the snow, making shadows of the tree limbs, but night has lifted now. He thinks about a hazy summer morning. About dawn in the garden, without her. And then he thinks about the slugs that hide in her bank of hostas, about taking the blade of the shovel to them, splitting and pulping them. She has done that herself. He watched her do it.

Jack is still in the bathroom but Paul has come up for a quick visit. He's wearing his grey teacher slacks and a blue shirt with a loosened tie. His jaw is his dad's, but clean-shaven. He is on his way to work, to his school, across town. He puts the *New Yorker* he's brought her on the bedside table and then he goes to stand like a guard at the foot of the bed, to hold her feet in his strong grip. Because this is what he does now. Holding her feet, he offers up all the strength he's got.

"How was the night?" he asks.

"Pretty good," she says.

"Sleep?" he asks. "Rest?"

"Some," she tells him.

"I just wanted to check in," he says. "I'll come over later, after supper."

"I know you will," she says.

He nods at her and gives her one last good squeeze and then turns to go, passing his father out in the hall, who walks him to the top of the stairs.

When Jack comes back she makes him stop at the small partners' desk under the window. "Get my journals out," she says.

He looks down at the drawers, where he has always half known her journals were kept. "All of them or some?"

"All," she says. "But bring me 1967."

He hauls them out of the drawer and stacks them on the desk beside the other books, the helpful, remedy-filled books that some of her visitors have left behind them. He has no trouble finding the year she wants because each cover is clearly marked. He sits down beside her.

"Now find late May," she says.

So he leafs through the pages.

She is being so good, he thinks. Crying, complaining so little. The strength in her stunned calm easily as strong as the force of his own, more fortunate, fight, with his heart. You hear about this. Only a few times, when she's looked straight at him with that face that says you have to help me, and it wasn't the pain, it was what the pain meant, has he seen that she is prepared to believe. She will not be coming back from this. Her oncologist's fair warning, to them both.

"What exactly am I looking for?" he asks.

"Yourself," she says. "You are looking for the name Jack."

He is quiet, like a sad scholar, and then he lifts his own spirits and says, "Here's something."

"What have you got?" she asks.

"'Jack's mother went over to Port Huron,'" he reads. "'She bought me two sets of striped sheets, which I will learn to love.'"

"Give it here," she says.

He shrugs, inept. "I'm going down to make us an omelette," he says.

"Just wait," she says.

And he does. He waits and watches her search through 1967.

Fifteen years ago, when Jack was led to believe that he was going to die first, all he could think was, no. Just that, with every godforsaken ounce he had. No. Now, watching her, getting used to her in this high bed but wanting her down at the kitchen table or out in the garage getting into the car or packing up for the lake or arguing about the kids' Christmas presents, he is catching on. He's getting it. Right from the start, when they first met, nothing else was ever going to happen for them. And all of it, the big ideas, the plans, the work, the money, the comfort of her body, his own body's strict and lucky habit of loyalty, the stubborn, costly mistakes, the laughs, the waiting, the kids, the luck, his discipline, hers, it was all only a way to use up time. Their short, short time.

They say you don't remember much about sickness but that's not true. He does remember the heart's pain, the severity and surprise of it, like any other muscle but bigger, worse. He knows that he cried and cried out, angry and ashamed, both. And that she sat there and cried out with him, with no shame whatsoever.

And even though he'd believed that the surgery was the answer for his plugged-up arteries, and even though he should have been grateful for all the expertise, he also remembers dreading, really fearing, the burning sting of that IV needle on the back of his hand. But then after his rib cage had been cranked opened and closed up again, he wanted the help. Whatever you've got, he'd tell them, let me have it. And he watched those suspended bags collapse as their magic syrup drained down into his blood. And then the whole mess went away and for all this time his heart has left him alone. And now it's going to be her. Christ, he wants to ask them, can you tell me exactly what we've done wrong? Haven't we eaten right? Didn't we walk? Swim? Haven't we taken holidays, taken ourselves away? Come down from our lives? Haven't we paid attention?

When she was first pregnant with April, Sandra told him that she'd always been afraid she would be loved by the wrong man. Or in some wrong way.

But he has not been the wrong man.

She is turning the journal pages one at a time, tracing words with an impatient finger.

"What is it you want to find?" he asks.

"Sex," she says. And then, "Here we go. This is the spring before we got married, when we were up at that leaky, rain-soaked cabin you borrowed."

He prepares himself.

"Cats and dogs," she reads. "It's almost morning and it is still coming down hard. And we've been at it since yesterday afternoon."

He lowers his head as if to deny his involvement. As if to ease his guilt in being that young, and so relentless. So good.

"Hunger has finally got us upright," she reads. "But we've baked our potatoes for something like eleven hours and now they're empty. They have disappeared inside their skins."

He laughs until he cries, which is not very long.

But she doesn't want to stop. She is ready with another page. She has found something else. "With him," she reads, pausing, making him wait, "it almost always feels like kindness. Or some part of it does, the beginning, the middle, the end."

Lunch

Sandra can hear Jack downstairs. He left her to check his e-mail, to see if there's anything from April or Michael or Jan, and now he's talking to someone on the kitchen telephone. The ringer on the phone beside her bed has been turned off so she won't be bothered, but she is bothered, because sound lifts.

She closes her eyes but soon opens them again to the sound of Colleen and Jude letting themselves in the front door. They have arrived with their Sunday lunch. They will throw together whatever they've brought and reach her with their trays not very long after the blast of cold air they've let in has climbed the stairs to find her in her high bed. Colleen and Jude can both rummage through her kitchen cupboards now, even with Jack standing over them, and they don't bother him any more with little questions. They have also learned to let her hang on to them when she's up on her feet bound for the bathroom, or for the armchair. They have shampooed her hair and made her up. These are the things that are most easily taken, and most easily given, away.

The three of them will eat their lunch at the shaky old bridge table, which has been set up near the front window and covered with a freshly starched, cross-stitched, creamy linen cloth. Because someone has dug through her linen cupboard all the way back to her early married years, when beautiful luncheon cloths were routinely given to young brides and, just as routinely, desired.

She has known Colleen since Richard married her forty years ago, and after so much time they can truthfully say that they are sisters-in-law who get along. The friendship got its start because, as was the custom, she was Colleen's bridesmaid and then three years later, when she married Jack, Colleen stood up with her. Like any good maid, Colleen helped her with the invitations and the trousseau, she handed her the shower gifts to open, the juice glasses and the toilet brush and the tart tins, and she made the paper-plate hat with the ribbons, for the idiotic picture. She had ideas about the bridal gown too, because she knew how to dress even then, but they were soon overruled by her mother's more determined choice, from a Vogue pattern book. The thing she remembers about her gown is that instead of a normal back zipper there was a long side zipper, running from her armpit down to her hip. The seamstress, a young Dutchwoman, made this change on her own, explaining that there was nothing worse than sitting in a church on a beautiful Saturday afternoon looking at a line of puckered satin running from a bride's neck all the way down to her arse. And on the way home, with the dress folded into a dressmaker's box in the back seat, her mother had lowered her head to ask what was the sense of avoiding puckered satin if you were going to have to live the rest of your life with such a coarsely described memory of it. But when the moment came, that was all forgotten, and Colleen had gone modestly ahead of her down the aisle, leading the way in her deep blue peau de soie gown, marching the slow march in her dyed satin spikes. The beautiful friend pretending, for the day, not to be.

The white, gold-embossed book of wedding photographs is still around somewhere, maybe down in the basement. The pictures were all standard issue for the era, the same as everyone's, except that the camera, as it always has, liked Colleen best. Still, she was the bride, wasn't she, and as pretty as she would ever be. And although Jack had no interest in zippers or tart tins, he did say, stripping her down that night, that he was glad to be legally tied to her. "I'm tied to you," he said, pulling her into the bed.

She and Colleen met Jude later, after the kids were born, and only by chance, because Jude and her son Liam had moved into the Oxford Street apartment, down and across the hall from Colleen's elegant, widowed mother. With April and Michael in real school and Jan and Paul finally in three-times-a-week nursery school, she often went along when Colleen checked on her mother. By that time the two of them were used to doing things without their husbands, and the visits became part of a shared routine. The morning they met Jude they'd been busy planning an excursion for Colleen's mother, a summer trip to Stratford to see a play, with Colleen arguing for lunch and *Hamlet* and her mother for dinner and *As You Like It*. They knew about Liam first because it was a rainy Saturday and he was pounding up and down the long hall with his soccer ball, kicking it against the walls, irritating them and probably everyone else within earshot. So not particularly angry but only motherlike, businesslike, she went out to speak to him, to ask him to stop his thundering.

And then Jude came into the hall wearing old green cords, a shapeless, purple, crocheted sweater vest and a tight, polite smile. Clearly ready for anything, she planted her bare foot on the soccer ball, put one hand on Liam's head and the other on her cocked hip. She was sorry for the noise, she said, but Liam was bored, because of the rain, because of the dismal day.

The day was an indisputable fact, so she told Jude that boys will be boys and invited her in for coffee.

Inside the apartment, Liam was given a banana muffin and put to the jigsaw puzzle laid out on a small table in a corner of the dining room, and Jude accepted a cup of strong coffee. They didn't learn much. It was only the two of them, Jude and her son, and Jude had a new job selling furniture at Kingsmills, and before they moved to London they'd been living in Woodstock and before that on some kind of farm north of Toronto. Then Jude rescued Liam from the puzzle, said her thank-yous and they left.

With things back to normal, Colleen's mother said that in spite of her circumstances, the circumstances being the long, out-of-date hair and the bare feet and the unattractive, even for casual, clothes, and all of it accompanied by a healthy, noisy, lonely son, Jude seemed to be a nice enough young woman.

Leaving Colleen and her mother to decide on Jude's niceness, she'd stood up to collect the cups and saucers. It had been a surprising morning. Although Colleen plainly didn't, she kind of liked Jude. And it was clear that Liam was not the only one at loose ends. Jude too looked like she could use a friend. Not needy, but plainly alone, a bit lost. On edge. Some kind of edge. Making a life, for an unexplained reason, in a strange new city. With a boy but without a man . . .

And here they are, one friend behind the other, with her lunch. They have come to eat, which means to talk. Because, even now, they still believe there is more to know.

She has never been able to discover what Jack and Richard and Gus talk about when they're on their own. There would not have been much conversation in the first years, when they took those hair-raising trips with all the kids, but later, when there was more money, when the six of them had flown away from the kids and she and Colleen and Jude had left the men to shop or to walk or to swim, they would have had plenty of time. Drinking rum, drinking tequila, had they told each other anything of importance? Gus must have had something to say to Jack about Richard's affair, and about Colleen, in Spain. And Richard might have had an opinion or two about Jude's earlier life, before Gus, at her communal farm with Liam's father, Tommy Davis. She has almost always known what Jack thinks, but he's not that good at reporting back. All she gets are the mundane facts. A modest lottery win, a shoddy car dealership, a tricky investment, a better gym, a coveted boat.

Colleen and Jude put their trays down on the desk and start to set the table. Colleen has just got one of her good haircuts and, as usual, Jude could stand a trim and an ash blonde touch-up. Today it's Colleen's turn to bring the food and there is dark molasses bread and a small clay bowl of cream cheese, tomato soup cut with so much milk it's barely pink, seedless grapes, and in quick response to a craving mentioned only yesterday, a pound cake drizzled with sugared lemon. They are saying that they made up a plate for Jack and are happy to report that he showed some enthusiasm for the soup.

Jude gets her up, bringing her first to a sitting position, finding the little black stool with her foot and then helping her stand by offering her own criss-crossed hands, which is a trick she picked up somewhere, the stronger hands crossed one over the other so the weaker hands can take a more natural, more productive grip. Her chair at the table is the comfortable one with the arms and she gets the midday view out the window. It's normal now, all of this vigilant thoughtfulness.

"So how is Jack doing, really?" Jude asks, spreading cream cheese on a slice of molasses bread and offering it on her open hand, hoping for appetite.

Now that she is plainly dying, evidence of appetite is one of the few things Colleen and Jude want from her. Like mothers of some stubborn, cranky child, they will be searching their recipes and asking themselves what can they fix that her wretched digestive system might convert to an ounce of strength. What aromas, what blend of colours on what handsome plate. As if she might let go more comfortably on a full stomach.

"He's not bad," she says, refusing the bread. "We had a bit of breakfast. He made us an omelette."

"I don't think my army father cooked one thing in his entire life," Jude says. "Unlike Gus."

And haven't they all been grateful for Gus's spur-of-the-moment feasts, his scallops grilled on a whim after midnight, his proud disregard for recipes.

"An omelette," Colleen says. "Good for Jack." She moves the grapes closer. "These modern men can be just chock full of surprises."

Colleen has only recently begun to call Jack and Richard and Gus these modern men, and hearing it, the men, whether annoyed or cheered, are letting it go.

"I'm not expecting many more surprises," she tells them. She drops a grape into her mouth. She has never put it any plainer.

She has, however, made it clear that they can lose any cheery small talk. "Hope abides," she said last week, at the first of these bedroom lunches. "I'm getting my fill without you two indulging yourselves." But then watching Colleen's green eyes glaze over and Jude's fists tighten, she diluted her decree with, "I'll try to stay open to idiocy." As if they have once upon a time agreed that idiocy is their one strength.

When she first told them, after the initial diagnosis, she told them together, expecting nothing but the automatic, certain hope that she and Colleen had given to Jude on her diagnosis. And they'd given her exactly that hope. And then left her to handle what she could alone because they understood that a fuss, a big, unnatural fuss, might have harmed her.

"No more surprises," Colleen echoes, wanting to give her the chance to say what she needs to say. Because, of course, Colleen will have imagined her long nights in this quiet house, conjuring and fighting her thoughts.

And she is ready to start, but then reaching across for another grape she catches her soup spoon with the sleeve of her nightie and knocks it onto the tablecloth. "Damn it," she says.

They watch the starched linen absorb the stain, a jagged pink footpath through the many-coloured, cross-stitched threads. Day after day, she has become more and more distracted. Clumsier. Because when health leaves you it takes everything with it. Grace. Skill. Patience. Ease.

But this time, for whatever reason, Colleen seems near frantic. "My mistake," she says. "I brought too much. The table's crowded." And then she's got the fix. "I'll get it out tonight. I bought this magic stuff at Costco."

And yes, Colleen *is* near frantic, but what she wants is to stop crying, at least here, in Sandra's house. She has always had a lot of respect for that one person in a room who can swallow grief whole, who can discipline herself to give full attention to the one who needs it. She has seen this at work, at the hospital, when a child is born severely deformed and dies, and the expectant grandmother takes her grown daughter's hand and tells her that it's all right, that it just wasn't meant to be, that all that matters now is her recovery. And then leaves, as if casually, to go around some corner and weep.

"The tablecloth should have been left in the linen cupboard where it belongs," she tells Colleen. "So someone can have it."

They decide together that the soup stain will be ignored. It didn't happen. And then, to change the subject, Jude says, "What about a little makeup? After lunch?"

For Jude, Sandra's plain, natural face is the most unanticipated change, because all three of them have always gamely made themselves up. Certainly no one expects Sandra to care now about the shape of her brows or to bother with little pots and potions, with shades of subtle, middle-aged red and sensible taupe, but her naked, sallow face, without the show and strength of colour, can make her look, some days, in the wrong winter light, like a woman they have never known. It bears no resemblance at all to Jude's own rebellious, left-alone, sixties face, which got along fine without any help, and it's not the plain, pure face of a child, either. Looking at Sandra now and knowing the time she just spent at her mirror at home, Jude feels not blessedly well but more like a made-up celebrity. Twice, she suggested to Colleen that they could scrub their own faces clean, that they should give it up the way some kids shave their heads in solidarity with another kid. She argued that there was a load of power to be had in any woman saying, if you want to look at me, you can look at this. Fourteen years earlier, when she was waiting for the results of her own biopsy, she had tried to imagine her way through to remission, and she'd got herself almost as far as power, likely because it's so easy to imagine. But Colleen said no, Sandra should not have to put up with their unimproved faces. She should see vigour when she looked at them. Or steadfastness. Something.

"No makeup today," Sandra says. "Or ever."

Because studying her changed reflection in the pocked mirror above the bathroom sink or in the hand mirror in her bedside table, and not truly hating what she sees because what could come of that, she has decided that a woman's natural face has the look of a country pond. Water still, with depth and sky, but calm. Inland. She thinks this image might have come to her because she's been reading poems in the *New Yorker.* It's Paul's wife Kelly who brings the *New Yorker*s, not daring to read any poem aloud but casually mentioning page numbers. She had forgotten all about poetry, its usefulness. Its accuracy. Certainly you can't find it in any Canadian magazine.

She is on her second spoonful of soup, and looking out the big window across the snowbanked street, she sees a woman and a young man talking as they gaze up at an old roof. The woman is too well dressed to be a midday neighbour so she must be a Realtor. There must be another sale in the works.

"Next fall you can tell my eager young neighbours on the corner to split off some of my perennials," she says. "They are to dig up and take whatever they want."

She means the odd, intrusive young couple who turned up in late October with an offer to put her garden to bed. For the practice, they said.

"You met them," she says. "That afternoon on the deck. I think they must have lost someone, and felt helpless."

Colleen is cutting the lemon pound cake into good thick slices. "Helpless or guilty," she says.

Colleen and Jude met the young garden couple that day because they'd come over to spend a last-chance hour out on her deck, pulling off their bright sweaters in the heat of the unusual afternoon. The roots of the roses needed protection from gusts of winter wind, and as the couple split and emptied their bags of mulch, they got into a muttering argument about the plans for their own recently purchased garden down the street. When the arguing got loud, not embarrassing but definitely boring, she called them over to have one of Colleen's Caesars and they leaned against the railing with their drinks and asked their questions about her arrangements of plants, about the painstaking timing of bloom cycles, and what, if any, success she'd had with holly, and where did Jack get his manure? Her assembly of deck pots had not yet been taken into the garage because some of them still held a bit of pretty decay, and when the young woman mentioned them, their charm and their extravagant number, Jude stood up to collect the empty glasses.

"She's fifty-nine years old," Jude told them. "She's got pots." And later, after the couple left, she said that sick people are treated to a hell of a lot of busy work. And busy talk.

Sandra wasn't surprised that Jude might be jealous of the young couple, of the easy pleasure they could offer, the straightforward, worthwhile distraction. Because, in truth, they had come in late at no cost and they could, whenever they decided to, and without turning back, leave.

Now, in looking out the window, in looking away from Colleen and Jude as she gave her instructions about the perennials, she has made her request equally, which will make them equally responsible. While the three of them have never been in true sync, she has been trying to keep everything, all of it, decrees and requests and questions and glances, perfectly balanced. And because she is determined to leave the two of them aligned, she no longer has the luxury of even briefly liking one over the other. There will be no more preferences, no more of what they once agreed to call their snarls.

She starts again. "The expected surprise is the bulk," she says. "Death takes up a lot of room." Her cake is gone and she's pinching crumbs from her plate, pressing down with a damp greedy finger. "Thank God for lemon," she says.

"Thank God for lemon *and* chocolate," Colleen says. But taking in Sandra's prayer of thanks, she is thinking that today might be the perfect time for them to cry together. The three of them.

Sandra stops pinching to make room for a second slice. "Nerve is all I've got, isn't it?" she says. "Perfectly innocent nerve. I'm guessing we all had it, just before we were born."

Jude looks like she needs a big, deep, noisy breath, but she's not going to take it.

"It's going to take that same nerve now," she says. "And the same innocence."

She watches Jude glance at the desk, at the bright, helpful books that have been mailed to her or delivered one at a time, in the hope. Against the dark desktop, the covers are inviting but the spines are still virginal, uncracked, and the slippery piles have fallen in on each other. Jude will be wondering who would have brought such books to this room, and checking too that none of them have been opened and taken to heart. But Colleen and Jude both know that there are friends and there are friends. That almost any woman is half surrounded, and that if the friends who might on the off chance bring along a helpful book are more outlying, they are still, by plain definition, there. With you.

They can both see the other piles too, beside the books. Her years of journals.

"Those are all your journals?" Jude asks.

"They are," she says. "Jack got them out for me. I thought I might look through them. Do some research. Maybe on my wasted youth."

"Yikes," Colleen says, as if this is some other day.

"I've been curious, for instance, about those Chinese pleasure spheres," she says. "Remember those aids to pleasure? In that dingy store in Toronto, after our trip to Spain?" She gives them a minute to follow her, to understand that she means self-pleasure.

"The balls," Colleen says, laughing. "The painted dragon and the bird. The rocking chairs none of us bought."

"Did either of you ever get yourself a set of those spheres?" she asks, straight-faced.

"No," Colleen says. "Not me." She turns to Jude. "But I'd bet you did."

Jude gives them not an answer but one of her well-timed pauses instead. And now they can all laugh at the very gratifying thought that she did get a set of pleasure spheres, or might have, or might still.

But Sandra's laughter has triggered the breathless cough. She looks at her bedside table, at the stale pitcher of last night's water that Jack forgot to replace. She takes three steady, disciplined, shallow breaths. "What I need is a glass of ice water."

Jude gets up to take the pitcher down to the kitchen, and when she's filling it at the sink Jack comes out of his den to wrap his arm tight around her. But then he has to let go, to help herd the skidding ice cubes she's dropped on the counter. He's been crying.

"That soup hit the spot," he says, leaving her to collect the ice cubes alone, his body smaller now, and his head held strangely high.

"You have to get me back into that bed," Sandra tells Colleen. "I can't sit here any longer." She half stands with both hands cradling her abdomen. "It's like being young," she says. "The day before my period." She takes Colleen's arm. "And who would have thought that this pain would show its ugly face again?"

Colleen helps her into bed and covers her with the sheet and then goes to the foot of the bed to the crank, because this was another of the decrees, *keep me upright.* Catching the last of her breath, she watches Colleen sit down again, so damned strong. Automatically swinging that one long shin bone over the other. The big show, Jude calls it.

And now Jude is back with the ice water and a clean glass, which she carefully fills and lifts to her mouth. She swallows as much as she can, like a needy child. Jude puts the glass down on the bedside table, within easy reach.

She should say thank you, she knows that. But saying it could break her heart.

If she had to confess, she might say that she'd enjoyed being given a drink, and that the enjoyment has caught her off guard. Being helped that way, a healthy child would want to bash the adult hand, to take the cup into its own anxious hands. And lucky the anxious child. She is going to tell Jack to get some of those straws with accordion pleats, milkshake straws. And then thinking about straws, she thinks about being a girl who has had her tonsils out and about the floating nuns who terrified her in their floating black habits and about the lumpy, milky hospital soup and the saucer of melted ice cream, and then, when she was home again in her own bed, her almost-sober father going up to the drugstore to buy a bent and sturdy glass straw, telling her, only the best for my lady love. The straw that her mother sterilized with almost boiling water and which she used for months, long after her throat had healed.

"Now you have to help me up to the bathroom," she says. "So sorry." She has allowed many unwanted things to be done to her in the last few days but a catheter is not among them.

Jude gets her sitting straight with her short legs dangling and they lift her down and walk her out. Colleen knows all the mechanics of nursing care, and many of the things they are doing for her they are doing the right way. Offering her their own locked arms, for instance, instead of pulling on her weaker arms, as people mistakenly do, helping someone. Neither of them objects when she closes the bathroom door, but they will be listening to hear that she doesn't turn the deadbolt lock on them, as she did yesterday. They will wait outside the closed bathroom door, leaning on opposite walls, and if Colleen's crying starts up, she can just duck into April's old bedroom to sink her nails into the back of her neck.

She realizes that Colleen cries behind her back, that it comes fast and full force, from nowhere, and that it humiliates her. Disappoints her. "Sorrow," she says, slapping her country-pond cheeks at the mirror. "Morrow." When she opens the door she ignores Colleen's bleary eyes and instead tells them that even with all the gifts of expensive concoctions, all those thoughtful gifts, she is still using only soap.

"But don't spread that around town," she says. "I don't want people to think I'm an ingrate. And take some of it home with you. Please. Get rid of those unattractive wrinkles." Jokes like this, simple-minded, awkward jokes, are new to them. But they will serve.

Jude flushes the toilet and they walk her back and Colleen lifts her into the bed as she was trained to do, working with whatever strength the patient can give her.

"Someone will be along soon to put me out," she says.

She has told them that the injections seem to be working again but she doesn't have to explain that this morning's is starting to wear off. The drugs, their effect, have been changing as she changes. A dose that a month ago would have put her away like Sleeping Beauty might now only steady her. Or it might not.

Jude sits down on the bedside chair and then, calmly, gently, she begins to smooth a hand back and forth over her forearm. Like the glass of water, this too is new and unusual, but it's an absent, irritating gesture, and almost before she knows what she's done, she has grabbed Jude's hand to put an end to the rubbing comfort. "Don't do that to me," she says.

Jude does stop, and then finally takes the deep breath she's been needing all through lunch. Although Sandra's rejection was slight, almost forgettable and even understandable, it was no less painful. But maybe she deserves it. Maybe she has to suffer it because she's let herself slip, too soon, into self-indulgence. Into heartache.

As far as Jude knows, Sandra doesn't pray in any accepted sense of the word. Jack's golfing friend, Father Tony, has come to see her several times, and while he can usually find a way to work *God* or *life* or *strength* into his conversation, he would not have touched on *salvation.* There is not going to be any last-minute transformation here. None of God's officials will be coming to this bedside to discuss what might be meant by the word *sin,* or the word *afterlife,* or by its accomplice word, *death.* For whatever reason, the timing of their birth, their arbitrary placement on the earth, some grudging chain of synapses in their brains, none of them are believers and there will be no leap now.

But still, even in the absence of heavy silver props to help them, with nothing at hand but this weary grief, couldn't she and Colleen perform some clumsy rite, some amateur blessing, on their own? Couldn't they borrow the phrases they need, or steal them? And if they did, would Sandra allow it?

She leans in with the thought of resting a finger on Sandra's sweaty forehead, on that central place where Catholics begin their known-by-heart, nailed-down prayers, where Hindu women wear their marks, their bindis, where smart fools smack themselves, after the fact, when they're alone. She imagines pushing out the two words, *bless you*, the push so bottomless it might deliver a good-sized child.

Watching Jude's pained endurance of Sandra's refusal, Colleen wonders about her own hand, about reaching over to cover Sandra's, their three hands stacked with Jude's down at the heavy bottom and then Jude pulling out free, her hand flying up to the top, and then Sandra's coming up right behind it, and then her own hand, and keeping on, all of them going for supremacy until something, probably laughter, puts a stop to it. But for as long as it does last, one or two or all of them might get the feeling, the illusion, of ascent.

Ascent can happen. She knows this because she was once a curious girl. Because she knows that if some part of you is held down firmly enough, your arms, for instance, pushed against the inside frame of a door, and then you step out, clear, you can get that leaving-the-earth sensation. "Levitation," she says, answering her memory's question.

But Jude has taken her hand away. And Sandra is ignoring both of them. So, lulled as they always have been by their separate thoughts, or maybe only by more lunch than they're used to, they wait.

Sandra is ignoring them because she is content with the use she has made of her late morning. Because she has said some of the things she intended to say. And made them laugh, with the pleasure spheres. Her temperament, a whim, an impulse, a wing and a prayer, all of it, has filled more time.

And now they can hear the young and lively voice of the after-lunch nurse as she pounds the snow from her boots and kicks them off in the hall. The nurse is questioning Jack to get a read on the morning when the front door opens again, and this time it's Kelly, her daughter-in-law. Kelly will have left her baby Annie with her own mother and come over either to tackle the laundry or to sit quietly reading some Russian novel while she sleeps her in-and-out morphine sleep. Whatever is wanted.

She drops her bare arm over the side of the bed to catch the cold, ascending air. The nurse's package, her hit of pharmaceutical relief, rustles in her hands as she hurries up the stairs in her woolly man-socks, with Kelly close in her wake.

Remembering where they are and who they are, Colleen and Jude stand up to acknowledge the younger women. They will wait through it all, the three-times-daily list of questions that Sandra alone can answer, the sight of those scars on her chest and the larger slash across a waist so narrow you can hardly accept it, the exposure of her blood-darkened, bony hips, and the quick syringe. And after the injection, if the nurse has the time and the goodness, the consolation of a sponge bath, which Sandra will mention until she gets her answer, one way or the other. It doesn't always happen. Sponge baths are a luxury from the old pampered days, the kind of thing a woman could hope for after a delivery, as a reward for not making a commotion, for accepting that the spectacular thing she had just achieved, pushing a separate human being out of her body, was not that spectacular at all.

The two of them will collect the remains of lunch and then talk on until they think Sandra is safely out of it. They will neither look away nor stare directly, because it's only a bath, only a waist, only skin and its temporary, life-saving scars. The questions will be routine and the answers not much different from yesterday's.

Kelly doesn't have much to say as she brings new sheets and towels from the linen cupboard and gathers up the soiled heap to feed down the laundry chute out in the hall. So while she waits, Colleen takes in the thick plaster walls and the dusty hardwood floor, the silk-fringed rugs, the masterful baseboard and mouldings. The stubborn builders of this house, she thinks, meant it to last. To outlast.

Listening to Sandra talk to the nurse, she wonders if, under the best circumstances, a woman's polished veneer might be the last thing to go, or second last, just before hearing shuts down. Hearing being the final accommodation given to the world? The last bridge? She saw a documentary once, when they were south on holiday, on the Pacific side for a change and just the four of them, she and Richard with Sandra and Jack. They were waiting in their hotel suite, packed and ready for the shuttle to take them to the airport, finishing off the last of the opened rum, because they still drank then when they flew. In the documentary, some obscure research had unearthed a witness to a beheading who had stood very close as the blade dropped and immediately called out the name. A witness who insisted that he had seen a responsive, commonplace blink of the eyes, who had called out again, for proof. And it would have been Jack who asked the idiot box, raising his last glass of rum, "And tell me who needs to know this?"

She looks at the desk, at Sandra's journals. She registered the journals when Jude mentioned them, but then talking and eating, she forgot.

She gets up to go over to the big bed, which Jack has left unmade, and after she fluffs the goose-down pillows and pulls the duvet taut and straightens the spread, she carves a crease beneath the pillows with a firm, slant hand. Finished, she comes back to the table to spoon more tea leaves into the big pot and, looking around, she sees that she'll have to get a refill of hot water from the bathtub tap because someone has returned the electric kettle to the kitchen, and she doesn't want to go downstairs, to Jack. Not after they've been laughing. But why in God's name is there only one kettle in this house? A teakettle costs nothing, Jack. Why not two? Or ten?

Bending over the tub, sweating, Colleen reminds herself that she has no earthly clue whether Jack is all right alone, so far away from any possible laughter. However it's the signal he sends and she isn't going to override it, she is not going to be the one who knows better. Back from the bathtub, she sits down at the card table and moves the pot in a small circle to hurry the steeping leaves. She fills Jude's cup and her own. The tea is green and weak and said to be good for them. "Tub tea," she says, wanting to be lighthearted. Wanting Jude to laugh with her instead of just watching and waiting.

Jude takes a drink of tea and nods her head to give Colleen credit for effort. Then she looks over at the nurse checking her notes in her big binder. Last night, in the middle of the night, she had almost cried herself out. Or that was what Gus called it, encouraging her. She has spent quite a few nights imagining just how bad things might get in this room, how impossibly hard. We can't do it, she thinks. We don't know how to do it. What she could use is a real drink but she stopped bringing even the wine because Colleen said she should stop. "She can't have it and it does us no good," Colleen told her. And then threw in the word *restraint* and let it stand there between them with its feet planted.

Kelly has taken the lunch trays down to the kitchen and now the nurse's work is almost done, the questions answered, the injection given, the roasting pan filled at the bathtub taps. The nightie stripped off and the towels laid down. Sandra's eyes drop shut and her relaxing body, her face, her hands, take on the signatures of sleep. She is dreamy, going, going, gone, and her shallow but easier breathing seems more private, more personal, than her nakedness. She has left them only her plain-faced gratitude, for the comfort now moving through her bloodstream and for its surface likeness, the pleasure of the bath.

Looking beyond the thin-blood bruising and the jagged scars and the absence of healthy breasts, Colleen and Jude both recognize the mottled shading of their own skin. But the thin legs look long, look wrong, and that narrow waist, which is now a stomach filled with soup and grapes and lemon pound cake, rises from her body in either distended pleasure or discomfort or both. Like a tumour.

"Next time you can do my nails," Sandra says, opening her eyes, startling them. She lifts her head from the pillow so the nurse can wash and pat dry the back of her neck. "But find some hot new shade," she says. "Spend some money."

She can always find a way to make them come back. One day it was the need to see specific photographs, some evidence of a time she was thinking about and confusing with some other time, another day it was an insistence that her good pearls should be restrung, and once the more practical necessity of a battery for her watch. The most recent, that craving for lemon.

The nurse continues with the sponge bath, but as she drops the cloth into the water to warm it again, she looks at the two friends, to catch their eye. They both understand that she means to advise them with her strict glance that nail polish is not a good idea, although only Colleen knows that holding the patient's hand and stealing a glance at clear fingernails is an effective, painless way to gauge the level of oxygen in the blood.

Quiet in her high bed, with her discomfort calmed and her skin soothed, Sandra entertains herself with two thoughts. That Colleen and Jude have already imagined a polish colour, imagined it done, and that no good nurse should be surprised by the complicity, or by the nerve, of loved ones. She lets her eyes drop closed again.

Deciding that Sandra has given in now to the deeper sleep, the nurse sets the roasting pan aside and gets her into the new nightie. Then after she's straightened the sheet and locked the rails, she turns to Colleen and Jude. "You don't need any special training to bathe a friend," she says. "You could do it."

But hearing this on the way down to sleep, Sandra thinks no, they can't. And neither should her daughters, when they get home, which will be soon, bathe her. And a nurse, young or not, should know this too, about loved ones. What Colleen and Jude can do is stay and talk and listen and pretend that her ruined nakedness can be endured. Because as wronged and defeated as she is in this high bed, even this close to it, she is still entirely herself, and the heat, the comfort of water on her skin, is still an intimacy. Like swimming. One that belongs to Jack absolutely, or to his hired proxy, this afternoon nurse, this detached, efficient stranger.

Because if their friendship has been true enough and necessary and lasting, it has never been beyond choice or control, or excessive, as it has to be when it's good with a man. As it was with Jack. What she and Colleen and Jude have done is bought this friendship, over time. Bought it with the right word found when it was needed and with just as many stupid and confused words. With necessary but soon-forgotten talk and half-baked thoughts and bitch sessions and small bouts of true confession. With good and faithful patience or with wine-prompted, rousing nights of saying maybe too much about their men, with doubts and pride and grudges and idiocy and high, passing joy, and all of it interrupted, on occasion, by their snarls. And bought now, today, with the two of them bending, like faithful maids, to decrees.

And all this time leaving that perfect space between them, for their men.

"There's really nothing to bathing a friend," the nurse says, packing up, watching them.

But Colleen and Jude turn instead to see Jack standing at the bedroom door, looking past them to the familiar, covered body of his drug-dreamy wife.

"You'll sleep now," he tells Sandra, as if he's certain she can hear him. Meaning to say, to them, you can go home.

Passing the journals on the desk, leaving her to Jack, Jude reaches to touch 1970, which is dark, dark blue, like a middle-of-the-night storm. And then Colleen does the same, choosing 1963, which is white, like winter.

Chicken Pox, Meat Pie

She's cold again, her arms and her legs. It's the middle of the night. She knows Jack isn't asleep because of the way he turns in the bed, with each turn a decision. Right now he is lying in his usual position on his usual side, facing away. All she can see is the dark mass of hair low on the back of his head, the only hair on his body that has not yet gone to grey. That maybe won't go.

"Are you asleep over there?" she asks.

She is using the weight of her hands against the discomfort in her abdomen. The sour cramping will mean that the uterus is involved now and the throbbing is only the heavy pulse of blood-the-advancing-hero. Brave blood cells called in from some other place in her body, ready to do battle.

When Jack wakes up she's going to ask him to find the old hot-water bottle, because that might do the trick. As it did when she was a girl, when the heavy, gurgling heat calmed her then still-mysterious insides. And today, instead of negotiating for a sponge bath, she might ask the nurse if she has some magic potion in her old kit bag. Although it's only a dull, menstrual ache, and not beyond bearing, she is not going to give the nurse that answer because pain can accelerate between nurses. Pain can grow, racing. It too can adapt.

Richard is across the hall again, taking his shift. Paul wants to help, of course he does, but his grief frightens him, he can't stand the quiet unease in the nighttime house. He can hardly touch her even in the light of day, although his wife Kelly can and constantly does, when they sit with her in the evenings. Michael and April and Jan, because they have their own lives in Boston and Vancouver and Orillia, are of little use now, or little daily use. Although they have been coming home more often, certainly. All of them have been coming generously home.

She has had time to devise a few strategies to protect Jack. Through the agitated nights she has got into the habit of fixing her eyes on that handsome black light standard out on the boulevard, on its steadfast, cut-from-the-dark cone of snow-filled light. Watching the snow fall through the iced-up branches, she can take herself into quite a nice trance. And this, as far as she knows, does her no harm. The weather station has promised her snow every night for a week, although twice there's been fierce wind and the flakes have fallen so thick and fast they almost smothered the light. Flakes like confused, bolting stars. Falling not just down.

"Bolting stars," she says to the night outside the window, thinking, a thought for my journal.

She has also devised some strategies for her children. One afternoon last month, when Colleen and Jude were leaving, when they asked if there was anything more she needed, she told them they could tell the kids to go ahead and plan their Christmases. Because Christmas was going to come, wasn't it?

In the beginning all four of her children were angry, understandably enraged that the thing that had once threatened their father, this early death, had come back for her. So she tried to ease them into it with dog-eared stories about a family driving great distances to investigate their unknown country, about the summer camping trips up north and taking that van through Quebec and the Maritimes as far as the ocean and the cliffs. And then later, flying out West to ski at Banff, in the Rockies. And building the pergola in the backyard and all of them ready to help with the design, laying out her garden for her. What she wanted from her storytelling was to make them understand that they had been good to her. But then she hauled them just as far in the other direction, to a roaring adolescent argument in the kitchen, to a thrown, broken plate of fish and chips, and the hair-raising, stubborn choice of a druggie boyfriend, a new car taken overnight with no one's permission, trying with these haphazard recollections to convince them that none of it had hurt her, not permanently. Not for eternity. And listening, they have allowed her to tell it her way. Disciplined by disciplined love, they have kept their interruptions, their own truer stories, to themselves.

And now they are all thoroughly back, or back and forth, wanting to make their grown-up affection for a mother seem spontaneous. They are not always that anxious to see her own heart on her sleeve, however, and while under other circumstances she might have been proud of their decorum, she's been working hard against their restraint. She has talked to each of them alone, saying to April the last time she was home from Vancouver, wearing what she hoped was her wondrous-mother face, "You have never told me this." And to Michael, home from Boston, "Out with it." And to Jan, most easily, because it was so easily the truth, "I appreciate the sound of your voice so late at night." And to Paul, as if stupid, "I think I do get what you're saying now." She knows they might have wondered if this kindness had been summoned for something other than their own comfort, although they seemed to accept it. But then even suspect kindness is hard to resist.

Another cramp is cutting a trail through the morphine, this one sharper, more acidic. She looks over at the parent who is going to live to see more. Jack is still out, still, she hopes, dreaming, but he has turned toward her. His face at rest has a look you never see when he's awake, when he disguises himself so successfully with worry and second-guessing, when you so often get that scowl and that hardened jaw. Which has been hard on the kids, and can be still.

He will be alone in this bedroom. In this house.

The cramping has stopped again, but she can feel in its place another tender bruise.

Jack was the one who wanted their marriage bed set up against the outside wall, the cold wall, when they moved into the house. Because he could never put out of his mind his sleeping kids, who could not have made any sense of their mother's low-pitched shouts in the dark. A little consideration, he told her as they assembled the bed, dropping the heavy steel rails into their slots.

"A little consideration," she says to him now.

Good enough. Waiting, patiently awake, she has got herself all the way back to moving day, in 1978. To Jack with his shoulder against the headboard as he positions a rail and to herself on the opposite side lifting the other one. With the kids loudly unpacking in their own rooms, pitching their emptied boxes down the stairs. All four of them in school and strong and healthy in their new, old house. But needing so much less of her.

She turns on her bedside light and reaches under her pillow for 1974, the journal she asked Jack for last night. And finds the page.

"The pox is upon us still," it says. "It was a hot spring day and I'm so tired I'm ready to die. But I probably won't because everyone is helping. I always need help now. It's a wonder my friends come near me."

Her mother Doris wasn't bothered by the heat. She was in the kitchen with the oven on, rolling out pastry for meat pies. And their new friend Jude was standing at the front door, holding two bottles of calamine lotion. Jude's hair had been pulled back and gathered high on her head, which was a good solution, and she was wearing a soft grey suit with a flared skirt, and electric-blue slingbacks. Her feet had already begun to swell in the heat, probably because she'd walked from the bus stop.

Usually, all of the kids ran to the door together, ran ahead of her in a me-first race, but that morning it was only Michael because the other three were sprawled out in the family room, half sick with chicken pox. The youngest two, Jan and Paul, were on old sheets on the couch, feet to feet, and six-year-old April, who was almost over it, was on the floor in her nest of sleeping bags. Michael's day was coming, although she and her mother and Jack were immune because they'd had it when they were kids, when most of the milder childhood diseases had been left to run their course unopposed.

"This is good of you," she said to Jude, accepting the calamine lotion. "Come in." She realized that an invitation into a house full of sick kids wasn't much of an invitation, not even to another mother.

"Thanks," Jude said. "But no, I can't."

Part of her was glad to hear this because she didn't really want more company. What she wanted was an empty house. "You're working this morning?" she asked.

"Yes," Jude said. Then she looked down at Michael. "Are you helping your mom?"

Michael said he was, and even after she told Jude that she couldn't manage without him, he continued to nod his five-year-old head in a promise of strength and dependability. And then they heard her mother calling from the kitchen in search of allspice, and not getting an answer, she came around the corner in her corduroy pants with their sharp crease and her white, ribbed turtleneck, with the sleeves pushed up. She stopped short at the sight of this person she didn't know.

"Mom, this is Jude," she said. "Jude, my mother, Doris."

"Hello," her mother said. "You're the furniture saleswoman, are you?"

"I am," Jude said.

And then the phone rang and her mother left to answer it in the kitchen.

She had told her mother about Jude, although nothing about her history. Nothing about the hippie farm or the divorce or her son's absent American father.

"I'm gone," Jude said. "Call me if there's anything. I'm finished at six."

"We're all right," she said. "But thanks for your trouble."

Jude had come a long way out of her way. She watched her start down the street and then yelled after her, just before she turned the corner to get the bus. "Give Colleen a call. She wants to see *Chinatown.* The two of you should go see it."

Jude lifted her hand to say that she'd heard, and she closed the door on the summer morning. She had not been outside in a week. She was going to throw open some windows to change the air in the house because she'd had all she would ever need of the smell of that lotion, and kids, she'd learned, could get just as ripe as the inactive old.

"Why isn't Colleen helping you?" her mother asked. She was in the hall again, waiting for her allspice. "She's your brother's wife."

Her mother had not begun to guess that Richard, her brilliant doctor son, might be messing around on the good and beautiful Colleen. And who among them would rat him out? Not her.

"She'll be sleeping, Mom," she said. "She works twelve-hour shifts. And she's on nights this week." She went to the kitchen cupboards to open the spice drawer, which was also the bills drawer and the pencil crayon drawer and the nail polish drawer.

Her mother found the tin of allspice and popped the lid to hold it to her nose, to see how old it might be. And then, starting to peel the mushrooms, she spat out, "Working. And can you tell me why?"

Maybe, she could have told her, because a demanding job can give a woman some of the security and satisfaction she deserves. Because you don't necessarily get that from a husband, Mom, as you would know.

Her father had kept on as always, coming and going and liking the ponies and smoking his vile, exotic cigars. Spending his mysterious money in spurts of responsibility, but maybe drinking a little less, or a little less obviously. Her kids, of course, sick or healthy, loved him to death.

"Richard works too hard already," her mother said. "They've got money enough. And what do they need more for when they haven't got anyone to spend it on?"

"Colleen might come over later," she said. She followed Michael down into the family room. "After I get them smeared, I'm going to open some windows."

She watched Michael sit down on the edge of the sleeping bag close to April, who was scratching her scalp again and then her forehead, guaranteeing herself a scar or two. April's mistake made her wince, but hadn't she been told, and just that morning, that she too had been unwilling to heed a mother's warning? Hadn't she gouged a deep scar on her temple and another in an eyebrow and another in an ear? Perfect little circles but no two the same, like pockmarks on Mars. Michael is sitting there, she thought, because he's smart. He wants the virus. He wants to get it over with.

"I'll get my pies in the oven," her mother called out. "And then if it's all right with you, I'm going to take my hour." She was sleeping on the sagging couch, but her hour was an hour alone up in a bedroom, in prayer. "That was him on the phone," she said. "He's threatened to come over for lunch."

"That's good," Sandra said. "That's fine."

Him was her father and *threatened* was just the way her mother liked to put it. It didn't mean that he would turn up at any specific time, or even that he'd turn up period.

She pulled Jan onto her lap and took off her pyjama top. The pustules had crusted and her beautiful little back had started to clear. She poured some lotion into her palm. It was pink and chalky and cold, just like the last bottle.

"I'm off," her mother said. Now her face looked dazed, looked kind and loving, as it sometimes did when she was in the vicinity of her grandchildren. "I put you and Richard right in the tub with it," she said. "Just poured bottle after bottle over you. Do you remember that at all?"

"Yes," she said, not sure. "I do."

Her mother turned to leave. "You'll listen for the timer?" she asked. "Because I'm not interested in losing a morning's work."

"I will," she said. "It's loud, Mom, remember? I've got myself a very bossy oven."

She looked down at her T-shirt, which was marked with a bright pink smear because Jan had leaned back to be held closer. When she finished Jan's legs and feet, she stripped Paul to check him and then she helped April stand up from the nest of sleeping bags so she could do her. Michael took some of the lotion from April's arm onto his finger to lick it, and then he touched his forehead.

"You funny muffin," she said, watching the pleasure melt him down, because at five he did still want to be her funniest muffin. He wouldn't want it much longer, maybe for two or three more years, but then he shouldn't, either, because being perfectly normal he should pull into himself and then away. Because, with kids, away was the only direction ahead of you. Although they could turn to watch you, later, still wanting your kind face. Just as she, to this day a daughter, occasionally still wanted it. And sometimes saw it when it wasn't there, and once in a while missed it when it was, or so Jack tried to tell her.

The hard work of parenting had not yet begun, she believed that. There was nothing to loving these kids. All they needed was a good house, a healthy dinner table, a little luck, and a pattern of regular sleep. That pattern of regular sleep being the thing they were not getting now.

She dried her hands and walked to the kitchen to crank open the window over the sink and then went into the dining room, to the sliding doors. That side of the house faced west and the sun had not come over the roof, so there was a chance for some cooling down. There was a breeze on the air, she could see it out in the yard in the corner spruce.

Cross-breeze established, she sat down with her feet tucked under her in Jack's big chair, a chair like a boat. It was the only piece of furniture he'd wanted, which had left her free to choose everything else. The one thing she was still missing was an ottoman and Jude was looking for one, maybe a paisley or a narrow stripe. Jude had suggested that it should be on castors, to go wherever, to serve more than one purpose.

Michael came close to rub against her like an old cat and then he wandered off to the kitchen, probably for crackers or juice, which he could get for himself. The others, relieved of their most painful itching, watched her with their quiet, bleary eyes. She looked at them as if to say that everything was just as it should be, the mother look, Jack called it, and the three of them fell into a light morning sleep.

Jack had promised that he would try to get away from the office early, but he was as tired as she was. He'd been contenting himself, and her, with the simplest, quickest sex, because nights could get long with sick kids. Strange to think that only eight years earlier, when they were first together in their illicit beds, some of which weren't beds at all but floors or cars, they had wanted all of their nights to be long.

She woke up with Michael nudging her and there seemed to be more life in the room, more energy. Her mother was coming in with a tray of apple juice and hermit cookies, which made April and Jan and Paul sit right up.

"You missed the timer," her mother said. "But luckily I didn't. And I've got some salmon and peas on the go."

"I can smell it," she said. "Smells good."

"So can I," Michael said, wanting them both to be happy.

The kids finished their juice and then they all heard the sliding screen door in the dining room. It was her father, using the wrong door, delivering on his threat to come for lunch. Her mother left to intercept him on his way through the kitchen, to take her wifely reading on his condition and then tell him, as she often did, just to keep himself to himself. But his loud voice wasn't making its normal retreat, it was holding to an outsized, outdoor cheer. Maybe her mother had decided that the house could use a little cheer and, for this morning, he'd have to do.

"Close all your eyes," her father shouted, giving the kids time before he came into the room. "All right now," he said. "Look."

Her unhandsome father was cradling in his arms a handsome pup, some dark-Lab mix, and the reaction he got was as uncivilized as any grandfather could have wished. The kids came at him in one pink-smeared, pyjama-clad mass, and after he walked over to lay a heavy, encouraging hand on her head, he put the quivering pup down on the floor. Then he rolled up his sleeves and squatted on his haunches to show the kids how gentle they should be. They watched and listened and then dove into him to pull him over, to thank him. Paul, who was three, reached to smash his monster nose sideways, which was their joke.

"Yuck," he said. "God. Yuck. What horrible kids." He pushed them away, a hoax that made them wiggle and snort and dive into him all the harder. Even the pup, who was looking a bit stunned, seemed game.

Her mother sat down on the arm of Jack's chair, beside her, to say, "A dog's not a bad thing for a family to have."

"Well, it's apparently a done deal," she said. "Isn't it?"

"Chicken pox and shingles," her mother said. "The two are closely related, you know. Your grandmother had a bout of shingles shortly before she died."

"Yes," she said.

"Shingles wraps itself around you like a belt," her mother said, lifting her arms to indicate her broad midriff and pointing in the general direction.

"It can go after your eyes as well," her father said. He glanced up at his wife and put a hand to his forehead just above his right eye, where shingles might get a start. "That's the thing you want to avoid."

"I can remember your grandmother in her bedroom, calling out for comfort," her mother said. "And all we could do was go in and talk to her to take her mind off it. Calamine couldn't touch it."

"It can be a terrible thing," her father said. "Either way it gets you."

"And it has little to do with cleanliness," her mother said.

"No, it doesn't," her father said.

"Of course not," Sandra said. "God. Who could ever think that?" Well, they could, maybe. Or had, once.

Although she always kept herself fortified against her mother's convictions, she could forget that her father had a few certainties of his own. And this could still surprise her, especially when she was feeling almost safe with them.

"It serves no purpose to deny it," her mother said. "People can bring things on themselves."

Now her father was nodding in agreement, which made her wonder if this was what had brought them together in the first place. A readiness to believe strange things. And what bad luck that their strange things had turned out to be so different. Different beyond surrender. Tonight, she would write some of this down in her journal. Heat and chicken pox and shingles and a dog. Bad luck and strange certainties. Differences beyond surrender.

Her mother was looking at the mound of sticky grandchildren that had attached itself to her depraved husband. And then she seemed to be studying the pup, who had finally stopped quivering.

"How about everyone comes out to the kitchen for lunch today?"

she said. She glanced down for after-the-fact permission. The kids hadn't been to the table in days. "How about we name that pup and eat normally and then we'll all have a bath."

Her mother didn't mean *all*, of course. She didn't mean herself and she didn't mean her husband or her daughter, neither of whom she'd seen naked in twenty years. She meant her grandchildren, who would be, from now on, the all-and-only flesh she would know, other than her own. And other than the once-a-month cube of soft Communion bread, dissolving in her faithful mouth.

The kids settled on the name Hank because their grandfather said the pup looked like a Hank, and, better yet, because it rhymed with Frank, his own good name. Michael tucked the pup into April's nest of sleeping bags, where it dropped on its side like a pull toy and immediately fell asleep, and they all got up to go to the kitchen. They waited as her mother filled their plates at the stove and brought them to the table, and when she sat down and lowered her head, they followed her example. She and her father did this as they had always done it, because it was necessary and easy enough, but with her eyes half open she could see that her tired and greedy kids, with their eyes so tightly shut, might be hoping for another surprise.

"Bless, oh Lord, this food to our use," her mother began. "And us to thy service."

As always, she was speaking informally, conversationally, as if to her oldest friend. What she meant to say was, God, pay attention to me. And keep me strong. And I'm so glad I can help my poor daughter with these sick kids. Someone else's mother, not Colleen's, who was restraint on wheels, but maybe Jude's, might have been able to say such things directly, to the people who should hear them. Jude had told them that her mother, an army wife, was soft-spoken and diplomatic by habit, but kind and bright and able, somehow, to hold her own.

"And make us ever mindful of the needs of others." Meaning, my daughter is tired and my grandchildren deserve the best there is in this world, because they are mine. Meaning, although I will never forgive my husband his failings and his beastly selfishness and his refusal to live as he should live, I will speak decently to him here in this house.

"In Jesus' name, amen."

And yes, she thought, amen.

They finished their salmon and peas and then her father announced that he could load the dishwasher, why not, and her mother led the kids upstairs to the bathtub.

She sat down in Jack's chair again, on holiday, listening to the scraping and rattle of dishes and the wasteful running of the tap at her sink. And then she could hear the more distant, muffled sound of excited, thumping feet as the kids waited for the tub to fill. The four of them couldn't all fit any more so there would be that push and pull of everyday quarrel, but she was going to stay put. She was going to wait to hear what might happen next.

Done with his dishes, her father left to go upstairs. Even in middle age he would still grab the newel post and in one big, enthusiastic swing, launch himself upward, maybe even take the stairs two at a time. And now she really wasn't going up there. Wild horses.

And, what luck, she was saved by the front doorbell. She looked at her watch. It would be Colleen. It was only ten after one, so she would not have had much sleep.

"You're still alive," Colleen said. She dropped her bag and then stood stock-still to listen to the racket coming from the upstairs bathroom. "Is Frank up there too?" she asked.

"You should have stayed home in bed," she said.

"Oh, well," Colleen said. She was studying the stairs as if she might decide to climb them, just to see Doris and Frank abiding each other in a small room. "I'm off tonight so I can catch up. And I wouldn't have wanted to miss this."

"Jude was here this morning," she said. "She brought me two bottles of calamine lotion."

"I forgot to call ahead to ask," Colleen said. "Sorry."

They went back to the family room and Colleen stood unsurprised above the sleeping pup, which meant she'd known that a pup was on its way. Then she went to the couch, stripped off the pink-smeared sheets, and dropped them in a heap on the floor. She sat down and half fell over and was soon stretched full out, but even this tired and with no makeup her skin still reflected all the light in the room. Certainly the new dusty-rose shirt, which would be the purest cotton, didn't hurt.

"Richard had to go in for a warehouse accident," Colleen said. "Just one guy apparently, but quite bad. Irene didn't know how long he might be." Irene was the woman she and Colleen had to talk to when they couldn't find Richard.

She got up to put the kettle on and, standing at the stove, she told herself that it wasn't getting any quieter up there, but then it wasn't getting any louder either. So she didn't have to climb those stairs, not yet. She could wait until her well-brought-up guilt grabbed her by the scruff of the neck.

"Do you think I'm lazy?" she asked, leaning around the corner to watch Colleen's answer.

"Sure," Colleen said, yawning.

There was nothing unusual about Colleen being this tired, because her hard-working body was always out of sync with any natural human rhythm. It was the price both she and Richard paid, Colleen working her long shifts delivering babies, none for hours on end and then an insane rush of them, and Richard either at the hospital or ready on-call to deal with his accidents, with his spinal fractures and chipped breastbones and crushed pelvises.

"He's sober?" Colleen asked, meaning Frank.

"I think so," she said. Sometimes she appreciated Colleen's cracks and sometimes she didn't. "You can check him out when he comes down. Or you can go up there and make him walk the hall."

"Make him walk a straight line," Colleen said. "Twice. Up and down and up and down. Come on, Frank."

Whatever Colleen thought of him, her father certainly liked her. He had liked her from the day Richard first brought her home. A racehorse for a daughter-in-law, he'd said. And then there was the speech about improved bloodlines, about traits worth passing from one generation down to the next.

"We'd hear it if she tried to drown him," Colleen said.

"Probably," she said. She went to the hissing kettle and came back carrying two mugs of instant decaf, fixed the way they drank it.

As Colleen sat up, she straightened and arched her stiff back. "How's Jude doing?" she asked. "Or more to the point, how's it going with big old hunky Gus? Is he still the one and only?"

"I didn't ask," she said. Jude had just found Gus but they could both guess how it might be going. "I did tell her to call you about seeing *Chinatown.*"

"We can wait for you," Colleen said. "I'd rather wait."

"Don't," she said. "Go ahead. I've still got Michael to get through it. Jack has to go in to work at night for a while, and no sane sitter would come near this house. And I can't leave Mom on her own with them. She's coming to the end of her rope, I fear. I do fear."

"All right," Colleen said. "I'll go with Jude and then I'll go again with you when this is over."

"Fine," she said.

They settled in, hoping to drink their coffee in peace, but it was soon broken by close and quick breathing and then a pair of lightly pitched, hesitant giggles.

Paul and Jan were standing bunched close together on the family room step, clean as whistles and naked as jay birds. So the first two had been sent down. The naked business would have been her father's idea, to lift everyone's spirits, or maybe it had been her mother's, in observance of her belief that God's good air was by every measure the best healer.

"Hi there, dumplings," Colleen said. Then, ready to do her part, she asked if the clean pyjamas were in the dryer.

"You stay here," she told Colleen. "I'll go."

But she didn't go. She looked over at her clean and shivering, scabby-but-healing kids. And because they were not sure what they should do, she put down her coffee and clapped her hands and opened her arms. . . .

The sour cramps have come back, so the naked armful leaves her. She wonders if Jan and Paul have any memory of that day. Clean and naked and straight from their grandparents' arms to her own. Her parents are both gone now, so she'll have to tell it herself.

She closes the journal and stashes it under her pillow. All those nights when the kids were small, when she was writing her life down, always at the end of a day, she thought it was to make that day more her own, or to make the next one easier to get through. To take control. Funny.

Across the room, Jack's breathing is heavier now, so he's sleeping. Good. She finds the top corners of the sheet and squares it neatly over her body. Recently, for a few obviously disturbing days, she had lost all modesty, abandoned it like a tart. They had to keep pulling the sheet over her wasted legs. But she can no longer worry about making it harder for them, doing or saying things she would not do or say. They can be confused or not, irritated or not, exhausted or not. That's up to them.

"Neither love nor dread is modest," she says, looking over at Jack. She could explain this to everyone, but they should know it.

The thing she doesn't want to live through is any kind of coma, lying there absent but still alive enough to hear every word. People forgetting not just her, but themselves, talking as if she won't mind what they have to say. Her children drained and weary and perhaps already lonely for her but plainly, and yes, rightly, relieved at an end. And all the love owed to her, which surely she will continue to crave, withheld. She knows this happens because she did it to her own father and mother, after they went to sleep. She did talk above and around them as each of their worn-out bodies worked so hard to put an end to itself. With each old mouth locked, so finally, open. And how could they have understood why the tenderness had left them? Although her father at least, maybe comatose-dreaming a lucky nag or a forty-ouncer of Canadian Club or an illegal cigar shared with some shady pal, might have fought back with one of his throwaway, standard lines. Life, he might have said. Or, screw you, Charlie.

Certainly she knows that last words heard can be no match for last words spoken. People listen for last words, even if they come from delirium. It was the last thing she wanted and didn't get from her parents. But can she manage, can she guarantee that the last thing out of her mouth will be dazzling or true or at least kind? With a little bit of something for everyone? And why do people need this when they've been offered a million conscious, intentional words? It is offensive. It's a waste of time.

"No," she says. "Nothing is a waste of anything."

People simply want their dying to say something familiar, or classic. To die intact. Although she often longed for a changed mother, a woman less devoutly self-satisfied, when it did come, she wasn't ready for it. She was not ready to see her mother become that unanticipated woman, not only regretful but suddenly, openly, kind.

Too much change at the end, dying change, proves beyond doubt that all along the woman people believe they know, the woman they watch and talk to, and now care for, has been nothing but spidery synapses, sparking or not sparking in the brain's frontal lobes. And like the breasts or the stomach or the uterus, that brain can become, just as naturally, diseased. She imagines a steel gate like a gate under water, locked, at her neck. She wants to die somewhere below her neck. Anywhere below it. This is her bargain.

"I'm all right," she tells Jack, ready to try again for sleep. "I am . . ."

Jack is glad that Sandra has started to talk to herself through the nights. Lone, loose words. Parts of sentences. There isn't much he can follow, really, however there's nothing to suggest that the pain might be outsmarting the morphine, either. But curled in bed, sleeping and pretending to sleep and sometimes just resting his eyes, he has almost not heard her this time. This isn't because he has heard enough but because he is more exhausted than he would have thought a man could be. It doesn't help that the nursing care is excellent or that Richard is across the hall or that the kids are doing all they can or that Colleen and Jude are coming over so much. Richard has told him that even if sleep won't come, you can still lose a certain kind of consciousness. And he wrote out a just-in-case prescription. But it's too late now for drugged sleep.

Jack has known since he was a boy that it isn't sleep that takes you to dreams, it's the other way around, but he can't get a dream going. He will stare something down, his father in an upbeat mood, giving him his old putter, or one of his sons actually listening to his advice, but then it gets overrun. By their shoreline on Lake Huron, the farthest edge of water just starting to darken as things gear up for the relief of a hot storm, and then the heaving and the belching of driftwood and garbage and sawdust from the old mills on the Michigan side. By a messy-haired granddaughter wearing his Christmas cardigan, dragging it behind her as she learns to walk, refusing his help but still aiming herself in his direction. By the old Sandra caught accidentally naked in her closet, or dressed and thinking herself so smart, closing a door hard after winning an argument against him. He thinks about the bedroom lunches with her friends and how they help her. Colleen and Jude come with the territory, of course. They've been coming with it for thirty years and there's no reason to think it might stop now.

She has told him a few things. About Colleen's screwing around in Spain, for instance, and, long before Spain, about Richard's own nonsense. Although he would have heard about that regardless, because it did hit the street, the golf course, the tennis court, the gym. Most men he knows are of several minds when they suspect a guy is stepping out. There's sometimes a round of that secret handshake laughter, the enjoyment of the thought, and some mild envy too, the wondering what it might be like for them. Or obvious guilt, that disciplined stone-face if they have done it or are doing it themselves. But usually there's just a shrug of confused contempt. The silent majority.

She has also told him a bit about Jude's murky past. Jude allowing herself to be passed around some hippie farmhouse like the sports section. Although that was not the way it was put to him. The way Sandra told it, it was Jude who made the decisions, taking her satisfaction from variety, no harm done. Which was easy enough to believe in theory. Still, he can't fathom how a guy could sit down to breakfast with someone who'd just been where he'd been. As if a woman was some shared bath, run with short-supply hot water. As if, after they built their hippie, wood-stove fire and enjoyed their weed tea, they wouldn't want to stand up and kill each other.

But he has always tried not to get involved because both Colleen and Jude have been so faithful to her. Regardless, Richard has long since settled down, he is sure of it, and Gus seems to have more than he needs in Jude.

He has never once asked Sandra any hard questions about where she was before he found her and she has never asked him any either. In spite of his routine prowling around, when he decided on her, for all intents and purposes he'd been a virgin. And he has always hoped she would say the same.

He is tired of all the people she needs. They both need. He has nothing to say to them and can't pretend otherwise, and because he can't, he has to look at their worried faces, their assumption that he is enraged, or afraid for himself too, already alone. Often he can't even manage the niceties, the things you say when you have nothing to say. Maybe this is depression, as Richard suggested. Normal, he said. Maybe it's only grief wanting some peace and quiet, wanting everyone to shut the fuck up. But no one, almost no one, will have it. And people want what they want.

According to Colleen and Jude, who carried her message to him, Sandra wants him to understand that she will be alive until she is dead. So there will be just that one split second, and then the rest of his empty life? No.

He gets up and goes to her in his pyjamas and kisses her hard.

"Yes," she says, joking.

"Why don't we clip your nails?" he says.

She holds up her hands to examine her nails. "If you like," she says. "Colleen and Jude are going to paint them for me, but you'd know that. They would have said."

"They did say," he says.

"And here," she tells him. She takes off her engagement ring, an emerald with two banking diamonds. "You should put that somewhere safe," she says. "It's loose anyway."

The thin wedding band stays where it is.

She drops the ring into his open hand but then takes it back and slips it on his baby finger, halfway down, to the knuckle. She isn't crying so he doesn't either, and how are we doing this, he wants to ask her, without sobbing?

"Looks good on you," she says, giving him her hand.

He pockets the ring and opens her bedside drawer to find his clippers. The drawer holds all the small things you need to care for a sick woman, and the joints rolling around loose at the back will be Paul's contribution. Although she won't use them.

Jack knows she doesn't like a straight-across, masculine cut but he's ham-fisted with a file and this is one thing he can do for her. When the kids were small he always did their nails, taking it on himself, holding their tiny hands steady in his own. And they all learned to watch and bring him their outstretched fingers when they thought it was time.

He's finished so he moves down to do her toughened toenails and then he searches the sheets for clippings. Satisfied that he's got them all in his cupped hand, he leaves to get rid of them in the toilet.

When he comes back he picks up his notepad to read her a few of the newest messages, skipping around and changing things as he reads. It's all, our thoughts are with you, with your family. Variations on that. Or, a bit easier to take, I've been remembering that time, or, even better, much better, we've been remembering that time. Two people together somewhere, talking about something that actually happened. Something with her in it.

"Nice," she says.

He begins to massage her legs and her feet but he isn't going to talk any more. If she can fall asleep now, he will stay in the chair beside her, awake.

And she does fall asleep. And he does stay in his chair watching her, and watching, he sees the waking strain leave her face.

He thinks about her strong, aging body, the body that belongs in their bed against the cold outside wall. About turning his back to the heat in her breasts and how long they held their saucy shape, even after she nursed the kids. About the smart little swimmer's ass he liked to study walking away from him, how he would leave his own ring in the bathroom and wait until she'd stripped down and, pretending to be tired, ask her to please get it. Just to see her walk away. And never confessing. In case she stopped doing it, or spoiled it, moving too deliberately, making it a gift to him. A choice.

Bridge

It looks like a normal winter morning and she wants to get up and sort through her jewellery to find her long rope of multi-coloured stone beads. The jewellery is in the chest of drawers where Jack put the poinsettia sent by his old accounting firm, the chest that had to be moved to make room for her hospital bed.

Their furniture was shifted around only once before, for painting, not long after Jack came home from his heart surgery, safe. After his body had been surprised and then, astonishingly, signed over to science. Because, as he told her when he was filling out the forms, donating himself, "Give me a reason not to."

"No earthly reason, Jack," she says.

She decided to redecorate the bedroom to celebrate his recovery, and she did mean to do the other rooms too. She meant to freshen things up, even to throw stuff out, but the enjoyment she got from their bedroom had been enough. The rest of the house stayed as it was when they bought it, the only addition their years of use, their habits and comfort and indifference. Maybe outside eyes did see a shambles here, but, aside from the kids' friends who could come and go ten times a day, they have never invited outside eyes in, or not often. When the house began to empty they did put some effort into getting a room painted, an unused bedroom, the kitchen, leaving the colour alone but still paying some attention, taking it semi-seriously. And after Paul finally got his own place, she even dared to think that the clutter would sort itself out somehow, and then had been a little surprised to learn that so much of it was her own. But too late now.

They have set up her bed on the plainer of her good rugs, possibly because someone, imagining the spoiling stain of an accident, thought it was the less valuable of the two, although it isn't. And while the grey velvet armchair has always been a mistake, she's paying for it now because, even when she encourages it, Paul's Jackson does not feel free after he's given her his kisses to climb up to comfort himself in a big chair. But maybe he's been warned by Kelly, his mother.

Writing out her list of bequests, naming her belongings, giving her most loved things to April and Michael and Jan and Paul, the corner cabinet in the living room, her mother's cream skimmer, her ruby anniversary ring, her one swimming medal, but then this to Colleen and to Richard, this to Jude and to Gus, to Jude's Liam and even to Gus's daughter Kate, she has gone to some trouble to dismiss the cost of things.

"They'll think they know the cost," she says. "But they won't. They will have no idea."

Paul has brought her a CD player and set it up on the chest beside the poinsettia, and the lovely resurrected Johnny Cash is singing "Sunday Morning Comin' Down," which is about another kind of drugged escape. They should have thought of music before. She likes music.

Jack is in the bathroom having not a shower but a bath, which is unusual. He was crying but he's stopped now.

Colleen will be here soon to sit with her. Maybe she can find the rope of beads.

Of course Jack wasn't around when she met Colleen because it was before his time. Before Jack showed up, when she was still convinced that she would have no one, Colleen had tried to make her see that she was worrying for nothing. "The right guy will show up," she said, in the phrase, in the theory, of the day. "They always do." As if she could know.

But she'd been ready for this. "I want to be loved in the right way," she told Colleen. "And I'm not going to get first choice, am I? So it could easily be the wrong guy." Because it was what she believed.

"You can't think that," Colleen said. "You'll make yourself crazy."

"I'd be crazy not to," she said. "Because we both know that it's going to take a minor miracle."

And here was her minor but indisputable miracle. They are all under its roof.

She'd met Colleen right away, when Richard was first going out with her, because in 1963 a family could still expect to be part of whatever happened to a son. She was eighteen and Colleen was nineteen. They were girls and soon girlfriends. That was what young women like them were called, at least until they were married and installed in some little starter house with a good set of mixing bowls and linoleum floors to wax and socks to sort, all of which could happen to you, or so it had seemed, in mere weeks. Then, for the first months after the wedding, in a kind of extended celebration, they would be called brides, and finally, with the celebration framed and hung on their walls, housewives. Or, when necessary, working wives. The unmarried women, who were assumed to be sleeping alone but who could become, for some wives, and eventually for Colleen, a persistent threat, got to be called, in time, in the mouths of the worst of the men, the old girls. Or the gals.

And most of the wives, the ones Colleen was trained and paid to help in their deliveries, to cheer on and envy and occasionally scold, were also called mothers. Women got to be called women only when they hit menopause, after the cycle, the buildup and loss, had stopped. And even then, not always. You often heard one grey-haired woman calling another a girl, as if that word held all the fun left in the world.

The spring she was Colleen's bridesmaid, they leafed through the glossy magazines together and made the lists and attended all the showers. They helped Colleen's mother make rich squares to freeze for the trousseau tea and had their fittings for their gowns. They drove to Toronto and Port Huron to shop for filmy peignoirs and satin shoes.

She wasn't used to money then, to the idea that quite a lot of it could be put to just one thing. All she knew about money was that it could set off her mother's nagging outrage, because her father apparently made it and lost it in mysterious and equal amounts. Now flush and now broke, he'd pointed the studious Richard toward scholarships and bursaries, and pointed her, even though she was easily as smart, nowhere. Because he loved her as you love a child. Which left her free after high school to answer an ad, on a whim, in the London paper. The job was acting as a paid companion, which meant light housekeeper and trapped audience to a tight-fisted, talky, eighty-year-old widow. A woman who became so secure in her care that she could announce to an unmarried, middle-aged son that homely girls were by definition the most reliable and loving. And this was the doctrine she lived with until she started competitive swimming and found a better job in a sporting goods store, where she met her first not-quite-suitable boyfriend.

But helping Colleen with all her planning, she had no doubts whatsoever about Richard's worth. She was more certain of it than Colleen. She bragged about the way he'd begun to change, about the way he had improved himself, prepared himself. He was going to have his own medical practice, she reminded her, his independence, their independence, and he'd become more careful with his opinions. She said that she alone could assign points for improvement because, like any sister, she'd been watching and listening all along.

Although there had been no serious contender in her own life that spring, she was dating an Australian she'd found at a swimming party. The guy had a good laugh and a full blond beard and a beer belly, but she essentially ignored him when he came to the house, which got him a load of sympathy. And she didn't want him at Colleen and Richard's wedding either, even knowing that this would make her the stray bridesmaid.

Richard didn't like the way she treated her Australian guy, and when Colleen defended his anger, she took the chance to explain herself. "They say they love you," she told Colleen. "And they do not." There was no need to paint the picture, the picture being that guys needed sex and would walk any walk and talk any talk to get it. "I couldn't do it," she said, tilting her face this way and that, pivoting her head as if to speak to different people. "I love you. I love you. I love you."

Then Colleen said that she had never been with anyone but Richard, who had said it only once. The way you might tell a child about gravity.

She and Colleen had talked again last week about how unlike three marriages can be. About her own holding fast, even through severe infant fatigue and the later, raucous, dishonest teenage years and then through Jack's heart attack and his wise and selfish fight, and about Jude with her two unlikely unions, the early, wilder one on that farm with Liam's father Tommy and now this stronger one with Gus. And about Colleen's having been so close to finished. She confessed that she knew exactly what she and Jack have been reduced to, that a couple as dull as they are, as dull as dishwater, is probably, in some quarters, the stuff of mockery. But she could say it bragging.

Of course, Colleen had not liked Jude, not in the beginning. Now there is always Jude to consider, she said once, jealous. Unwilling then to comprehend an approach to life, a risk, so different from their own.

She reaches to the bedside table for 1974 again and finds the late summer.

"We had a go at teaching Jude how to play bridge," it says. "Colleen was borderline obnoxious because my brother is making her insane. If Richard isn't careful, he's going to find himself beyond reach. Gone."

They wanted Jude to play bridge because it was something they did with the men through the winter, and it would be easier to put a last-minute foursome together if six of them could play. That was the idea. And Jude insisted that she was ready to learn.

It was a muggy evening and the sky wasn't yet dark. Jude had brought Liam along and he and Michael were back in the family room but Jack, bless him, had taken the three other kids upstairs. They could hear the high-drama rumbling of his voice as he read from one of their storybooks, or maybe he was winging it, making up another convoluted adventure with the kids themselves at the centre of the action, with one of them stepping up to be the hero and another, because didn't every story need one, the arch villain. Once upon a time there was a girl named April, a boy named Michael, a girl named Jan, a boy named Paul. There were nights then when the chance to be a star or a villain was the only thing that could settle them down.

Colleen was in a sundress and she and Jude were in baggy shorts and T-shirts, and they'd all kicked their sandals off under the card table. Jude had just got her ash-blonde hair cut, it was now chin-length and shaped, but they couldn't mention the cut because that would have meant they'd seen the need.

Colleen was plainly annoyed about the bridge lesson, maybe because she had some story to tell, about Richard or about work at the hospital. There were not that many work stories, birth stories, she could repeat, ethically, but she seemed to be very good at pushing women, all kinds of them, to do the thing she herself might never have to do now, or get the chance to do. Although Colleen had always expected to see her own legs up in the stirrups, after ten years of trying, and the last time refusing even to cry, she had never been able to hold on to a pregnancy. So she'd had to learn the urgency of birth the hard way, by watching it, by persuading it and cleaning up after it, her only proclaimed weakness sometimes letting her sympathy go to the bravest, as a reward, rather than to the frightened, who might be able to use it.

Jude had brought a Mama Cass tape, because she'd just died, choking on something, and as they listened to "Dream a Little Dream of Me," she said they should pay tribute, they should raise a glass to that strange, heartbreaking voice. And then they talked about Jude's recent promotion to manager of the furniture department, with some responsibility for inventory, finally, which meant that now she could exercise her good taste and her natural instinct for scale and colour.

It was decided that they should play a few hands with their cards laid out on the table, so Jude could see how it worked. And that she and Colleen would take turns bidding for the absent fourth player.

"Again," Jude said. "The point count. Ace, king, queen, jack, four, three, two, one?"

"Yes," they said.

"Well, that's got some logic to it," Jude said.

"A lot of logic," Colleen told her.

There was a bowl of mixed nuts at Colleen's elbow because she'd quit smoking, but she wasn't afraid of the nuts. Given her metabolism, which was her mother's, there wasn't going to be much weight gain. She had decided to quit because of the miscarriages, because, although no longer so sure of her marriage, not with Richard as he was, she said she suspected a connection.

Colleen wasn't allowed to smoke in the house anyway because if Jack smelled a cigarette he'd want one and find it. "Jack gained twenty pounds when he gave up the evil weed," she told Jude, picking out a big pecan. "He got the weight off," she said. "But it wasn't easy and it certainly wasn't pleasant."

"That's so encouraging," Colleen said.

"I absolutely need thirteen points," Jude said. "And if I've got seventeen or eighteen, I'm laughing?" She was counting her points a second time, double-checking herself.

"You're laughing," Colleen told her.

They bid the hand and Jude started to play it out. Then Jack came down and stopped in the hall to stick his head in and say that the kids were almost asleep. "How's the lesson going?" he asked them.

"She's a genius," she told him.

"And who would have guessed it?" Jude said.

"Genius is always good," Jack said. Then he left them to go back to his big boat of a chair, to the only peace he could get in a day. Except that Michael and Liam were on the family room couch and Michael, at five, was old enough to want to hang on to the remote, and to argue hard for *Hawaii Five-O*.

"Nope," Jude said. She had thrown in her cards because the bid couldn't be made, which seemed fair enough for such a compliant beginner.

"It's like anything else," she told her. "It gets easier."

A new hand was dealt and they arranged their suits and laid their cards face up on the table again. This time Jude had a long string of hearts, six of them, king high, and the board had two, including the ace. They talked her through the appropriate bids and she began to play it out.

"Pull your trump," Colleen reminded her. "You want to kill everything that's out there against you."

"Five of them," Jude said. "There are only five low hearts against me."

"You're catching on fast for a one-time hippie," Colleen said.

"For a what?" Jude asked.

But then Colleen told them her work story, about a young father who was enraged, who had lifted his arms in the air, imitating a woman, and yelled at her, because his wife had been given a surprise C-section. Because Colleen was beautiful, she was used to her calm and beautiful face putting an end to things, if not always in women, almost always in men, but she said that she had not handled the guy very well. However, the C-section had been necessary and a success, so nothing else mattered as far as she was concerned. She said people would soon get tired of listening to the guy's blow-by-blow, and later, given the odds, he and his wife would get to watch the baby girl with her father's eyes sit up and crawl and then stand and walk and finally run off, safely delivered, to her life. Then she said that she knew she shouldn't be interrupting Jude's concentration, but if she wanted to play bridge with them, she should maybe be prepared for it.

So Colleen wanted to be funny. To stop herself.

Jude had done a pretty good job of ignoring both Colleen's hippie crack and her hospital story. Her hearts were long gone, she had run her clubs, and now she was cleaning up.

"Where did Gus learn to play bridge?" she asked, to enforce the peace.

"His wife, I think," Jude said.

"His ex-wife," Colleen said, coming back for more.

They all liked Gus, there was no not liking Gus. They hadn't been told why his marriage had failed, but maybe it was the years-on-end strain of raising a damaged child, because Jude *had* told them about the complicated birth and about Kate, the difficult adolescent daughter who could be wildly destructive. Or maybe his marriage had failed for the usual reason, although it was hard to believe that the Gus they'd met would have messed around. But how to know? It could have been his disheartened wife who made the mistake. Or found the solution.

Certainly she had tried to help Colleen with Richard's mistakes, advising her to forget his young women, that he'd just become one of those men who gave off the scent, that it probably leaked through his sweat glands now that he was a big-time surgeon. And that it wasn't as if this was unique to him. She'd told her that the young women would keep on a-comin' and that there was nothing to be done except maybe have an informal talk with some bulldog lawyer, to find out exactly what she could say to Richard if one day she did need to hold his attention. Because that's what she would do.

And then she'd offered her best theory, which was that looking outside a marriage was about nothing more than sexual boredom, and that if someone did a survey, they would likely find that first marriages were vaginal and second marriages oral. Whether Colleen was grateful or appalled, she couldn't tell.

"The vagina can lose some of its dark appeal," she told her. "At least," she said, "that's Jack's thinking."

Jack who had sworn, having got in her both a first and a second wife, that he would never, ever be bored. *Realpolitik*, she'd called it, shrugging her shoulders. Or, if Colleen preferred, growing old together. She had also suggested that maybe Richard didn't realize the lasting effect of his behaviour. And that she was willing to confront him. She could tell him clearly enough what he was doing.

"And then what?" Colleen asked. "Tell him that I selected him, above many others, when he was nothing but raw potential? Or that I still want it, every time, to start with me? Which would make me the most deluded woman in history?"

Jude had pulled off a make-believe slam but the points had been there for her. She was taking a handful of nuts as her reward.

It was Colleen's deal, and when they had their cards, she looked over at Jude as if studying her, as if she belonged to a slightly altered species. "After Tommy," she asked, "before you met Gus, when you were out there on your own . . . ?"

"What exactly are you getting at?" Jude said.

If Colleen had just looked across at her instead of at Jude, she would have seen in her face what was going to happen. Jude was going to take her handful of nuts, call Liam from the family room, and walk out the front door.

"Why don't you just lay your cards down on the table," she told Colleen. "Or we'll quit for tonight."

And not waiting for an answer, she turned to Jude. "Had enough?"

"I think I have," Jude said.

"We'll stop then," Colleen said. "You did really well," she told Jude. "Having you and Gus is going to make the winter a lot shorter."

Jude left to go back to the family room, to Liam, so Colleen helped her fold up the chairs and the card table, although not with anything like the same force. Usually when Colleen went too far, which wasn't that often, given Richard's conduct, she could just turn her back. And then, because she made herself, she could forget it.

"Was that necessary?" she asked.

"I'm sorry," Colleen said. But she didn't look sorry.

She wondered then if Richard's newfound, reckless pleasure in women, his power and his glory, would ever be something that she and Colleen could describe to Jude. Maybe Jude did know why so many unattached women allowed it, or needed it. Were they only lonely, only stupid? Or did they think that a wife was a small thing? It was quite the mystery, a woman's ability to realize and in the same instant overlook the fact that another woman, and maybe a strong one, strong enough to win at any cost, existed.

But for tonight she would throw a snack together and she and Colleen would join Jude and Jack and the boys in the family room. Faithful Jack would continue to pay Jude a little extra attention because she was still new, and then he might tell them about something he'd just seen on television, from the real world, and the tone of the conversation, everything, would be corrected.

"Do you think this cheese is all right?" she asked Colleen. She emptied a box of crackers onto a plate. The cheese was a leftover half-round of Gouda with a few specs of white mould at the one edge, but she wanted it saved.

"Hand me that paring knife," Colleen said, saving it. . . .

And now Jack is standing beside her in his bathrobe, glistening from his bath, so she drops the journal on the bed.

"Where have you gone?" he asks. "Are we having sex again? Tell me what we're doing."

She can smell the steam pouring out into the hall, so he must have used something in the bathwater, one of her potions. He would not have realized the enormity of his mistake until it was too late.

She can hear Colleen taking a minute with Kelly down in the living room and now she's climbing the stairs to relieve Jack.

"The cramps are worse?" Colleen asks from the doorway, looking at the hot-water bottle on her distended abdomen.

"Pretty obviously," Jack says.

Colleen comes toward the bed. "How about a massage?"

"Just sit down," she says. "And talk to me about your fascinating life."

Jack steps back to make room. "I think I'll give the life a miss," he says. "I'm going to call Alice." He lifts the tray from the desk to take it downstairs. "To see if she can't prescribe something more cramp specific."

"Tell her to remember being fifteen," she tells him. "Fifteen and doubled over."

He leaves them to make his phone call and Colleen sits down beside the bed. "Alice will have something up her sleeve," she says.

She lifts the hot-water bottle. "This thing needs to be filled again," she says. "Not scalding hot but as full as you can get it." Then she thinks she needs to sit up.

"The bathroom?" Colleen asks, pulling the sheet back and helping her stand, giving her a locked arm. She stays out in the hall, but keeps her hand on the bathroom door, to hold it open.

She sits on the toilet, waiting for the small pleasure of urination. "Is Jude coming tonight?" she asks.

"That's the plan as I know it," Colleen says.

"I should feel guilty, shouldn't I?" she says. "Taking everyone's time. Is Richard getting any sleep at home?"

"He is," Colleen says.

They both listen as the weak stream of urine, no more than a tablespoon or two, which is not enough, hits the water in the bowl.

"And what's Gus doing with himself?" she asks. "He and Jack could do something. It would help Jack." Having said this, she knows that she doesn't mean it. Because what would they do except sit around and think about her? And does Jack need to have his thoughts doubled up? No, he doesn't.

"Gus is probably shovelling snow," Colleen says. She helps her back and into bed and, fussing, tidies the sheet and then moves to the wall side of the bed to tidy it there. "If Jack wants Gus here, he'll call him," she says. "Jack's a big boy."

"I guess," she says. She reaches for the water pitcher on her table but can't lift it, so Colleen comes to help her. . . .

Earlier this morning, hours ago, Colleen had opened her eyes not wanting to take her turn today. And then, coldly awake, she remembered more clearly what it was she didn't want.

Watching Sandra lift the glass to her mouth, she notices the shaking she has seen in her mother's hand, at the seniors home. This has nothing to do with fear, it's just the overtaxed nervous system shutting down or misfiring or simply worn through, like brittle wiring in an old house. Some other time maybe she'll remember the hard science, the dutifully memorized physiology.

"Jude's out shopping for nail polish," she tells Sandra, sitting down to wait for the next thing. Our friend Jude, she wants to say, still and always half aware of her cool resistance the day they met her, when a lost and lonely Liam annoyed them with his soccer ball as they sat visiting in her mother's apartment. Jude the ex-hippie, messy-haired, single mother of a boy.

She wasn't particularly embarrassed by her mother's reaction to

Jude that first day, by her tight smile or her practised restraint, because there was no need to be, because Sandra was on to her mother, to restraint's trick of giving so much force to the unspoken judgement. Besides, Sandra had her own mother, didn't she? A woman who was both deeply religious and, once in a while, casually brutal. And neither of these of much use to a daughter. Or to a son.

She had been getting a bit impatient with mothers and thoughts of mothers the year they met Jude, and she'd been thinking that what she needed was a friend in her own situation, a woman who had no children, and who was ready to say goodbye to her mother. Someone who was, like her, tired of all that connective tissue, that attachment. Maybe it could be a woman she worked with at the hospital, some other nurse. Certainly Jude had not looked to be a candidate. Which just proves.

"Nail polish," Sandra says. "Good." She lifts her hands to examine her clipped, blunt fingernails. "Look what he did to me," she says.

Even a month ago Colleen's line would have been, Oh, relax, you can fix them the day after tomorrow, when they grow out again. Because Sandra has always been lucky with strong nails, which means that her bones have also been sound. She looks at Sandra's profile on the pillow, at the disproportionate nose, the too-short neck, the unpretty, undercut chin. Like Richard's face, it was a gift from their undomesticated father, hard-wired and beyond easy correction. But then neither of their faces is actually seen, not any more. So if my husband and my friend went missing, she thinks, I wouldn't be able to describe them to missing persons?

When they were young women shopping in Toronto for filmy peignoirs, for her wedding night with Richard, Sandra told her that she was afraid she would be loved by the wrong man. It was the first deeply private thing she'd confided and it sounded so ridiculous, so vain, that she laughed. And laughing, not getting it, she hurt her.

"But I have to make a move soon," Sandra told her. "Or I'll be the only one left, the only one without a house and a bedroom suite and three bratty kids. So I'll say, fine, all right. You love me. Let's tie the old tie that binds."

She did know what Sandra was saying. Young women like her, without the easy appeal of prettiness, and with the confusion that must create, had to look at things a little differently if they were going to survive. Sandra had probably been looking at things a little differently all her life, or at least since she'd first noticed, when? at five? at six? that absence of pretty-girl appeal given back to her from other faces.

Although he was just as unpretty, Richard had grown up unscathed, and after she got home from that holiday in Spain he decided for some reason to explain that he knew why. He said that he'd watched Sandra in school, walking up the big double staircase with one of her friends, laughing off the mockery he never got. Or didn't get openly. If they hated him, he said, it was because he was so much brighter than they were. And they kept their comments to themselves. It didn't matter and wasn't going to matter that he wasn't standard-issue handsome, he said, although he always knew that he'd have to wait for the sex.

But then when she reached out for him, wanting to ask why all that waiting for her had not made him faithful, he told her that he never wanted to talk about it again. "And anyway," he said, "look at Sandra now. Now she's got it all, hasn't she? A good and faithful husband, those kids, that house. You and Jude. Me."

"I do," Richard used to insist in the uncomfortable back seat of his old Plymouth. "I do." Or, "Come on, I need you to believe me. Find a way." And if he never talked about love, didn't he talk about joining forces, about building a life together? And wasn't that love? A girlfriend, a bride, a wife, did you have to take it all on faith . . . ?

"Where are you?" Sandra asks.

"I'm nowhere," she says. "I'm right here."

She is dizzy from sitting so she stands up and walks over to the window, to the desk piled with the journals and with all the brighter, supposedly helpful books. Then she gathers the helpful books into her arms and lugs them out to the top of the stairs, where she stacks them in two piles, erect as soldiers. She comes back empty-handed.

"What if your dumping those tomes was a mistake?" Sandra asks. "One of them might hold the answer, if someone would just take the time to look."

"The colours were all wrong," she says. She goes to the opened drapes and pushes them open wider on a winter day that is as bright as you can expect in December. "Crass yellow?" she asks. "Black? In a room this good?" Although it has been years since they redid the bedroom, she knows that Sandra is still proud of it, that she still likes to be told that it's a good room.

"What do you think I should do with my journals?" Sandra asks.

All right, she thinks. She sits down again. "I would say that depends," she says. "Doesn't it?" Disposal of journals is not a problem she herself will ever have.

Sandra is waiting.

"Have you asked Jude?" she says.

"No," Sandra says. "Not yet."

"How many are there?" she asks.

"One every year," Sandra says. "Some of them not finished, some fairly raw, maybe, depending. I guess if I don't want them read, I could tell you to take them with you today. I could say, get rid of them."

Then she has to stop because so many sentences in a row have interrupted the rhythm of her breathing to make room for the gasping cough. They wait for the cough to do its work and when her lungs are clear, or almost, she says, "I could ask you because you might be the only one who wouldn't cheat and read them." She is concentrating, working to reset the rhythm of her breathing. "You would restrain yourself, I know."

There is a certainty in her words because right at the start, soon after they met, Sandra had been told the miserable story about the pink plastic girlhood diary and her elegant, worried mother's thieving betrayal, reading it. And if she's had to let some of the oldest stories go, and who hasn't, she will have hung on to that one.

"Yes," she says. "I would behave myself."

"We've been quite different in our mothers," Sandra finally says. "Our imperfect mothers."

So this time Sandra knows exactly where she's gone as she sits there ready to do anything asked of her. One more time she has understood that, like the half-submerged, slippery rocks that can take a girl down a Lake Huron creek, some thoughts will gladly lead you on to the next.

"There must have been times when I could have been a better friend to you," she says. Risking the next rock.

She doesn't mean anything like betrayal, she means only a faltering, a hesitation, some undeserved hesitation. Not taking the time. Wanting to take it and then holding back, tired, or busy with some self-indulgence. With adultery, for instance.

"Oh, I don't think so," Sandra says. She lifts the hot-water bottle from her stomach to turn it over.

"Is any of it in the journals?" she asks. "Our loyalty. My lapses?"

"Where else?" Sandra says. And then, to the pain, "God."

"I'm sorry," she says, standing up. Useless.

But here is Jack coming through the door with a high-held tray of weak tea and arrowroot cookies. Once again turning up, as she had promised Sandra he would.

"How was the life?" he asks, not wanting an answer but apparently strong enough today for a word or two of upbeat gallantry.

"Not long enough," Sandra says, accepting her cheap plastic mug.

They have their tea together and then Colleen leaves them to get her coat. Driving away, she can see that the sun is trying hard, but it feels colder.

Soon another nurse will come bounding up the stairs to help Sandra into the bathroom again and then, with a bladder only half emptied, she will sit for a while in a velvet chair and try to answer the list of necessary questions buried, sometimes absurdly, in the nurse's chat. The vital signs will be taken, and after the notations have been made and the bedding changed, the needle will be lifted high in the light for inspection and then lowered to a bruised hip.

When she gets home Richard is just waking up but he says that he's had another good two hours and then he throws back the duvet and she drops her clothes and climbs in beside him. He is in no mood for any of what he calls the fancy stuff, and she is ready to take his lead. It makes perfect sense that he would want only the most straightforward, most elementary sex. The kind he imagined as a boy.

They seem to be finished and he is curled behind her with his arms and legs wrapped around her own, guarding her, like an animal. He is quiet but his jaw is worrying her shoulder blade. He didn't get his satisfaction and neither did she.

"Next time," he says. As if she might doubt a recurrence.

They have been on this plateau since her episode in Spain, although she has to believe that it will disappear, eventually. You see it all the time at the grocery checkout and in doctors' offices, articles encouraging people like them, the patronized aging citizenry, to try to carry on regardless. So an end or a very serious tapering off must be out there, lying in wait for them. Certainly nothing they were doing now could match what they did with each other in the beginning, but neither is it the confused, numb, dishonest thing that got them through the years between his messing around and her own. It's just that there are no more surprises, not unless you count their occasional, generous patience with each other. Short of joining some swingers' club or dressing up in each other's clothes or playing around with pain, which, given who they are and what they know, would be impossible, from here on in surprises are going to be unlikely.

He has told her that he wouldn't touch Viagra with a ten-foot pole, but he can say that, can't he? So far. So far so good.

Gus is on Viagra. She knows this because he was so pleased with himself that he told her one morning on the phone, when she was waiting for Jude to pick up. He sounded like a young man who'd discovered transatlantic flight and she had shared his good news with Richard, just as a matter of interest.

All through these months, Richard has been refusing to say anything specific about Sandra's cancer. Eons ago, when she was in nurses' training working her butt off to finish with spectacular recommendations, the young Dr. Richard McKellar had been very eager to explain the things he was afraid she might not comprehend, both to help her and to impress her, but after she married him the explanations got fewer and farther between and then they stopped entirely. Leaving it at the office, he called it, telling her that he simply could not spend his days in the operating room and his evenings at home rehashing it all. And that was when he started to talk about death with what sounded to her like ease.

Of course he knows Sandra's surgeon and the oncologist at the clinic out on Commissioners. And he knows Alice, her family doctor, because they graduated together. He will have made his inquiries and muscled his way into the results of X-rays and ultrasounds and blood tests. He will have understood the codes. But now, this week, watching over Sandra, watching the pain's cost grow on the face that is his own face given back to him, he can only take his overnights and then come home to lie in this bed, catatonic.

His hand is cupping her belly and she rocks her behind, as if looking for comfort. As if calling his name.

She can feel him rising behind her. "Let's go again," he says. "I need this."

Richard has never confused his honest need with anything he would deal with on his feet. It's just their bodies doing them a kindness, he told her. One of the last favours from their middle-aged bodies.

Right from the start she has never been much good at reading his need. It materializes, it doesn't. Certainly she's had her years of wifely assumptions. A brutal morning in the operating room, a tetchy but unavoidable nurse, an admired patient badly lost. A passing fondness for her or a slight but frisky inebriation, with its usual hopefulness. The wanting of forgiveness, or its gruesome mirror image, some twigged memory of that treacherous young woman, his sweet and stupid young thing.

"But do *I* need it?" she asks. Such a savage thing, she wants to say, and so late in the game. But it will not be stopped, not yet. And what exactly is its purpose now? Can it really be prompted by pity? By rage? Is it just gratitude for her own safety, maybe some deep fondness for him here, in the face of death? Or is it only the savage and endless body-long plunge of blood from her aching heart down to her pelvis.

It will make no difference. She knows that. Because from here on in, whatever prompts it, their need will have to both carry and hide their loss.

When they're done she's going to make him a comfort meal of poached eggs and maybe some peameal bacon, and while she stands at the stove he will open the *Globe and Mail* to read something aloud and she will ignore him, because as much as he insists on the reading aloud of random horrors, with all her aching heart she hates it.

But for now he is kneeling above her with his clever mouth, a mouth like a child, dancing, buried in her neck. Her hands find the small of his back and quick as a storybook bride she lifts her hips to meet him in the air.

Showgirls

Jack put together a hodgepodge meal from the casseroles and the last of Jude's maple custard and then the supper nurse came to give her another injection. And now Jack is seeing the nurse out.

While he's down there he will be checking the phone messages and his e-mail, looking for something from Michael or April or Jan. He won't call anyone back tonight, although he will write down a few things to read to her, from neighbours, from acquaintances. And he'll load the dishwasher or try to organize the fridge, all the best of everyone's everything piling up, waiting, spoiling. He complains that he can't keep ahead of it, his food-the-hardship routine, Jude calls it.

Jude should be here soon, but she's alone for a few minutes so she picks up 1979 from the pile Colleen brought her and finds October.

"Hunky Gus has moved in with Jude," she reads. "So that's done. Colleen and I didn't help much, although he did have everything he owns wrapped in newspaper. I think I love him too. Or could. The guy Gus brought to help made a sleazy move on Colleen, so none of us loved him."

Jude's parents had been killed six months earlier, coming home from their winter in Florida, she'd bought a house with an inheritance she had never given any thought to, she had finally met Gus's daughter Kate, and now he was moving in. By any measure, it was a lot.

They had seen five years earlier, at the Wonderland dance, that Jude was ready to be smitten, but she insisted that she'd made her decision because Gus liked her to laugh out loud in bed and because only a fool would not lust after his competence. She had her new and regrettable security because of her parents' deaths in those hospitals in North Carolina, but she'd applied for a job in admissions at Western, so no one could accuse her of wanting a meal ticket. They weren't going to bother to get married, although Colleen had planned an intimate party, in November, after Gus was settled.

Liam had been taken out of school to fly down to Texas for a rare visit with Tommy, his father, so he wasn't around to help with the move, but Gus had hired one of his part-time construction guys and the two of them were muscling an oversized trunk through the kitchen down to the basement. It was the trunk Gus's parents gave him when he left Sweden. His tools were already out in the garage in their locked cabinet, or in his truck.

"Can any of you tell me why I didn't have a yard sale?" Gus asked from his end of the trunk.

She and Colleen were sitting in the breakfast nook in their work jeans and sweatshirts, drinking moving-day coffee and being no help at all. They'd come over partly to show their enthusiasm for the move but also to unpack or to haul upstairs or at least to break down some emptied boxes, but Gus had told them, please, just sit there. Along with the coffee, one of Colleen's sour cream cakes had been set out to tempt the men into slowing down, and when they came back up from the basement, they were ready for it.

Jude's parents had been hit by a drunk driver. The phone call came when she and Liam were eating shepherd's pie and then Colleen and Richard had taken Liam so Jude could fly down with her brother, although their rushing around hadn't done any good. They found their army father and their loyal mother unconscious and alone in different hospitals. And even the funeral in Woodstock was shocking, with the two closed caskets and the minister trying to describe not one life but two lives together. When Jude finally told them the whole story, about her mother being taken away separately in an air ambulance, and her father's mangled legs, and the taxis she had to take back and forth between the hospitals, she said that even if her parents had regained a battered consciousness, she would have had nothing for either of them but hurried, amateur prayers. Regretting so much. Promising everything.

Jude was able to get the house with her inheritance, but she said it was the Hopper print that was bought in her parents' memory. The scene was typical, a house and an outhouse and a tall lighthouse sitting together on a low rolling dune, but she put it in the hall so she could see it from her red living room chair, in the winter, when she swivelled away from the backyard. She said that Hopper was the painter for her because his eye had gone to the things she herself would go to, strangely routine things, like houses with bay windows and quiet, suggestive people, blue water and dunes and casually crowded pines. And because in asking her to look at them in his convincing light, he was asking her to do some work. She said Hopper caught both things at once, pure escape and no escape. And if loving him could do you no practical good, it could remind you of those two-at-once things.

After Jude got the print up Sandra was invited over to have a look at it, and standing both close up and as far away as she could get, she told Jude that loving a painting was new to her, and that she was glad to learn that such a thing was possible.

Gus had helped find the house, of course, and given it the okay, because of its sound structure and the new furnace and the wood trim. It was in Old North too, only eight blocks away, a storey-and-a-half built near the end of an era, before the fifties ranches took over. It sat closer to the street than a newer house would and it had a nice high-pitched roof and a sturdy chimney. And some work had been done. The garage had been torn down and replaced with a double, attached garage, for bad weather, with a small family room tucked in behind it. Jack said that the generation that built these grand old houses had wanted the grace of solid workmanship and they'd got it because they didn't second-guess or hurry their workmen, because even money could move slowly, once upon a time. Then the generation that built the big ranches, like Colleen and Richard's, wanted both larger, spread-out rooms and the luxury of isolating space, with the cornfields simply put to grass and the grassy distance between the houses allowing them to say, we hardly know the people behind. We never see them, hardly hear them.

The day of Gus's move Jude told them that there wouldn't be much to do because he'd got rid of most of his apartment furniture, handing it off to a couple of his guys who had families. She said he had already pitched a lot of her basement junk to clear space for his winemaking, coming up the stairs with his arms full, checking with her but clearly decided.

She also told them that at her age, at thirty-eight, getting to know a live-in man was a brand new game, because now you knew that a man's stories, his past, might be told more selectively, and that you would have less time to sort it all out. Although Gus had tried to ease her mind. Early on, like some perversely honest used-car salesman, he had disclosed his defects, his annoyances, he called them, parading them past her one at a time so she would never be able to say she hadn't known, hadn't even dreamed. What you see is what you get, he'd told her, although this wasn't true because it never was true. There would always be more, of everything.

Aside from *MASH* and the weather, Gus would watch nothing but news on television, and only some of it, and the last time Jude got him into a theatre to see a critically acclaimed film, she'd decided that that's what it was going to be, the last time. She said she'd coaxed him and she should not have coaxed him, so she paid. He was already shifting and muttering in his seat before the critically acclaimed carnage began, and when the slouching kid in front of them turned around to say, shut up, old man, Gus had leaned forward and booed, loudly, holding his cupped hands to his mouth as if it were vaudeville they were watching, as if they were a hundred years old.

And on weekends, when he stayed overnight at her apartment, he would sit at breakfast looking through the Saturday paper for contrived photographs, often urging her attention over to his side of the table, to a heavy-handed shot of arranged children holding war-battered toys, or of desolate, meticulously overturned shoes. Or of souped-up boy soldiers charging the first-world cameras. Boys with guns strapped over their backs like guitars, or aimed high, as if it were the night sky they wanted to kill. War stars, he called them.

"Journalists," he told her. "They seem to think we can't be stunned by something they've just stumbled across, by accident, something they haven't framed." When he found a photograph he could credit, and there were some, he would tell her, "There. That's the real thing. Can you see it?"

Gus had been a boy in Sweden during the Second World War, and he had never forgotten the proximity. He eventually told Jude that near the end of the war some guy had convinced him to climb a woodland hill with five other boys, his friends, and that they were told to crouch, to take aim with their air rifles. So six skinny boys had posed like warriors and, pretending to be dangerous, had got their village fame. This boy-during-the-war story had been his best told and least reluctant, and Jude said what she'd learned listening was that, with him as much as with her, it was anger that kept some stories alive.

In the beginning, when she started in about Tommy leaving her at the farm to go back home to Texas to sign up for Vietnam, about what he'd done to her and to Liam, wanting him held accountable by everyone and for all eternity, Gus had stopped her short. So she'd given that up. Although it could still rear its ugly head. On bad days when she wanted more anger she could still find it, easily, in Tommy's appetite for sacrifice, in his anguished readiness to serve a cause, his country's cause, that was greater than his own son.

Thinking that Gus might have been scraped clean by the wife who'd divorced him or by Kate, the daughter who'd been known to hate him, Jude had tried, unsuccessfully, to make him keep talking, to make him believe that things would be different for him now. But except in relation to Kate, Gus never said anything about his first wife, although he had once taken Jude to an old Toronto suburb to show her the house he'd built and lost. Well over two hundred thousand in this market, he'd told her, accelerating. The house had been so huge and severe and modern, Jude said, although not modern any more, that she could not imagine him living in it, with anyone.

Jude and Liam had been invited to meet Kate together, at the group home in Guelph, where she lived with some older women. The home that her mother found for her after she and Gus accepted that it had to happen. And Gus too wanted Kate protected from the world, from men and from herself, because when she was living at home with her mother there had been a bit of trouble. Two guys once, smuggled up late at night to her room, their snorts of laughter giving them away and then their outrageous condoms offered to Kate's mother as evidence of their common sense. And sixteen-year-old Kate both laughing and enraged. And strong. Pounding her mother into the bed.

There was the birth control pill of course, but apparently there was no cure for Kate's wildly perfect lust, only a drugged smothering. North American sex had long since been sprung from puritan shame to take its rightful place among the other necessities, like shelter and food and work. But not for Kate.

Gus and his guy were bringing in the kitchen boxes and putting them on the floor at their feet. And then they carried the last of it, the clothes, up to the bedroom closet. When the truck was empty Gus started to tell them about a job he'd just got out at the lake. His client had bought one of the finest old lakefront cottages and he thought he wanted to level it. Gus said he was going to make him see that there was no good reason to do that.

Then he took his guy back down to the basement to help him set up the winemaking equipment and Colleen grabbed a knife from the sink to attack one of the boxes on the kitchen floor, a box labelled Maybe. The dishes were hit and miss but everything, even the bags of pasta, even the Tupperware, had been wrapped in newspaper. Jude said that with the exception of the food and the four onion soup bowls, she was going to encourage Gus to take it all out to his cottage.

The men had decided to leave the winemaking equipment for another time so they came up for a last coffee and, pretending that he had to get at the sugar, Gus's guy leaned close behind Colleen and put his hand on her neck. Colleen squirmed him off but, undefeated, he turned to Gus to say that he'd forgo the day's pay if Colleen would stand up and show him those long legs. And now that he'd made his move, now that these women could see that he was a performer, he waited for them to laugh. But they wouldn't laugh. Instead, they stared at his fingers, two of which had been taken off at the first knuckle. So still performing and still hopeful, he brought his fingers close to Colleen's face.

Gus moved as fast as any man could be asked to move, using his own beefy hand on the guy's back to steer him down the hall and out the front door. And coming into the kitchen after it was done, he told first Jude and then Colleen that he was very sorry. That the guy just didn't know.

"He knows," Colleen said.

Nothing remotely like it had ever been done to Sandra, and for the first time she was wondering how often it might have happened to Colleen. Judging from the way she'd squirmed him off, so automatically, there had been other creeps. "We should bring back the outraged slap," she told Colleen, almost meaning it.

"And what distant planet are you living on?" Colleen asked. "Do you really think the guys who need a slap would take it from a woman?"

"Then a good, deep, life-threatening gouge," Jude said, still mad but laughing. "Some significant loss of blood."

Gus quickly poured the last of his coffee down the sink and told them that he should take his truck in because the oil was low. He said he'd see them later. Then Jude started to load some of the unpacked dishes into the dishwasher, so she and Colleen got to work on the rest of the boxes.

"I'm going to be all right with him," Jude said. "From now on. That's what I believe."

The boxes were all empty and broken down by the time they heard Gus open the front door. He'd been dropped off by someone from the garage, and coming into the kitchen he didn't slow down but went straight out to sit on Jude's side patio, on one of the two forgotten summer chairs. The patio was covered with cold-stiffened leaves from the big maple and it was windy out there.

Jude started the dishwasher. "All right," she told them. "That's it for today, thank you very much." They had all caught the scent of the day's sweat on Gus when he opened the patio door, and now he was half turned away from them.

Watching him relax in his chair, in the cold, she told Jude that Gus's body would be used to extremes. "He's likely been chilled a thousand times," she said. "Building his houses." As if that might be exactly the kind of stamina that could make a woman all right, from now on.

"He wants us out of here," Colleen said.

Jude got Gus's parka and her own jacket from the front hall and went out to sit with him, leaving them to rinse their mugs in the sink. But before they left to go home they locked arms and leaned their coordinated, mock-showgirl bodies through the patio door to blow the sweaty man a kiss.

Gus mustered a deep nod to tell them yes, he could see that they might have had careers as showgirls, but as Jude reached across for his meaty, callused hand, she shook her head to say no, not in a million years. . . .

And now the million years are gone. She can hear Jack on the stairs coming up to her, so she closes the journal on 1979. Because, memory aside, she wants to be here, with him. Living this day too.

Jack's climbing has been getting slower, neither of them has run the stairs in a while, but it is no less faithful. Listening to him climb you would never imagine him hesitating. She watches him come through the door, carrying his notepad, which he drops on the bed, and after he gives her a drink of water and smears some Vaseline on her lips, he leans in to kiss her, kiss her and lick his lips, his eyes their darkest hazel, like Michael's. And then they hear Jude on the stairs, lighter and faster than Jack.

She decides that tonight she will try to make Jude go back again to her parents' accident in the States, to those separate hospitals in North Carolina where they died. Not for long, just for a few minutes. Because she wants to lift the horror off Jude. She wants to see if she can take it with her.

"Hi," Jude says. "How are you doing?" She empties some of the contents of her satchel on the desk and turns around holding up a bottle of nail polish. "What do you think?" she asks.

"It couldn't be much redder," Jack says on his way out.

"Oh, you might be surprised," Jude tells him.

Now her nails have been painted, and Jude is at the foot of the bed with the razor, because, having no idea how to lift her horror away, or even how to approach North Carolina, she has asked Jude to please shave her legs. Because she knows as far as Jude is concerned, it could be this, it could be that, it could be anything.

"Jack hates stubble," she tells her. "You should keep that in mind to share with any woman who turns up."

"That's enough," Jude says. "There won't be another woman." She grabs the towel to dry the finished leg. They can both feel the weakness in the calf muscle, the atrophy.

"It wouldn't be the end of anyone's world," she says. "People do take their second chances. You, for instance."

Jude pours lotion into her palm and works her hands together. "Are you done?" she asks, rubbing the lotion into the dry skin. "I've got another leg to do here. It should be possible to shave two in one go."

She does not reach down to feel her first smooth leg, as she would if she were doing the job herself. She is trying to keep still, because of the returning cramps, because as she knows from her cramping adolescence, total stillness can work.

"No," she says, talking to her discomfort. "Please." And then she lifts her head to look at the bedside table. "Paul got me some pot," she tells Jude.

"Are you thinking you want some?" Jude asks. She opens the drawer to see the three fresh-looking joints rolling around loose at the back. "Do you want me to find some matches?"

"Probably not," she says. "But he asked me to try, to consider it, so I said I would."

"It's apparently a lot stronger than it used to be," Jude says. "In days of yore. But they say it can help."

"I'll keep them there," she says. "In case. And because Paul will check that no one has made off with them."

"Is the heat helping?" Jude asks, putting her hope back in the hot-water bottle. "Is that thing hot enough?"

"It's the weight that helps," she tells her. She lifts the bottle and lets it drop. They both hear it gurgle as it settles on her stomach like a well-fed, cuddling child. "Did you stop shaving when you lived on that farm?" she asks. "With Tommy?"

"Nope," Jude says. "I did not."

"I'm surprised," she says. "I've always thought that was part of the freedom. No bra and nice hairy legs."

"Not for this hippie," Jude says. "I left my face to fend for itself, but I hate hairy legs and I could never, ever go without a bra. Not even in my prime."

This was the truth, Jude has never let herself off. Although she's told them that lately, when she's hooking up one of her overpriced, fortified, middle-aged bras, she sometimes thinks about the more elegant structure, the more graceful mechanics, of a horse harness.

"And remember, I was a fraud living at the farm," Jude says.

"As you've tried so hard to convince us," she says. "Although didn't you . . . ?" But she doesn't finish because her eyes are heavy. Her eyes want to close, which could mean sleep, so she turns to face the wall.

Jude knows that Sandra's discomfort and exhaustion have been gaining ground, that now they can just take her. She puts the razor on the night table and sits down to wait, and waiting, she looks at the old carpets and the crafted furniture, the carved detail in the mouldings and the high green ceiling. Workmanship, she thinks. Love for a future you won't see.

I was a *true* fraud, she thinks.

Altogether, she'd stayed on the farm for almost five years. There was that first year and then the year of her pregnancy, which was 1967, both the summer of love and Canada's centennial year, and then the months before Tommy went home to Houston to sign up for Vietnam, and finally the last two years waiting for him to come back. She can see now, counting from this bedroom, that five young years was maybe too much time.

There were a dozen of them in the ancient farmhouse, all true believers living in casual squalor, thinking their important thoughts, and she was so eager to share their scorn for the things they'd left behind, the careers that threatened, the mortgages, the sparkling appliances, the baby showers. The compromises strung out like rattling chains behind their parents, behind that supposedly miserable, middle-aged defeat. A woman's proper place. The hidden machinery of government. Corporate greed and its older brother, war.

At first she had loved the long, late hours of enlightened men and women arguing the fine points, and she'd believed, doggedly, in their communal rules about work and food. Even the children, three of them, seemed to be loved communally. There were drugs, of course, soft as clouds by today's standards, but there was also music, serious, good, political music. There were stacks of LPs: Joan Baez and Dylan before he went electric and Judy Collins and Buffy Sainte-Marie, Woody Guthrie and Pete Seeger. And authentic Irish ballads, political ballads brought back to life by the Clancy Brothers and the Weavers and the Chieftains. "The Wild Colonial Boy" and all those other songs that needed not just a good strong tenor but companion voices too, in harmony, to hold the tenor down. There were guitars and banjoes and floor-sitting circles of singing, and most of the guys who couldn't talk did have their instrument, or they had something. A good ear or the shelter in a big heart or a sun-darkened, naked back, which they let you watch as they stacked and stoked the campfire. To make it last, sometimes, all night.

She had dreamed the customary dream, of course, when she was a girl. One solid man. Cushy, warm exclusion. But she got to like the farm's harmless, informal sex, the easygoing variety. And who wouldn't? Who would not have believed that it was only the outside, corrupted world that corrupted love? That sex, taken honestly and for nothing more than itself, was perfectly innocent, only the simplest of pleasures. That all you had to do was give. Not her.

But then Tommy sat down at the fire to sing to her with his Texas twang, sometimes forgetting his words or not making his notes, and night after night, sitting that close and singing so badly, he saved her from believing. Or wanting him, just him, exclusively, saved her.

After Liam was born they hitchhiked to the nearest town to get married, and she borrowed the communal beater of a car to take Liam home to Woodstock, to show him off to her parents. She was sent back to what her army father called that spiteful life with overflowing boxes of food and clothes and books and toys, which someone, which he, had stubbornly bought. The innocent bystanders, her mother called the children. Collateral damage, her father corrected.

And then when Liam was not quite one but proudly walking, Tommy became preoccupied and agitated and nervous. Her first thought was that he might be lonesome for some of his old harmless variety, and she briefly stalked the other women to find out who might be loving his twang while she napped, curled up with Liam. But that wasn't it. Tommy's convoluted American conscience was taking him bravely home to Houston to enlist, to train. To become strong enough to drop out of a low-flying helicopter, drop with his soldier's load into a misty, faraway jungle. Which meant that she would be alone. Alone enough to change her mind about a few things.

Although even now she can feel a remote gratitude for the physical demands, the sweating, the muscle tone, the best skin she would ever have. And at the end of the day it was only one farm, with probably the exact wrong combination of true believers. Believers whose own mistakes and appetites had eventually aped the outside, corrupted world's.

After Tommy joined his army, things were better with her parents at least, and with her father in particular, because he'd been forced to show a little soldierly respect for the son-in-law he had refused to meet. But she didn't move home to them. She waited on the farm, filling her time with Liam, who, in spite of the throng, had exclusive love written all over him as he rolled in the snow at her feet or stumbled through the rows of vegetables in his diapers, which she'd made from Tommy's forgotten shirts. Left on her own, she had learned to find a use for everything she laid her hands on. She'd got shrewd.

And when his tour was over she sat outside the farmhouse in a lawn chair, reading his Houston letter. His, I can't come back, we probably made a mistake, letter. And reading it she learned that the thing she had been sitting still for, for two years, was desertion.

So she had to compose her own difficult letter home, and then there was a small going-away party, with a carrot cake and only a few questions, and everyone threw in a little cash so she and Liam could be dropped off at the nearest bus depot. This money has been here waiting for you, her father told her, sitting in his big chair with Liam on his knee, handing over the cheque. You've put your eggs in the wrong basket, her mother said, winking. Just get them back. And put them, she'd wanted to ask, where?

Accommodations were made. She and Liam lived in her brother's basement and she worked for a friend of his, a disorganized, obese lawyer. Her mother watched Liam until she found a sitter, but then her sister-in-law started to ask too many self-satisfied questions, about the farm, about Tommy, about the kind of costly mistakes a woman can make, so she found a real basement apartment with a shuddering furnace and off-and-on evidence of mice. She was stuck in that damp basement for another two years. Cosmic punishment was what she called it, to amuse herself. To keep herself going.

Still, she was not exactly sorry. So Tommy had got to her with a guitar and mediocre singing. A man could use worse things. As could a woman. And she did have Liam, and always would.

The disorganized lawyer took care of the long-distance divorce and Tommy began to send his first small cheques. There were no more real letters and never the suggestion of a loss anything like her own, but there was finally a note from Tommy's Texan father and that first, bombshell mention of the shot-up hip. The note asking for pictures of Liam, which she did send, by the dozens.

It costs her nothing now to concede that the farm transformed her. A raw and pretty and vacantly open-minded young woman had somehow become a woman who could survive any number of things. Being essentially unqualified, for instance, for a job, or having to watch Liam try so hard to comprehend the changes in his small life. Or getting used to her own life, without Tommy. Although the worst of it didn't last long, only a few years. And she doesn't kid herself, she would not have survived much of anything since without Sandra and Colleen. There could have been other friends, just as there could have been another farm. There might have been some different life. Without Gus, for instance. She just can't imagine it. . . .

"I've always kind of liked Tommy," Sandra says, with her eyes still closed.

After Liam got himself a second father, in Gus, Tommy started to fly up from Texas more often, and he and Sandra had both been at the graduation party and at Liam and Julie's wedding, so, yes, Sandra can say that she knows him.

"Oh, yeah?" she says.

"You bet," Sandra says. She pushes the hot-water bottle off her stomach.

"I'll fill that," she says.

She takes the bottle into the bathroom for a refill and comes back holding it by the neck, like a dead, burnt-orange goose. For the laugh. Then after she wraps it in the towel and lays it down she reaches for the shaving gel to prep the second leg.

Although Sandra is aware that she slept for quite a while, she doesn't feel rested. But she's got used to this. She has also got used to someone sitting close, watching her, waiting for her to wake up, rested.

"Tell me something you have never told me," she says.

She waits as Jude thinks for a minute, searching.

"I have never told you about Tommy's photographs," Jude says.

"How very interesting," she says, imitating someone.

"There was a makeshift darkroom," Jude starts. "Out in the barn, in an old stable. His specialty was black-and-white nudes. Glossies."

"Sounds promising," she says. She straightens her unshaved leg.

"He used to take Liam from my breast and put him in his basket on the floor," Jude says. "And after he arranged me on the bed and lit his candles, he'd jump around like a goofy pro trying to get an interesting shot, struggling to capture me."

"That would be young love," she says.

"Perfectly run-of-the-mill people can take good porn shots all the time now," Jude says. "And with all the privacy in the world, because the technology is so cheap. But it was tricky then. The developing. Other people hanging around wanting the darkroom, with their communal curiosity."

Sandra wants to laugh. She's just waiting for her cue, for Jude to give the permission.

"You have to let me know if I'm hurting you," Jude says. She begins near her foot, working up. "Tommy wanted his photographs to be the study of shadows. The beauty of light against its absence. All that mystery in the coming and going of light."

"Art," she says. "Could it exist in the dark, do you think?"

"No," Jude says. She drags the blade up through the gel. "Nothing can."

"Oh," she says. "I was hoping the answer would be yes."

"He made me look like a woman in a cheap film noir," Jude says, ploughing on. She wipes the razor on the towel. "Like a woman hoping against hope to be a star."

And this is the permission. The words *star* and *hope* together have thrown the door wide open. "A star," she says, laughing. "And where are those glossies now, I wonder? Did Tommy keep them for himself?"

"I got rid of them," Jude says. "Right after we moved here, I made Liam go inside at Whiteoaks Mall while I stood in the rain over a garbage can, ripping them into shreds. Bits of chin, bits of leg, bits of enormous but very firm, nursing breast."

"What a crying shame," she says.

"Do you remember how hard they were when you were nursing?" Jude asks, lifting the razor away. "Really like, exactly like, supermarket melons?"

"I bet you'd give a bit of right arm to see those pictures now," she says. "I know I would if it had been me lying there nude, hoping to be a star."

"Maybe," Jude says. "I never paid much attention to my body. But it didn't need much attention then. Not from me."

"No," she says.

Although the grin hurts her parched lips, she has enjoyed this confession, this nod back to something done, or allowed, in a strange time. Colleen should be here, she thinks. I was only young, people like to say. Yes.

She twists her leg so Jude can shave the back.

"I couldn't even describe that body now," Jude says. "It's possible that Tommy could, I guess, if it hasn't collapsed in his brain into all his other bodies. Do you think that men in their middle-aged dreams call up one woman's boobs, another's mouth, another's beautiful feet?"

Although Sandra knows that Jude still talks to Tommy, because of Liam, Liam and Julie now, she doesn't think she would be wise to bother him with questions about her pieces and parts.

"Maybe we should try to remember the bodies of our many young men," she says. "To see what we've done with them."

They erupt together. Once again they have got themselves, or their talking has got them, right where they want to be. But this time the laughter has brought along her wrenching cough. From my boots, she thinks, I am coughing from my boots. And my dead mother's phrase, here with me in this room. Laughing, coughing, my mother's words and . . .

"Damn it," Jude says. "Damn."

Because she has done exactly what she was afraid she would do. She has nicked the skin, on the sharp ankle bone. Sandra's blood streams out and the shaving gel is running pink and red, like tinted icing.

"Shit," she says. She reaches up to the night table for a wad of Kleenex. "Well done, Jude."

"Don't panic," Sandra says, with the coughing almost conquered. "It's worth it to me, having it done."

The blood won't clot so Sandra hands her more Kleenex and she presses harder against the cut.

"Give it a minute," Sandra says.

And she's right, it just needed a little more time, and now there is only the soaked fistful of blood.

"Keep going," Sandra says. "It doesn't matter."

Jude takes her fistful into the bathroom to flush it away, and after she washes her hands and watches the last of the watery blood circle the drain, she stands at the mirror gripping the pedestal sink. There will be no crying because the crying has crouched low in the sockets behind her eyes, and hiding there, it transforms itself. This is crying's best magic, transforming itself into withdrawal and weariness and a low-grade, humming strength. So, she thinks, looking into her bloodless eyes, now you want us to think you're strong?

Back again at the foot of the bed and with her mouth holding the shape of a smile, she picks up the razor. "That's how barbers got to be surgeons," she says.

"I've cut myself worse," Sandra says. "Believe it." She nods toward her leg. "You've likely cut yourself worse."

"I have," she says. "Yes, I have." She starts again near the cut, carefully, as she would have on her own leg.

Sandra is quiet too. Enjoying something.

She wipes the razor. "What about all your journals?" she asks. "What do you want done?"

But Sandra is looking beyond her, toward the window, and now she seems to be annoyed. Probably she planned to ask the question herself, and was just waiting for the right time.

She should have waited too. Damn again. But she asked because she's been thinking that the wrong person might decide that the journals should be opened and read. God alone knows what Sandra has written. Given the right frame of mind, a woman can have herself some pretty ugly thoughts, about kids, about a husband, about her truest friends. But maybe some close-mouthed visitor, or one of the nurses, has agreed to load the journals into grocery bags and get rid of them. Or maybe, some other day, after, she will take them herself. And tell Sandra's kids or Jack, if he catches her, that she is doing what? Looking for earrings she was promised? For some library book that should be returned? Better, as it always is, not to get caught.

"What do you think should happen with them?" Sandra asks.

"Whatever you want," she says. "I have no opinion."

"Neither does Colleen," Sandra says. "I think they should stay where they are."

"That's good then," she says. Ready to commit to this.

But Sandra has turned to the wall again, toward sleep. Toward, she hopes, some generous dream.

"There," Jude says. And although it isn't true, "You're done." She runs the towel over the leg and quickly applies some lotion and then she pulls the nightie down and the sheet neatly up. "Like a baby's rear," she says.

She clears everything away and sits down again to wait. Dream, she wants to say. Dream being young with randy Jack, or with those kids. Dream swimming.

It's no surprise that Sandra has already asked Colleen about the journals. Because that's the rank. Because she and Colleen had known each other, had known so much, before she even met them. Before Liam helped her meet them, kicking his soccer ball.

She'd been alone inside her apartment, half asleep on the couch, successfully ignoring Liam's racket out in the hall, but she did register the racket's abrupt end, and then the muffled sound of what was likely a neighbourly, and not unreasonable, reprimand. So she had to get up and go out there, both to defend Liam and to shut him down.

She found Sandra nodding at Liam, as if the two of them had come to an agreement. She pulled him close and apologized for the noise and then Sandra said that boys will be boys and invited them into Colleen's mother's apartment for coffee.

The first thing she learned, as Sandra and Colleen sat across from her on a white silk sofa, was that Colleen's mother didn't really mind children. And then that Sandra, with her odd face, who seemed to be equal parts tired and friendly, had four kids under seven. And then that Colleen, with her paisley skirt and expensive boots and her thick dark hair and well-shaped head and elegant, wide-set Jackie Kennedy eyes, had none. Or none yet. And that they were related, by marriage. As she listened to them she was thinking that although they were not old they did seem to be confidently set, like those moulded jellied salads you saw in magazines around Christmas. They were secure middle-class women who had never thought to try for anything different.

Apart from the fact that she had a son, and was about their age, just into her thirties, she realized that she had nothing to offer. But drinking her coffee, and still always a bit raw from the life she'd left on the farm, from some of the things the two of them had never tried, she became interested in their interest, and in their easy kindness to Liam.

They talked and drank their coffee and then they all turned to look over at Liam, who was holding jigsaw puzzle pieces up to his nose to study them, to divide pieces of ocean from pieces of sky.

"He looks like he's just one of those kids," Sandra said.

"A kid who needs his daily dose and more of activity," Colleen said.

Whatever the nature of Liam's problem, to solve it, he was invited over to Sandra's to connect with her son Michael, who was both close in age and apparently just as buzzed up with calories loaded into him but never entirely spent. And that fast, it was decided. The next afternoon she was to bring Liam over to play with Michael. How she was supposed to find them out in the suburbs, they didn't say. She put down her cup.

And then she was back on her couch with Liam on the floor beside her, half expecting to be reamed out but also waiting for the verdict, for whatever she was going to say about those rich women across the hall. But he got tired of waiting, so he left her to kick his ball around the kitchen.

The reason she had nothing to say to Liam was that it was obvious, it was always going to be obvious, that he would be better if she could be better. Safer if she could be safer. It was like that caution, that in-the-unlikely-event warning you got on the plane on your way down to Houston, Texas, to visit the other grandparents, when the flight attendants instructed you not to panic about your son, to secure your own oxygen mask first. Because, they meant, if you didn't take care of yourself first, it could be game over, for everyone. With no one left breathing.

But she and Liam have both been left breathing.

Sandra still looks pretty rugged when she finally wakes up, and she confesses that the discomfort has got much worse. But then she wants to talk about Jan, who even with Sandra's face has always been more Jack's daughter. Jan, who should be getting home first, because she lives the closest, in Orillia, and who often finds something else to do, who can find an excuse, any excuse, to leave her mother's side. So a daughter gains strength by keeping herself occupied, like the biblical Martha. It makes sense to Jude, or at least she's prepared to tell Sandra it does. Grief being grief. Being, like everything else now, itself.

Then they have to stop talking about Jan maybe being shortchanged because Jack has come in with a box of Midol. He says that Alice wonders if the cramps might respond to that, so Sandra downs two of them, and then throws back the sheet to show Jack her legs. To make him touch them.

"Very nice," Jack says.

She collects herself and leaves them to it.

The dark streets are not bad for December and when she gets home Gus is waiting with cinnamon toast ready to go. After they eat they go up together to fall into bed and, although she is past tired, she can feel him stiff behind her, and he's rubbing her back to keep her awake. She rolls over to tuck into him and reaches down to find him, which is easy because in refusing pyjamas Gus has always made it easy.

"What have we got here?" she asks, a bit deranged. "Lord have mercy."

Sometimes he tells her that what she has is his youth-come-back, or his store-bought love, the store being the pharmacy at Masonville. When Gus made his decision to try Viagra he didn't ask what she thought and it's too late now because he's hooked. And so is she.

"It's like your new kitchen," he told her the first time, walking in from the bathroom, naked and proud.

"It can make ice?" she asked, surprised but guessing. "It can grill chicken?"

Being with Gus was nothing like being with Tommy. With Tommy, she had given everything over. Or up. She had taken leave of the world, delirious. To make him smile his foxy, God-we're-good smile, she had turned herself into another, better woman. And not even that was enough because he always wanted more, and so did she. Anything, as long as it was more. And using his need against him, she had made him talk, made him say all the right things. She'd squeezed the words right out of him.

When she tried to coax that kind of talk from Gus, he'd looked at her as if she were out of her mind. "Not my kind of love," he said. "Sorry."

But when she was away in Spain, fourteen years ago, he had built her a new cherry kitchen as a reward, as his gift for coming through her own breast surgery without a peep of whining. And both her house and his cottage have been reinsulated and rewired, with all the lights miraculously coordinated because he said that one of the things he learned in a lifetime of building was that lighting could be everything to a room, and not least to a bedroom. As if the right light on a body was as critical as ventilation in an attic or substantial baseboards or triple-glazed windows. So the light in their bedroom had been improvised at some expense to be a friendly, softened, empathetic light. Gus has used his experience, and she could not have stopped him, to make many practical and aesthetic improvements to the way they live their lives. You can never look at a house, he insists, as done.

And they have become a little more focused in bed. They have given up passionate kissing, for instance, because neither of them likes it any more. Certainly, they did their share at the start, but now it seems to be for kids, or for actors, for people who like to be watched. Watching it on television, they will often look at each other to share a stumped expression, knowing that they've seen the last of desperate lust, and that they are going to be all right without it. But plain appetite is another matter. Gus still has his big Nordic bones and his sturdy, square face, and one of his techniques, unnecessary but no less appreciated, is to lie back on his pillow and look her over, as if he has never before seen a woman. He is still as strong as an ox and almost from their first night together he had her angle down. Watching her face and listening to her, he has taught himself how to make his plunging dives play off against the much slower threat of his leaving, and he goes on until she's had enough and then he'll want just that last few minutes. And sometimes, to make his day, she will take on a second wind or just stare down at his mastery, or give him a stupid encouraging grin. Making a joke of his magic. His storm of movement. Her luck.

Gus has never wanted to delude himself, not even when he was alone after his divorce. He will always have to find his comfort in the use of his body, and of hers. But tonight he has no nonsense in him to temper his storm. Tonight there will be no jokes. No jokes, no magic, and no luck. She crawls up to straddle him. She plants her bum on his broad belly and throws her nightie off.

He lifts her onto his youth-come-back and dives up into her, his hands rough on her heavy breasts. And then he is finished. Finished and crying, with bone-dry eyes in a collapsed face.

She slides off him. "Talk," she whispers.

His arm is resting across his face. "I don't think I can go," he says.

"What are you saying?" she asks. "To the funeral?" She pulls the duvet up to cover them.

"When it was you . . ." he says.

She leans over him again. So down in the dark kitchen, ready with the cinnamon toast, he had let himself go back to her own smaller, almost forgotten cancer and now he wants her to convince him that she is alive. To promise him. That in this house, things are different. He is forcing her to say it, that everything Sandra is, now, she is not.

"This is only a very bad night," she tells him. "A bad time."

"When it was you, I thought . . ." His arm is still shielding his face.

"But it's not me," she says. "Not yet and not soon." She lifts the arm away. "You better look at me," she says.

And then with no more warning than at its start he pulls himself together, and this she can take as a kind of love.

"I think I'll drive to Guelph in the morning to see Kate," he says.

"All right," she says. She falls back on her pillow. "Good."

Of course Gus needs to be with his angry, grown-up, suffering daughter. Because given one hard thing, there are people who do go looking for another, more familiar hard thing, people who can use a well-tested strength to brace themselves for something new, and Gus has remembered that he is one of them.

Kate will want to know what is happening with Sandra, and she will certainly care, because even with all her difficulties she does remember kindness, and who has sent it her way. Although there is no point in telling her that Sandra is dying. Kate has got far too used to dying, living where she does.

She thinks about the last time Sandra went with them to visit Kate. Kate was not having a good day, so the conversation wasn't the best, and although Gus tried to defend her as a woman he loved, no, not Kate's real mother but nevertheless a woman he loved now, she still had to duck to avoid Kate's raised hand. As they talked on and ate their little squares, the unpredicted snow, a true snowbelt storm, started to come down hard outside the window, and later, when they were ready to go home, they couldn't navigate the slippery front steps. So Gus had to shovel them clean while she and Sandra waited on the big porch. With nothing to do, Sandra began to stomp out a snow angel in the porch drifts, and then, out-of-the-blue, she lifted her cold-blushed face to insist that Kate was lucky to have her, and to say that, like any woman, she likely had more kinds of love in her than she knew.

"Because it's not the amount," she said. "It's the kinds."

Painting

JACK HAS TOLD HER TWICE when the others should arrive. Thursday. Two days, plus. Soon. Things have been gaining on him. Last night he didn't even bother to undress and he's so tired he is flat on his back, snoring. But Michael and Jan and April have made their arrangements, and there is nothing to do but wait. Which means that today when it comes and tomorrow are going to be long days. She wants her kids.

She looks over at Jack, alone in their bed.

If all is right with the world, Colleen and Jude will come with lunch again. Their lunches are just a way to fill time now, to make it hurry up and pass. Today she plans to ask them about gowns. And she might ask for the biggest mistake they might be willing to own up to, or the worst thing they ever witnessed, someone else's mistake. There will be no entertainment in asking about the towns they grew up in or their parents or their childhood friends, because she's heard it all before. And she won't push for first or worst or best sex because neither of them has ever wanted much talk in that direction. The things she told Colleen, about what Jack liked to do and to have done to him, she mentioned only as a last resort, to help her. So mistakes it will be. That and a few magnificent gowns.

She and Colleen were the ones with the gowns, of course, because when they were doing their dress-up dancing the unknown Jude was still living on her farm. On that boinking hippie farm, Jack calls it. Although Jude has had a couple of boss dresses and she's confessed to keeping one of them, a black French velvet with a long, flared skirt and a white, stand-up, linen collar. She said that she wondered if Liam's wife Julie might be interested in having it, and wanted to know if you could do that. Could you offer a second-hand but exquisite dress to your unfriendly daughter-in-law?

She has never told Colleen and Jude that she kept her own gowns, that she moved Jack's defunct wardrobe of business suits into Jan's emptied closet, to make room. Or that she continued to swan around in them even after they'd begun to look not just tight and dated but preposterous. Although they did zip up again after the surgeries.

She is going to enjoy the lunch talk but it isn't doing anything for her now because the pain is reproducing itself. Pain like a fungus. And she's crying again.

"You are only tired," she says.

Twice through the night, Richard has crawled out of April's old bed and crept in to check on her, sticking his head in the door first in case she might be sleeping, and then lowering the rails to help her up to the bathroom. He worked with her surgeon when he was at Old Vic and he knows her oncologist and his sterling reputation. And he knows Alice. Richard will have worked himself into her care as far as he could, given the restraints of medical etiquette, and there will have been telephone calls, test results read over the phone and respectful, insider talk about the final mix of morphine. The best, most humane dose, given the progression. Morpheus, he told her, is the God of dreams. A good God.

Colleen has bought Richard a new wool housecoat, a deep burgundy, and looking up at him in the near-dark she could see that he wasn't yet comfortable in it but that he wanted to be presentable, which might have made her mock him, another time. She didn't ask him to sit down to talk to her, and he would not have wanted to anyway, because he'd be afraid of upsetting her, robbing her of her rest. You learn a thing or two having a doctor brother, and one of these things is that doctors put a lot of stock in simple rest, although not necessarily their own. She did ask him to get 1990 from the desk, and to turn on her light.

"We painted the bedroom green," she reads. "And April is gone. She has chosen her druggie boyfriend over us. Over everything."

The day they painted, dependable Paul had got up early because she needed his help moving the furniture. Other than April, who showed up when it suited her, Paul was the only one still at home and with Paul came Sailor, the dog he got after Hank died. Michael had done a year in business at Western but then he'd moved out to the University of British Columbia and then to MIT in Boston, and Jan was in her second year at Ryerson in Toronto, studying graphic design and happily living in sin with Cliff. They liked Cliff, although Jack, maybe jealous, said he thought twenty was a tad young for that much sin.

Paul decided that they should get everything except the partners' desk out of the room. Jack had bought the desk at a client's estate sale and although it isn't full size, it's the heaviest thing in the room. They had to take out the drawers to even begin to move it.

She's the only one who has ever used the desk, to write in her journals, and by 1990 she'd stowed more than twenty-five years of them in those deep, dove-jointed drawers.

Paul put Sailor in the closet and they carried the mattress and the broken-down bed into April's room and leaned them against her window and her closet. They put the cherry chest and the butternut trunk and the rest of it out in the hall, and because she and Jack would need to get into the other bedroom and the bathroom, Paul pushed and piled everything tight together, like a puzzle. They rolled up the floral rug and threw it on top but they had to leave the other rug where it was, under the desk. Both staircases, the one down to the front door and the narrower one up to the big, gabled third floor that was now just Paul's, were left clear.

They put the drawers back in the desk and covered it with a sheet, and if Paul noticed her stashed journals, he showed no interest. Then she opened the closet door for Sailor, who, because he could not be insulted, bolted happily out and began to run wild in the upended bedroom, skidding on the hardwood floor. He had a thick golden coat and a good disposition, but he was essentially a middle-class, loyal-by-necessity mutt. They'd named him Sailor because of the way he locked his legs when he stood waiting, and because of his concentration, as if he were standing guard on a heaving ship. They had all tried to love him, to allow for the fact that he wasn't Hank, but he demanded too much from them. Even coming up to his dog middle age, he remained annoyingly hopeful, prancing around for the attention he believed he deserved. Jack said that Sailor was just in the wrong house.

"You'll have to stand on the desk to paint that," Paul said, meaning the plaster medallion and the old light fixture in the middle of the ceiling. He was spreading the drop sheets to protect the hardwood floor.

"Yeah," she said. "Your aunt Colleen is coming over this afternoon after she's had some sleep. She might be willing to climb up there."

"But Jude shouldn't help," Paul said.

Jude had had her lumpectomy in early June. Richard promised her that he'd get her the best guy available and he did, and they hadn't had to take the whole breast. The prognosis was good, or good given what it could have been, but she still looked tired. For relatively healthy people they'd had a bit of a run, with Jack's heart operation the year before and then this with Jude.

Paul patted his thigh and Sailor high-stepped it across the rustling drop sheets and the two of them went upstairs to the third floor so Paul could carry on with his packing. He couldn't give her any more time because he was leaving the next morning for Ireland, for the trip he'd planned with two of his friends. Sailor, who did not have a ticket to Ireland, would stay behind. It was no surprise that Paul wanted to see more of the world. She and Jack had taken the kids on lots of trips across the country, in the summer to learn, in the winter to ski.

While she envied Paul his age, she didn't have to envy his Ireland because next month she was going to Spain, with Colleen and Jude. Although twice lately Spain had been touch and go, the first time when the police brought April to the door and then the second time, six weeks ago, when Jude was diagnosed. But things with April had settled down, and Jude was insisting.

When she'd first broached her painting project Jack had raised his talking eyebrow to suggest that it would be a lot faster to hire someone, and she'd pretended to think it over, but then she promised him that the upheaval wouldn't last long and, besides, a penny saved. But the real reason she didn't want to hire a painter was that she wanted the challenge, because didn't the theory go that if you were stressed out, you should find something to occupy your mind? And even if she was a little slapdash impatient with a paintbrush, this didn't mean that she wanted help from Jack or from Jude. The tumour had been in Jude's right breast so her stiff arm was her painting arm, and although Jack had been back at work for months and was still, as he liked to say, passing his tests, she wasn't about to push her luck. It was enough that Jack had April to deal with.

She was going to bring the high bedroom ceiling down with colour, by painting it to match the walls. She'd picked a mid-range, mild green, named something or other. Ironstone, she thinks. Something stone. And when she was done, she was going to have the floors sanded and stained a bit darker and get Jack's mother's armchair done in pretentious dove-grey velvet, and she was going to try to find the same grey for drapes, just for the change. But she would put their bed back against the outside wall, and she would stick with the two old rugs, the one a green that would likely fight the walls and the other a deep grey with a floral border, green again, some peach, some blue, some rose. The day would come when the kids would need to sell off some of the contents of this house and she knew that they wouldn't get what they should for that floral rug. Watching morning television down in the kitchen, she'd learned that floral patterns were today held in contempt, although flowers themselves were desired in even the smallest yards, and the more unheard-of, the better. Every wretched thing now, even tulips, for the love of God, was just one more way to climb above the crowd. Or to step outside it. As if life could be better if you were alone, if you alone were chic or clever or shrewd. Although what they probably meant was not alone, but first.

One of the things that she and Colleen and Jude were old enough to know was that a good part of garden fashion, house fashion, any fashion, was sustained by ordinary loathing. Because people didn't necessarily buy a thing to replace the worn out or the broken down, they bought it because they'd begun to hate the old thing, begun to regret even the time when it was new, when they'd fallen for it. Like Flokati rugs, for instance. Like brass floor lamps. Like bar stools for the dark basement.

She was halfway down the stairs to look one last time at the paint chips when she saw Jude standing on the front step in her worst clothes, holding a paintbrush in front of her face. She opened the door.

"I'm not good," Jude said. "But I am available."

"I'll give you a coffee first," she said. "So you can come to your senses. You can drive over with me to get the paint but that's it." She had never helped Jude with any kind of work, except for the move from the Oxford Street apartment after her parents died, and the little bit they'd done when Gus moved in. She'd helped with Liam, certainly, but that was measured on a different scale.

"I've been told to keep moving this arm," Jude said, lifting it. "And painting is moving." She dropped her things onto the hall chair. "You're thinking green, I hear."

Jude knew about the recent business with April because everyone knew. Michael and Jan and Paul had known before they did, of course, and then Richard and Colleen and Jude and Gus had to find out because it had to be told. Told in strict confidence, meaning, I need you to hear this but you cannot speak of it, except to me, now. Now and maybe some other time, when and if I decide.

Although April had not been charged, she'd been brought home by those two policemen. They had stood under the porch light, one on each side of her, to ask if she was who she said she was. And then they'd described what they called an incident, and as they talked April had turned around to smile at Brad, who was shaking his arrogant head in the back of the police car. Brad the bloody dope, Jack called him. As far as they knew April had got through her teens untouched, but now, with this new guy, who'd come out of nowhere, and apparently from a family just as well off, just as fortunate, she seemed to be enjoying a reckless, drug-assisted reappraisal of her life. Although anyone who looked would have seen the privileged aggression in both of them. If it hadn't been so all-round awful, it would have been ridiculous. When Colleen and Jude were helping her rip April's bedroom apart, looking for the drugs that Jack eventually found in the basement, Jude, to help, said it was likely just cultural. Because it was everywhere now, wasn't it?

After she and Jude got back from Home Hardware with the paint and the trays and the rollers and the extension handle, Jude persisted, so they began the tedious part, the prepping. They took down the drapes and dusted the high ceiling and taped the trim, all one thousand miles of it, and Jude asked about the closets, which had not been emptied.

"Closets should stay white," she told her.

Jude started to tackle the cutting in on the big front window, so she wouldn't have to do much bending or stretching. They heard Sailor first.

"Jude," Paul said, filling most of the doorway. "What are you doing here?" Sailor galloped over to a tray to stare down into the paint, maybe to watch for some imagined fish to break the surface.

"So, me boy," Jude said. "You're all packed?"

"Nearly," Paul said. He was looking around the room like a foreman, to see what they'd achieved. "You need some music," he said.

He ran up to the third floor and came down with a handful of tapes and his small tape player. He squatted low to plug it in and give them some Paul Simon, and they went back to their cutting in. But moving their hips now, with the music.

"*You* would understand about drugs," Paul said, over the music. They both turned around pretty fast but of course it was Jude he was looking at. "Maybe you could help Mom see," he said. He shook his big boy's head. "I don't know."

Jude was waiting for her to say something, because Paul was her kid. It never would have occurred to her that Paul might hold some opinion about her past life. That even in this house, where she was safe, there might be some speculation.

"Jude took off," she told Paul. "She wasn't living under her parents' roof, pretending to go to class every day. Pretending that she'd used her tuition money for tuition."

"So do you want April to take off?" he asked.

"Maybe I do," she said. She was looking at him hard, willing him not to speak. "Maybe that would be an improvement."

"It was a different time, Paul," Jude said.

"Bullshit, different time," he said.

"Hey," she said. She slammed down her brush but then Sailor was beside her, barking.

"Sorry," Paul said. "I'm sorry, Jude. That was out of line. Big time."

"You just want things to be all right," Jude said. "I know."

But he was gone, with Sailor close on his heels.

She had never once hit Paul, but now that April had surprised her so badly she realized that she could. Even if it wouldn't be fair. Even if when she was dealing with April, she was as kind and as reasonable and as careful as it was possible to be. And what she would give not to know that she could hit her enchanting son, and not to know that he would be able to take it, to accept a mother in the wrong and go on, and that April could not. Or would not.

Although her pumping heart could be precisely quartered and handed to the four of them, she had never been able to treat them equally or fairly because, looking from one of them to the other, she had never been able to hold to any one state of mind. Most of her blunders, and her guilt, had come from that looking from one to the other, that staggering around. Regardless, for a while she'd been thinking that they had all made it through. April likes to shine, as Jack said, and to win, so she'd tried to help her do this. Michael wanted acknowledgement for his brain power, and she'd given it to him. Jan had to keep her perfectly contented distance from all of them, which she'd finally stopped fearing and learned to respect. Paul wanted to please, with hard work, with wit, with listening, and she was pleased. So each of them had made of her a different mother. It didn't matter.

The worst of it had been the thing she'd never confessed, to anyone, that earliest, blazing fear, those cold sweats when the kids were so new to her. Certainly she had known, every time, that the thing tearing itself out of her was a distinct and separate life, but it was too easy to forget that. Because even before the kids had enough balance to walk from one handhold to another, she knew that very real things could find them. Diseases. Accidents. The most offhand, casual hatred. The kinds of things, the oldest news, routinely reported in any newspaper. To justify her fear-mongering she told herself that it was an undervalued skill, that she was just a magnet pulling danger to itself, a functional thing like a lightning rod on the high-pitched roof of a barn. Women like her, like Jude with Liam, like the best witches, simply meant to ward things off. Once, when the kids were small, watching a documentary with them about the plains of Africa, she'd felt an immediate connection to those beastly, four-legged mothers. To that turn of the head, that lift of the nose, that alarmed scenting, and then the commanding, brutal nudge. Run.

Then later, when she was tested with the kids' first convoluted but apparently necessary adolescent lies, or evasions, when they were hours late coming home to their beds or nowhere near where they were supposed to be, and fed up with her worry they would say, Damn it, Mom, you do it to yourself, you convince yourself that we're trapped in a mangled car on some highway, she would tell them, You bet I do. And it works, doesn't it? Because here you are, safe home.

And then later still, persuaded by a blunt-talking Colleen, she had disciplined herself to back off, to watch from a fake detachment. If not with April and Michael, because it was too late, then at least with Jan and Paul. And to her amazement she began to enjoy this. And she didn't seem to care what kind of mother it made her.

What kind of mother? And who wants to know? They fuck you up, your mom and dad. What fool could have said this, and with such bone-headed conviction? It was that poet, that Brit in the slumpy tweeds, with no kids. Of course with no kids because you did need to have them, and *have* is the operative word, to understand that the pleasure of accusation is just like the family silver, that it moves on down the line. You blame your parents, year by year you heap it up, you build yourself a sweet little shelter of blame, and then this helpless body comes squirming out of you and you are changed and new mistakes begin to accumulate, and in no time, in ten years, or fifteen, or twenty, there's a brand new story and that treasured heap of accusation is aimed at you. You are no longer the pitiable object of misery, you are its pitiable cause. You are weakness itself, stupid and inadvertent, with every wrong thing that's loose in the world originating in you. In your words and just as often in your running out of them. You do resist the guilt but eventually you just pick it up and carry it because you would be plain crazy to refuse, to keep heaving it back for ever and ever, amen. Because if you heaved back far enough, you would find nothing waiting for you but original sin and that sin would want to call up innocence. And neither of these exist, not in real time. Not in this real time.

"Simon was better with Garfunkel," Jude said. She was looking through Paul's tapes for something different. "The Highwaymen," she said. "The best of the bad boys. Ha."

They soon lost themselves in the rugged harmony of Johnny Cash and Waylon Jennings and Willie Nelson and Kris Kristofferson, all of them very rich bad boys now, and when they finished the cutting in it was eleven thirty, so they went down for a quick sandwich. Then she sent Jude home, telling her that Colleen was coming and that they would just trip over each other. Jude left without an argument.

Back up in the bedroom she could see that she would have to get the old wood ladder from the basement to do the high corners. The green was not what she'd imagined but there was always the possibility that it would look better dry, and anyway, what difference did it make? She was going to say she loved it and stick to that.

Not very usefully, her mother had told April that this new boyfriend was no earthly good. But it would have been a waste of breath to try to get her mother on board, to get her to work with them in a joint offensive, because the concept of reverse psychology was lost on her. It wasn't exactly stupidity, it was that devout, unyielding, wrong-headed directness. Her father had been dead for five years and just recently her mother had claimed to be lonely for him, which made her want to remind her that she hadn't actually cared for the man when he was alive.

"Now that's a full hall," Colleen said.

She turned around. Colleen was carrying the ladder and even in her grubbiest clothes she looked put together.

"Paul let me in," Colleen said. "He was leaving to get his money changed." She stood the ladder in the corner. "He told me to bring this up."

She assumed that Colleen had already slipped Paul a few hundred dollars for Ireland. He'd saved up a chunk of money waiting tables at Michael's on the Thames, but Colleen and Richard had both said they could leave the kids money or they could watch it help them, and that they wanted to watch. Still, after their cheques were cashed, or after the excitement of ripping open a present, there had always remained the tuition and the clothes and the lessons and the dog and the camp and the teeth and the bikes and the various short-lived passions, the kites and the Barbies, the birdhouses, the fishing rods, the poor gerbils.

Six years earlier, when she turned forty, Colleen had announced the end of any trying for a family because she said her eggs, being more or less as old as she was, would be too old, and neither she nor Jude had argued against that decision. They knew that obstetrical nurses saw some pretty difficult things because, going silent, Colleen had said as much. She had never described any specific infant, of course. She had never talked about urgent prayers or the hope for a merciful death. She and Richard could have, and should have, adopted, but they didn't, and you couldn't ask why. "Hope can put off good decisions," she'd told them after the last miscarriage.

"I like the green," Colleen said.

"I'm not so sure I do," she said.

"Well, let's get it done," Colleen said. "And then we'll know."

Colleen had brought a couple of stretchy caps, like shower caps, from the hospital. Although her paint-smeared fingers had already touched her hair a dozen times, she put a cap on anyway and they began to work as she'd worked with Jude, back to back. Listening to the Highwaymen.

Certainly there were days when she wished that she'd done things differently, that she'd had a career, or even a job. That all along she'd been building up a lifetime of experience that would be worth big money now. Fifteen years ago, when she was thirty and before Jude knew her well enough not to say it, she'd suggested that not working could put her at risk, which had been without a doubt the truth. But then no life she knew, and certainly not Jude's, had been failsafe.

There could have been a different Jack, of course, someone who'd taken on more of the work here, the dullard work stripping the beds and mending the sleeping bags, pricing the running shoes and reassuring the teachers, making the applesauce, lancing the boils. But if she'd been too busy and tired and he'd been too busy and tired, well, what would have happened then? The kids hadn't asked to be born. No one had twisted her arm. She could have prevented any or all of them.

So her life was a done deal. Jack made the filthy lucre and she handled the rest of it. But even if she did believe that it had been a fair division of labour, it was hard not to count the money she could have made. To give to Paul, for instance, for his trip. She'd joked once about the alimony a mother of four might get, to prove how secure she was, but she'd done it just that once, because Jack couldn't see the humour.

And no amount of money could help April. April had to be prepared to help herself, that was the only answer. That was the advice.

"Paul asked Jude to explain drugs to me," she told Colleen. "To help me understand."

"Did he?" Colleen said. "And did she?"

"No," she said. "But maybe he's right. Maybe April's right. I'm overreacting. I'm blowing this up."

"If any of Jude's friends fried their brains," Colleen said, "I don't think it was with the drugs they used on that farm. And Jude has never mentioned Tommy stealing any televisions to feed his habit. Not to me, anyway." She set her tray of paint on the desk and climbed up after it to do the plaster medallion. When she finished she stood on the edge of the desk and threatened to fly. But she didn't, she jumped down and they carried on with the walls.

"Is Richard on tonight?" she asked.

"He is," Colleen said.

"Then you'll stay," she said. "I've got steaks, I think. Or maybe Jack is bringing something. Yeah, he is."

What Jack brought was Thai food. Paul was back so the four of them sat down at the kitchen table with the food still in its containers. They'd never eaten much takeout when the kids were all home but they did now, sometimes, because she'd advised Jack that she was semi-retiring, she was taking the early package. And being semi-retired she realized that it wasn't really all the cooking she'd hated, it was the twenty-plus years of deciding what six people should eat.

Sailor heard April first. Before the sound of the front door had even registered with the rest of them, Sailor sprang from his bed in the pantry and bounded down the hall. And then they could hear April up in her room moving the torn-apart bed out of her way. It was only one more upheaval, but this time it was loud, which meant that she'd made up her mind about something.

Jack and Sailor were waiting at the bottom of the stairs when April came down. She had stayed at the table with Paul and Colleen, shaking and listening, and what she heard April say was that she and Brad were going to British Columbia, and don't worry, she had money. They had money.

Jack would have been waiting to hear something better, something that made sense to him. He would have been hoping that his restraint might slow April down, might make her hesitate and think again. But April didn't have time to notice restraint.

And then Jack and Sailor were in the kitchen again and, with no comfort on offer, Sailor crawled back into his bed in the pantry, aggravated and dog-quivering.

"Did you give her some money?" she asked.

"I did not," Jack said.

Then there was nothing to say, but Colleen and Paul were ready to say it anyway.

"You have to take this the way I intend it," Colleen started. "Vancouver is not exactly the other side of the moon. It's a fantastic city. When Richard and I went out to that conference . . ."

"A conference," she said. "At a posh hotel."

"You took the kids out West yourselves," Colleen said. "You took them all over the blessed country."

"I know a guy who went to Whistler for a week and just stayed," Paul said. "He loves it."

"Richard and I were almost ready to move out there," Colleen said.

"Strange that you never mentioned it," she said.

When April was slamming around upstairs Paul had got up from the table to find the chopsticks he'd given Jack for Christmas, and Jack, having discovered his pair beside his plate, was holding them high above his bright, confusing food.

"It's like a dog run off with a bone," he said. "Backing up to a cliff. Playing. He's crouching there and taunting you because he doesn't realize the cliff is behind him and it wouldn't matter anyway because he doesn't know a goddamn thing about falling, does he? He doesn't believe in falling."

"It's not even about you guys," Paul said. "It's nothing about you."

"Good try," Jack said. "But you could be partly right. Because I refuse to believe that she wants to hurt us this much."

She watched the peppers and onions glisten as Jack lifted the food to his mouth. And then Paul leaned down to bang his forehead against her paint-splattered head.

Jude and Gus were able to walk right in because April had left the door open and Jack hadn't stayed to close it. Jude called from the hall. "We've come to pass judgement," she said. "And to ask why your front door was wide open."

"There's a squirrel sitting on your stairs," Gus said.

But when they got to the kitchen they had to wait because, looking around, neither of them could ask.

"April's going to British Columbia," Colleen said. "She's gone."

"That far?" Gus said.

Because Gus was no stranger to great, sudden distance or to uproar caused by a daughter, she was sorry that he had to be part of this.

"How old is April?" Paul said. "Twenty-two. Getting out of here might help her straighten herself out. Maybe she'll even see Brad for what he is."

"I have known her forever," Jude said. "She'll protect herself. Self-preservation is the strongest instinct we've got."

"So I've read," she said. Her back hurt and it would hurt even more the next day. "But not if that self has disappeared from the face of the earth."

"The only thing you can control is the way you think about this," Colleen said. "Just hang on."

"Just," she said.

She could have withstood Paul's optimism, and even Jack's hunkering down, but not Colleen and Jude together, promising something they could not hope to deliver. What did they think they were doing?

She wanted all of them gone. She wanted April on her lap and none of the others born, just April in her peach sundress with her wispy hair, or better, April not yet born, not born so soon to a woman so young, so dangerously, so stupidly unequipped.

And now there was only Richard to tell. And then Michael and Jan. Richard would pace around and think it all through and then he'd decide that he should get on a plane to track her down, and, like Paul, Michael and Jan would begin one more time, in whatever new way they could, to understand their careless, dangerous sister. Or they would not. . . .

She drops the journal on the bed. Hard times, she thinks. Hard times gone. She looks across at Jack.

"Fire," she whispers.

Then she turns on the television, keeping the sound low.

Through these nights of remembering and of practice runs, of dread, she has been keeping herself occupied with junk television, both confusing and annoying Jack with her nervous channel surfing. A few nights earlier, after an hour of flipping around trying to avoid another beautifully lit, half-dressed corpse of another beautiful young woman, and finally giving up and turning it off, she came awake happy to be crying not for herself. In pity, maybe. Or humiliation. For the all-death-all-the-time world of entertainment. For the low-pitched, sleazy, low-rent voices of the men who announce in loving detail the week's upcoming brutality, men she believes to be backwoods television cousins, sallow-faced carnys making a buck.

Still she can't stop distracting herself, amazing herself, alarming herself, some nights flipping around to count three or four beautiful dead women in the span of just a few minutes, the only real and slight difference the not-quite-handsome men bending over the corpses in experienced dismay. And every one of these women so perfectly made up, bruises, bloody gaping wound and all. And she has also discovered the fashionable, dramatic effect of some character, a man or a woman, it doesn't much matter, alive, very alive, with a mouthful of gun. The reference, so kindergarten clear, once upset Jack to the point of grabbing for the remote. Now she wants to ask someone what the writers of such pretty scenes might be after, if the men who can get themselves off on the image of the muzzle of a gun in a mouth might represent some advertiser's demographic of high disposable income. But who is there to ask? Not Jack. Not Richard or Gus. And probably not her sons.

Deadly fellatio, she thinks. For my pleasure. For my entertainment.

"Thug pleasure," she says. And then, "Jack."

She wants the feel of him again, turning tight to her in their bed, nudging her rump with his erect and perfectly innocent nerve endings. She would never have been a man, with the need so obvious. With so little chance for contradiction.

She does have other entertainment options, of course. In the middle of any night she can find well-dressed, blow-dried soul savers, smiling men with attractive, loyal wives at their side who are keen to explain it all, the world's present, its past, its certain future. They can lay out her own future too, and she doesn't have to take just their word for it because they can prove everything with prayer and raised fists, they can hold up the threat of the Good Book, sometimes shaking it above their big shaking heads. Wanting so much to save her, to rescue her. If only. And scrolling across the bottom of the screen, telephone numbers like a reading from the stock exchange. Just call, they beg. Please pick up that phone. We are here and we do take Visa or MasterCard. We know your pain. And we need your help so very badly. God needs your help.

On other, higher channels, more generous crooks have schemes that they too are compelled to share, so astonished have they been to discover how easy it was to triple, even quadruple, their incomes. And she has discovered so much to buy, things that will make her life easier and more exciting, the best so far a clunky, hand-held contraption that nails sparkling sequins to your jeans or to your best spring jacket. The Bedazzler.

And so many cures. Exciting vitamin combos for aches and pains, and magic potions for the obese, and help for that once-mighty but now undependable penis.

And on the highest channels, just below Jack's baseball, and moving their bodies to the puzzling accompaniment of the same music used by the weather station, dull men and women, often with good hair, go at it, with the women usually on top, their strong backs arched for balance. Sex not as an art but as consumption. Although her muscles do know that balance, and that stamina. Stamina was the reason she went to the gym with Colleen and Jude.

"Should I be getting all this down?" she asks the room. "What your mind does with itself when time won't budge?"

She has decided to leave the journals where they are, on the desk. It won't be Jack who goes through them. It will be April and Jan, and she hopes they will be curious enough to read even the entries about themselves, some of which they won't appreciate. And they are welcome to the early entries too, written by a mother before she was a mother, and by an even younger woman who was sometimes stupid and often frightened. They will discover how much she'd liked sex with their then just-as-remote but always-randy father, and how many times she had rewritten their first months together, when Jack would lead her and then let her go, so sure of her. An old-school gentleman, she called him. They could read all about the things he did now, or not now but not that long ago, like waiting until she was naked and then asking her to please fetch his forgotten ring from the bathroom sink. So he could watch her rear end.

But maybe tempting her daughters wouldn't be that smart. Certainly she would not have done it under normal circumstances, because how could you carry on normally with daughters who knew you so well?

Still, they are not children. If the journal reading unnerves them, it could just as easily toughen them up, and hasn't this always been, and hasn't she always known it, her job? Loving and toughening each of them in equal, complementary doses? And couldn't learning something about the inside of a mother's head make them more at home with their own thoughts, which have to be no prettier, no more pure, than her own? Regardless, they will have their easy out. They can always read a page or two and toss the journals away, as a gesture of respect.

"Enough," she says. "God."

She wants Jack roused from his rest. She wants him to come and hang on to her in this high narrow bed. To forget everything else and just be in love with her. Crazy in love with her. Didn't she climb up into his hospital bed? The night he was at his weakest, when for that one awful hour they came so close to believing in his heart's end, the last thing he said before his surgery and then his drugged, healing sleep, the thing that could have been his last complete, sensible thought, was that her breasts were warm against his back.

But she isn't going to ask because there are things you shouldn't ask, not even from a husband. Easy, conspicuous things.

She looks across at him. "Get over here," she says.

But instead of making him leave his warm bed, she can do something else, can't she? She can make his staying so close, every night so close, sleeping or not, enough. And to coax her own sleep closer she can look again to time passed. Because time passed is a bloody banquet table.

She can go back to her girlhood bed, which was as narrow as this bed and almost as high. And lying in it she can dream a young girl's dream, about what might happen. About happiness. She can feel the gurgling, rubber-stinking comfort of the hot-water bottle brought to her bed by her mother. A devout mother who could not bring herself to explain either the womb's purpose or its moon-timed, sweet-and-sour pain, but who did stand guard over her young body with that discreet, tight-lipped reassurance.

And then this too passes, as any time can.

"Come on, morning," she says. "Come on, Jack."

When the house comes to life today she is going to lift the atmosphere. She is going to take some of the pressure off everyone.

Oh, a new sort of cramp, lower in her pelvis now but less severe and in the unlikely shape of a boomerang.

She closes her eyes to sink and this time she dreams Jack's lonely, undemanding cock, sly against her rump. As soft for a time and as warm as her breasts must have been.

But that good dream feeds another and now she is in her younger, perfectly distended body, high in an earlier hospital bed. She is wincing at the glare of harsh fluorescent light in the cheap-tiled ceiling, and repulsed by the smell of stale blood and by something else too, maybe some antiseptic solution they've used on the tile floor or on the stainless steel instruments, or on her. She is huge, a monstrous, stranded turtle, and cold, and her tanned legs are hung high in stirrups. Her turtle belly is a hard, cramping vice in the last throws of first delivery. And then Jack with her sweaty hand tight in his own is leaning away from her, leaning down to look between her legs, like a boy. God in heaven, he is saying. Can you sit up? Can you look? And for all she's worth she is trying, pushing up on her elbows to find the promised mirror. And in it, the promised miracle. April . . .

"A hard promise," she says, still the woman who made it all come true.

And now her feet are warm because Jack is at the foot of the bed, holding her callused feet in hands still warm from sleep. Smiling one of his dry-mouthed smiles. A switched-on, obligatory smile. She has thrown off the sheet again and her nightie is hiked to her waist.

"I see I'm regressing," she says, reaching to cover herself.

"Did you sleep?" he asks.

"I did," she lies. "And I think I feel a bit better."

"Good," he says.

"I've been thinking about that year with April," she says. "But I've also been watching you in that bed and now I'm wondering about your future, and I've decided that you can't be alone."

Mexican Doors

It's mid-morning and she's got 1979 again.

"We've had our trip to Mexico," she reads. "For the change instead of the rest. The pyramids were something to see, but I didn't much like the Avenue of the Dead. Then we met an artist, by chance, and went to his house and to his studio, and I bought a great print. My Mexican doors."

The print is still down in the front hall. It's a series of simple, rustic one-of-a-kind doors, five rows of four beautiful doors, each of them crafted and boldly painted according to one man's idea of a door. When she saw the print, in Mexico City, she wasn't sure she would still like it when she got it home, because she was never sure so far away, but Jude had understood her hesitation for what it was and stepped up to convince her. Jude has a good eye. She doesn't worship art but she is grateful for it, and for the people who make it. And she has wanted the same from them. It was Jude who taught them, who coaxed them into the museums in Europe and into the big galleries in Vancouver and Toronto and Chicago and New York. She has no training and she can't do anything herself, but she can trust her instinct. And she has always wanted them to trust their own, to go with their gut reaction, because there would be something behind it.

The day she put the print up, Colleen and Jude were sitting at her kitchen table and she'd got out the hammer and the coil of picture wire because she'd finally found a frame. She and Jude were in old jeans and T-shirts and Colleen, of course, was not. But Colleen has always justified out-dressing them by reminding them that she spent half her life in scrubs. That day she was wearing her two-hundred-dollar black cotton pants and one of the white embroidered blouses she'd found in Mexico, and the combination of black and white was, as usual, good on her, because of the near-black hair and the pale Irish skin. And because the jealousy had become tedious by then. Worn out and boring.

She remembers the market and the girl with the white blouses, the coarse blankets the girl had spread over the dust to protect her embroidered goods. She remembers in particular the girl's bare arms, because it was the closest she got to that Mexican skin, skin apparently without blemish. Like amber satin, if you could have touched it. It was obvious that the embroidery had not been hand done, that would have been a different part of the city and it would have cost Colleen significant money. And it was obvious too that dozens of identical blouses would be sold that same afternoon to other tourist women, women who would have been interchangeable to the girl. But the white cotton seemed to hold the Mexican light, so Colleen was ready to buy.

Jude had put down her morning coffee to untangle a length of picture wire, and Colleen pointed to a dark turquoise door in the bottom row. "Different colours are more at home in different parts of the world," she said.

"Yes," Jude said.

"You wouldn't see that in London," Colleen said. "That colour would be ridiculous in London."

"England does better with green and gold," Jude said. "With time and money." Whenever they said the word *London* out loud they almost always meant England.

"And who does blue then?" Colleen asked.

"France," Jude said. "Sweden."

"Red?" Colleen asked.

"The States," Jude said.

"And white?" she asked, knowing the answer.

"That would have to be us," Jude said. "Canada. Or Russia."

Although none of them had ever been anywhere near it, they knew that the Far North was up there, barren under the endless snow and the unstopped winds, the ice-bleak winters, sea to sea to sea. Their own London was not much farther north than northern California, so the colour she would have named wasn't white but a dirty-slush grey. Or the crimson of fall, or the tinted sky, after a pastel sunset on Lake Huron.

The print was safe in the frame behind the glass and she was using her kitchen shears to cut the picture wire to length. "I'm going to put it in the front hall," she said. "Doors and doors and doors. My little artistic joke." She twisted the wire around itself.

"We'll probably laugh," Jude said.

When they got to the hall she gave the print to Jude and the hammer and nail to Colleen because she had to stick a small piece of masking tape on the plaster, because the household-hint book said that this would stop a spidery hairline crack from coming off the nail hole. Then after the print was up they all stepped back, pleased with her decision. And she was sure that her doors had found their place.

Now she has closed the journal because Jack is sitting beside her with his laptop. They've been talking to April and Michael and Jan, who have also been talking to one another, by e-mail. And they've been looking at recent pictures of the Vancouver and Boston grandchildren, the teenagers.

When Colleen arrives, Jack turns the laptop to let her admire them too. "So pretty, so handsome, so accomplished," he says, mocking Sandra, taking a chance. On his way out he leaves the laptop open on the desk, but the pictures soon disappear, leaving a pulsing, starry night.

"It's true," she tells Colleen. "They are."

Colleen agrees wholeheartedly, as she does when grandchildren are praised. And then she slides her arms under Sandra to change her position, because bedsores can erupt quickly and, once established, are so hard to defeat. She grabs the bottle of lotion. When she was taught in nurses' training to do back rubs she was told that the lotion was more or less a ruse, that it was the massage a body needed, to stimulate circulation. But for Sandra, now, it's the lotion. She rubs her dry, shaved legs and then moves to her feet, to the cracked soles. She and Sandra and Jude have known forever that their feet are at their best at the lake in the summer, in and out of the water and then buffed naturally by the sand. She notices Jude's nick on Sandra's ankle, sees that the skin has begun to scab over, oblivious.

Now that she's done everything she can think to do for her, Sandra seems content. Her breathing is better, less laboured and less suggestive of pneumonia. When this last part began she promised herself to let Sandra take the lead, to let her say what she needs to say, but she doesn't feel that strong today. Today, although she's not going to go anywhere near Spain or her courtly, afternoon Spaniard, she wants to have one last talk with Sandra about Richard's confession. There will be some thoughts about it in her journals, no doubt whatsoever.

Although she had been blind sided by Richard's confession, the one thing she wasn't going to give him, standing in her kitchen at 1 a.m., was the satisfaction of surprise. As if she'd been completely fooled. As if she had not been afraid.

"Tell me why," she asked him.

He was leaning against the kitchen sink in his pyjamas and he didn't know the answer. "I can't tell you," he said.

"Run a few things past me," she said. "Because I'm interested."

"I think I tricked myself into thinking that it could be self-contained," he said. "Detached. Or maybe, and just as stupidly, for the first time in my life I felt free."

So he had rehearsed this little talk. He was ready to use his honesty as a weapon.

"And I've been lonely, I think," he said.

"You can be free if you want," she said. "We can make that happen."

She'd said *free* the way she would have said *discarded* or *forgotten* or *relieved* of a few hundred thousand dollars. And relieved too of the lake house. So she *had* got a little surprise after all, her rage waiting just offstage, the eager, warmed-up understudy ready to go on. Screw it. Whatever he thought he might want, she would keep the lake house. Because it was the one thing she might be able to love on its own, without him in it.

"Freedom is not what I want," he said. "I've learned that much."

She had fallen headfirst into this swamp because of a sobbing midnight conversation, which she'd overheard because she picked up the kitchen phone, assuming that a midnight call on their private line meant bad news of some kind, from someone. She hadn't listened through to the end, just long enough to get the drift. The drift being that a young woman was in love and Richard was not.

"And you've also learned that she's in bad shape," she said.

"That's been coming," he said.

"Which means you have two things to fix," she said. "Doctor."

He turned his back to her to run a glass of water.

"Turn around," she said.

He filled a second glass and came to sit down opposite her.

"What did you tell her about me?" she asked. "About all this?" She opened her arms to the house. "Why don't you tell me your sob story?"

"I didn't tell her anything about you," he said.

"Does she know me?" she asked. "Does she work at the hospital?"

"She's a radiologist," he said. "Just starting out. She knows you to see you, that's all."

"Nice," she said.

"She moved here two years ago," he said. "From Denver."

"That's enough," she said.

She was not going to allow herself any more curiosity about a sweet, manoeuvring young woman, about the quick, attentive little smiles or the rollicking, slowed-down sex or the not-quite promises that Richard might have promised her. Somewhere in the city there was a woman who was going to cry very hard for a few lonely months, and, Oh, Sandra was going to say, doesn't your heart go out, maybe make another one or two pleading phone calls but then cry less and then stop crying and eventually move on, with her memories intact, to some other man. Maybe even to a man, if she got smarter, she could have.

What she wanted to explain to Richard was that his sobbing young woman would never need to forget anything. For the rest of her life she would be free to ask herself if her time with him was either a complete waste of her young body or sublime. And it wouldn't matter either way. For as long as she had brains in her head she could remember every loving detail she was able to conjure up: his smooth chest, his heavy arm across her stomach, his slow nighttime voice. If she wanted to, dreaming backwards, she could fall in love with him all over again. With her secret, treacherous Richard.

"What do you want me to do?" he said. "I'll do whatever it takes. I'll sign the house over. Or the lake house. We can separate some money off, now, in your name. I need my marriage."

"I'm going to bed," she said. She had not expected him to break down but the move straight to the pragmatic had been fast even for him. "Stay away from me."

"Of course," he said.

She had to hurry to the bathroom to vomit, which she did until the slate floor was cold under her knees and there was nothing in her but bile, so she didn't hear him go to bed. But when she passed the guest room she saw that the door had been closed.

Lying awake, she reminded herself that she'd had her chance. She could have listened to Sandra. She could have confronted him, could have stopped it before it got legs, when he was only discovering his potential, enjoying it the way another guy might enjoy a life-threatening hobby, like skydiving. Because it wasn't necessarily the start of something that could ruin you, it was the momentum. Momentum and assumptions. Maybe she'd ignored Sandra's advice because she had assumed that, when and if the crunch came, he would just not be that kind of man, the kind who might compromise himself for some imagined better happiness. Because right up to now, when she could assume it no more, she had savoured that lofty thought whenever she heard about some other dope who had thrown it all away.

She let herself fall into nightmare sleep but was soon awake again to the faint taste of bile. She told herself that she could, in time, rescue herself from his wreckage. She could do this the way other people did it, with discipline and adjustment, although it could be years before she stopped wanting to brain him with the cast-iron skillet as he slept that soundest of sleeps, the sleep of the confessed and reformed. He should take the hit because she was going to have to take it, because what he'd done was going to make them common fodder. He had turned their good lives into something of interest, into one more amusing bit of news to be indecently mentioned at a hockey game in Toronto or at some fundraising dinner, by people they didn't like. And she had to keep going to work at the hospital, where it would never be mentioned but would be known.

He was gone in the morning but there was a note on the kitchen table. "I've got surgery this morning," it said. "But just one."

Although she hadn't slept much, she could see applying her mascara in the bathroom mirror that her face at least was not going to betray her. She had the day free and she'd promised her mother a trip to Canadian Tire and, touching blush to her cheekbones, she was thinking that maybe she could pull it off. Because she was going to have to do something. She looked out the bathroom window to gauge the weather. The leaves had been turning for a week and there was enough wind to bring some of them down. She watched a maple leaf float sideways and then up again, as if to music.

When she got to her mother's apartment she found her ready with her coat on. She had been sitting counting her Canadian Tire money. There was a small multicoloured pile of it on the coffee table, maybe enough to buy the Drano she needed.

"What's wrong with you?" her mother asked.

Her account was more cold-blooded than she would have believed possible driving over.

"That's disgusting," her mother said. "I am just disgusted." She was sitting very still and she had covered her face with her hands. "And I have to say that I'm disappointed in you for letting it happen."

"No," she said. "You don't."

When she was a girl being trained for her life, being taught, among other things, to acknowledge a mistake when she made it, her mother's disappointed guidance had always taken the indirect tack. It was never the kind of blunt but disregarded scold she heard in the houses of her several guilty friends, it was never that loud smack of words that was usually the same, basic question: Why in God's name did you do that stupid, awful thing? At her own house it was the more subdued, and only once-mentioned, Oh, I wish you hadn't. I just wish you'd think.

As if she had not been thinking.

"Could we go to Canadian Tire another day?" she asked. Her mother was studying her pile of counted money. "I don't think I can do it."

"Of course you can't," her mother said. She took her coat off and hung it up again in the front closet. "You will need to get your own lawyer, you realize. Some big gun he doesn't know." She pointed to one of the brocade chairs, the deceased husband's chair, by the window. "You will not be going hungry."

It was what she'd come to hear.

Living alone, widowed in her high-rise apartment but coming over to the house for dinner or to watch a movie and being neither blind nor stupid, her mother must have seen or heard something. She must have noticed. So it made sense that she would be ready with her standards of conduct, with her disgust and disappointment. Her big-gun lawyer.

"But what if I've been thinking that I might want to work through this?" she asked.

"Well," her mother said. She'd gone into her narrow galley kitchen to fill the teakettle and she had to call out over the sound of the water. "The brain is not always a friend, is it?"

"I don't think I can stay," she said. And then she was out the door fast, because she'd heard the teakettle bang hard against the stove.

Sandra wasn't home so she had to drive around for twenty minutes to find her, or to find her car, which was parked outside Loblaws. And then she had to sit and wait, parked beside it, until Sandra came out, terrified, because why would anyone have to track her down at Loblaws?

She told Sandra that she was sorry, and that it had nothing to do with the kids or Jack. Because these were Sandra's nightmares, and she had been thoughtless, careless. Sandra got into the car borderline mad.

"It's me," she told her. "It's Richard. There's a young woman. She phoned him last night and I listened and he confessed but he says he doesn't want out. Let me follow you home. I'll be right behind you."

She had gone to Sandra for two legitimate reasons. Because she could find no good reason to protect Richard from his sister, and because she believed that if anyone could come up with a way to help her it would be Sandra. She was the one who had the stamina, the heart, to take this in. To take it in and make something of it. Because she would want her brother saved from divorce, want him punished, sure, but then put back where he belonged.

"Where is he now?" Sandra asked.

"At work being a hero," she said. "Firing up his saw. Likely rebuilding some grateful guy's hip."

But this was the easy talk and what she needed was to be saved from it. Because she could waste the whole day, such an important day, with bitter talk.

When they got to Sandra's, after they unpacked the perishables, Sandra said, "It's not entirely what he's done, is it? It's what he'll do now."

"More what I'll do," she said. And then, "Did you know about this?"

"No, I did not," Sandra said. "I've only ever known what you've told me."

"And what Jack has heard on the street," she said.

"Some of that, yes," Sandra said.

"Do you want to go over when he gets home from the hospital?" she asked. "To talk to him?"

"Yes and no," Sandra said.

"You don't seem enraged," she said.

"And neither do you," Sandra said.

"My mother is mad enough for both of us," she said.

"You've told her?" Sandra asked, stalling, adding, "It's only that, you realize if you get past this, your mother will be left out in the cold, hating him. Or repulsed. Something."

"The word was *disgusted,*" she said.

"And what's your word?" Sandra asked.

"I haven't got one," she said. "And I haven't had a coffee either or anything to eat."

It took them just one piece of toast to come up with the word *shock*, because even believing something might be coming, you could still suffer the shock. And then Sandra told her that she had to go home, because Richard could be there, waiting. "Just try to say less than you want to say," she said. "Let him talk too much if he wants to. And don't interrupt him."

"Let him hang himself, you mean?" she said.

"No," Sandra said. "I mean something different."

She rinsed her cup. "We won't be bringing Jude into this," she said. "Jude's got enough on her plate."

But she didn't go straight home. She drove south instead, toward Port Stanley, toward Lake Erie. She crossed both overpasses, the 402 and the 401, and after the traffic thinned out she was able to appreciate where she was, to take in the barren fields. In the yard at one of the roadside houses there was a small family of cut-out, snarling pumpkins, and above the house, geese, flying in a wavering V. Watching them climb, she changed her mind and turned around for home, because Port Stanley was one of her favourite towns and the last thing she needed to see was a lovely summer town in October. And because if she did keep driving, she would, to forget herself, to lose herself, begin to imagine things. The people who first settled this area, for instance, where they came from, and why. The working boats and the men, the husbands and fathers and brothers and sons, who harvested the perch. Their loss in Lake Erie storms. The burned-down dance hall on the beach, the music drifting out over the water. The couples, and the people who longed to be couples.

When she got home Richard was lying on the sofa with a sandwich he'd bought somewhere but he sat up when she came into the room.

"You've been for one of your drives," he said.

"I have," she said.

"And I'd guess that you have already talked to Sandra and Jude," he said. "And to your mother."

He waited.

"How is that supposed to make me feel?" he said.

"Damned if I know," she said. "Excluded? Forsaken?"

She had been only twenty when she married him, and everyone was so happy for them, especially their parents, so confident on their behalf. Or that's what all the wedding pictures suggested. She would have been amazed, when she'd stood in that church listening to Richard utter his public vows and repeating her own, to know what could exist outside a marriage. What was best kept outside it. All this time and she and Richard had not become one. And now she'd never know what they might have become.

"It began," he said. "It's over. I am sorry."

"That's movie dialogue," she said.

And then he told her that the gate, the *gate* had been slammed shut. And swore to her that he had never once thought of walking away from it. The *it* being, she guessed, her body and the house and the friends and the future. The slight possibility of children. The life.

"I'll give you five years," she said, not knowing she was going to say it. "And don't worry about the money. If and when I want your money, I'll get it."

Although she realized that she was being wildly generous, because in five years she would be forty and past babies, she could not have explained exactly what she wanted from the time she was offering him. Maybe nothing. If he could manage nothing.

"That's fair," he said. "You are being more than fair." And then his most vicious words. "Thank you, Colleen."

Like some stranger, he had used her given name. Because he wanted to put a formality to their agreement? To be a grown-up man? He looked as close to crying as she'd ever seen him, which made her think again about the skillet. Had she told Sandra about swinging the skillet? About the imagined spurts of blood?

Later, when she got back over to Sandra's again, they decided they needed some air so they went out to the deck, for some last rays. Hank followed and left them to find his place on the far grass and they sat in their chairs to give their faces up to the October sun, because it was strong, and they had a long winter ahead of them. They sat with nothing to say and then, for some reason, Sandra started to talk about Liam, who had been secretly skipping out on his music lessons.

Although she was not his aunt, she had eventually come to love Liam as much as she loved April and Michael and Jan and Paul. But she wasn't going to talk about anyone's kid today, not even one that she would happily take as her own. She'd decided to stop back in on her mother on the way home, to begin to bring her, if she would be brought, around. Sandra was right, it had been stupid to unload on her mother. She should have waited for the first wave to pass. But where else could she have found those rigid standards of conduct? That immaculate disgust?

"I've had enough of this sun," Sandra said. She stretched her arms high in the air and then they both checked the back of their hands in the hope for a little October colour.

"I should go," she said. "I was supposed to take my mother to Canadian Tire."

"You're a good girl," Sandra said.

"Yes I am," she said. "A good, disappointing girl."

"Are you going to leave him in the guest room?" Sandra asked.

"To answer your question," she said. "No, he hasn't touched me. Or tried."

"Maybe you'll have to go away," Sandra said. "Pull back from everything and have yourselves a little forgiving sex, and then come home with that first big step behind you. Richard is sorry because he has to be, which is a damned good reason. You should believe him."

"Should I?" she asked. "And away where?"

She did know that you couldn't leave a wound hanging open. You only had to have seen the dark rot or inhaled that septic stench to know how an open wound can affect the people who love you. But, aside from Richard's being sorry, which was no great achievement, what should she expect from him?

She hadn't thought of going away. Trust Sandra. But she did know that she would have to touch him first because if he dared to reach for her she might have to find one of his scalpels and cut his little heart out. . . .

Now Sandra is wide awake again, and watching her. "Are you going to tell me what's on your mind?" she asks, yawning.

"Do you think?" she starts. "Do you think it would have been better if Richard had never told me about his sweet young thing?"

"Never told you and carried on?" Sandra asks. "Or never told you and quit?"

"Quit," she says. "God. Quit."

"No," Sandra says. "I don't. I hated what he did but he had to tell it."

Sandra realizes, of course, that her loved ones, sitting so close, will not be sitting idle. She knows they must leave her, sometimes, to go to their own thoughts. But even being certain that Colleen had discovered some level of cure with her own episode in Spain, with her Spaniard, she can't take this any further. Because when the going gets tough, often you can say only so much. And she too had to forgive Richard. She too had to accept what he'd done.

"Why don't you go curl up in that armchair," she tells Colleen. "Because you're tired."

Colleen does as she's told, tucking her feet under her and spreading the afghan, which was knit by a neighbour's mother, across her lap.

Sandra is going to have to remind Colleen, maybe tomorrow, about Richard's kindness, about some instance of unimpeachable kindness. It won't be hard. What comes to mind most readily is his relationship with Colleen's father, when, after eight years of illness, he was approaching his end. The worst had been at the beginning, Colleen said, when they didn't understand either the disease or the future, and she was so frightened. And then later when her mother and father together decided to keep the inevitable to themselves, to protect her, to allow her to float like a child in her newly married happiness.

Colleen had told the unimpeachable story herself. She said that she'd gone over to the hospital cafeteria for a quick sandwich and was coming back down the hall to her father's room when she overheard Richard talking to him. Except for the patient in the other bed, who was sadly quiet, they were alone, and she stood outside the door thinking that the two of them had never had much time. Richard was asking her father about being an Ontario farm boy during the Depression and her father was explaining his determination to be free of want, to never again have to depend for his happiness on any one person or on any one bit of good fortune. Which was why he'd taken so long at university, he explained, because he was slowed down by the need to work for money. And then he had to stop talking because he was sick to his stomach and Richard must have lifted his head from the pillow and held the kidney-shaped tray to his mouth. Colleen heard the retching, and when it was over Richard went into the bathroom to flush the tray's contents down the toilet. And then he ran the taps, and went back with a cloth and a toothbrush. Her father was embarrassed and crying in protest, but he would have had no choice, he would have wanted to be clean because her mother, his wife, was on her way back to the hospital. Then he told Richard that she had been the best wife to him. And that the High Church attitude, the snobbery, was just her wishing everything could be better. That it should never be held against her.

Women like Colleen's mother won't exist much longer, she thinks. All those strict expectations. The manners and restraint, the taming of a situation. The silence. The teacups and silver. To her everlasting credit, with the exception of Colleen's near divorce, that morning when she was so angered on her daughter's behalf, she did always try to practise what she preached. And maybe still tries, in her room in the seniors home Colleen found for her.

Colleen said that a nurse stopped in the hall to ask her if she needed help but she said no and then walked into the room to catch Richard and her father holding hands. Or, not holding hands but Richard holding her father's and her father allowing it. But when they saw her they pretended they had only been putting in time. Her father said they'd been wondering where she'd got to and then Richard said he was going down to admin to make the switch to a private room, as if sharing a room was the unbearable thing.

They had all heard about Richard's kindness with his patients. That the ones who could thrived on it. But why did he have to hide it from them? Why was it so rigidly controlled? Was it because he felt like an amateur? She thinks about him in the middle of the night, standing over this bed in his new burgundy housecoat.

"I want to go downstairs," she says.

"Downstairs?" Colleen asks. She gets up from the armchair and comes over to the bed. "How? How are we going to manage that?"

She throws off the sheet and starts to sit up. "One step at a time," she says.

"Wait," Colleen says. She goes to the top of the stairs and calls Jack and he's soon climbing as fast as he can.

"What do you think you're doing?" he asks, recognizing the look on her face.

"I want to see my Mexican doors," she says.

Colleen knows what Sandra means. She means the print she got in Mexico, the twenty multicoloured doors. "We'll bring them up to you," she says. She turns to leave, to go down and take the doors off the wall.

"No," she says. "Just help me."

Jack finally gives the okay and they get her up and walk her slowly into the hall and over to the top of the stairs. Her nightie drifts around her, too big, and she is breathing carefully, taking all the time she needs.

"Put me on the first step," she says. "And I'll sit and go down on my bum. Maybe one of you should go ahead."

They get her in position and Jack goes ahead and she starts, like a kid, taking one step at a time, bracing herself with her feet.

"Bump, bump, bump," Colleen says, encouraging her.

Paul and Kelly have heard them and come to the foot of the stairs.

"Can you get a chair ready?" Jack asks.

She's at the bottom and now she has to stand up, so Colleen lifts her under the arms, from behind.

"That wasn't bad," she says.

They walk her over to her Mexican doors and, standing in her nightie with Colleen on one side of her and Jack on the other, she leans forward to touch the doors through the glass. "That turquoise stays with you," she tells them.

Then she looks behind her at the bench and at the shelf high above it.

"Where are the ball gloves?" she asks.

In the dining room, Jack's mother's cherry dining room suite, all eleven pieces of it, which she'd had to grovel to his sister to get, glows.

She turns to look into the transformed living room. The furniture is still where she wants it but everything else, the stack of magazines, the fuzzy red throw, maybe some mending, maybe a package of get-well cards bought on sale, has disappeared. And then she understands from Kelly's face who has done this.

"I'm really sorry," Kelly says. She is ready to cry. She is ready to leave.

The mantel has been cleared and is now covered with an arrangement of framed photographs, and she's in all of them. The doors of her corner cabinet are wide open and her silver, the last of the wedding gifts, the fish platter and the crumb butler, the pickle cruet and the Wedgwood ice bucket with its silver lid, has all been polished. The morning light from the mullioned front window goes to the silver as if there's nothing else in the room.

They help her into the softest armchair and lift her feet up onto the small red, tufted footstool that had been left to her by an aunt. The footstool has always sat in the corner, under a stack of Jack's old LPs. She hasn't seen it in years. "Imagine," she says.

Then she claps her hands and opens her arms and Kelly comes to her to lean down. And now they are free to laugh.

"Do you want to see the kitchen?" Kelly asks.

"No," she says. "The kitchen is just a kitchen."

"What about lunch," Jack asks. "What do you think? Could you eat?"

"Yes," she says. "I could eat some salmon and peas on toast."

Colleen and Kelly both bolt at once and, like clowns, they nearly knock each other out when they hit the small doorway to the kitchen.

They eat their salmon and peas in the living room, or the others do, because all she can manage is two good bites, and Kelly is just gathering the plates when Jude comes in the front door, bringing another blast of cold air with her.

Jude stands under the arch and looks around the room, the last one at the party. "What's all this?" she asks. "What's going on?"

Colleen explains the desire to see the Mexican doors.

"And now that I've seen them," Sandra tells Jude, "I want to go back to my bed." Because her gut has had something to say to the two good bites of lunch.

They help her stand and walk her into the hall and then there's the question of how to get her up the stairs.

But Colleen knows how. She grabs her own wrist and reaches for Jude's with her other hand, telling her to do the same thing, but in reverse. And it's done, they have made a human platform. Kelly turns

Sandra around to face the front door and she lowers her meagre weight onto their locked hands, wraps her arms around their shoulders, and up they go. Paul follows close after them, standing tall, intending to break any fall. But it's working because the staircase is wide, like a staircase in an old church. They have to stop only to laugh.

"What is this called?" she asks Colleen.

"God only knows," Colleen says, and they stop to laugh again.

"Is it the fireman's lift?" Jude asks.

"I think it is," Jack says. "I think that sounds right."

Summer-Night Happy

The lunch nurse has come and gone and Colleen has left too, because this afternoon is Jude's. That's the way they talk. Her time has been parcelled out among them. Although it would be wrong to complain, to ask for just a little normal chaos instead of all this deliberation, this management.

She is back in her bed, and tired, and her bony rear end is sore, both from the bouncing down the stairs and from the ride back up, but she doesn't regret seeing her doors. And something has happened. Either the Midol is kicking in or there's nothing left in her to cramp. Maybe she's been hollowed out.

"Do you think I've been hollowed out?" she asks Jude.

"What do you mean?" Jude asks.

"Nothing," she says. "Nothing."

"Do you want some music?" Jude asks.

"Yes," she says. "But make it something you want to hear."

Jude goes over to the chest. Everyone who comes into the room has been bringing CDs, so the choice has grown. "Sarah Harmer?" she asks.

"Yeah," she says. "That would be Paul's, I guess."

"She's very good," Jude says.

They listen without talking, but not for long. She looks beyond Jude's head.

"When I was eight or nine," she starts. "When Richard and I were no longer excused, our mother made us attend a great-uncle's funeral."

Jude waits.

Jude and Colleen have both heard so many of the collected essential stories about her time in her parents' care, but she hasn't told this one. And it's no great mystery why this particular girlhood drama has come back to her. The Mexican doors down in the hall, a Mexican holiday, lots of sun and food and history, but then the pyramids, the Avenue of the Dead, with its murderous history. The worshipful butchery, the priestly promises made as the hearts were carved out. Because it wasn't only Abraham's God who liked this kind of thing, it was Almighties the world over. Or so the holy men liked to insist. She imagines a strong, brightly robed priest whispering, trust me, my screaming, sacrificial friend, because this is what the gods demand of you.

"I didn't know the uncle and the church wasn't even our own church," she says. "There was no altar, no scarlet carpet down the aisles, and, hardest to believe, the shining blond pews had been carved all of a piece."

"Workmanship," Jude says.

"I guess," she says. "The man doing the service, 'preacher man,' our father called him, was standing at the casket as he talked to us, and the top half, the lid, had been propped open so we could see the quilted white satin and the profile of the uncle's face, which even with its sunken cheeks was still a strong profile, like some king on a stamp. And just as the guy wrapped up what he had to say about the tribulations and the wrath of God and the licking flames of hellfire and the wrenching anguish of eternal damnation, someone behind us called out a loud 'Yes,' and then, as if he had practised his timing, the preacher man dropped the coffin lid closed. And not respectfully. The bang echoed off the damned rafters."

"Shit," Jude says. "Couldn't you have run? You were a kid. Kids run."

"No," she says. "And the guy knew exactly what he'd done. He had meant to grab the attention of his captive sinners. He'd meant to terrorize the grieving."

"To terrorize the bone stupid," Jude says.

"But it didn't work on me," she says. And she can still feel it, sitting there in the pew not being what she was supposed to be but doing something else instead, which was body blushing. She and her mother both watched the flush of blood move down her arms to her white church gloves, and then down her skinny legs to the cuffs of her dress-up socks in her patent-leather shoes. And all of that blood rushing out from her heart not for her own salvation but on behalf of a stranger uncle. It had happened to her once before, after something else, her father acting drunk in a public place, at her school.

"I was blushing," she says. "I was hot pink because everyone in that church had witnessed his humiliation. The lunatic preacher had used his body like a summer carny with a two-headed calf."

"Well, they do, don't they?" Jude says.

"But why didn't I know this?" she asks. "That a horrible thing could happen and no one would move a muscle?"

"Maybe you did," Jude says. "And just forgot."

"When it was over, I thought we were leaving but instead we joined everyone for egg salad sandwiches in the church basement. It was a half-basement, you know, just six steps down, and when we got inside some strange woman who stank of Noxzema bent over to hug me, as if I had been a good girl. Leaving sweet Richard free to stand behind her and smirk."

Eventually her mother gave her father the signal that it would be all right to get out of there, to go home. He had his Matinée lit on the bottom step, she heard his Zippo snapping shut behind her head, and then they were inside his big luxury car, with its drifting streams of smoke.

"Driving home, my father said, 'Maybe after their lunch they'll all be taken, and their self-satisfied guilt with them.' He said that was a service he'd be willing to sit through."

Jude was laughing because she had known her father, because she'd heard so many of his catchphrases.

She and Richard were in the back seat because on any trip it was always just their parents in the front. Her mother sat halfway between her father and the passenger door, holding his hat in her lap and playing with his pigskin driving gloves, which he always kept around but never wore. She never once saw him pull them on.

"My mother reached over to put his hat on his head," she says. "And then she told him, 'No, they probably will not drop dead, not even for you.' Because she could still pretend, sometimes, not for herself but for our sake, that he was only a boy-man having fun, ribbing her, trying her patience. She could still pretend that she didn't despise his godlessness as much as he despised her God. But really she was just saving it for a better time."

Unlike her mother's, her father's belief in her had always been incidental. And she let him off because of his loud and secret sinful ways. His worldly charm, his nerve. And because he wasn't home that often. There were never any daytime quarrels, although some nights she did lie awake to listen to the whispered spats, recognizing one word and then another and then that one more. Her mother had already told her, speaking softly as if she were talking to a friend, that it was her father's godlessness that took him and his money, loaded, to the races.

"And later, when I could finally say some of what I'd been saving up for her," she tells Jude, "years later I asked who those people were, and where were the parents who should have saved us from such rank hysteria? Or at least saved me, from a hot, stinking hug."

She had been picking up her mother's stack of Christmas cards, to mail them, and when she asked the question her mother told her that the uncle was someone she'd been fond of when she herself was a girl, although why, she couldn't say. Probably some connection with a pony or humbugs or forbidden gum.

"And the answer?" Jude asks.

"Her explanation," she says. "Her reasoning was that the funeral must have been right around the time when she'd started to believe that Richard and I were old enough and smart enough to take in a bit of what the big old world has to offer. That it looked like we might be halfway intelligent, so perhaps she could relax her hold a little and enjoy some hard-earned, sweet Jesus relief."

The story has come to its end and now Jude will want to give it a marker, a tag, something they can recognize if they ever want to come back to it. If they ever want to talk about how careful you have to be with children, with your own grandchildren, for instance, when they are faced with their first death.

"Your mother did not say that," Jude says. "Doris would have jumped off a cliff before she'd say 'sweet Jesus relief.'"

"The blasphemy was rare," she says. "So you are almost right."

"You could take it as a measure of her faith in you," Jude says.

"That's one idea," she says.

"I liked your mother," Jude says. "I used to think that she put all of her kindness straight into her cooking. I remember the stew and dumplings she made for us in your red Dutch oven." She gets up to change the music and comes back with a handful of CDs, to let her choose.

"I was angry at that God for a long time," she says. "But I'm not angry now." She closes her eyes to let the morphine try to take her.

"No," Jude says.

Watching the drug do its work, watching Sandra's unadorned face go calm, Jude sits down again to wait, and the music can wait too. Hard-earned sweet Jesus relief, she thinks. It's not a phrase she has used, but she's used others, of a similar nature. And so has Sandra. God have mercy comes to mind.

She gets up to go over to the armchair, to the afghan.

"God have mercy," she says quietly, not to be heard. "And on me."

Because how can she survive now, without this friend who knows her as well as she knows herself? Because that's what it is. It's the knowing.

Sandra had helped her with Liam just when she most needed it, because they both believe that complicity is good for mothers. And from the time their friendship began she's been able to keep Liam safely clear of her trials and tribulations, her confused, brutish stretches.

She told Sandra and Colleen all about Liam's birth at the farm, of course. Although she'd lost a first baby, very early, she carried Liam as easily as a good meal and his arrival was both fast and lonely. Although communal too, because she couldn't keep the others out of the room and Tommy would not.

When she first got to the farm, she'd waited alone at the kitchen table, suffering the heat from the wood stove as she listened to another girl's pain rise up undefeated through the voices that crowded around it. But when it was her turn she still listened to the solemn advice offered by the two other young mothers, who promised her that the age-old thing they were describing was something she'd be strong enough to bear, that her uterine muscles were smart, and ready. The pain natural. She'd listened because they had her cornered in a place that was filled with corners, even out in the cut-from-the-bush yard.

And she did try to prepare herself for their long, natural hours of labour, their possible days of natural grievous pain, for making a fool of herself and being forgiven. But Liam didn't come their way. And it didn't matter that she was surrounded by people she soon didn't want near her, cheering her on and touching her without relief, or that someone had clumped in the door with more firewood, yelling, we're going to be fine. Because Liam took almost no time and within minutes of it starting she'd taken a last good look at Tommy and disappeared from the soaked bed. And they could not have found her.

She'd left them to go to Liam inside her and she stayed with him until it was over, as astonished as he must have been by the rupture and the rock-hard spasms as her very smart uterine muscles pushed him out of her bruised body, a pit from a plum.

Maybe it was only because she'd had no truly generous help with Liam since the farm, but she'd been happy to compare wins and losses with Sandra. To put a name to the worst things they could imagine for a child, hating and fearing those worst things out loud and then hauling themselves back from the brink. And Sandra was always eager to match her stupidities, some of them invented, she is sure of this now, to her own. "I've got one," she'd say. It was like soaking in the tub and discovering a strange, wonky nub of bone in a knee and then finding the exact wonky nub in the other knee. Symmetry making all the difference.

She and Sandra both knew what it was like, having to outsmart the kids when they were small, manipulating their every move to keep them safe, how exhausting it was, and finally how insulting, to the kids themselves. And they were equally bewildered by the way a child could create himself, could become a small person easily pleased, for instance, or too quick to sulk, or spaced-out funny, or bossy but so relentlessly cheerful. They served up both the kids' occasional successes, which were not their own, and their occasional defeats, which were. They talked about deserted women who were forced to do impossible double duty, who would be tired beyond tired, and sometimes, for their resentful entertainment, they imagined pearl-draped, well-travelled European mothers, with their trusted, lifelong nannies, with staff. Women who could go away and return to nothing much changed, and who could leave again, the way men left. When you had kids, they decided, all you had was luck.

And after Gus moved in, Sandra asked, just in case, if there had been any change. If, for instance, Gus had started to offer a few helpful suggestions about Liam. Nothing as bad as give that kid a smack, but maybe some smaller thing. She said she'd seen a lot of this, people with advice about kids they hardly knew, expecting to be heard. And both Sandra and Colleen had made sure that Liam was acknowledged, that he too was consoled, for the loss of his grandparents in the accident. Colleen even told him that he looked like his grandfather, which wasn't very true. But he'd liked it. He had.

And Sandra encouraged her working life too, telling her when she applied for the job in admissions at Western that she was unusually but still perfectly qualified. Because she was smart, and no stranger to chaos, to the pressure people can put on a woman . . .

Sandra is awake now, and almost rested this time, but her eyes are tired and her focus is off. Jude is over in the armchair, staring into space, but she doesn't want to disturb her and she doesn't want to worry about her eyes, either, so she gets 1974 from the bedside table and finds June. Because now that she's been downstairs, she wants to go dancing.

"A night out," it says. "All six of us together for the first time, at Wonderland. It was crowded, which is good, and I wore my backless black dress and I taught Gus how to dance. We watched some older couples dancing to swing. Everyone watched them." And then, "Jack was wide awake when we got home, so this morning with a week's laundry to do, here I am aching the good ache."

It was June, the easiest month of summer, and she and Jack and Colleen and Richard and Jude and Gus had gone to the open-air dance. The night out had been her idea and after Jack said all right she called Colleen and Jude so they could get to work persuading their own men. There could finally be three couples because Jude, divorced from Tommy, had just met the equally divorced Gus. They were not going to try to drag the men into it, but she and Colleen and Jude were in that celebratory frame of mind, absolutely.

They arrived early enough to pull two good tables together at the edge of the terrazzo dance floor, halfway back from the bandshell, and then the men went into the pavilion to buy the bar tickets. Eddie Doan's Big Band was just ten-musicians strong because the outdoor stage under the bandshell with its elegant, sheltering arch was not as big as the winter stage inside, but it made no difference. The smaller band could still play whatever the dancers might want, and from across four decades.

She was ready to dance because she had her four one-after-the-other kids at home, and she'd bought the new black sundress with the shameless low-cut back to show off her early start on a tan. Colleen, in long, white linen with a black sailor bib, was game because she always grabbed a chance to wear her beautiful clothes. Jude had probably said yes because she wanted to know if Gus would come, and if he could dance. Jude had found a soft print twirly skirt with a matching tunic top to camouflage her bothersome breasts, the print not floral but abstract and muted, and she'd splurged on beautiful shoes. All three of them had splurged on night-out, high-heeled summer sandals.

Jack and Richard and Gus were in short-sleeved pastel shirts, blue and peach and apple green, and they'd kept their ties on, although like most of the other men they had been quick to get rid of their jackets, because it was a warm night after a hot day. Jack was still solid and compact, which was one of the reasons she'd wanted him, and Richard could finally carry himself as if looks made no difference because he was established in his practice now, and he was very good, with privileges at the city's best hospital. But only Gus, with his long arm resting on Jude's turned chair, was perfectly made.

The place was packed with loud, laughing couples, and if they weren't up dancing, they sat drinking and talking when they could, in short and sometimes baffling bursts. They watched the other dancers move past them, circling the floor like slow, clockwise skaters.

When Eddie Doan's band stopped for a break, Jack and Richard and Gus left with a small crowd of other men to go over to the parking lot, to stretch their legs. And with the men gone, instead of trying to get into the washroom, she and Colleen and Jude turned to look back into the dark, where they could see the Thames River through its flanking trees. The steady current was doing its best to cut the humid city air and the water reflected all the light it could catch, from the tall light standards and the incandescent bandshell. In the absence of wind, the oaks and the maples and the big willows were quiet, but she knew that on a more ordinary night they would have heard the crickets, or the mallards coming in from the near-distant fields, or a fish or two breaking the surface of the water for a feed of fat June insects.

After the band and the men were back, and after some teasing insinuation and a small dose of manly taunting, it was decided that Gus should learn to dance. To really dance. And so, not beautiful but adequately seductive, she offered to pull him through the other dancers to the far edge of the terrazzo floor, where it met the manicured lawn, where they would have some privacy. Standing close at his side and moving with the music, she nudged him with an elbow to relax him and then took all of the steps forward, as he would have to take them, repeating the pattern until he said okay, he got it, and she could turn into his arms to follow him, to take her own steps, the same set pattern, but in reverse. And Gus had, and much faster than Jack or Richard when she'd taught them, got it.

Richard had just brought a new round of drinks when they got back to the table but Jack stood up to lead her onto the dance floor again. The band was playing Duke Ellington's "Mood Indigo" and the singer, a lean man in a summer tux who was clever enough to stand very still at his microphone, was singing the lyrics with a convincing mix of hesitation and deep melancholy, as if he had just that night found a way to speak about his heartache. The others got up too, and moving through the crowd they caught glimpses of each other, she and Jack moving close and slow, Colleen and Richard floating around like tall, disinterested pros, and Jude content to follow Gus's careful, hesitant lead. And then the music changed.

The band had left Ellington and the Beach Boys and Stevie Wonder behind them and switched it up to Count Basie, to swing. The change in tempo was for the regulars, for the half-dozen older, middle-aged couples who had no doubt requested it, who had been dancing all night to everything but waiting for swing. These older men, who looked to be in their late fifties, sported strict and recent haircuts and polished summer shoes, tan or creamy white, and, hot or not, they had kept their jackets on. Their partners, robust uninhibited women, followed them onto the dance floor almost skipping. Although they were not as well dressed as they might have been, and a couple of them hadn't bothered to update their hairstyles from the war years, their hair was obviously tinted and the shoes were definitely dancing shoes, the heels solid but high enough to show off the muscles in their legs. One of the men was missing an arm, from the elbow, but his partner bravely threw her body into his and just as bravely fell away, pretending that the arm would be there to catch her.

The couples had the whole floor so they spread out, taking it. Watching them, the band came to new life and, championed by the musicians, the dancers' late middle age began to look more like mastery, like wild but absolute control. Soon the younger couples sitting at the tables started to clap in time. Some of them stood up clapping.

"Before this night's over," she told Jack, "I'm going to ask one of those old guys to dance with me." She was on her feet, clapping for the sheer energy of the performance, for the spectacle. "And he can be dripping with sweat, I won't care."

Colleen got up beside Richard. "Aren't they a little old?" she shouted, laughing over the music. "Aren't they as old as the bleedin' hills? Maybe even heart-attack old?"

Jude was leaning close to Gus so she wouldn't have to yell. "When is the last time you've seen anyone that happy?" she asked. Plainly willing to confess that for her, at least, it had been a while.

Because they belonged to a fortunate generation that had not been handed a war to fight, Jack and Richard and Gus might have been wondering what it was, exactly, that the old guys were dancing so expertly to forget, what slow-to-heal wound, what lost friend, what blasted, blood-soaked stretch of foreign soil. But not even this would have stopped them from taking account of the older women's bodies, the well-shaped dancing calves, the hips gone solid and the strong enthusiastic arms, the breasts both heavier and softer than they would have been.

And watching the dancing men, she knew that they had once been even stronger and more courageous, when they were boys. Courageous enough not to collapse weeping when they were sent from their families, in their dull Canadian uniforms, across the cold North Atlantic. And gauging their wives, taking the measure, subtracting the years from the made-up faces and from the heavy bodies, she was just as convinced that the men would have been handsome, or irresistible, or dashing. Whatever the word used to be.

But more than anything she was summer-night happy, just happy to witness such roaring stamina. And then to notice that the pale southern Ontario sky above them had gone dark, which meant that now she could see everything. This always happened when she wasn't looking, the empty sky taken over by the night, by the night's arrangement of random stars and its high-flying, buttercup moon.

She lets the journal drop to the floor but Jude, still in the armchair staring into space, doesn't seem to notice.

And now handsome Jack is standing at the door, defeated, and crazy in love with her.

If only Michael and April and Jan would get home.

BABE

SANDRA HAS COME AWAKE *not awake. First she hears Jack and then Richard and right away some other voice, a murmuring woman, the morning nurse or maybe Alice, her good doctor. The woman has used the lone word* unresponsive, *and now Jack is trying to get his breath. Choking. But she can't find him because her eyes won't look and now he is standing aside to let someone rub something cold on her skin, but what skin? She feels the lifting of her hips and a downy diaper and the rolling push onto her side with the pillow braced against the small of her back, to hold her. And then she catches sight of the sleep beneath sleep.*

Jack has sent a reluctant Richard home, and looking out the window above the desk, he can see that the snow has slowed down, and that the street light will soon be outdone by morning. It takes a lot of power to light this city in December, when the days are so short. There's a book around somewhere with old photographs of the streets when they were lit more modestly. He bought it for her at the Oxford Book Shop. And now she'll never see it again. The other kids have not made it home in time, and he is ready to kneel at her bed.

But he doesn't kneel because he is determined to keep talking, to keep thinking of something to say. He will stay clear of anything she loved too much and well away from what can't be changed, and from the things she never wanted to hear. But her face is so still now, and without her tics and twitches, without her signals, how can he know what he's saying?

Earlier, down in the hall, pulling on her boots, Alice told him that each body shuts down differently because there are simply so many levels of consciousness, such an unbelievable range. And she also said that there might be a change in the level of pain, a lessening, because of her body's natural morphine, and that the nurses will know what to watch for and how to proceed. She has left a note for them.

How did people die, he wanted to ask her, before the drugs, before the help? How did they stand it? But of course they did not. *Anguish,* once upon a time, would have been a very common word, as common, as routine a word as *death.*

Richard and Alice have both promised him that there has been no anguish here.

He is going to tell everyone that now is not the time for their grief. And that they should choose their words carefully. Because even when he was souped up after his surgery he had heard some of the words, absolutely. Although it was more like being in the next room, busy in the next room, overhearing. Nevertheless, it's something they have to keep in mind.

"It's Wednesday morning," he says. "When you wouldn't wake up, I called Alice and she's been here to see you. I sent Richard home but Paul and Kelly are on their way and Jude and Colleen will come to sit with you. When the lunch nurse gets here we'll give you one of your baths." He takes a breath. "Jan will be here soon," he says. "And I've talked to April and Michael. They'll be in the air today."

Her mother is hovering over her bed because she smelled smoke on her summer jacket hanging in the back hall and then dug around in the pockets until she found the pack of du Mauriers. Now she's busy explaining that her father is not in any way to be admired, and that while men smoke, women can't. "We are not in the least like them," she says. "Men work hard, yes, but it's their money that buys the vice. The liquor, the horses, the women. Booze is dangerous," she says. "Horses are dangerous. And as for those things," she says, gesturing with her disappointed head downstairs toward the stinking jacket, "you listen to me breathe," and she breathes deeply, twice and twice again. "Now, next time you get the opportunity, you listen to your father." Across the room, her exhausted father is stretched out on his couch and she is going to him with her girl's kindness to cover him with a blanket. But he tosses her a turquoise cinch belt and some of the money he won at the track. Eighty bucks, in fives. "Don't spend it all in one place," he says. "And don't, for God's sake, mention any of this to your blessed mother. She'll get hers." She can always smell booze on her father when he gets back from the city but this time he smells like Noxzema, and when she tells him that, he says, "Oh, my little lady, I've given the booze up. Long since." Her father is the best, the most persistent and genuine liar she will ever in her life know. "Now give me one of your hugs," he says, "and go away. Go nuts. Get yourself uptown. I'm played out."

Jack straightens her nightie and the sheet and then he walks over to their bed, asking himself, why have I left her with only the thin, guest-room pillow when all along she's had her own, right here where she can see it? Why hasn't she asked me for it? Back beside her, he lifts her head and throws the guest-room pillow across the room. He puts her stashed journal on the bedside table and eases her head down on the better pillow.

"More of my stupidity," he says.

And now he has nothing more to tell her, nothing to do. So he picks up the journal, 1979, and lets it open where it wants to open.

"Last night," he reads, "after a baking hot day, we had a terrific perch supper out at Gus and Jude's. Along with everything else he's got to offer, Gus can cook. We are going to call this our high-summer supper and do it every year until we're dead."

He looks at her and waits but there is no way to know if she's heard.

"Gus has built a covered porch across the front of his cottage," he reads, "which changes your view of the lake. Or, I guess, the sky. We had a small difference of opinion about that view, but what a storm."

He can hardly see the words now, but he does remember that in 1979 Gus sold his boat and built the porch. And he remembers that Jude was too quick to say that it was only an ordinary porch, but then Sandra said that it looked like it had always been there, which was what Gus had been waiting to hear.

Gus had found a local guy with some recently caught Lake Erie yellow perch to sell, and he pan-fried it in butter just as it was, but when they took their places at the kitchen table they started to argue about his new porch, about whether it was better to sit under the open sky or to sit tucked under a roof, getting the same breeze and almost the same view, but protected from the worst of the elements, so you could stay longer.

After they'd eaten all their vegetables Jude gave them butter tarts for dessert and then they got a chance to put their opposing theories to the test, because the wind had changed and the thunderhead that had been hanging out over Lake Huron decided to come ashore, hard and fast. Lightning flashed in the steamed-up kitchen window and the booming thunder made Gus's exposed timber ceiling the skin of a drum. And then the power went out, killing the lights and everything else with them.

Jude got a candle from Gus's prized French-Canadian sideboard and they took their coffee out to the porch, to watch what Gus was calling its first storm, its first real test. The thunderhead held low and black and heavy and the undecided wind made even the thickest branches of the few trees wave around like twigs. Most of the lightning shot down in the usual, crazy bolts but when it came in sheets it caught everything, sky, water, and beach, at once. The pocked surface of the lit-up lake heaved as it threw the light around.

Because of the thunder, Sandra had to wait for a break at the end of a rumble to insist that what they were watching was only a narrow, limited part of the storm, because their sightline, framed both by the roof above them and by the porch's protective half-wall, had been reduced by horizontals.

Colleen and Jude agreed with her, of course, and he and Richard and Gus said nothing, although they all knew more than enough about limitations, of several kinds. And any of them could have taken Sandra's reduced-by-horizontals lecture and run with it, because they were not without perspective. None of them had to be told that they had been nowhere and knew nothing, not even with all of their trips and their working lives and the six kids they had between them. They knew exactly how secure, how lucky they were, sitting in early middle age on a porch at the lake, even in a storm that bad.

Satisfied that he had no leaks and with his argument for sitting under shelter so indisputably won, Gus rubbed a bare foot on his dry cement floor and looked up to thank his sturdy porch roof. And then he lifted his mug in a toast, to himself. Which Sandra saw and liked, and remembered, and told.

They sat out until the storm moved on, inland, toward the towns and cities.

Although she has no one in particular to marry, she is trying on wedding gowns, one after another. She has cut herself shaving, so there's a little blood on some of them. Between gowns she stands, cold, in a silk slip. A semi-trailer brought the gowns, racks of them, to her parents' driveway. Her law-abiding mother is convinced that they've been stolen, "a hot shipment," she calls it, but she is trying to be a good sport, fussing with the small satin-covered buttons and with the long bridal trains, some of which reach all the way into the backyard.

Colleen and Jude are out there keeping watch over the pristine trains. And now they are screaming because clumps of dirt are falling from the sky, or from the walnut tree. But her mother wants the sky and the tree and everything in them ignored.

Sandra is making a different, deeper sound now, like impatience but worse. He gets up to turn her, to change the blood flow, and then he half lifts her to hold her. When her face seems relaxed again he releases her and tries to arrange her more comfortably on the pillow, but then there is nothing more to do so he takes another journal from the bedside table. Because he wants more. More of her, in summer.

In 1990 their high-summer supper was at Richard and Colleen's, in late spring. They'd had to miss it the year before because of his heart surgery, but as soon as he had his energy level back he told Sandra that he wanted their routine returned to normal. He told her that he was ready for every damned, routine thing anyone could dream up.

Richard and Colleen's place was really a winterized house built high over the lake, twenty yards back from a steep drop, and it was both relatively new and miles south of all the older, more typical cottages. The people they bought it from had built it as their home because it was under an hour into Sarnia where they worked, and just off the all-season highway that followed the lake until it narrowed, like a woman's womb, to flow into the St. Clair River. Colleen had ripped out the kitchen and designed what she called a better layout, and all of the panelling was gone and the wall-to-wall replaced with slate tile.

"Richard has put in a motorized lift down to the water," he reads. "A rich man's toy. But he calls it insurance against our old age. We had an extremely sensible supper and went for a ride. Down and up."

Because the nights of lobster bisque and crown roasts and double-chocolate whatever were behind them, they were having a stir-fry. Richard stood at the stove managing the chicken in one wok and Colleen waited at the other for the vegetables, which he and Gus were madly chopping at the table with two of her excellent knives, cutting on the slant as they'd been instructed. Dessert was already set out, Colleen style, berries and melon from a highway fruit stand and a couple of expensive cheeses, including the one that Jude would call revolting. Jude circled the room with the ice and the bottle and she and Sandra cheered on the cooks and the choppers. Then, with the vegetables done and their supper minutes from ready, he wiped the table so Colleen could set it. He remembers that because it was the first table he'd ever wiped clean.

The television in the living room was on because Saddam Hussein had just invaded Kuwait. Gus had the remote and he'd been flipping around, calling the invasion "serious business," saying that it was only the start of something because Hussein was a beast and oil was oil. Richard had been watching all day and he told them what he'd learned, and then Sandra wanted to know if they could imagine being young enough to sign up to fight a world-away, bloodthirsty beast. But before they got a chance to tell her what they could imagine, Colleen asked them to take their places at her table.

Richard wanted the television left on, and although they couldn't see it, they could hear it. But after he and Richard left the table, twice, as they would to catch a replay in a hockey game, Sandra got up to turn the television off, which he remembers because it was nervy even for a sister. So they finished eating without the invasion and then with nothing cleaned up, as though there would be a servant along, they took their coffee and liqueurs out to the patio.

The talk slowed to a Cointreau-muted, after-supper crawl, with Sandra counting off the seconds between the sun's meeting the water and its disappearance beneath it. And when the sun was gone, but not its after-colour, Richard announced that no one would be getting another coffee until they tried out his new chairlift.

Richard had put the lift beside the steep stairs to make it easier to get down to the beach, or more to the point, to make it easier to get back up. He'd done this not because any of them were decrepit, they were only in their late forties, early fifties, and his heart surgery had not been the worst kind, but simply because he'd thought of it, and he had the money. Because when you had no kids, you had the money. The rails dropped at a slope that looked to be about forty-five degrees but the cable on the pulleys was a good inch thick. Standing over the motor, Gus said that it could power a riding mower, or a small freight lift. There were two switches, one at the top of the hill and one at the bottom.

Jude and Gus rode down first, with Gus telling Richard that he'd throw the switch himself, thanks, and then clowning around, clutching the safety bar like a nervous kid on a not-to-be-trusted midway ride. If he and Jude thought there might be a little metal-on-metal squealing and maybe some jerking around, the drop, as Richard promised, was as smooth as butter. Then, laughing like a kid, Jude took her turn at the switch and everyone watched the car climb up again, faster empty.

He and Sandra went next and after Richard and Colleen came down they stood in a row at the edge of the water, with the last of the sunset still on the lake. Sandra and Jude threw off their sandals to wet their feet in the foam and make their pigeon-toed impressions in the sand, and then Sandra hopped around on one foot, back and forth and sideways, to confuse any bad guy following her trail, she said. They watched the unimpressed waves take the footprints and he and Gus offered Richard their chairlift praise, what a great idea, and what did it cost you? If they had been just a bit younger, one of them, probably Jude, would have stripped and run in for a skinny-dip, and then someone else, likely Richard, and then Gus, would have followed her, howling. But they were not a bit younger. And they were cold.

Richard and Colleen rode up first and, rising backwards, Colleen, sitting erect with that face of hers, smiled a flat smile and lifted her hand in a cutting wave, like the Queen of England. A Canadian joke.

And when Richard finally figured out what was funny, he turned to wrap his arm around her, which, Jack understands now, was not that common.

She and Jack are in bed with April and Michael and Jan, who are taking turns being lifted high into the air on Jack's strong legs, the helicopter, they call it. And now Jack has his hand on her rounded stomach because they are ready to tell the kids about their new brother or sister, about Paul. There are no questions about how the baby got there, because they know. "That's what sex is for," Michael explains, proud to be the one with the hard facts. And now they are down in the kitchen and the kids are teenagers and Michael has brought her a computer that looks like a placemat, telling her that she has no choice, she simply has to learn. But she's busy cutting the girls' hair with her good scissors. And when she's finished they turn on her, begging, to make her sit in the chair to have her own hair cut. "Willy-nilly," Jan says. "That's how we're going to cut it. It'll be great." And although she doesn't let them see it in her face, she's a little afraid, and being afraid she starts to float up toward the kitchen ceiling. But then Paul catches her by the feet and pulls her down.

Sandra is perfectly still, which must mean that Alice is right, the pain has lessened. And he wants just one more. One more summer, sitting here beside her, alone. He puts 1990 down and goes over to the desk to get 1999, the year before she found her first little bastard bullet.

"Our turn," he reads. "Sausages from St. Jacobs, and a sprained ankle because Jack went over on it looking for a Christmas golf ball in the damned rough. And for whatever reason, Colleen was hard on him. She should have been stopped."

He and Sandra had used that morning to get the cottage presentable and then, risking more heat than they could take, he and Richard and Gus and Father Tony spent the afternoon on the posh new golf course, which was essentially a gold mine, a mile inland. Gus told them that the conversion from farm to leisure land would not have been hard, that you could dig out the water hazards, the ponds, with heavy machinery, and not even that heavy, in two or three days. And then you could use your dug-out earth to build a few challenging slopes. And sod could patch anything.

But they didn't finish their round because he'd sliced his drive off the eighth tee, and when he walked into the rough to try to find it, because it was one of his good Christmas balls, from Michael, he tripped on a hidden, fallen branch, and overcorrecting, lost his balance and turned the ankle. Father Tony was riding in the golf cart with him, and when he heard him yelp and saw him go down, he stood up to call Richard and Gus from the middle of the fairway. Not unreasonably, they were all thinking another heart attack.

Tony had to get back to the city for his marriage-counselling sessions so Richard and Gus put him in Gus's truck and lugged him into the cottage like some warrior on a shield. Richard used tea towels to rig up a makeshift tensor, and with a little help from the edge of the table or the back of a chair, he was able to get around on his good foot. But then, fed up and worried, Sandra put him on his chaise on the deck with the foot on a cushion and a heavy bag of party ice resting on his swollen ankle. Gus had to cut the bag open to grab a few cubes to mix the drinks, although there was no drink for him because Richard had loaded him up with the painkillers he kept in his golf bag.

Gus took over at the barbecue with the bratwurst. He remembers it was bratwurst because Colleen had coaxed Sandra into a quick trip up to the Mennonite country north of Kitchener, to the markets, and they'd brought home all kinds of sausage. Sandra had made her garlic-cheese toast things, and Jude tossed the compulsory green salad, the roughage that was supposed to save them.

After they finished eating, and with Sandra standing behind her like some consultant, Colleen lifted the ice off his ankle to see if anything had changed, to see in particular if a dangerous pool of blood might have gathered under the skin. Finding no evidence of this, and because, she said, not everything can be learned by looking, she pushed a finger down into the swelling. And that's what Sandra meant, in the journal, when she said that Colleen was hard on him. Ankles were not Colleen's field, her field was babies, but she was familiar with the concept of measuring pain by prompting it. He knows he didn't cry out but he hopes he swore at her.

Then Sandra started up again about driving in to Emerg.

"And to what end?" Richard asked, because he was sure there was no break. "It's Sunday so they'll be light on staff and he'd just have to wait around and he'd likely rather wait here tonight and get his X-ray tomorrow."

"So be it," Sandra said. "You're the bone doctor."

"We'll see," Richard said. "When the swelling's gone down, maybe." Because she would not let it go unless she got at least the possibility of a changed mind.

Sandra offered to bring out the coffee and her hermit cookies, but with things mostly cleaned up, everyone said no. Jude and Gus left to walk down the beach to Gus's cottage and Richard and Colleen took off in Richard's old Mustang convertible.

He and Sandra stayed out on the deck as they usually did after people went home. And sitting out there studying the stars, she asked him, "Would you say that we're luckier than we know?" Meaning the friends.

But he had never thought of it as luck, knowing Richard and Colleen and Gus and Jude, eating these meals together, talking freely, keeping some things to themselves, now and then giving or getting a bit of advice. He believed they deserved it.

She got him into bed and climbed in and held him, at first only held him, but perfectly. Then he told her he was afraid she might be the kind of woman who would take advantage of an injured man, and she did. And nicely done it was. But because he could never make her see her perfection, he had to praise her for something else altogether. . . .

"So nicely done," he tells her now.

He can hear Paul and his boys downstairs and Kelly has come into the room carrying Annie, with Jan and Cliff, who have just arrived from Orillia, behind her. Waiting for his absent kids, he has been timing them, getting out their suitcases and loading the car or calling the taxi, locking their doors. Now he gets up to hug Jan and to shake Cliff's hand, and then he's ready to leave, to let them have their time. But Cliff tells him not to go so he sits down at the desk. He puts the journal back on the pile.

After such a long drive home, Jan stands alone beside her mother and cries until Cliff is beside her, to hang on to her.

Kelly has curled up in the armchair to nurse Annie and, after Annie has had her fill, she stands up and gives her over to Jan, so she can do Sandra's lips with the glycerine. Jan stands close, to supervise, and then Kelly pulls Sandra's sheet back. "Let me have her," she tells Jan, opening her arms.

"She's not a doll," Jan says, looking over to Cliff, who has gone to sit on the bigger bed, who can only lift his hands. "She's not some prop," she tells Kelly. "What if she's frightened? What if she starts to wail?"

"She's not much of a wailer," Kelly says. She lifts Annie from Jan's arms. "Only for a minute," she says.

Having lost, Jan leaves the room shaking her head and, by the time she's down the stairs, sobbing.

Now Kelly is looking over to Jack for approval. Kelly has worked very hard here these last weeks. She has done everything asked of her and more. But he knows his daughter, doesn't he?

"It's just too much for Jan to watch," he tells Kelly. But because he wants both of these women near him, he can't say which one is right.

Kelly snuggles Annie and lays her down in the bed beside Sandra. "There you go," she says.

Annie opens her eyes wide to see where she is and then she lets them fall heavily shut. Although she can't be hungry, she turns her face blind into Sandra's arm, searching out the breast. And not finding it, she heaves a quick, surrendering sigh.

"She thinks she wants to call it a day," Cliff says on his way out. "She's remembering other sleeps."

"Yeah," Kelly says. Then, "It's as if Mom can't fill her skin any more and Annie's can hardly hold her."

And as good and kind as Kelly is, this was something Jack didn't need to hear. He is ready to call all of them together down in the living room, to lay down the law, to tell them what they are allowed to say.

But someone is out in the hall, so Kelly takes Annie back.

They are at Richard and Colleen's for their high-summer supper, and she has got them up to lead them across the dark grass, not sanely over to Richard's stairs but straight ahead, straight down the steep, sandy drop to the water. And they all step over the edge after her. They lean back into the dune and reach out for whoever is close but they soon have to give that up and just slide down on their haunches, night-rowdy loud. Standing in their ragged row on the shore, they take in the lake, under stars they never see in the city, and then, although they might be shivering hard and just as sorry after, they strip to their underwear to swim, to swim and float around in the dark. They have to keep their bodies low in the warm lake, because the night air is cool, but unexpectedly, Jack dives under her, between her legs, to lift her high on his shoulders. She doesn't always appreciate this but she does tonight. Then after they've had enough they come out and gather their clothes, and turning to see the climb ahead of them, ignoring both the stairs and Gus's sensible suggestion of an easier switchback climb, they crawl straight up on their hands and knees. The night-rowdy laughter is not as loud now because they have to concentrate, they have to find the surface roots of the scrub that holds the dune. But reaching the top, they can brush the sand off one another and spit it from their mouths, completely satisfied with their idiocy.

Kelly and Annie have gone downstairs so Jack sits holding her blunt-cut, painted fingernails, which are blue-red, like a showgirl's.

The ragged pounding in his chest, a hammer, a claw hammer, is new and it is not what any man could call love. He looks at her parched mouth and at her chest, as hard and flat and cold as a boy's, and at the weak expansion and shallow collapse of her lungs, that mock breathing. Sheet or no sheet, he can see the body's ruin, the wasting and the bruising and the pale rubbery scars.

He doesn't care. She could be inside out, he wouldn't care.

And then like a fearful boy put to a test that he has in fact prepared for, he is able to say the thing he should say.

"Love you, Babe," he tells her. "More now."

The Jacket

Colleen is standing at the big bedroom window. She would have said that she has steeled herself but now that it's here, here and coming, she knows she hasn't. Theory and practice, she told herself in the shower at dawn. What you can see yourself doing against what you can actually do. What you can hear yourself saying against what you can finally say. She wants to talk to Jude but she's taking part of the afternoon again, and Richard has reminded them that they have to keep spreading themselves out, to stick with the schedule, because it could still be, well, it could still be some time. Paul was here earlier and now she's watching Jack out on the street, helping Paul load up the kids, because he brought all four of them. Jack is securing Annie in her car seat.

She is taking shelter in a small, steaming tent, from a thunderstorm, just before dawn. The lightning, sheet and fork and then sheet again, lights the air, and the wind whips the thin canvas walls, making them breathe, in and out, in and out. The storm is almost on top of them and she counts as she waits for each boom of thunder. One Mississippi two Mississippi three. One Mississippi two. One. She is naked on top of a sleeping bag because the air is so close and now the guy beside her is breathing just like the tent. He is young too and for a minute she thinks he might be frightened. When she asks what she can do for him he says, "Help me relax." So still counting, she pushes him onto his side and begins to massage his back, digging her fingers into the muscle. Before the storm hit he was saying that he thinks he loves her. But she doubts this.

Jan and Cliff have gone back downstairs, and April and Michael and their families are in the air, heading home. All these last days, Colleen has known that Sandra wanted to save the best of her energy for her kids. Watching Sandra and Jack raise them, and watching Jude with Liam, she could have told them that this was what children got from their parents, the best of their energy, and the worst. Which was not necessarily what you would wish on them. Now there's another car. It will be more food, which someone will have to find a place for, throwing out something else to make room. She is sick of food.

Kelly has moved the hopeful, helpful books into Jan's old room so after she refills the hot-water bottle, on the off chance, she goes to root through them. And when she finds one that looks half promising she sits down beside Sandra again to check the index. She is looking for references to *coma,* the indicators, the depths and variations, but she suspects that she's wasting her time. What she needs is a recently published text from Richard's crammed bookcase at the hospital, or access to the Internet. When she trained at Old Vic they certainly covered the unconscious mind, but that was forty years ago. And all Richard will say is that the mind can fool you.

She's a bit unsteady because she has not really slept, because it isn't exhaustion that gives you the sleep you need, it's belief, it's hope. Even the slightest amount. She puts the book down to take Sandra's wrist, to count the faint-hearted beats. Then she gets up and lifts the sheet to check her feet, which are even colder than they were twenty minutes ago. But maybe they aren't. Maybe it's only that her own hands have got warmer. It could also be true that Sandra's sleeping feet have always been a little on the cold side. She works some cream into Sandra's skin and then goes to the bedside table to dip a Q-tip into the lemon glycerine, to clean her mouth. She lifts her head from the pillow to turn it. "Is that better?" she asks.

They have been advised by Alice to keep talking. But talk is hard now.

Until this morning, there has never been a reason to kiss Sandra. Kisses are for babies or irresistible children, for a boyfriend or a husband or an afternoon lover, or, very long ago and by far the most optimistic kind of kiss, for a parent. A kiss takes the place of something not said, something you don't need to say or know how to say. It's the solution to the one problem that she and Jude and Sandra have never had, not even in the grip of one of their snarls. The snarls being only words held back, massing, like some army. Waiting for her or for one of them or for all three of them to smarten the hell up.

She is lying on her blanket down on the beach. It has started to spit but she isn't moving because she doesn't believe the rain will last. Jack is up in the cottage with Colleen and Richard, trying to get the kids settled, reading to them or playing one last game, Snakes and Ladders or crokinole. She has just taken a quick dip to cool off after the heat in the cottage kitchen and she can't understand why she's been excused from the dishes and from getting the kids into their pyjamas. Has there been a blow-up? Is she mad at someone? At Jack? She doesn't like to think that she would have a go at him in front of the kids, but such things happen. Or maybe she has her period. Is she just a little bitchy, a little on edge? She can feel the sour menstrual ache, the ache that is to birth what clouds are to a storm, and now someone is singing. Some woman with a pitch-perfect, unsteady voice.

Colleen can hear Jack down at the front door again, almost shouting. Maybe a visitor has asked to see Sandra, or said some other wrong thing. Someone, probably one of his sons, should talk to him.

She glances over to the window again, at the bright, cold morning on the other side of the glass, then at the desk. On Monday, when they were talking about the journals, Sandra said, "I *could* ask you to take them." And as she remembers from her compulsory composition classes, from sitting in her dutiful row reciting the rules aloud, such a sentence, such a way of speaking, is conditional. It is used to indicate a stipulation, to say that one thing depends on another. What Sandra meant to say was, I could ask you if I wanted to. And it seemed she did not. She'd used the word *trust,* too, something like, you are the one I could trust not to read them.

She looks at Sandra's closed face. "But what if I need to know what you thought about something?" she asks. "What if I need that?"

Certainly Sandra's journal entries might have been slanted, like anyone's, but how many Sandras had there been? How much of the truth had she told herself and how many words had been wasted, for instance, on her, the good-bad sister-in-law. Had the times and the ways she disappointed been noted?

She looks through the small pile of journals on the floor by the bed and when she finds 1990 she leafs through the pages until she finds Spain.

"Colleen's Marco" is the heading, and the entry begins, "A rough landing at Pearson Airport, but home again in my own bed with some sleep behind me."

Because what Sandra thinks will be near the end of their holiday, she skips past the descriptions of the flight over and the hotel and the tour buses that circled Barcelona, and Sitges and the pickpocket and the paella. The olives.

"Colleen has apparently found her cure," it finally says. "It was the guy who sold her the suede jacket. It didn't take long, only an afternoon, but Jude was offended. Or maybe just left out, and therefore confused? And now we have to find a cure for that. Because Jude counts."

They were in Spain for only ten days and the plan was that they were not going to talk about Jude's luck-so-far with her breast cancer or the radiation to come, and they weren't going to talk about April taking off to go out West, either. After a good dinner in their first recommended restaurant, they joined the other tourists to walk along La Rambla. The wide pedestrian boulevard, so sensible and beautiful, dropped from the Plaça de Catalunya down to the massive, get-your-bearings statue of Columbus looking out across the Mediterranean. Hundreds of years earlier La Rambla had been a lesser road outside the city walls, but now, with its exclusive shops and artists and mimes and flower stalls and its small, tempting side streets, it prospered on saved-up holiday money. The evening was perfect, the holiday begun.

The next morning they went back, ready to give the boulevard the whole day, and partway down, like three Alices, they walked through a small passageway into a huge and noisy, sprawling market. Beyond the fruits and vegetables and fish and meat, the fish obviously fresh-caught and the meat maybe too reminiscent of the animal it had just been, yesterday or even that morning, they found stall upon stall of everything anyone could think to sell. Out in the sunlight again they stopped to watch a thin young man standing perfectly, absolutely motionless, a split-dressed statue, half-clown, half-angel.

And then she saw the leather store. It was narrow and the window display was limited to just one rusty-red bomber jacket and one pair of black leather pants, which were big again even at home.

"I'm going to buy a jacket," she told Sandra and Jude.

"Here?" Sandra asked. "Are you sure?"

"Markup," Jude said. "Think criminal markup."

She told them that she wanted suede, and black or fawn, and long, at least to her hips, and when they got inside they separated to search through the jackets hanging high against the walls.

Then she heard "*Hola,*" followed by a heavily accented, well-mannered "Can I help you?"

"*Hola,*" she said. "Yes, please. I'd like to look at a jacket. Suede, and fawn or black, and long." She made a line with her hand across the top of her thigh.

He was looking at her thigh and nodding. "I have it," he said. Starting for the farthest depths of his store, he turned back to say, "And my name is Marco."

"He's got what you want?" Jude asked. "Good."

And he did have it, except that to get the length she wanted the jacket had to be a bit roomy. But the fawn was like Lake Huron sand. Not the minuscule, multicoloured mix of grains you hold in your hand but the seen-from-a-distance colour of sand. Marco walked her over to the three-way mirror, where she saw that she could carry it off, both the muted colour and the butter-soft suede. This didn't surprise her because she could always wear pretty much whatever she wanted to wear, she could make almost anything look better simply by putting it on. Not everything was that easy, of course, but her mother had suggested a long time ago that she had only the two choices, either try, honestly try to set the beauty aside or use it to everyone's advantage. Because people did not necessarily dislike beauty.

"It's too big," Sandra said.

"This will be fine," Marco said. "It's not unusual and I have my factory close." He lifted her arm up and away from her body and pinched the side-seam suede in his fingers. His other hand was resting heavily on her back, to convince her.

"Where are you from?" he asked.

"Canada," she said. She found the price tag. The jacket was no doubt overpriced but she was there and it was there and it was not beyond her. "How much for the alterations?" she asked.

"Nothing," he said. "It is so straightforward."

She turned around to Sandra and Jude, who wisely shrugged in case the jacket was a mistake.

"How long to take it in?" she asked Marco.

"Two days," he said.

"All right," she said. "Then I guess it's mine."

With the sale made, they were joined by his staff, two very well made-up young women.

"*Hola,*" they said together.

"These are my sister's kids," he said, helping her out of the jacket.

Out on La Rambla again, they had a salad and carried on through the afternoon. They followed another passageway through to more ordinary stores selling furniture and fabric and drugs and then they came back out to walk down to Columbus and along the waterfront. There was a large marina filled with pleasure boats, but no apparent hope for a ride on the blue, blue water. So they found an empty bench, a place to sit to watch things.

"What if I go over there?" she asked Sandra and Jude. "What if I stroll over to one of those yachts and charm the pants off a skipper?"

"That could work," Sandra said. "You check it out and let us know."

Jude looked tired so she and Sandra slumped on the bench as if they were tired too. Gus had been worried about Jude's exhaustion, and he'd asked them to gang up on her if they had to. She knew, they all knew, that bouncing back from surgery could cost you more than you'd bargained for, that after the initial high, your recovering body would take exactly the time it needed. It had been weeks since Jude's surgery and almost two weeks since she'd needed to talk about it, to talk it through again, but that was what you wanted, wasn't it? You wanted to get past the time when it was always right there, on your mind. Still, they were watching her for fatigue, for any clue, or for a false bravado, some pretense that she was unchanged. And they helped her in the ordinary ways, taking her luggage from her, finding an elevator.

Rested or not, Jude stood up from the bench to announce that she didn't feel like waiting until nine to eat, and that she could stand some North American food. So they got a taxi and found a Hard Rock Cafe, where they were completely out of place among the young, tourists and locals together. "Sore thumbs," Sandra said.

The next day they walked more slowly and more at home through the dark, damp streets of the medieval section of the city, and after they'd ducked under the arches and climbed the stone staircases and crossed the connecting balconies, they overheard a guide explain, bragging, that this was how the nobility had lived. And then they found the Picasso Museum and bought the expected postcards.

The day her jacket was to be ready, after a quick breakfast and a morning on the Bus Turístic with a stop at Plaça d'Espanya with its 244 steps and its city view and then at Poble Espanyol, which was a replica of a Spanish village where the nobility had never lived, she told Sandra and Jude that she would go down to La Rambla alone. But when she got to the leather shop her jacket wasn't ready.

"My apologies," Marco said. "Please, let me call them."

She waited, looking out the window at the clown-angel guy, wondering if he slept in a tight ball. Because she would, if she had to stand that tall, that still, all day.

"It's finished." Marco was back, with a smile. "I will go to bring it for you."

"How long will that take?" she asked. She had travelled enough to know that time, in different parts of the world, could be a different animal.

"Twenty minutes, at most," he said. He pulled on his own fawn jacket and then, with a still stronger smile, he issued his invitation. "You should come with me to see my factory. To meet my sister."

And was this it? Was this what she'd been waiting for? "All right," she said. "I'll come to your factory."

He collected a few recently chalked-and-pinned garments to take with him and they left through a back door to get into his van. They drove turning and turning again and then he stopped not at what she would have called a factory but at a stone building that might have been a large middle-class house.

The door was locked but he had his key. When they got inside and no one was around, he looked at his watch. "They have gone," he said. "My mistake."

It was midday, when many establishments still closed down because of the heat. He dropped his chalked-and-pinned armload on a long table. Looking around, she saw her jacket before he did.

He stood behind her to check the fit, to check the shoulders in particular because any garment has to hang right, and satisfied with his sister's work he led her through to the back to show her the sewing machines, which were industrial, to take the thickness of the leather. There was a high, clean window and below it a cutting table covered with sleeves and partial backs and pant legs, and with handsome baskets of buttons and zippers. The uncut leather was laid out in low piles on the floor and there were several stacked bolts of heavy satin, for the lining. And beyond the bolts of satin, his cot.

He took her jacket off as if he still owned it, and she was too tall for him, but not when he laid her down. She could guess what he believed. Believe away, she thought.

He was not young but he was swarthy-dark and he had once been heavily muscled, which pleased her, and at forty-six, and pleased, her body's nerve could still overcome the evidence of its age. So she let herself go, although not as far as trust, because it would be wrong to put weight on a phantom limb. She had adjusted to her marriage, of course, which was bolstered now not by trust but by a regretful longing for it. And regretful longing, it turned out, could be just as tough-minded and as thoroughgoing as trust.

After it was done she stayed beside him longer than she should have, feeling protected and safe. Or excused. This was just her own little drama, she realized that, because while he continued to be considerate and well mannered, he would be enjoying something entirely different, maybe the drama of a good, choice collection, over time. She stood up to get dressed and find a bathroom and become herself again. Instinctively, like a snapped rubber band.

Then she watched him roll off the cot slowly, a little tired, and walk over to the rack near the front, where a dozen garments hung ready to be returned to the store. She helped him carry them out to the van and when they got back his nieces said their mother had been in and was sorry to have missed meeting her. They told her how exquisite the jacket was as they wrapped it in pale blue tissue.

When Marco announced that there was one more thing she had to see, she'd already said thank you and was almost out the door, but she turned around, with that last bit of curiosity. And they hurried down La Rambla to the Marine Museum, where he paid for her admission, because they were in public, he told her after they were inside. He took the bag with the jacket and began to explain what she was looking at, which was all raw, massive timber. In its heyday the museum had been both a shipbuilding centre and a giant repair shop and it wasn't inland as it was now but right at the water's edge. The ceiling looked to be five storeys high and there were long ramps and high-strung pulleys to haul the great sailing ships inside and then to release them, restored. She was astonished, and wanting exactly that, Marco was finally quiet. Then he pulled her into a room off to the side to see a life-size, dry-land replica of the kind of ship that had crossed to North America, hundreds of years earlier. And, more astonished, she told him that there were people at home with bigger boats for nothing more than pleasure. And yes, he said, he knew, and here too. Then he stepped onto the dry-land replica, as you were meant to do, and turned to take her hand, but just as she boarded, ready to set sail, a storm broke. The ship began to roll and heave and the room went dark and there were loud cracks of deep, resounding thunder and pretty convincing sheets of lightning. And she could see in the lightning that he was grinning.

"They were braver even than us," he shouted. "You see?" He expected her to laugh so she got her footing, as she would have to anyway, and laughed.

Outside in the sunlight again he found a side-street taxi and, putting her in it, said that she and her friends must go to the 4 Gats for dinner, because it had been one of Picasso's haunts. And, all right, she told him, thinking, you are going to forget all this, starting now. Riding back to the hotel, she wondered what she was going to tell Sandra and Jude to explain the extra time she'd taken, because they had a right to be worried. If they had convinced each other that she was only in some holiday sulk and wanting a bit of space, all to the good.

But speeding through the Barcelona streets, explaining the extra time to herself, she began to like the sound of the word *unplanned,* which could be just the right word if she could find a little innocence to go with it. But no. She was not surprised by what she'd done. The episode on the cot had been the reward postponed and the only question was why she'd taken it now, this late. And this unnoticed. She would never see Marco again and she would never confess, either. Deceitful? Yes, of course. Wasted? Maybe.

It turned out that Sandra and Jude were just back themselves, from Gaudi's Sagrada Familia, which they'd decided to see without her. She told them that after she picked up her jacket she had gone down to the Marine Museum, because it was so close and she was curious. She said she would tell them about it at dinner, which Marco said they should have at the 4 Gats. She had a shower and some sleep and three hours later they were sitting up on the narrow balcony at the restaurant, overlooking the other diners, and Jude was feeling rested enough to fall in love with the maître d'. They ordered a bottle of wine and their lamb and shrimp and chicken and she didn't see Marco until he was halfway up the open staircase.

Sandra and Jude remembered him right away, and because his standing at their table was making things difficult for the servers, Jude asked him to sit down, to join them. But he couldn't, he said, because he was not alone.

"I am with my father," he said. "We come every week."

He turned to wave at a small, very old man sitting alone below them, who acknowledged them with a courtly nod of his old head.

"I just wanted to check if your enjoyment is high," he said. And saying it, didn't bother to look at Sandra or Jude.

"It is," she said. There was nothing to be gained by asking why he had climbed the stairs to betray her.

All three of them watched him go down. When he was almost at the bottom, to avoid touching a woman on her way up, he flattened his body against the banister. And then he found the maître d' and arranged to have a better bottle of wine sent up.

"A gentleman," Sandra said, making eye contact with neither of them as she leaned back to let their server place her plate of lamb.

"Oh, I don't think so," Jude said. Catching on so late, waiting for one of them to say something, she looked completely betrayed.

She and Sandra had kept Jude in the dark about Richard's confession and now, still in that dark, she had reason to become aggressively confused, which would spoil everything. So she should be told something about the history, about the reason. Which would also spoil everything.

Sandra began to eat, telling them that she was glad Marco suggested this place because, Picasso be damned, the lamb was the best she'd ever tasted.

"How thoughtful of him," Jude said. She had not picked up her knife and fork.

"Jude, don't let your chicken get cold," Sandra said. "Please don't." And ploughing on, ploughing on, "I'm looking forward to tomorrow."

Tomorrow was Montserrat.

"Then I guess I'd better look forward to it too," Jude said. She was watching Marco, who sat below them, listening politely to his father. "Given my limited options."

In the morning they took the metro to the train and at the end of the line, in the mountains, a cable car. It was cold that high but the hotel clerk had warned them so they'd dressed for it. The cable car wasn't half full, and as they moved up through the cloud, with the exception of a woman who clung to the centre pole with her eyes clamped shut, everyone stood at the windows taking pictures. She and Sandra and Jude were all able to look down, which was something else the hotel clerk had warned them about, and she guessed that the drop to their deaths could have been calculated. Two children who should have been enjoying the mountains were staring at the woman clutching the pole and she wanted to warn them that they were making a mistake. But then Jude was staring too, probably because the terrified woman could have been April's older twin.

"Look," Jude said, pointing, taking Sandra's arm. "The mountain is jagged there, but just over there it's been worn smooth."

"The work of the wind," Sandra said. "Exposure and direction."

Then, because she was not going to let Sandra and Jude talk around her, she mentioned the stubborn growth, the trees and shrubs in the jagged crevices, even near the top where the air would be thin.

The cable car landed with a confident thud and they poured out to join maybe a hundred other visitors climbing the last slope up to the church. The church was dark and beautiful and, up at the front, the beautiful, towering Christ on the cross was black. They took their places in the lineup, but when they got to the cross an old woman she took to be Spanish was refusing to move. The woman was crying or praying and reaching up to caress the dark legs. She was reaching in wounded supplication to touch the Christ.

"This is just too awful," Sandra said, too loudly.

"Is it?" Jude asked.

And then they were outside, walking down to inspect the many kinds of honey for sale on the tables near the souvenir shop, and Jude had stopped in her tracks behind them.

She and Sandra stopped and turned to her, to hear it.

"I've always thought you didn't tell me about Richard so the whole thing could just die a natural death," Jude said. "Which was fine. I didn't care."

So she had known all along. Because Jack had told Gus? Or maybe it was just all those years of crumbs left for her to follow. Either way, she'd known and said nothing. For all that time.

"Hang on," Sandra said.

"Jude, it was just so damned awful," she said. "I didn't want to talk about it at all."

Jude took off her sunglasses and folded them in her hand. "Like Richard," she said, "I had a bit of a run myself. When I was young." They moved closer so she wouldn't have to speak so loudly. "You both know that. And some of it wasn't very pretty. Before Liam, some of it might even be called a mistake."

And now she was ready to come to Richard's defence?

"You're not implicated here, Jude," Sandra told her. "And neither, believe me, am I."

Jude obviously had more to say, maybe about the cruelty of late-in-life retribution, or about Spain being ruined, but their concentration was broken by the old woman who had reached to touch the Christ. The woman was rushing between them not praying but laughing as she tried to grab the hand of a boy who was getting away from her, who had a scar like a horseshoe on his shaved head.

Then Jude put her sunglasses on again, maybe to hide her eyes.

On the way back down, standing on the opposite side of the cable car, away from Jude, she noticed the snaking switchback highway, the safer ascent that she'd missed on the way up. Now that she too had enjoyed the pleasure of delusion, she saw that she might have offered Richard's sweet young thing a bit of counsel, a heads-up: Don't ever let yourself believe that it was better than it was. Because in one afternoon, Richard's betrayal had finally been recast. Now it was something she might be able to manage, now it was only his unremarkable lust, which was not, she was beginning to believe, connected to his heart.

Following the toy cars on the switchback highway, and understanding exactly what it was that Richard had done to her, she began to recognize in other people, the people with them in the cable car and back at the church, people at home, people not at home, other degrees of loss. The loss of hope, for instance, of wanting what might come next. The loss of a child being the worst, the one worst thing that could give you truly catastrophic anguish. But the loss of Richard would be hard, too. And so would the loss of a faithful friend, like Jude.

So loss was to be *measured* in mid-life? And measured not against good luck or even against your occasional honourable decency, but by holding your own damage up against other damage? As if everything had been equal, once, and everyone with the same chance?

They were flying down now and faith, faith in forgiveness, was becoming a possibility. If she let it, that faith might grow big enough to displace her thinned-out faith in God, and maybe it would stay just that size. Then it could move the way her rage liked to move, from one place in her body to another. It could swim behind her eyes. It could throb in her fists.

The truth was that she had stayed in her marriage because, even after Richard's sad-sack confession, she had still wanted it all, the man and the house and the money and the job and the kids. And if people thought that any self-respecting, betrayed woman would be anxious to give this up, they had been misinformed.

So, like an animal, like a mother, like anything but a wife, all this time she has continued to keep watch on Richard's contentment as his young women have continued to drift around him. And drift more openly now, ignoring her, lightheartedly. Watching these young women she can see exactly what they think they see in him because, although she would never have acknowledged it in herself, she too must have perked right up when she found him, hoping for a glazed, middle-class life. Because she would have known, even then, that there are worse things. Even without the children. And if her hormones have let her down, at least they did identify, when they were young, that chance for strong children.

And if Richard had made them both the subject of cheap talk, that was the one thing she had not done to him. So maybe the far away secret could serve as her innocence. Because even when they were old and beyond desire, even on the day she buried him, if she did bury him, she would half expect a few suggestive comments from the crowd. Comments coming fast and loose from guys just like him, men who would not know how to believe that they had become old and past desire . . .

"Jude can't really comprehend," Sandra has written. "And neither can I. So on we go."

She is at the fridge organizing the artwork, giving each of the kids their exact one-quarter of the white door, even if it's left half-empty. The unmade bed is piled high with all of their other gifts, years and years of them. There are a million earrings, both delicate and huge, because after the girls got their ears pierced, sitting bravely in the chair while she sat out on a mall bench, disapproving and afraid for them, they convinced her to get her own done. And there's an alarm clock from Paul and dozens of CDs and several expensive belts to show off her small waist, one of them, the best one, a fawn suede. There is the cappuccino machine, which she got tired of bothering with, and picture frames, silver and gold and leather, filled with the kids' faces and with the faces of the people they have found to love, and newer frames for the smaller faces of their miracle children. There are pictures of her, too, with a horse, with a hat on, with a broken wrist in a cast. And now she's resting in that gift-laden bed and Jack is at the door frowning, warning her to get organized.

Beside her, Sandra makes a sound like regret, so Colleen puts the journal face down on the bed and gets up to pull back the sheet to lift and turn her. And then she starts to massage her legs.

"One of the things Marco enjoyed," she tells Sandra, "was to watch me as if he knew me. Isn't that funny?"

She works Sandra's muscles, pushing the blood up toward her heart. "Forgiveness can ambush you," she says. "A woman can almost count on it."

But how much easier it's been to live with Richard since Spain, since she's had her own guilt to exhaust on him.

"A very brief and lovely affair," she says. And then, "Oh, what a cartload." If Sandra would just wake up, they could laugh. They could see it for what it was, all of it. But she won't wake up.

What she really learned in Spain was that people like her would be smart to denounce their lesser miseries. Even to feel a bit of gratitude for their lesser lives. Because it is possible to forget what you know to be true, initially for short times and then for longer times, and this can become a habit as odd and as much beyond your control as the habit of remembering. The going back to it and back to it, the calling to account. If Sandra wants to sit up now and tell her that her losses were nothing special, that she has only worked her way through a commonplace life, she will be happy to hear it.

But a friend's life over and with it a great part of her own? And rage as useless as a stranger? There is not going to be anyone to tell her how to take the measure of this loss.

Sandra's mouth is becoming a hardened oval, like that painting, that scream on a bridge. Or like some soloist angel. But it's only the jaw muscles, unhinging as the nervous system shorts out.

She gets up to check her feet again, and standing with her back to the door she knows that Jack is behind her, with Paul. Paul has brought up a new CD, some kind of jazz, and soon a young woman is putting a nice, crisp clarity to familiar, mournful words. Jack sits down in the chair beside Sandra's bed, which will still be warm.

"You have been such a friend," he says.

Of course Jack's loss will be the most monstrous.

"I did her feet," she says. "But it wouldn't hurt to do them again. This house is so damned dry." As if someone has made it so, deliberately.

She is swimming, to win, in an Olympic pool. She knows the pool is big because of the high, wet echo and the difficult length of the lanes. But she's an old woman. Ninety-eight, they keep insisting. And doing so well, they tell her. But knowing her true condition she would have to say that standards have taken a dive, because her back has the curve of a scythe and she has lost all bladder control and she can't see much or hear it either. When the young people come to see her now, grandchildren, great-grandchildren, once a year, once every two years, she pinches her skin for them and they see that it stays pinched. And then she lets them do it. It's always the smallest child who is the least afraid of her, or the most afraid. Her three surviving kids are old too, with problems of their own. Which one has died? She can't say. Which means she is worthless. It can happen, you can fool yourself into living too long. She has buried Jack, with his bad-luck heart. And Colleen and Richard and Jude and Gus, all of them. So finally there is no one to know what she knows. As good, as her old mother liked to say, to be dead.

Now Jude is at the bedroom door, and Colleen turns to tell her that she was supposed to come after lunch. She was supposed to sleep in.

"I was," Jude says. She sits in the desk chair. "Gus is downstairs," she says.

It looks like she might have had some wine with her breakfast.

Jack gets up half stumbling. "You know you should talk to her?" he says. He waits at the door, and Paul takes his hand. "And you know to be careful what you say?"

"It's all right," Jude says. "We're fine."

"I might have promised her a bath," he says.

Then, in a tone of voice that Jude would never use, but Sandra would, Colleen says, “Jack.”

As soon as he and Paul are gone Colleen wants to tell Jude not to be afraid, that once you get started, it isn’t hard to find something to say. And that she can never blame herself for living through her own cancer, because no one, no one here, ever will.

Instead she walks over to Paul’s music set-up on the chest of drawers, to look through the stack of CDs. She is looking for an instrumental, but not jazz this time. Something less personal.

Saved

Sitting with Colleen beside her, Jude notices that one of Sandra's journals has been left on the bed, half covered by the sheet.

When Richard phoned early this morning he'd used just the one word, *coma.* After the call, Gus got their medical book down from its shelf beside the breakfast nook, but then he just sat there with it, drinking coffee after coffee. When he offered to get on the Internet she had to tell him that it didn't matter.

"Are you ready?" he'd asked.

She got out the bottle of wine because the phone was going to ring again, soon, and it would be Jack or Richard with not one but two words, and all the rituals would begin, the just-to-let-you-know phone calls, the visitation, the service. And then they would have nothing left but the time ahead of them.

She has made her biggest pan of lasagna and a banana cake with fudge icing because it's April's party and that's the rule, the party girl gets to decide the menu. April has been away for a long time so she wants to welcome her properly. But she's brought some new friends home with her. Jack doesn't think much of the friends and he tells them not to go near his liquor. And he won't give April his car keys because she has lost her licence, she has actually misplaced it. Now one of the boys is saying, "That's okay, Jack," and lighting a fat joint. A huge stack of pale American money has been dumped on the kitchen table, thousands of dollars. "Who are these kids?" she asks Jack. "Do we know them?" Now Hank is barking and Jack wants to call the police, but she says she doesn't see how that would help. And then the boy with the joint stands up and hits her hard enough to leave a bruise. And Jack is going to kill him.

Jan and Cliff have brought lunch up to the bedroom, grilled cheese and bottled juice, a pot of tea and a plate of squares. Gus has gone home but Jack stayed downstairs to eat on his own and as soon as Cliff finishes his sandwich he goes back down to him. Jan cleans everything up and follows her husband, explaining that she is going to deal with the fridge once and for all, which any other day would have made Jude laugh, because what grown woman bothers to say once and for all?

She and Colleen wait quietly until the after-lunch nurse comes in. They move back to give him room to work and he takes Sandra's pulse and leans down to look into her mouth before he gives her the injection. They turn their backs when he pulls out the new diaper, but they do watch him rub his beefy arms, hard, as if they might be chilled, before he slides them under her to shift her in the bed. After he adjusts the pillows he wants the mixing bowl filled, so she takes it to the bathtub taps and then comes back to watch him. Bathing Sandra's face, bent close over her, he tells her, "That feels better."

He drops the cloth into the water and, wringing it out in his big hands, he turns to look at them.

"I should go," Colleen says, leaving quickly.

Alone with the nurse, she stands up to encourage him with a smile and an empty nod of her head. "Is warm water better than cool?" she asks.

"I don't see why it would matter," he says.

With Gus, and even with Liam now, in imitation, she is half surrounded by people who say less than they could. And she doesn't have to take it from this guy.

"Why not?" she asks. "Why doesn't it matter?"

"Because there's no fever to speak of," he tells her. Then he packs up to go on to another patient.

The water has got tepid, neither here nor there, so she takes the bowl into the bathroom to refill it and, back again, she lifts the warm cloth to Sandra's face. Although she was not close enough to see it before, there seems to be movement in the face muscles. As if she isn't unconscious but just not bothering to respond, taking some kind of time-out.

Talk, she thinks. And then she wonders about singing. Because doesn't she have a substantial repertoire, and isn't she the one who can always come up with the melody? Can't she still hear Liam's dozens of old tapes, and all her hours in the car, and even the easy, ancient, popular stuff, from high school and university? And the much better, more important music, from the farm? But no, there won't be any singing. And for two good reasons. Because Jack or Paul or Jan might catch her, and because even if her rusty voice could stay in key, words might not be so easy. Not alone.

Then her decision is bolstered because it's obvious that the pleasure moving across Sandra's face is in answer only to the warm cloth. The pleasure is coming from the most fundamental part of her brain, from the darkened back of the cave, where words and melody won't register.

Talk, she tells herself. She wants Sandra to sit up and snap, can't you try just a bit harder? Can't you think of anything that might interest me?

Colleen is in that white linen Wonderland dress with the sailor bib and Jude has on her soft print two-piece with the twirly skirt and the tunic top. They are all in their bare feet and they've told the men this is because they are feeling young but really it's because they can't dance any more in their high-heeled sandals. They are wearing their bathing suits under their dresses, secretly, because after the dance they hope to go for a midnight swim. To mark their last night together. Then Gus is handing out air rifles because tomorrow he and Richard and Jack are going to China, to war. "But you're so old," Jude is saying. "What possible good could you do?" And then Colleen, tall and enraged, is asking, "Shouldn't the boys go? Don't the boys have to go?" But Jack says, "Everything has changed. Now it's the old men who fight, the men who are done raising their children."

Along with Paul's joints there should be an eyedropper in the bedside table but Jude can't find it so she pulls a straw from the box to suck up some water from the pitcher, using her finger to make an airlock and then breaking it when she gets the straw to Sandra's mouth. But Sandra doesn't or can't close her mouth. She doesn't or can't stop breathing to swallow.

What else? she thinks. She takes Sandra's hand, getting back nothing but thin surface warmth. She looks at the stark white sheet floating over the forfeited body. Camouflage.

She is tired, but they still need her help here. They still need her hour or two. She wants Gus beside her.

Sandra takes a deep, gasping breath, as though waking up but too quickly, or coming up from one of her deep dives, but then she settles down again, insubstantial.

Tonight, instead of sitting alone in her dark kitchen, chilled, or lying awake beside a half-asleep Gus, she might take one of the sleeping pills he keeps in his shaving kit. He never finishes his prescriptions and he never throws them out either, and she has given up telling him how foolish he is, on both counts.

She knows that there are people who retaliate with delusion, keeping someone alive by talking to them, by finding them and hearing them in daydreams. So maybe she can do that. Maybe Sandra can continue to live, saved, as the pious might say, from suffering. She will know all there is to know and her voice will still heat up the winter-morning air as it did when the three of them were walking, getting their tedious exercise. There can be new and better arguments, and if she wins one, a maddened Sandra can storm out an imagined door, or she can laugh her loud, bent-over-double, imagined laugh. They can have a snarl or two and it will be easy to tell a conjured woman that she is pushing her luck, or that she'd be smart to think again.

Delusion, made to order.

Her eyes settle on the half-hidden journal and she reaches for it. "Colleen has found her cure," it says. "It was the guy who sold her the suede jacket. It didn't take long, only an afternoon, but Jude was offended. Or maybe just left out, and therefore confused? And now we have to find a cure for that. Because Jude counts."

She takes Sandra's hand again. So their trip to Spain was recorded. Of course. But she doesn't want to read that. She turns the pages, skipping ahead, surprised at her nerve. But the journal was open on the bed when Colleen was here, so she doubts she's alone.

"The three of us went into Toronto for the day," she reads. "And it looks like we've been saved by a pair of pleasure spheres. Sex toys in a red silk box. I'm glad, because I've had enough. God. More than enough."

"But I was the one who found the spheres," she tells Sandra. "Where's my credit?"

Their trip into Toronto had been planned to celebrate her recovery. Her clearance, they were calling it, because she'd had her radiation right after they got home from Spain, and now it was behind her. They'd had five days of Indian summer, the reprieve like an Alberta chinook with bright, warm skies, and just after dawn, waiting for Sandra and Colleen to pick her up, she found a dazed crocus at the front corner of the house, and had to bend down to tell it, no, you are confused.

Then she got into Sandra's car and Sandra and Colleen both turned around to get a good look at the shiny new boots she'd bought to wear with her long Black Watch skirt. Before she was diagnosed she'd been taking a computer course, where she met a retired, widowed economics professor who told her that his late wife could have been her sister, and he gave her the skirt one night after class. Sandra was wearing her old camel pants and a cream sweater and her rope of stone beads, and Colleen was in a black pencil skirt with the fawn suede jacket.

They spent most of the morning at the Art Gallery of Ontario and then they walked through the University of Toronto campus. Only one of them had been a student there and London's more expansive campus was more impressive, but they liked the dark architecture and the close shade of the trees. And it was Liam's university.

Before Liam even decided which courses he wanted Gus had told him that he'd give him whatever help he needed, absolutely, but that he was not to tell his father this. His father, Gus said, should be offered the first opportunity to come up with the money. As a courtesy. Although he had displaced Tommy in every way, outdone him in every possible way, Gus simply didn't care that Liam might forgive, or maybe not even blame, the man who had sired him and then disappeared with his conscience and his time and his energy and most of his money. And even if she pushed Gus now, hoping for some late-in-life disdain, for Tommy, for the mistakes she'd made, he would limit himself to the words he used on his own life. *Water, bridge. Twenty-twenty.*

So Liam and Tommy talked long-distance about tuition, which, being Canadian tuition, must have been dirt cheap from Tommy's perspective, and doable now that he was solvent again. Listening and ready to take the phone if Tommy started to dig his heels in, she guessed that he was more than solvent, that he had survived the alimony payments to the second, short-lived wife, who was American and more likely to expect it. Tommy had been much luckier with her, because she hadn't even thought to ask for alimony.

Standing in the dappled university shade, Sandra announced that she was getting hungry, although she was more likely thinking about her, about the aftermath of fatigue from the radiation. So they stepped back into the city that surrounded the campus to look for a place to have lunch. The sidewalks were busy and the people of interest, but there was nothing to like about Toronto traffic, which was just something to hold your nose against and try to raise your voice above. Because they couldn't easily talk, they were looking around and they were soon drawn to a sidewalk show of blowsy, out-of-season cut flowers. Then they followed each other into the narrow and dark and dusty store, which was crammed to the hilt with one-offs and worldwide miscellany, all of it piled like junk. Colleen stayed up near the front but she and Sandra went deeper back, more curious, and standing dead centre of the store she could see vacant birdcages and a heap of ivory chopsticks, embroidered gloves she'd never wear and a stone mortar and pestle. A basket of tarot cards with one of the decks in French and a white beaded evening bag that looked slightly Middle Eastern, a child's slippers. They had seen a lot of the imported stuff in its country of origin, not just in Spain, but that morning they seemed to be, equally, open-hearted. Which she had assumed would never happen again.

Certainly there was a good chance that the open-heartedness had been prompted by nothing more than the late-summer–like day, or by the skill of the artists in the gallery or by the university's architecture, the stone's grace or the shade of the old trees. There was also the chance that it was a fraud. A collaboration.

Nothing had been said about Spain, which meant that nothing was going to be said. They had lived through snarls before, usually when they'd had a little too much of each other, and they knew that their approaching menopause, the paws, Sandra called it, might be getting ready to knock them around. But Spain had been different. In Spain she was exposed as the odd man out and then, too sure of herself, or too angry, she had overstepped the boundary they'd drawn.

"I want to move away," she told Gus when she was unpacking from the trip.

Because if she had given, over sixteen years, just as much as they'd given, if she had invested as much, which she had, well, wasn't that worth its weight? And now they wanted to have it both ways? Excluding her, for years, but ready to insist that they needed her to survive her cancer? And celebrating, believing she had?

It was Sandra and Colleen who'd had to say the words *breast cancer,* after Gus tried and couldn't. And they were the ones who had to listen to her fear, to her apprehension about disturbed cells, who endured the thought of the mass that would be so gingerly sliced from her cut-open breast. Who enjoyed as much as she had the way Liam came home to take charge, to boss everyone around, even her in her hospital bed and even Gus, who let him. It was Sandra and Colleen who took such pleasure in describing how obnoxious Liam had been. How admirable he'd been.

And before Spain, it was Colleen who heard her complaints about the sterilized chill in the operating room, and met her surgeon, and listened as he reassured her that his arcs of tough, unyielding stitches would not have to be removed because they would disintegrate into her flesh, into nothing. Reassured her because he seemed to have guessed that she could still feel the thick, barbed-wire threads in her childhood chin and their painful, slow extraction.

And then after they got home it was Sandra who came to the radiation clinic to meet her reputedly brilliant oncologist with his small, warm, aggressive fingers and the confusion caused by his too-soft Asian accent, Sandra who agreed that the confusion wouldn't matter a damn if the guy could enforce a permanent peace in her body. Sandra who counted the lead barriers the radiologists use to shield a person's still-healthy organs from the deadly, bouncing rays, the shelves and shelves of thick lead blocks like heavy toys in all their many shapes, and each shape unique unto itself, like every human organ in the body.

Gus seemed better with it behind them, but he'd never once acknowledged the scar, not even when it was new and purple-tender. After the surgery he took her into the bathroom to empty the drainage tube bag as if it was all just plumbing, the kind of problem he had seen and fixed before, building his houses, and even with his mouth resting on the concave depression, he still didn't know anything about any cancer. Gus was using his obstinate vision to keep the body he loved, her near-to-normal body, alive.

She did wonder if this could be healthy, for either of them. At her final checkup she was ready to ask her busy surgeon what he thought, because wasn't reality something you should face in middle age? But then she calmed herself with the suspicion that most men, and most women, would be forced to imagine something other than their diminished, naked bodies, eventually. Or they would if they could still imagine.

Colleen had stayed up at the front of the narrow store and now she was holding an ice bucket she didn't need. Sandra was near the back, likely looking for something for Jack because, since his heart surgery, he was often, or more than he used to be, on her mind. Her little gifts were pointless, Colleen had suggested, because it's women who expect to be kept in mind when you're shopping, not men.

Then she was ready to leave because she was hungry too, and she'd had enough of the useless cast-off, sundry stuff, all of it hauled around the world on monstrous cargo ships, and to what end? But when she started to go over to Sandra to make the push for lunch she noticed a small, red silk box. Its hinged lid had been propped open to show off two spheres the size of golf balls. The spheres had been hand painted with delicate brush strokes, one with a black, fire-breathing dragon and the other with a wide-winged copper bird, in flight.

"Those are for stress," Sandra said, coming to stand behind her. "You hold them in your hand and roll them around." She made the motion with her empty hand, to explain herself.

"Oh, they're for more than that," she told her, knowing.

"What?" Colleen asked. "What are they for?" So she'd decided to join them.

"You insert them," she said. "And then you settle into a rocking chair. And then you rock. They're Chinese. An ancient remedy."

Each of them took a second to register the intimate placement, that smooth and solid bulk. And a quiet evening with a brand new rocking chair, beside a fireplace.

"We should get out more," Sandra said. She pushed in closer to touch the spheres. "They're not used, are they? They couldn't sell them used."

"They'd probably go in the dishwasher," Colleen said.

So they'd got themselves back to it, to the brink of laughter.

Sandra picked up the spheres to roll them around in her small hand, to see how much stress they might alleviate, but they were heavier than she'd guessed, probably solid through, so she dropped her hand, fast, to describe their weight. When the sudden drop made the spheres chime like loud and merry church bells, she yelped and pitched them back into their little silk box.

There was barely time to make it down the narrow aisle and through the open door to get their breaking laughter outside, where it wouldn't echo, where it wouldn't be so loud. Because they had been caught before, laughing too hard in too small a place.

She had to lean on a parked car and Colleen's eyes were soon streaming tears but Sandra stood stock-still on the crowded sidewalk and roared, forcing everyone to go around her, the Toronto Red Sea.

Then when the owner came out after them to see if they looked like thieves, they had to stop and sober up. They had to give him their best and most honest, out-of-town faces, their public smiles.

There was a busy sidewalk café across the intersection, Italian, but they could see at least one empty table. Staid London didn't have sidewalk cafés. In London you could eat good Italian but you had to eat it inside. They followed the waiter through the cigarette smoke with disciplined faces, as if they'd had some small dispute, and then they sat down to take his oversized menus and study their pasta choices.

Sandra began to tell them about the attention-hogging chair of her fundraising committee for the hospital, but then she gave that up. "Sitting in my brand new rocking chair going to town," she said. "Sharing a fire with a very puzzled Jack. Who, ding-dong, ding-dong, thinks there's something wrong with his hearing but won't admit it."

"Watching a Leafs game," Colleen said. "And Richard losing track of the shots on goal, growling at me, 'Could you please keep it down over there?'"

"Liam coming in with some new girlfriend," she said. "And the girl saying, 'I can hear soft cathedral bells.' And Gus telling her, 'You are mistaken. That is not a cathedral.'"

Now they were laughing their most consolidated laughter, and when the annoyed waiter came back to stand over them, they stared up at him as if they couldn't guess who he was or what he might want. Then Sandra remembered and told him, "Oh, give us all your special." Which could not have been much better.

They realized that the other lunch patrons were watching them, overhearing and enduring them. Deciding what they were. Harmless, offensive, mindless women on the loose, probably in from the suburbs or from some small town or a farm. Probably shopping, bargain hunting in the big city and, oh, what fun for the ladies.

But realizing didn't mean they had to stop themselves. Not in the open air they didn't.

She can't see Jack's face but his spent cock is content. She is in their bed against the cold outside wall with her head at his thighs, which explains the residue of pleasure, the blood-heat in her neck and her cheeks. "Like a girl's cheeks," he sometimes says, although he has nothing to say now. He has locked the door so they can tend to each other, enjoy each other, and then sleep through, in peace. They are not going to take a chance on morning, on one of the kids barging in to ask if he can take her car to school today, or if she can wear the green cashmere sweater, or her new lace-up boots. Jack's hand, a friendly hand, is tangled in her hair. The sheets are twisted and damp but they will sleep in the bed as it is, as they like to do.

Why Sandra and Colleen took her on when they were so secure in their own lives, and knowing nothing about hers, has remained a mystery to Jude. She has never asked why and they haven't told her. And now, because she has never been anything like them, and never wanted or pretended to be, she knows it was nothing more than chance. Circumstance. The coincidence of an apartment building and a loud, energetic boy on a dull morning, and then the good luck of Sandra's impulsive, offhand kindness, with Colleen in its wake, all of it triggering the friendship. Although her initial suspicion, that having only each other might have been too routine, too bleak for them, could be just as correct. Maybe, in the beginning, they were simply using her to take the pressure off, to make their own compulsory friendship less cumbersome. Or less fragile. But if that was what they wanted, they have been betrayed. Because she has not made anything easier, not intentionally.

Now she has to let go of Sandra's hand because her own is cramping. She does let go, and massaging her one hand with the other, shaking it, bending and pulling the fingers straight, she thinks, this is why the nurses shift her in the bed, to keep her blood moving, to lessen the chance of cramps. Submerged, invisible cramps that would be a hell of a lot worse than any absence of talk. She stands up and walks around to the other side of the bed. Why didn't the nurses tell them that they had to keep doing this? She lifts the sheet away and the two pillows and then slips one arm under the back and one under the hips, because this is what she has seen. Sandra is warm, like an exhausted, pungent child. She turns her just a quarter turn because there isn't any logical need for more and then she shakes and punches the pillows and uses them to brace the new position. She covers her again.

"That's better," she says. She has said it as a parent would, not as a question but as a guarantee. And then, as if it's the one thing you do for a friend in difficulty, she pushes the hair back off Sandra's forehead. The gesture that Liam always refused.

"Why do we do that?" she asks Sandra. "Where did it come from? What was it for, before?"

She puts the journal on the desk with the others and when she's back she dips her finger in the glycerine to rub it across Sandra's mouth. "You were right, weren't you?" she says. "*Saved* was the word."

She takes the mixing bowl into the bathroom, dumps the water in the tub, and adjusts the taps until she's got the perfect temperature. She carries it back slowly, so the water won't spill on the hardwood, and makes room for it on the bedside table. Then she hikes up to sit on the bed, in the bend of Sandra's body. She pulls the cloth from the water, wrings it out, and takes it to her face again. And again, the response. There is nothing else you could call it.

She and Colleen and Jude are at a funeral in an unknown church, standing up at the front, and, although she has only recently learned to walk, her nails are painted dandelion yellow. She has been told to be quiet and to keep her nosy hands away from the big box near the altar, but no one is looking so she stretches and reaches up into it and, bang, the lid comes down and her hand is trapped. Not bleeding but trapped. She is yelling but no one notices her. Not even her own kids, who are standing around with everyone else enjoying themselves, eating egg salad sandwiches and drinking Bloody Marys. "I'm sorry," she says. "Never again," she promises. But they won't notice her. So she uses her free hand to push against the lid and Colleen and Jude push with her and when they get it open wide enough she can see that it's Jack lying there in the box. "You are okay, Babe," he tells her. "You are going to grow up and find me because I am not moving."

Still bathing Sandra's face, she hears movement and turns to see that it's Jack, with Paul behind him, coming around to the other side of the bed. They have caught her with a smile, which has set off a spark of shock. She considers telling Jack that she is guilty of nothing but thought. Just the thoughts that have come to her, on their own. Instead she hands him the cloth, giving him, and with some affection in the handing-off, his proprietary rights.

Jack takes the cloth and leans across Sandra to buzz her cheek. So he isn't shocked, it's something else, but from the shock family. "What would I do without . . . ?" he asks.

She looks at Paul, who seems to be drifting with no place to land. "She should be turned," she tells him. She gets down off the bed and pushes up her sleeves. "It's good for her," she says, coaxing him. "She needs it. Let me show you."

But Paul, disappointed not in himself but in her, has walked over to the music on the chest of drawers. And she can hear Colleen, and Richard, who has committed himself to the nights, coming up the stairs. Richard's carefully constructed schedule is falling apart. Having devised his plan to conserve everyone's stamina until the other kids get home to help, it seems he can't stick to it. So what hope for the rest of them?

Paul has found a Peggy Lee CD and now he's come to put his gentle hand on her back. And who knows why but she remembers that Peggy Lee came of age in the American Midwest, on the generous great plains, which is not what you would expect listening to the edge in that sexy, big-city voice.

Silence

Even though Jack stood over Sandra through most of the night, he didn't understand it, not right away.

Now it's six-thirty, Thursday morning, Alice has already come to sign the death certificate, and Richard is letting Colleen in the front door, telling her that he is sure he wasn't asleep, that when he heard what sounded like silence he got up to check that she was comfortable, and found Jack standing beside her, wondering. And then he explains that it would have been the accumulation, that any system can take the others out with it. "A house of cards," he says, leaning on her, wrapping his arms tight around her.

Colleen answers Richard's embrace and then, because an embrace cannot begin to touch it, she parks him on the hall chair below Sandra's Mexican doors. He is in shock and talking to him won't help, not now. She starts to go upstairs to Jack and Jan and Cliff, but Jude and Gus come in, and before they get their things thrown off, Paul is on the porch behind Kelly, who is carrying Annie. When they are all inside, because he wants to be himself, to be useful again, Richard takes Annie.

Jack told Colleen yesterday that Michael and Jing and their children have had to wait for an early-morning flight out of Boston. April and Jason and theirs are on last night's red-eye from Vancouver, and by now they should be rousing one another from insufficient sleep and washing their faces with steamy facecloths. Or maybe they've already piled into a Robert Q van from the airport to fight the westbound Toronto garbage trucks on Highway 401. When they came home in November, April and Michael had tried to coordinate the arrival of their flights, to take the last leg home with all of them packed into one rented SUV. But Sandra told them not to complicate things for themselves, because there were simply too many of them now.

Jan has come downstairs, and with everyone in the crowded hall and Annie still content in Richard's arms, there is a round of quick hugs. Then, after that's done, Jan takes her phone from her pocket to try to get April on her cell and she does get her, waiting at a luggage carousel at Pearson. And before anyone can think to stop her, she tells April that she has left it too late, and still holding Annie, Richard stands up to grab the phone to tell April that it's all right. It is all right. So he *has* got back to himself.

Then everyone but Gus and Kelly, who stay in the living room with Annie, go up the stairs. And because Jack will not be touched they have to stand around the bed a little apart from him.

"We have to consent to this," he tells them.

But Colleen is feeling only a strange absence of panic. Thank you, Jan, she thinks, because it must have been Jan who smoothed the sheet over her mother's body. She must have run her fingers through Sandra's hair, too, because it looks tidied. And someone has pushed the bedside table out of the way. Maybe Jack, getting ready for them. She wonders if Paul's comforting joints are still rolling around in the drawer. She watches as the rest of them look or don't look at the body, and when she sees Cliff, who is a lifelong if subdued Catholic, lower his head and genuflect, that quick burst of his hand seems to her like some second language, like a tongue a man might switch to in the hope for a better explanation. Without any words of her own, and none threatening, she is very close to grateful for Cliff's unheard prayer. And caught off guard by that appreciation, she almost lifts an agnostic hand to her own forehead.

They leave Jack alone and come down to the immaculate living room. Some of them sit hunched, some stand at the windows, some pace the small distance between the windows and the sofa. Paul is half sitting, half lying on the floor, near the fireplace, near the mantel with its photographs, with Kelly crouched above him, trying to quiet him. And now here's Reg from the funeral home with his van left running in the driveway, its back door hanging open. Seeing Reg and the young man who helps him approach the door with their empty stretcher, Richard doesn't wait to welcome them into the house. He stands up quickly to say that everyone should go back to the kitchen, and then he prods and bullies them until they are on their feet. Colleen leads the way because Richard is right. No one should have to watch the descent down the stairs.

Reg lets himself in and he is efficient and discreet, all business. He lowers his head in a deep, near-bow, but he doesn't wave toward the kitchen. Richard and Paul follow him and his man up the stairs and then Jan is behind them. Watching from the kitchen doorway, Colleen thinks that this efficient removal, these two strangers taking Sandra away from her house, will be the last worldly thing. After this she will exist briefly in Reg's underworld and then nowhere. She sits down in a kitchen chair to put her head between her knees.

She realizes that not everyone in the kitchen, not Cliff, for instance, would agree with the word *nowhere.* Sandra always ignored Cliff's silent resistance to a godless family argument or joke, but Jan, if not herself a believer, has been ever watchful, ready to defend her husband against her infidel family when they threaten to get out of hand. Like many wives, Jan can sense an outbreak coming, and moving away from them, and from Cliff too, going to a different chair or to a different room, she will say, Let's not go there, not today. As if

Cliff's faith might be exposed to be a delicate, flimsy thing, which this morning it does not seem to be.

Downstairs in Sandra's hall, in it and not in it, Jude had watched Jan and Paul reach out for their uncle and their aunt, and then for her and Gus, as if they'd known they couldn't be enough for one another. And when their standing around Sandra's bed was over, she was the first one down the stairs and the first to turn her back to the sight of the van in the driveway. Then she was pouring cranberry juice for everyone left in the kitchen and making Colleen drink it, insisting. She was insisting because when she was getting the tumblers out, standing in a frenzied kitchen with people who had never had the chance to know her parents, she'd come up against the memory of them, obscenely demolished and unconscious, waiting for her in those separate American hospitals. Then she'd made herself think instead about Sandra's splendid bedroom, the ironstone green bedroom. And about Jan and the five men, Jack and Richard and Paul, Reg and his assistant, all of that male strength surrounding her body. Although it would be the professionals who touched her, because they would be responsible for everything from now on.

Reg leaves with Sandra's body, and when the van can no longer be seen, Paul gets up and puts his coat on to collect his boys from his mother-in-law. Colleen and Richard and Jude and Gus leave too, and they agree that it's going to be cold later. But so far there's just the stillness, that morning stillness.

Jack takes Jan up to her old room, to sit for a while beside her on her bed. And then he comes down to the couch in his den to listen to Paul's son Jackson run up and down the third-floor stairs, and work on the obituary.

After a flight from Vancouver that was late and long and rough coming in over the lake, April and her family have gone upstairs to rest. April told Jack that she'd done her crying on the plane, because she knew, she told him. She knew. Michael, who won't cry, is up in his mother's room, alone, and Jing has come down to sit with the others in the kitchen. Since they've known her, Jack thinks, no one has ever needed to tell Jing anything.

In truth, Michael is probably his favourite, but not because he was any piece of cake growing up. And not because he's achieved anything more with his life, either. They are all doing well enough. He approves of Michael for two reasons, because he has developed a good head for numbers and also for recognizing the long-haul impact of choices, and because even when he was a boy he'd stood up to him, as if he'd been practising. And so, like anyone who has held his own for so long, Michael can be fair-minded, even affectionate.

Last night, not imagining today, Jack had asked Paul and Jan to stay with him and their mother through the last part of the evening. He suggested pictures, that they could look through some of Sandra's haphazardly assembled albums, but Paul said he wasn't up for that and then Jan said she wasn't up for it either. So they sat and talked about work, and listening to them, he watched the street light behind their heads, a dull glow against the pitch-black sky.

Paul was content with his wife and kids but he was no longer satisfied teaching. "Teachers have been abandoned," he said, like a mantra. "No one would believe what goes on in my classroom now." That too, heard before.

Teachers have crashed pretty hard, Jack thought, in a big wave of father empathy. Because ten years earlier the good citizens of Ontario had elected a government that despised them. He imagined a math class filled with restless, spaced-out, snarky kids who refused to nail their logarithms, who could laugh at the thought that anyone could force them to do anything.

More than Sandra, he was ready to accept that Paul would never be satisfied, because didn't all kinds of people have to work an unsatisfied lifetime? Sandra had wanted Paul to get another degree, an escape hatch. Maybe dentistry. They had offered twice in the last year to help.

He will be thinking about it, she'd promised.

And then Jan talked about her job, which she'd just landed, managing banquets at a resort hotel. She had stopped working twice, but she'd lost both of the pregnancies, late, and she was still angry at the cost. The cost to her, she called it, correctly.

"We had a big wedding on Saturday," she told him. "And when it was over the father of the groom, a real nice guy with a tiny, beautiful wife, walked off with the big lobby flower arrangement. By mistake. Instead of the one he was supposed to take, the one he'd paid for, the hydrangeas and curly willow. And when he brought it back to us, he kept saying, 'I must have banged my head.'"

She was laughing the way her grandfather, Sandra's reprobate father, had sometimes laughed, silently, with only her shoulders and belly.

But he had heard enough. They'd gone too far afield. Give an inch, he thought. These two were young and healthy, they had good partners, they had enough money. They'd been given every chance and every second chance. Why couldn't they find something worth talking about? Why couldn't they talk about their mother?

Once or twice in the last ten years he has caught himself thinking that they failed in some unique way with each of the kids, and one night out at the cottage he'd said this out loud. But Sandra wouldn't hear any of it. That's not true, she told him, getting up from her chair on the deck and smacking him with *Lives of Girls and Women,* hissing as she left him, you complete fool.

So he has tried to stop thinking it.

And Jan and Paul had talked about their work because, unaccountably, he'd asked them, how is work? Were they only wanting to pretend to be, to remain, sane? And some of it, maybe, in service to him?

Still, he was not sure that he would have had them all, or at least not that close together. But she'd liked having babies around. She was at the top of her game with babies, talking to them as if they were fully grown and perfectly capable, as if they could interpret her meaning.

And carrying them so close, as if in being born they had not moved out into the world but simply from the inside of her body to its other, unprotected side. So they kept at it, one pregnancy after the other. Rational enough at the time.

He could have taken Jan and Paul out into the hall to remind them that their mother might be hearing the insignificance of their words, but he didn't because it wouldn't matter if she heard. She would not want them shut down. She would want them to keep saying whatever they had to say. The theory being? Something she alone knew.

He has told Colleen and Jude to take the rest of the day for themselves. They've been carrying a significant load here, filling in the cracks. Sandra seemed to appreciate their lunches and their talk, about the usual stuff, he assumed. The old stuff. Their history. He heard them up there laughing, but she trusted them. She had never gone many days without them.

Now April and her husband Jason have showered and come down to adjust to the time change, and after they get their son and daughter reintroduced to their cousins, Jason goes out for a cold jog. April finds him in his den to ask some of her tangled questions, most of which he can't answer, but she leaves when she hears Michael on the stairs. He can hear them all talking in the kitchen, the lulls, the sobbing, the accounting of the order of events. The ones who had to fly home have landed from another planet and they will want to say the right thing, to come to the right understanding. Every one of them is going to need a generous dose of praise, so he's trying to think of something she said in the last week or two. He can hear the muffled uproar of his teenaged grandsons, who are down in the basement now entertaining, or better, exhausting, Paul's boys.

"Oh," Jing says. She's hesitating on the threshold of his den but he nods yes and she comes to stand over him holding two mugs of coffee and, balanced on one of the mugs, a small plate of cinnamon buns. He sits upright on his couch to make room for her, this gentlest daughter-in-law on the face of the earth.

"I'm sorry," she says. "Lonely Jack."

She gives him his mug and, putting the plate down on the ottoman, she sees his open notepad, so she picks it up, probably to read some of the kind messages she's heard about. But it's only his rough draft, his start on the obituary.

It's only *with family and friends by her side* scratched out. And *peacefully, bravely, ready to meet her maker*, all scratched out.

And then the word he was left with. *Suddenly.*

The Overlook

When Colleen and Richard got home, she crawled into bed and watched him strip and stumble around, but he still wasn't talking. And she was no longer the kind of wife who could argue, even in the privacy of a bedroom, that a man simply has to talk, that it's the best and only way out.

Turning naked to look at her, Richard said that he was cold, and he would be, from both the night without sleep and the drive home in his ice-cold car. Then he said, "Saturday is all right for the funeral? Do you think?"

"Two days seems quick," she said. "But then so would a month of Sundays."

She waited for the slam of the shower door but it didn't come so she listened to the water hitting his cold body. Steam curled out the bathroom door. She watched it move across the ceiling toward the open window on her side of the bed.

Richard had not been with Sandra as he might have hoped to be. He didn't see the breath that must have looked like all the others but then was not followed. When he called home she was half asleep, half waiting for the loud mechanics of the garage door, and his voice on the phone, his first call and just the two words, was tight as a drum.

Come over, he said, and she'd dressed fast in yesterday's clothes. Fast and all in the dark, like some practised, predawn drill.

She knew that Richard must have done something before he made his calls, touched Jack's hand or put a hand on Sandra's body, wept without sound or maybe said something like the truth, something like, we are right behind you. People commonly do and say such things and Richard has become a man who is able to believe, sometimes, in the common gesture. Like kissing an unfurrowed forehead, for instance, as she did when her father died. But whatever he'd done, he had not yet described it to her.

Then he was out of the shower and telling her that he and Jack discussed the funeral arrangements, although there wasn't much to decide. Sandra apparently had her own wishes and in the last month she'd invited Reg up to her bedroom and then sent him away with written directions. Reg must have filing cabinets filled with directions, she thought, with strict instructions from people who are afraid of a service they won't see but wouldn't like if they could, who think they might be forgotten just that bit too soon. The casket is to be nondescript, something mid-range rather than cherry or oak because Sandra wouldn't want the waste. She could have guessed that much. And she did know, because Sandra told her after the last surgery, that she'd decided that the United Church minister could do her service because there were some, more than some, whose only comfort would come from the requested presence of God. But no one else should speak unless they were determined to do so. They could argue over the eulogy, or not. They could please themselves. Paul should pick the music and she wanted not that southern Ontario restraint but a full range of sentiment, like a banquet table, with something for everyone. And after the service they should go to a better place. Buy one another strong drink. Or crowd her shambles of a house and finish the last of everything in Jack's liquor cabinet.

There was to be just one day of visitation. Friday afternoon and evening, two hours, twice, to shake all the sorry hands, to remember or get to know every sorry face, to hear what they want to say, to try to comprehend why they've come. It used to be said of Richard and Sandra's father that if he knew you he would keep you ten minutes, and if he didn't he'd keep you twenty, because he needed the extra time to make your acquaintance. Like letter writing, like good correspondence, Frank's big-talking habit is on the endangered list now. Because people seem fine with the buffer, with the limitation of casual, imitation talk.

Then it was nearly nine o'clock and they were down in the kitchen when the phone rang and it was Jan, wanting to know if she and Jude could come back to the house after lunch. And she told her yes, although she didn't ask why. Had Jan already started to go through her mother's things, to give herself something to do, and maybe noticed the journals, maybe read a few unfortunate pages? And was she now wondering what to do with that unexpected mother? And wasn't this exactly the kind of thing that can pounce on the grieving child?

Richard was sitting at the breakfast table with his cold towel wrapped around his hips.

"You should sleep," she told him. She kissed his bare neck and poured more decaf into his mug.

She wanted him to go back to bed because, exhausted, he wouldn't be much help to anyone and he would regret that. In these last weeks his regret had once or twice become anger, directed at her, because she had not corrected or stopped or supported him when she should have known it was wanted. It is easier with Richard, sometimes, to overpower him, to outguess him, to take your far-flung chances.

But he picked up the remote to turn on the small television squeezed in above the fridge. He flipped through the morning talk shows and the home improvements and weather and then lingered at the news. "Listen up," he told her. "Today's women are more complex than ever before and, wouldn't you know it, when it comes to relationships, men continue to be off, just that half-beat off. And given a microphone, people will talk the most appalling shit, and shame on us, shame on you, this house could stand improvement. Last and least the weather this winter morning is not exactly what was anticipated, but other news is good. Good and bad."

She was going to have to leave him flipping and summarizing in his towel, because what she had to do now was drive fast on some empty highway. She just didn't know in which direction. And then Bayfield came to mind. His Buick would still be cold but she'd take it anyway, because it was heavier and safer.

"I won't be long," she said, grabbing the keys. "Try to sleep."

Thankfully, Number 4 has been ploughed clear and the morning sun, hot and bright on the windshield, is pulling the wavering mist from the ditches, back to its warm self. She turns up the heat. The fallow fields are almost entirely blanketed now, the snow either grey under the shadow of small clouds or that truer white. The only real colour, apart from the evergreens and the salt-dirty paint on an occasional passing car, is in the winter-blue sky.

The traffic going north is light so she slows down to notice things. A long-haired cat balanced on the roof of a doghouse, the Arva Flour Mills, several ongoing corner-of-a-field rock piles, a lone but obstinate sway-back spruce. Deadfall in the distant islands of bush, which seem to be getting smaller every year, and a white barn and a black barn and then the more common grey barns. She passes a small sign advertising colts for sale and watches the parents, a handsome blond stud and a big dark mare, taking their morning exercise, their hot breath steaming and trailing behind them as it did from trains a century ago.

She likes this countryside at any time of the year and she thinks they are lucky to have it, the spring crops with their irregular growth, the weaker rows, the stronger rows, and then later, the dried-out, ripe maturity. The food. But she likes the fields better when they're dormant, as they are now, because without the crops, you can see the earth's true curvature. You can see the real horizon and the long, smooth rises, the twisting creeks marked by the braid of scrub brush. And mile after mile of fence, barbed wire or small evergreens planted in a straight row, with their claim of ownership. The work the land takes is more obvious in the winter because you can imagine its unsettled past, and if you get out there before the sun burns the mist off, and if you've studied the past at all, you can often, almost, see it. Driving this same blacktop she has imagined first settlers who had brought with them intricate memories of such different, more civilized places, people up against it here, men made rough by risk, and the wives who came with them, changed, stern women who made do, who warned themselves to be content with smaller pleasures, with babies and bread and root vegetables. Or, who did not warn themselves. She has read about prairie women separated by bigger distances and colder, more deadly winters, women without the comfort and help of another woman in the same boat, an easy quarter of a mile away. And all of them, men and women together, adapting not just to long-delayed possibility but also to the lesson that you could not fight everything. That some things, the unhinged madness, the loss of limbs and years, the careless deaths, were bound to happen.

On other mornings she has imagined a slow-moving village of implacable natives. Women and old women, old men and children, following a day behind their hunters, moving slowly south across the unfenced snow, their travois, loaded with skins, hitched to their shaggy, sweating ponies. When she was a white girl in a white school she was taught how to build a travois and she painted her watercolour teepee and cooking fire on the brown paper, like butcher paper, that lined her classroom walls. And all of this as if in respect. But for what? For history? And what old farmer doesn't have his horde of arrowheads turned up by the plough. She used to know a woman who kept a grandfather's arrowheads on her living room mantel, who said each time she held them up to show them off that it was like ancient history. Which it was not.

And she has also imagined, driving alone through the winter dark, through distress caused by another one of Richard's women or by some incident at the hospital, that the rolling furrows could be waves, that it could be water she was crossing and the road she was on a narrow, iced-up bridge. On one of her longest, aimless drives, soon after Richard's confession, she convinced herself that the actual bridge ahead of her, a perfectly ordinary, rebuilt, concrete bridge, had been destroyed by a land mine, one mine among thousands left over from a war. And that even forewarned, even knowing the bridge was gone, she would not have time to brake. But then everything had been blown up that year. Changed. Made more dangerous, Sandra told her, by stress.

Now she almost wishes she hadn't got this far, but she has.

The last miles into Bayfield are slower because there is always more snow near the lake. And more wind. Turn to the weather station on any winter day and you stand a good chance of seeing that thick, bulked-up cover of snow-filled cloud, poised over a Great Lake.

Like all summer towns, Bayfield seems unnaturally quiet in its off-season, with many of the residents and most of the visitors, the people like her, gone. The main street is one long, mismatched run of stores and shops, some of them southern Ontario yellow brick and solid, like the serious town buildings they were built to be, and some of them cheaper, squat and rambling frame, brought back to life with gabled porches and new, high-pitched roofs and summer siding, grey-green or salmon pink. Lemon. The oldest of the yellow brick buildings, having stood tall for at least a century, have the kind of handsome, modest facades that small committees sometimes work hard to keep standing, accepting as their challenge the tilt of foundations and the pitiful heat-leaking windows, the brittle wiring and the clanging plumbing. The entire length of the street has been decorated for Christmas shoppers and, with that and the snow, the oldest buildings look if not European then at least reconciled to their status. Entitled to their place in this old town. The morning's accumulation of snow is getting a touch-up by a guy in a small tractor with a blade, so she waits at the top of the street, where it splits. When he's finished he passes her without so much as a nod, driving too fast.

The first of the old hotels looks to be open, or the dining room does. And so do the year-round businesses, the grocery store, the post office, the hardware. The second gallery, the one where she and Sandra bought their good-luck glass turtles, is dark inside but the path to the door has been shovelled. Probably limited hours. Then she is glad to see Mary, the woman who has the bookstore, a terrific bookstore, crossing the street in front of her with a bag of groceries, lifting her hand in a cheerful, hopeful, don't-run-over-me wave.

Coming to the end of the street and deciding not to stop for tea or for anything else, she turns to follow the shoreline road past the big cottages that overlook the lake. The land here meets Lake Huron abruptly, so the cottages are up on high ground, many of them with their own long-weathered plank stairs leading down to the beach. And maybe some of them with a small motorized cable car, like Richard's, because he can't be the only one. The best of the cottages is an old fieldstone with a broad front porch and a low, shake roof, but it's on a side street she sometimes can't find, and won't today. Instead she parks at an overlook. She leaves the car running, for the heat. She isn't going to sit long.

The ice where it meets the open water has thickened like a scar, because of the waves, the heaving push to shore. And it has been crusted, stained amber and grey, nicotine and ash, by the filthy air. Today's new snow will cover the stain for an hour or a day, and then it too will give evidence of what the air holds now. She watches the gulls as they busy themselves in the ice crannies, flying from one dirty crest to another in search of whatever it is they eat. The lake out beyond the ice could be the summer lake, clear and placid and safe, except that the blue carries with it that weighted tinge of grey. Beneath her coat and sweater, she shivers. Because how could you not, looking at that water?

Another time, from this same overlook, she saw a winter-dressed man in his sixties, or maybe his early seventies, walking with an almost imperceptible limp down on the flat, icy beach. He was wearing a red hockey toque and high boots, to the knee like riding boots, and carrying a cane, and as she watched him he lifted the cane and swung it in a wild circle high above his head. He did this in a show of strength, as if getting over some operation or injury. Then she watched him go down and she stayed watching until he was safely on his feet again, although certainly she could have managed the icy, snow-packed stairs, could have taken them in full slide if she'd had to. But he'd known exactly what to do, he'd known how to get himself upright. And then there was a woman beside him, wearing identical riding boots but with her big parka hood pulled tight around her face, for protection from the wind off the lake. She was holding on to his arm and plainly yelling at him. A life partner, no doubt.

She opens her coat and reaches under her sweater to unhook her bra. Lifting her left arm and pressing with her right fingertips, she starts the rote examination. She pushes deep to the chest wall and then comes back up to the more shallow depth, deep and then up again, around the clock. Finished, she pushes her fingers into the concave hollow under her arm. Then she switches hands, switches breasts, and lifts her right arm. She is clean, there are no lumps but the known lumps. Before she married Richard a doctor had plunged an astonishing long needle into her to drain a cyst. He'd used only a local and told her she was lucky. And since then, nothing has changed. Even Richard insists, nothing has changed. She puts herself together.

She turns the Buick around to find a street that leads away from the lake through the town to the highway, but finding her way in the mishmash of Bayfield streets, taking an easy right and then another too-quick left, she loses control in a fishtail, and in the split second before she can correct by steering into the skid, she's got her rear end caught in a low-drifting snowbank at the side of the road. She gets out to look, stomping and annoyed. There's a small running ditch just beyond the bank of snow and if she'd gone two feet farther, she would have been in it up to her axle. She climbs back into the car and puts it in low gear as her father taught her to do when she was learning on her mother's stick shift. She straightens the wheel and rocks forward, throws it in reverse, rocks back, forward, back, forward, back, each time gaining more of the street but also coming that much closer to the running ditch. Then giving herself a minute, she hears light voices and a shout and she can see two girls in the rearview mirror, both of them bare-headed in dark, matching peacoats, like Great Lakes sailors, their faces disguised by the falling snow and by the car's exhaust rising in the cold air. There is no need to get out and talk this over. The girls see that there's no room to push from the back so they march, laughing, to each side of the car and open the back doors to try it that way. They've seen this in some movie, she thinks, but she waits to hear them shout, now, and puts a steady foot to the accelerator. The girls give it everything they've got and slam the doors and the car is free, sideways in the middle of the street.

Another time she would have got out to thank them properly, probably made a how'd-that-happen joke and pressed some money on them so they could treat themselves uptown at the tea room. But sliding into the skid, feeling the back wheels go out from under her, she'd heard Sandra say her name, and not in shared, laughing lunacy or with her cool-headed, we're fine, we've been here before conviction, but with something like fear, or disappointment. So Sandra had come along to Bayfield for the company, as if she'd had nothing better to do with her morning. And she was counting on her to drive safely, to at least keep the damned Buick on the road.

Now the car is a dead chamber and the echo is only her own shout. "I'm sorry."

She lifts her hand from the wheel, hoping that the girls will recognize the universal sign for gratitude. But they have run up beside the car to talk to her, to check that she is okay. One of them, the heavy-set one with the glasses, the brave one, dares to reach in to touch her arm. Now they can go straight to their friends and describe this city woman in a big white Buick, getting herself stuck in a nothing snowbank. They will be the heroes of the day who have discovered in themselves the capacity for quick-thinking competence, and it makes perfect sense that they will want to hold the attention of their friends into the afternoon. But to keep the talk going they might have to conjure up a few interesting details, maybe an expensive brown sweater, no, it was more rust. A big, but actually a little weird, diamond ring. Great hair and, for once, not too much of that thick middle-aged makeup. And then they can brag, rightly, that they calmed her down. That she seemed nice, just upset. Kind of wrecked.

On the way out of town, as alone in the car as she's ever been, she wonders how the girls got to be loose on a school day. Were they, in their matching peacoats, truant? Or have the Christmas holidays begun? Even having Sandra and Jude and all the years of their kids and their kid talk, she has never been that attuned to girls at large. To the way they get along in this new world, to what holds them steady or to the chances they can take now, with everything changed. Maybe she should start. Maybe it's time to become what Jude's ex, Tommy, liked to call Sandra, with her chaos of kids and her speaking right up and her neglected house and her magnificent, bone-deep laughter. A *feminista.*

The highway is still almost empty and the snow is lighter, drifting low, driven by a lighter wind. The landmarks move past in their reversed order but the fields have lost their polish now, because the cloud cover blocks the sun. So all there is to do is drive. Just drive home.

She pulls into the garage and gets out to walk behind the car to check for damage, a scratch or a dimple made by a nugget of gravel buried in that Bayfield snowbank. Over the years she has earned herself a small reputation for allowing harm to come to Richard's cars. She has sheered off a side mirror, left a moon roof open, just a crack, in the car wash. But this time there's nothing.

Tomorrow she will send Richard to pick up their suits from the cleaners and while he's gone she'll give his dress shoes a once-over and then try to find her lowest and only comfortable black pumps, because formal visitations can be hard going. The people who come through have the advantage of moving along, but they will be on their feet in place for two long hours in the afternoon and another two in the evening. And to acknowledge that moving-along-grief, they will put on their best public faces, their most considerate public words. They will do this because grief has troubled itself to gather, because it has got dressed up with nowhere to go but to them.

For now, she will go inside to her husband, who will be waiting with messages and regrets about this double death, of his sister and her friend. She can feel the loss in her heavy, arthritic, nursing hands but it's suspended too, in her brain, like a bird of prey. Like a hawk waiting high on a cliff. On an overlook.

Her Shoulders

When Jude and Gus got home she called Ottawa but she had to talk to just Julie because Liam was in Minneapolis at a conference. Then Gus left a message on Liam's cell and he soon phoned back to say that he'd arranged to fly directly into London Friday morning, but that he didn't have the right clothes with him. So Jude had to bother Julie again to ask her please to bring his new dark suit.

"Of course," Julie told her. "I'm the one who knows what he packed." Then she stalled to compose herself, to say what she'd forgotten to say. "I'm sorry for your loss, Jude. You must be . . ."

After the phone calls she made some coffee and Gus noted the arrival times on his pad by the phone. Then he got out the Mini-Wheats and milk and the bowls and spoons and laid it all out at their places.

"Flying is nothing to these kids," he said. "Less than nothing."

Neither of them wanted the coffee and she didn't want the cereal. Gus ate quickly because he was tired, and when she got up to put everything away, he pulled on her arm to come upstairs. He stretched out on the bed and helped her down beside him and then he wrapped himself around her, fully clothed. If you want me now, she thought, I might have to run out the front door.

This was ridiculous but it was a phenomenon you saw in trash movies. Some monstrous shock has been delivered, someone has drowned or a bloodied child has been found in the woods, and soon there's that loving guy, stroking a woman, trying to comfort her, and it occurs to him, what the hell, we're touching anyway. But Gus only wanted her as close as he could get her. He had wrapped himself around her for warmth. What he needed was nothing more than the furnace of her post-menopausal body.

After a few minutes he turned away, and she turned too, but then he'd had enough so he stood up. He said he was going to get the recycle boxes ready for tomorrow's pickup, and, "God," she asked him, "why would you think of that?" and then he said he was going to do the driveway, and go back over to Jack's, to shovel them out. So he wanted to be cold again. Fine. She went into the bathroom to get the cup and the Cutty Sark.

The good scotch, one Glen or another, it makes no difference to her, is kept down in the kitchen cupboard. She started to buy the Cutty Sark for upstairs after Jack told them that there was nothing more to be done. She liked the name, Cutty Sark, and the picture of the ship, which no doubt had been a courageous, doomed ship, which would be its cachet. The day she brought the first bottle up, Gus had followed her and stood beside the bed with his arms crossed. Still and forever the immigrant who had made his own way, with not one goddamn thing to depend on but his own seat-of-the-pants resources, he'd described to her their soft, modern life, with the upstairs bathroom, the upstairs telephone, the upstairs TV, the upstairs laptop. And now the upstairs bottle. Convenience, he'd said. The thing we have worked so hard for.

But she had surprised even herself with the scotch. It didn't make sense to her either.

She was half finished her drink when the phone rang and she could hear Gus downstairs talking to Colleen. He came halfway up with the message, that she and Colleen were wanted back at the house, this afternoon.

There was going to be a lot of this in the next few days. Phone calls and messages involving all the households, calls to be returned, back and forth, names and times to be written down, arrangements to be sorted out. There were people who liked to whip up this escalation, this fit of activity, people who took great pride in jumping right on things. When she finally got her parents home to Canada to bury them she had seen the way whipped-up activity could lend comfort to people, or help them withstand its absence.

She wondered if Jan, keeping busy, had discovered her mother's journals, if she'd begun to read them and found herself hesitating. Fumbling. If Jan had been digging around and discovered a moral dilemma, she and Colleen would need to be as clear-headed as they could be.

But maybe it wasn't that. Maybe Jan wanted them to come over to choose a keepsake, something from her mother's jewellery box or her closet or the corner cabinet in the living room. She hoped that wasn't true, and not because she wasn't greedy for something to look at or to hold or to wear, maybe that pickle cruet, maybe that rope of chunky beads, but because she wanted Sandra to have made the choice herself. She wanted the instruction to be written down somewhere with her unmistakable name in Sandra's unmistakable hand. Even knowing how disheartening it can be, wanting too much, too precisely, she wanted it.

She heard the garage door open and then she could hear Gus's shovel, stubborn and loud, scraping into the new snow. Sometimes she watched him from the bedroom window, watched his rhythm become so quickly established and then hold steady, with his cold job quickly done. But this morning she was too late, because his car was backing onto the street.

Gus had not left her on her own since this last, worst part began. Other than for short minutes when she was in her car going from someone to someone else, she had not been alone in weeks. You have no good reason, she told herself, looking at the last inch in her cup, to drink. Except that it might hold you down.

She picked up the phone to call Nicholas, to see if he could squeeze her in for a cut. Then she put the bottle back in the linen cupboard and stretched out face down on the unmade bed. Before the surgery on her own breast, she'd always got her deepest, most childlike sleep on her stomach. But not since.

Now she's awake, and it's just after ten, which will give her enough time to shower.

Not entirely dry, she dresses and hurries through the mud room for her jacket and boots. If Gus were home, he would follow her to open the garage door, to tell her to watch herself at the corners.

Nicholas is waiting at the front of the salon, ready to shampoo her himself. People do such things on days like this, taking pains. They shovel other people's driveways, work someone in for an overdue haircut, are careful to say not what they're thinking but a little less. Massaging her scalp, sniffling and catching his breath, Nicholas gives no indication that her own breath might have any connection to a proud, doomed ship. And she isn't going to let his sniffling set her off.

Nicholas came over to Sandra's once, like a doctor making a house call, and she and Colleen had attended, washing Sandra's hair in the bathroom sink before he got there. He has been in charge of their heads forever but that at-home appointment was the only time the four of them had been together in one room. Sandra sat on the chair by the desk and he was very careful moving her head around but otherwise he was a bit wired and soon energetically indiscreet, laughing his big laugh. He would not have betrayed his other clients, not even if they'd coaxed him, especially if they'd coaxed him, but he made a game of letting them in on their own reputations at the salon, what his staff said about them after they left. Nothing about what he told them had been particularly brutal, or likely strictly true, given the things people feel free to say about standard-issue, middle-aged women.

Still, she was mightily impressed by the goodwill Nicholas brought to Sandra that day, and by his skilled use of bravado. Although a week later, when she was sitting in his chair at the salon and tried to slip in a quick word of admiration, he'd told her that he had mastered bravado quite early in his life, and by miserable necessity, thank you very much. But saying even this, he offered up his loud laugh. Then he leaned in to see how bad her hair had got and told her, as he sometimes did when she finally showed up, "Well, sweetie, you'll be getting your money's worth today."

Now he asks, "Does she have lots of siblings and things?" He is lifting her hair into sections, starting the cut. He has not bothered with the charade of asking what she wants.

"Just Richard," she tells him. "Colleen's husband. Her parents are gone."

"Oh, yes," he says. "I cut Richard's hair once. Doesn't talk. And he didn't come back either."

"There are the four kids," she says. "And they have their spouses and their own kids. So the funeral will be hard."

"And don't my people know all there is to know about hard funerals," he says. Then, because it is his habit not only to laugh but to think aloud, "I've never believed that children should attend funerals. I just can't see it." Nicholas holds all of his convictions pretty firmly, although she does wonder, depending on the client, if he ever has to make minor adjustments, perhaps even the adjustment to restraint.

"She hasn't worked since the kids," she tells him. "But her fundraising friends will be there, from probably half a dozen committees, and Jack's colleagues." She wants to give him the complete picture, lifted from what she can already see. "And I expect there will be a lot of neighbours because she'd become pretty neighbourly, with her garden."

"Neighbours are usually all right," he says, pushing her head around, cutting faster. He is concentrating, thinning out the back where her hair grows disproportionately thick, because of the blood flow in her lower brain, he told her once. He would describe his own neighbours some other time.

"The visitation comes first," she says. "And then the funeral."

"I know the drill," he says.

Lately, whenever she and Gus have found themselves in Reg Martin's serene, carpeted rooms, she has noticed that many of the mourners, the people their age, seem to be making a new effort to be aware of each other while they were still taking breath. They pick up on interrupted conversations from the last unhappy gathering, and say pleasant, excessive things that might have been taken, when they were young and guarded, as false and humiliating flattery. She has seen even slight acquaintances touch each other for no reason whatsoever, and the cynics among them, working the room for laughs, have their work cut out for them now. Soft-spoken, telling incidents are passed around like joints. Kindly thoughts hang in the air like angels. Joints, she thinks. Angels. That's how old you are. How worn down you are.

"She had such good shoulders," Nicholas says from his concentration. And isn't this exactly where it likes to go? Into praise? Into the naming of some specific, maybe unheralded, trait? Nicholas means to tell her that they have been lucky to know a woman with rare, wonderful shoulders and his testimony would have been ready before she walked in the door. "She had no idea how good they were," he says. "Some women know all about themselves but she didn't. I admired that."

Sandra herself had been able to use the word *admire.* As in, I admire Kelly's ease with those kids of hers, or, maybe we should just admire my young gardening neighbours, or, you could at least admire Colleen's middle-aged willingness to take a chance.

Now, pulling her hair down to her ears to check that his cut is perfectly even, Nicholas catches his breath again, for the loss of such an oblivious woman. And finding his distorted face in the mirror, she doesn't mind that he knew Sandra so slightly, that oblivious was the last thing she'd been.

She sits up straighter. "I expect to see Mrs. Granger at the funeral," she says. "You know. The kindly old neighbour woman with her blow-by-blow description of the life to come."

"Oh, her for sure," Nicholas says, relieved. "They always turn up."

She and Colleen had not appreciated any small part of Mrs. Granger's promised afterlife, and it should have been the last thing Sandra wanted to talk about, but the day Nicholas came to the house with his scissors she had told him about Mrs. Granger's heaven, and, of course, he remembered.

"Sandra said it was like a tour of St. Petersburg, right?" He was smiling.

"I'm afraid I'll go right to the woman's side," she says. She looks at his scissor hand, aloft, and then at her hair, an improvement even wet. "I'm afraid I will be nicer to her than to anyone all day."

He is finishing the top, going through one last time, taking the smallest snips.

"I can't seem to break the habit," she says. "I talk to the person I most don't want to talk to. And I'll go to some trouble to find them." Whatever this means, it stops her from crying, so she keeps on. "I stand there thinking, don't say it. Do not say what you are on the verge of saying."

"So don't pay any attention to them," he says. "It never does us one damned bit of good anyway." He grabs his blow-dryer to quickly style his excellent cut. "Does it? Do you think it does?"

Finished, he whisks her neck with his silky, soft-bristled brush, but when he tries to take off her smock, maybe because he's a little angry, or trying too hard, he puts a knot in the satin tie, which, working away, bending his big body down to study it and working away again, he only makes worse. "Help," he says, turning to his staff.

Two of them do help, and with the smock cut off and her reluctance to commit to the next appointment duly noted, she leaves the salon and starts the car and turns on the non-existent heat. You have to wait for the engine, Gus never tires of telling her. Because it's the engine's heat. She adjusts the rearview mirror to check the haircut and to wonder again why she lets herself go.

Now that she looks presentable she should be able to think of something to wear to the visitation. There was a time, and not that long ago, when black was the only decision possible, but now, with the exception of big-name funerals, no one expects women to turn up in head-to-toe black. It's like those super-relaxed, new churches, sanctuaries tarted up to look like concert halls, or stadiums with big-screen televisions. Or those grubby weddings in Vegas. But maybe reaching into your closet for something you feel comfortable wearing, the kind of thing you might put on for some normal evening, is just a sign of acceptance. Death taken as a part of life. Or maybe, in throwing off the darkest rituals, in losing those antiquated, collective gestures of humility, people mean to say that death doesn't deserve a damned thing, and especially not a costume. But, remembering her parents, and living through this day, she knows otherwise. Death should not be accepted, and it deserves everything.

Sandra would have told her what to wear. Wear your white pants, she might have said. The ones you bought for the cancelled trip to New York, right after the attack on the towers. Or, wear that slate-grey two-piece, with smoky stockings and your suede shoes. Grey is good on you now, she would have said, with that hair.

The car is finally getting warm, and as she watches people go in and out of the salon and the pasta place next door and the dentist's office on the other side, she can see that a lot of lives are being improved on a Thursday morning. The unexpected sun has turned the parking lot snow to slush, and if it stays with them through tomorrow, and if the snow holds off, everything will be that much easier. The last of the ice will be gone and they won't need their boots or their gloves or their scarves held tight against their faces. And they won't have to rush from their cars.

She wants Liam to get home.

She is sick. Her churning gut, with not even a slice of toast at breakfast, is squealing. She wants to be young, a sober, innocent girl, because then she would not have known Sandra, and wherever in the world she might be, Sandra would not be dead. She waits, offended, for the corruption to work its way through her body.

And now she isn't alone because a guy who must have wanted her parking spot and had to wait for another one knuckle-raps her window as he walks past the car. He carries on, and not even bothering to look back, he flips her the bird.

She lowers her window and yells, "*Mange.*"

But he still doesn't turn around, he just shakes his pissed-off head at one more old woman taking up space. And he's right, she is taking up space. But *mange* what?

"Fine," she says.

It doesn't matter. It can't matter because she should get home to Gus. He might be worried again or he might be hungry after his long morning of hard shovelling. Or maybe he'll have something already underway, grilled cheese or one of his famous open-faced concoctions.

"He's an accomplished man," she says. "Our Gus." And then, astonished, "Oh." And again, "Oh."

Because what has come out of her is not her own voice but Sandra's. Sandra's exact words, spoken casually but with that unmistakable certainty. And there's more. Although the guy is long gone, the forgotten curse has come back to her, like a gift. It's *merde. Mange merde.* She kills the heat and puts the car in reverse. Okay. So now she knows and will know. And will be free to cry, for the rest of her life. Because now she has every reason to believe she'll be heard.

The Celery-Green Suit

Colleen finds Richard where she left him, in the kitchen. But at least he's dressed. She takes a Kleenex from the box at his elbow and suggests a bowl of vegetable soup.

"The phone won't stop ringing," he says. And to prove him right it rings three times in the few minutes it takes her to heat the soup. The last call is from the young neighbour couple who put Sandra's garden to bed, who must have come home for their lunch, and heard.

"Everyone we know is very sorry," he says. "Some of them are wondering if they should come over here."

"But no one is coming?" She sits down in her chair and looks to him for reassurance. She is not going to make a big pot of coffee and sit around with sympathetic, speechless visitors. "People have trouble coming up with something to say," she says. "Understandably."

Richard has not used his time for sleep. In the middle of the night two weeks ago, when he wasn't actually watching over Sandra but with her nonetheless, she'd come down with him for cornflakes and an hour of old-fashioned double solitaire with the beat-up camping decks. But neither of them could even try to win. Sandra knew Richard couldn't save her and now it's his turn to accept it, to believe that he did absolutely everything in his power. But it's not going to happen today.

She drops her soup bowl into the sink and throws the tap on. And then she goes up to change, because she's still wearing yesterday's clothes. She wonders about a dress but decides on her long wool skirt with the teal turtleneck. She pulls her hair back and clips it.

When Jude gets home from the hairdresser she finds Gus sitting at the table, searching for something on his laptop. He tells her that he has been worried sick. The streets, he says, the black ice. She's had it wrong, of course. In not leaving her side these past weeks, he has been keeping her at his own.

"The streets aren't bad," she says.

He pours her a coffee because he wants her to stay downstairs with him. "Don't go up," he says. "Eat something."

So she sits down to a warmed-up plate of his meatballs and a bit of salad.

Because Gus has never allowed himself much carelessness or excess or stupidity, he is waiting for her to ride out the drinking, and he'll want it to be quick. Quicker now. He will be counting on his own patience to get them through it, but he has made no secret of his wish that she should drink downstairs in her red chair, one of the two chairs that swivel to overlook the backyard, which is where they sat when he first moved in, when they would have a drink together, planning or recalling. Beginning to recall.

Pulling into Gus's driveway, Colleen wants to stay in the car because Jude should be ready and watching for her. The driveway has been cleared of snow and Gus has probably taken his shovel over to Sandra's too. The sidewalk is clean enough for summer hopscotch and now Gus is at the open front door, standing in the cold with his arms wide, so she gets out and goes to the hug like a home-again child. Except for his daughter Kate, Gus has no capacity for the everyday embrace. Gus keeps his embraces in check, saving them for unusual times.

Jude is sitting halfway up the stairs, holding a coffee, but Colleen isn't going to take her boots off because Jan is waiting for them and she said they'd be there.

"The hair looks good," she says. And then, "Can we get going?"

"What should I wear?" Jude asks.

"It matters not," Colleen says. "Wear what you've got on. Jeans will be fine."

She can see that Jude has probably been into it. Her mascara is sloppy, the lines at her eyes and mouth look carved and, sitting halfway up the stairs with an innocent mug of coffee, she is giving off that attitude, that take me on, you two, go right ahead. So she isn't going to call up her own strength? She's going to sink? She didn't sink even when her parents were killed in the States, and she hadn't even told them the real story until recently. She'd held on to that story for twenty-five years.

"What do you think Jan wants from us?" Jude is standing up now.

"Don't know," she says.

"Can I shower?" Jude asks.

"No," she says.

Gus stands between them studying the palms of his hands as if they map the floor of the Pacific. But Jude is looking to him for an answer, wanting to be soothed, wanting him to take up his duty to her. Then she turns and climbs the stairs, asking them to give her two minutes.

"I could have brought you some vegetable soup," Colleen tells Gus.

"Another time," he says. And then, "It looks like this could last a while." He means both Jude's vague indecision and the upstairs bottle. He isn't asking for anyone's help, he is just describing the future.

How strange, she wants to say, that someone's else's grief can want to overtake your own. But Jude's sinking will meet its end because you always come up against something, if not a thud against bottom then blinding exhaustion. People know this and they still let go.

She asks Gus when Liam is coming. One more time she has said Liam instead of Liam and Julie. Then she wonders how seeing Liam, or any friend who is this day unharmed, could do anything for Sandra's kids.

"Friday morning," Gus says. "But straight from Minneapolis. He was already there when I got him, in two days of meetings. Julie is coming tonight, Pearson and then the Robert Q. I should go in to pick her up but I don't see how I can do it." He looks at the stairs, at the mug of coffee halfway up. "I hope to God they're on top of that highway. It wasn't good through the night." Without saying it, Gus is cursing the hulking, thundering trucks, the semis that carry the goods that belong back on the damned countrywide railway tracks.

"No," Colleen says. "It wasn't good. And you're wise not to go." She has spun out, of course, driving in bad weather, and not just this morning. But who hasn't? They have all done it, driven through conditions that should have kept them home.

Jude comes down the stairs in navy slacks and her long navy sweater. And she has made herself up. Gus goes to the other closet to get her scarf and gloves and a beat-up wool hat. "Only the gloves," she tells him, buttoning up and lifting her collar to shield her neck.

With the door held open to the cold air, Gus leans down to kiss their cheeks. "Whatever they think they want over there," he says. Meaning, give them.

"We shouldn't be long," Jude tells him, taking a second kiss.

They walk to the car on Gus's shovelled sidewalk. "We're safe on this," Colleen says. And when they're in the car, she asks, "Have you talked to Liam?"

"No," Jude says. "Just to Julie."

The residential streets have been narrowed by a month and a half of snow, and the ploughed banks are waist-high and stained with urban soot. The distant kids have arrived from Vancouver and Boston but there's room for them in the driveway because Cliff's car has been parked out on the narrow, no-parking street, probably by Gus, Jude guesses, when he was shovelling. He would do that, go inside to get all the keys, tucking them into his many pockets.

Cliff and Kelly are sitting in the living room on their own, as if their marriages might have dissolved, but Kelly gives them a smile. The only child in the room is Annie, who is calmly nursing. If Paul and Kelly's older and likely overtired, complaining boys are in the house, they will be downstairs with their cousins, sitting on the old sofas, watching videos.

Jack is in his den but Jan and some of the others are in the kitchen drinking bottled water. Sandra's kids look exactly as Colleen expected, grown up and dumbfounded. Because she'd left the house before Michael and April got home, she goes over to hold them for a few seconds and to say how good it is to see them, to have them where they belong. And then Jude does it too. The fuller, clumsier embraces, the ones given before dawn, are impossible now because everyone has retreated. After she holds her niece and nephew, Colleen sits down at the table. Whatever this involves it looks like Jan is going to be the spokeswoman. Or maybe it's her idea and hers alone.

"Reg called to ask us to bring some clothes over," Jan says. Her eyes are red and their sockets puffy and she hasn't bothered to disguise or improve herself. She has a photograph in her hand. It's a close-up, maybe five years old. Sandra has just begun to take on a tan. She is wearing that paisley sundress.

So it's only this. None of them wants to choose what their mother will wear in her casket.

Jude understands immediately. "Is there a favourite thing?" she asks. "Some memory?" But there are no suggestions.

"I'm not sure he'll need the photograph," Colleen says.

"He asked for it," Jan says.

Colleen puts the photograph in her pocket and stands up and Jude follows her down the hall and up the stairs. The bedroom looks the way Sandra meant it to look when she imagined it, the year they painted it. The partners' desk has been cleared of everything but the journals and the poinsettia, her beautiful trunk is at the foot of the bed and the chest of drawers is back where it's supposed to be. The high hospital bed and the bedside table have been taken away and the window has been opened a few inches, for the fresh air. Neither of them has ever been anywhere near Sandra's closet, and she hadn't told them that she'd taken over Jack's.

They open the mirrored doors and switch on the fluorescent lights, and then they back up to sit on the bed.

"What the hell are we looking at?" Jude asks. "She kept everything she ever bought? From the dawn of time?"

Years of clothes are packed tight in both closets but it isn't disorder they're looking at. There are skirts here, jackets there. Silk tanks and carefully folded sweaters on the built-in shelves. Shoes and evening bags. Pants. Dresses in their own corner. All of her colours, her shades.

"The only order in this entire house," Colleen says. "Or it was," she adds, remembering Kelly's work downstairs. She stands up and walks straight to a celery-green linen suit. "This?" she asks Jude, turning it on the hanger. "Didn't she get this for Liam's wedding?"

Jude nods yes to the suit and, still sitting on the bed, leans forward to look deeper into the closets. "How about we tell Jan we'll come over next week to deal with this."

Colleen lays the suit across Jude's lap. Although the thing they've come to do has been done, she walks into the other closet and resurfaces with an overstuffed but surprisingly light garment bag. When she unzips it on the bed the first thing out is a pale lavender strapless gown with an organza overskirt. Both the boned bodice and the organza are embroidered with small wildflowers and there's a narrow, yellowed, white velvet cummerbund. She half closes one of the closet doors and holds the gown up to her reflection in the mirror. Because she is taller than Sandra the gown stops at mid-calf, but she's sure she remembers the dress, or maybe only that she wore one like it, once. The pumps would have been peau de soie and dyed to match, the jewellery a lone pearl on a gold chain, with small, matching pearl earrings. A pair of long white gloves is pinned to the cummerbund, gloves with slits at the wrist and five or six tiny buttons, because they would be tight to pull on. They are over-the-elbow gloves because the gown is strapless. Immodest. It was a strict rule. You paid the price for exposing your shoulders by hiding some of your other flesh, your arms and your hands. They'd all had very short wrist gloves too, Jackie Kennedy gloves, to be worn in the light of day, when their shoulders were covered.

"Evening length?" she asks Jude. "Or cocktail length? What did we call this?"

"I never called it anything," Jude says. "Do you remember seeing me or anyone remotely like me at your dances?" It isn't often that Colleen has to be reminded that she lived her early life a little differently. "Although I suppose I did have skirts that long. They were more what you would call earth-mother length, or, there's-no-sewing-machine length. And the gloves were a bit heavier, with stiff leather cuffs. And thicker, to save your hands when you hauled wood or tried to thaw the godforsaken pump."

"But you were after pretty much the same thing," Colleen says. "In your work gloves and your earth-mother skirts." She turns from the mirror and puts a half-smile in her voice. "What were the skirts made of? Hemp?"

"Yeah," Jude says, with no smile of any kind. "It was all hemp all the time. Hemp or burlap. Just as you would imagine."

She waits but Colleen isn't paying attention. She's going back into the garment bag.

"I wouldn't have been there anyway," Jude says. "At your Cinderella balls. Making believe. Not if you paid me."

"No," Colleen says.

"Most people weren't," Jude says.

The second gown out is a dark-as-night taffeta, the skirt narrow and tight but with a helpful dancing slit in the back, up to the knees. Colleen thinks she might remember Sandra practising her walk, swishing around the bedroom as she asked for advice about the shoes, shoes that would have been black, maybe patent-leather slings but certainly spikes. And although this gown has rhinestone spaghetti straps, it too would have required long gloves, black like the shoes, because spaghetti straps didn't count. The neck would have been left bare of jewellery but the earrings would have been long and extravagant. And Sandra would have been scrupulously made up and very close to happy, released for a night from her near-unmanageable kids. And she would have stood in the middle of a dance floor swaying in place as she waited for Jack, who would have stopped their dancing to talk to a colleague about something that didn't matter to anyone, not even to him. She reaches in for the next gown.

"Leave it," Jude says.

"So the suit or the taffeta gown?" Colleen asks.

Jude puts the suit on the bed and goes over to the chest where Paul set up his music, and when she opens the top drawer she sees that it's subdivided for categories of jewellery and lined with felt for its protection. What she's looking for isn't Sandra's old pearl choker, and not the much better, single strand that Annie should get, but the long rope of rough-cut, multicoloured stone beads that she wore for years, everywhere, with anything. And never telling them why or where she got it.

She pockets the rope of beads and walks over to the big closet mirrors to hold the pearl choker up to her neck. "Wow," she says. "But probably better on you."

Colleen takes the choker but then drops it on the bed. "What else will he need?" she asks. She is stuffing the gowns back into the garment bag. "A slip?"

"We're going," Jude says. She grabs the suit and walks over to Sandra's big window overlooking the street to wait for the sound of the garment-bag zipper. The journals are still roughly stacked on the desk. So no one has looked?

They let themselves out the front door, and after Jude buckles in with the suit laid neatly across her lap, she drops the multicoloured, chunky rope of beads over her head.

Noticing, Colleen says, "Maybe, but then maybe not."

It's snowing again, with an edge of threatening wind, but they will be at the funeral home in minutes because the streets are quiet. In this part of the city the traffic is heavy only for an hour before and an hour after the normal workday, and all the ploughing is done in the empty middle of the night. As they drive, the houses continue to be similar to Sandra's, two storeys high and some with third floors under high-pitched roofs, their design belonging not to the same builder but to the same era, which is a different thing. The masonry on each house is so plainly the result of one artisan's time and deliberation, and all of the windows, and their placement, have been tailored to the house.

They've both been to the funeral home many times. With only a few exceptions, for Jewish acquaintances, for people new to the city, it's the home most people they know use. The senior funeral director, the father, buried Colleen's own father and he'd been professional and kind. His middle-aged son shares his name, Reg the younger, Gus calls him, and while no one ever saw much of the senior wife they do know the younger wife, Betsy. Betsy is one of those ever-present, supportive, tenacious wives, and she always tries to make an upbeat appearance. You could go to school on Betsy's supportive tenacity, but Reg the younger likely chose her with some deliberation, given the circumstances of his dismal day-to-day. It doesn't matter who they have under their roof, a child, a once capable but now ancient, skeletal pensioner, a mid-life golfer with a secretly failing heart, Betsy refuses to wear anything downbeat. And standing in front of you in one of her bright and expensive abstract numbers, she is ever eager to explain this, to chant some blather about the here and now. Like others of her kind, Betsy is a woman impervious to slight. A woman you don't waste time thinking about but automatically brace yourself against.

The funeral home has been renovated. Reg the younger has installed a classy black canopy over the entrance for protection from inclement weather and inside the heavy glass doors, in the small anteroom, there is a small elevator up to the living quarters. Deeper inside the main floor, several of the walls have been taken away to facilitate the steady flow of mourners, and to bring in more natural light from the broad front windows. It's almost revolutionary, Gus said, the amount of light Reg allows into those rooms. But he also said that Reg made a big mistake not putting in a ramp, for all the aging boomers.

Colleen rings the bell and they soon hear the buzz of the lock release. Jude pulls the door open but before she walks in she looks up to find the security camera, which is tucked into the corner like a small wasp nest. She nudges Colleen. "What's to steal?" she asks, frowning for Reg.

"Richard has bought shares in security technology," Colleen says, looking at the camera. "He thinks we might get rich."

"You could implant that thing," Jude says. "A camera in your forehead."

Now they are inside and Reg is there to greet them, extending his business hand and then wanting to take each of their hands in one of his own, an enclosing gesture that they have been too slow to prevent. Acknowledging the suit on Jude's arm, he says, "That's very nice."

Jude is wondering if Reg ever offers anyone a drink and then she thinks that if she reaches over to take Colleen's hand the three of them will make a circle and this possibility brings back a game from summer camp, played in the lake, something about joined partners and blasting through, outsmarting your enemy, leaving your enemy behind as you pushed out deep enough to swim free. She had not caught on to the finer points and she was too intimidated to ask the counsellor to explain the game again, but she does remember working hard to win, and that she was on the victorious team, lots of times.

Reg drops their hands to take the suit and the photograph. "You are friends to her children, too," he says. His low voice rocks with the tried-and-true rhythm of the trusted service provider, although the high praise is still heard, and appreciated. A man like Reg would be smart to take a reading not just on the family, Jude thinks, but on the friendships, too.

Betsy is not in sight, although any minute she could jump around a corner with her sympathetic grin, both astonishing and not astonishing either of them.

"Do you want to see the casket she chose?" Reg asks, nodding to something beneath them.

Colleen looks at his elevator. Of course it goes down.

"No," Jude says. "We haven't come here to see the casket."

Jude has been borderline rude but Colleen can say nothing to counter it. Although it is Reg's legitimate business to encourage people to give some thought to caskets, he'll know that such thoughts will be temporary in the extreme. On ordinary days, ordinary people don't care one way or the other about his caskets, or about the clothes and the makeup, the preparation, the lowering into the earth.

When the elevator motor starts up Colleen feels a shudder, a vibration, in the floor, like the first hint of a coastal earthquake or the end of the world. Someone in the house is moving.

"They're saying that the worst of it should stay out over the lake until Sunday. So we might get lucky." Reg has accepted with his professional reserve that Sandra's casket is not something they care about and now he's suggesting that the weather might hold off.

And Jude is staring at her, blank-faced.

Reg opens his heavy glass door to see them off and when he says, "I look forward to seeing you tomorrow," Colleen turns away but Jude takes his hand again, because she wants his handshake, because she always appreciates any firm grip. Reg the father never did give you the satisfaction of a strong handshake and, remembering this, she knows how right she was to teach Liam how to take someone's hand. Making him feel in her own practice-hand the authority he would need.

The slow glass door is closing behind them and they have started down the sidewalk when they hear, "Hello, girls."

Betsy's voice is filled with equal parts cheer and displeasure and regret. One more time, she is afraid she has missed something. But they're not waiting. They are not going back.

"That woman could cost him some business," Colleen says. "Mine, for instance."

"Run for your life," Jude says. She grabs Colleen's hand.

Whatever unusual circuitry makes Betsy tick, and there will be reasons because reasons exist, Jude will not this afternoon listen to her. She will not let that sweet voice say that she too loved Sandra, that she too has been thinking about her, so much. She holds Colleen's hand tight as they hurry across the parking lot. They are going to escape. Run away home.

"Sorry, Reg," she says.

Colleen is almost sure that Betsy has heard their nasty words and that their cruelty will be taken to heart, although probably not repeated to Reg. But she can't slow Jude down.

"And now we laugh?" she asks in the car. "Is that what we're going to do?"

The Receiving Line

After a long afternoon at the visitation, they have come back to the house for a quick supper, and Mrs. Granger, Sandra's neighbour, who is wearing a dark felt hat and a black wool coat with a fox collar, is at the door with a large box of Timbits, apologizing to Colleen. Her hat shimmers with melting snow. Colleen assumes that the coat has been a gift, or a suggestion, from a daughter who wants her mother to continue to dress well. Beyond the shallow porch and the bright porch light, the snow is being driven almost horizontal. The howl of the wind comes into the hall, into the house, a sound to make you cold. She invites the woman inside and shuts the door against the wind.

Mrs. Granger is telling everyone that she is sorry she can't come to the visitation. And she says that she had to drive all the way out to Tim Hortons this morning because she can no longer be trusted to bake, because her family has made her promise to leave the oven off. "I have to follow all the rules," she says, sighing heavily. "I have to swear to do whatever I'm told."

Richard is standing with Gus under the living room arch. "Her family might also give some thought to taking the car keys away," he mutters.

"Horrible to live so long," Gus says. "Bullied and bossed around."

Jude comes in from the dining room and when Mrs. Granger sees her she steps forward to take her forearm in a fierce grip. "You must be delighted," she says. "Knowing your friend has gone to her certain reward."

Even half expecting it, Jude needs a few seconds. Then she decides to take the advice she got yesterday from Nicholas. There is no reason to be particularly decent to this woman. If everyone could only be a little indecent, people like Mrs. Granger might learn to keep their paint-by-numbers consolation to themselves.

"No," she says. "I am not delighted."

She imagines the woman in her useless kitchen, praying for Sandra's soul, which she will now believe to be winging its way to God's estate, to his loving hands. But Sandra a fistful of soul in God's loving hands? She would only drift away, provoking the other angels with her inattention, her curiosity. Her insistence on having a look around. And on looking back, still interested. She turns to Colleen. "Are you by any chance delighted?"

Colleen puts the box of Timbits on the hall chair, pulls on her boots, and grabs her coat from the hook. "I'll walk you home," she says.

"Oh, no you won't," Mrs. Granger says. "I'll be fine, dear. I'm just a block or so down."

But with relative youth on her side, Colleen can insist. "That wind is foul," she says. "And the sidewalks are treacherous. I'll just see you safely inside." She looks back at Richard. "I won't be ten minutes. But start without me."

Stepping off the porch, she sticks out her locked, bent arm, and at the end of the sidewalk they turn to fight the wind.

"We have to eat," Gus says. "So we might as well get on with it."

Someone has brought them a big platter of chicken with thyme and several loaves of French bread, and there's a new broccoli salad and a couple of untouched jellied salads in the garage. There is also an angel food cake and two apple pies and a tray of butter tarts, the best in the city, from Sullivan's Old North Market.

This bounty is no mystery, at least not to anyone over fifty. It is more an echo. Of deep obligation in the time of heartache, a rural custom brought forward. Because there was a time, and it isn't ancient history, when not even death could put a stop to work. When a family's chores still had to be done, wood cut, fires built, eggs collected, animals fed or slaughtered, jars of peaches brought up from the cellar, water pumped and heated on a stove, in anticipation. When a day was filled morning to night and sometimes through the night with work that could not be neglected, and all offers of help had to be welcomed.

Liam describes a Christmas party last year where he remembered all the food from the last party, the generic shrimp rings and stuffed mushrooms, the cheese balls and factory cakes and squares, and everyone over fifty is sorry to hear about it. But then Gus promises him that honest bounty could return, if and when the young get sick enough of their passable factory food.

April, who has no interest either in the overabundance of food or in folding herself into a dated ritual, because she is all future now, all environmental action and responsibility, runs up to her mother's bedroom to bring down the poinsettia, for a centrepiece. Kelly and Jing arrange the salads on the buffet and Jan stacks the plates on the dining room table.

Then a raw-faced Colleen comes in with nothing to say except that the cold air has made her good and hungry, and Richard, tapping his watch, says that they should get a move on. So the bounty is quickly gone and they return to the funeral home for their second two hours.

Like almost everything else, visitations at Reg's have become routinely informal, with small, broken groups of family and friends milling through the rooms. But Jack didn't want that. He wanted a receiving line. He has seen too much discomfort, he told them, too many big talkers taking over, too many awkward people on their own, and too many bored little kids skipping around while their parents, enjoying themselves, let the lack of courtesy go. He said that sensible people wouldn't want to stay long anyway and that if anyone thought they had more to say they could join them at Jude and Gus's tomorrow, after the funeral. Where they could be handled more easily. He told everyone to arrange themselves according to their descending ages. "We're not Irish," he said. "We'll line up and they'll line up. Reg can seat the elderly and I'll speak to them when I get the chance."

Richard has asked April to stay tight to her father at the casket, and to move people along if they threaten to turn it into a picnic. "Just take the arm firmly," he told her. "And walk the yakkers past." April has always been one of Richard's fans, so she'd been open to his advice. Sandra's kids have all known, in varying degrees, about their uncle Richard's offences. But for today forgiveness reigns. And April is ready to save her father if she can.

There are only the two floral arrangements on the casket, Jack's and the kids'. The others, from Colleen and Richard and from Jude and Gus and Liam and Julie and Kate, from Jack's old firm and from the only living uncle, flank it. Donations have been pouring in, both for specific cancers and for cancer generally, and Reg's wife Betsy is somewhere out of sight keeping a close and appreciated account, so Jan can write the thank-you notes. This afternoon, before the first two hours of visitation began, Colleen had found Betsy to give her a quick nondescript hug.

The people who have come out into the cold night to pay their respects are lined up now, and because Reg always sets his thermostat to keep the immediate mourners comfortable, his assistant, who is largely ignored, hovers at the door to encourage the removal of coats.

Because Jack has no intention of chatting about how much Sandra looks like herself, he turns away from the casket to greet people and then to introduce them to April, who often doesn't know or remember them. But as she helps the self-centred and the devoutly, loudly cheerful and the wretchedly sad, the people who have had no choice but to bring their own grief with them, past her father, April is gently effective. Jack did see Richard lean down to advise her and now, hearing her, he can see her willingness to save him.

Richard and Colleen stand near the start of the line beside Paul and Kelly, who have left their boys at home but are taking turns holding Annie as she either dozes or squirms in their arms. When the stooped, wispy-haired man who was once Jack's mentor reaches to touch Annie's foot, as if for luck, she gives him the other foot too, hoping for play.

Jude stands beside Colleen and because she's a little unsteady on her feet she has stepped out of her suede shoes and kicked them behind her. Her breath has been sweetened with mint on the way over, to kill what Gus called the perfectly obvious. "But who will notice other than you and me?" she asked him. "And what do we matter?"

Gus is the first to offer his hand to people, he's the one who has to ask for the name and the connection, to pass along. But most people are smart enough to assume the normal shock and exhaustion and are willing to tell Gus who they are, and to explain their connection. Only a few walk past with their hands withheld and nothing to say, and only one, a complete stranger as far as he knows, says, "You don't know me from Adam." And only one says, "Who do you think I am?" As if Gus, like Annie, might want to play. Which he does not.

With nothing to oversee now, Richard has weakened to the point of offering only one or two deadened words to whoever is shaking his hand. And standing beside him, Colleen is waiting for the perfect condolence. For someone to say, you loved her, and then not one more word. She doesn't care that other people have been fond of Sandra, or that there are so many flattering things to say. Or that Sandra looks so good, considering.

More neighbours come through, and some of the people Sandra worked with years ago, raising money for the shelter and the hospital clinic and the library. They are followed by a bunched-up group of Paul's old friends, who must have assembled at someone's house to drive over together. These are the kids no one sees now, kids who have married and moved either away or out to the newest suburbs. Young men who once sensibly slept it off up in one of Sandra's beds or helped themselves to a beer from Jack's garage fridge or to late-morning cereal from the kitchen cupboard. Young women who sat with Sandra late in the night on the stairs to tell her private, confusing things while she listened in her housecoat, understanding, certainly trying, but often wishing that they could just accept that tomorrow was a new day and go upstairs to fall into teary-eyed sleep. As they would one day have to learn to do, she'd told Colleen and Jude.

"She was so great," one of these young woman is saying. She calls both Colleen and Jude by name, as if they too, sitting with their weekend morning coffee in Sandra's kitchen, watching the drama unfold, had exercised some fleeting influence. Perhaps with a tossed-off, knee-jerk, older-woman opinion or just a pleasant, placid nod of the head. Or maybe even with real interest or a compliment or a mild disagreement, a test. All of which, Jude thinks, any young woman should want.

Next in line is the couple who put Sandra's garden to bed.

"A mighty strange pair," Jude says, watching them approach. "Very close to offensive."

"No, they aren't," Colleen says.

The young man introduces himself and his wife to Gus, who has heard about them and approved of what they did, because it was work. But when she's shaking Jude's hand, the young woman, Sarah, breaks down, so Colleen starts to explain that they are to take some of Sandra's perennials, whatever they want, in the fall.

"Split off whatever you like," she says. "Help yourselves."

Then seeing that this hasn't helped, she passes Sarah over Richard to Paul, who will just have to do what he can with her.

But the young husband has stayed behind. "We'll be careful," he says to Jude. "And not too greedy." And, smiling, "You are very kind."

"Oh, it's not me," Jude says. "It would never be me. I don't care about your garden."

And then he too moves past Richard to Paul, to catch up with his wife.

"That was a bit rough," Colleen says, taking the next hand.

"Why should she get to cry so damned hard?" Jude asks. "Because she brings a spade to a stranger's garden?"

"Stop it," Colleen says. "There's no point."

More of the kids' friends come through, Jan's this time. Father Tony arrives, in tears, and then a few former neighbours, the people who have downsized. And some friends from the lake.

It is almost nine thirty when it's done and there is still a night to face. The snow that started during their supper break has turned to a driving sleet. "The lake," Richard tells them, "you are a fool to forget it." Wanting to please Jack and wanting to do something useful, the younger men collect the keys and get all the cars, scraping the windshields clean and pulling up close, like car jockeys, under Reg's black canopy.

Jack mentions a nightcap, which no one wants, so he climbs in with Michael and Jing and April and Jason to go home, and the others wave them off.

When Gus reaches to hug Colleen good-night, she tells him that she and Jude need to ride together, which is news to Jude. And although he is prepared to argue sleet and ice and a long day, Colleen's stance suggests to him that it might be a wasted argument. He looks to Richard, who just lifts his what-do-I-know eyebrows.

Sitting in the cold car with the last of her buzz worn off, Jude waits. Whatever is on Colleen's mind, she doesn't have that many blocks to get it said.

"You were cruel tonight," Colleen says. She pulls onto the slippery, empty street. "Unnecessarily." The wipers are already sluggish against the weight of new ice.

"What?" Jude asks.

"To the young garden couple and earlier, at the house, to Mrs. Granger," Colleen says. "And yesterday, to Betsy."

"I don't think *cruel* is the right word," Jude says.

"I can't stand it," Colleen says. "I won't."

Jude leans forward to see what she can see through the steamed-up windshield. To help.

"You can't keep this up," Colleen says.

"Wait and see," Jude says.

"No, I won't," Colleen says. "And the drinking on your own . . . You should be careful because it will change you, because it does, and asking us to watch is just selfish. It's heartless. Don't you remember Sandra and Richard's father?"

Jude holds her hand over the vent on the dash to check that warm air is being sent up to the windshield. "And you," she says. She has always told herself that she would never do this. "You would never be selfish or heartless."

Colleen has sometimes wondered when Spain would come up. And what Sandra might say to defend her. "Get it said," she says.

"Making us wait in that hotel, for instance," Jude says. "While you waltzed off with that smarmy creep. And then turning up with your lies, and so well rehearsed. So pleased with your good luck. So damned satisfied."

"I didn't care," Colleen says. "I realize now I should have."

"A day late, my friend," Jude says. "And a dollar short."

"Sandra told me she could understand," Colleen says.

"No sale," Jude says. "When did she tell you that?"

"At the time," Colleen says.

"Sure she did," Jude says. "You know it's the reason Jack and Gus can't entirely trust you?"

"Then they can stop trusting Richard too," Colleen says. "And we'll all be square. God," she says. "Sanctimony squared."

"That's your answer?" Jude asks. They are on Gus's icy driveway and the car is still cold.

"I had never been with anyone but Richard," Colleen says. "That's why I was so damned terrified when he was messing around with my life."

"And you decided that having another man would make you less terrified?" Jude asks.

"I had a right to wonder," Colleen says.

Jude is shaking, not with the hurt and rage she felt in Spain, but with tonight's. "You were thinking about nothing but yourself," she says.

There is no mistaking the profanity in the word *yourself.* "But I'm thinking about you now," Colleen says.

"Now?" Jude says. "Keep your *now.*"

"Do you think she liked your drinking?" Colleen asks. "Try to tell me you believe that."

Jude opens the car door.

"You can guess again," Colleen says.

Richard has come out of the house because he wants to get home to his bed. Gus is standing under the porch light and he has thrown on his overcoat but the sleet, coming at him aslant, is soaking his face and his thin hair, his scalp.

"Oh," Jude says, watching the sleet cut through the light.

She gets out of the car, but when Richard comes to take her hand to get her safely up the icy porch steps, neither one of them looks safe. It's the first and only time Colleen has seen Jude helped, the first time she has seen her want it.

"Stop the drinking," she calls through the open car door.

After Jude is inside and their coats and boots are off, Gus pulls his shirt free to dry his face. And then he says, "Only bed." Their last words for the night. Although Gus did tell Jude about Richard's nonsense, she has never told him about Spain, not the full story. If he knows anything, he knows it from Jack.

Richard gets into the car quickly because he hates the winter now, even the best of it. And from the way he closes the door, from the way he is pulling himself together, Colleen knows that Gus must have broken down again, when they were inside waiting, taking Richard with him.

"Man, it's bad," he says. "I'll drive?"

"Then why did you get in on that side?" she asks. She starts to back out of the driveway. "Things are pretty quiet. No one will be out in this."

"Whatever you say," he says.

After he sees that she is likely going to be all right with the slick streets, Richard wants to talk about the people who came to pay their respects to his sister.

"You can never actually grasp it," he says. "The impact you have. And on so many people. People who don't even know each other and never will. From different times. From different circumstances."

"We could imagine it," she says.

"What could we imagine?" he asks.

"Our own visitations," she says. "We could make ourselves a master list. Age everyone a little. Leave a few people out."

"We could do that," he says. He has taken off his gloves and when he throws them against the windshield they drop to the floor. "Or we could just get ourselves home."

"All right," she says. "That's what we'll do." More last words for the night.

Concentrating on keeping all four of the tires in heavy, muscular contact with the ice, Colleen knows that there's a stop sign coming up. Given such an ugly, empty night, she might have ignored the stop, but she has to make her turn north, and, as she was reminded in Bayfield, turns on ice are better made slow. She thinks about tomorrow, about the funeral, and then she wonders how much sleep they'll get tonight at Sandra and Jack's. In that crowded, empty house. In that grieving house. . . .

And certainly sleep is what's wanted in Jack's crowded, empty, grieving house. All the kids have gone up to bed, exhausted from travelling and from the time change and from talking with people they don't know any more. Jack has put April and Jason in the green bedroom because he doesn't want to sleep there anyway. He wants to sleep in his den.

But before sleep or anything close to it can happen he has to soak his swollen feet. Other nights, coming home after some similar event, Sandra often brought him her roaster filled with warm salty water. Sympathetic Sandra with her narrow, never-swollen, blue-blood feet. He finds the bag of salt and the roaster and gets himself set up in his den, sitting on the couch.

The service will be at the funeral home instead of a church, and it's going to be a rough combination of the instructions she left and at least some of what the kids have said they want. She named the United Church minister and a poem, which she read to him a month ago, and Paul gets to pick the music. The kids didn't know what they thought about a eulogy but April was sure that things should not be left open, because she doesn't want any spur-of-the-moment speeches to take the service off in some bizarre, personal direction, which she claimed to have seen. Michael and Jing have put together a small display of pictures, Sandra's life over time, all the eras and the shifts, from a good, competitive swimmer to a cheerfully exhausted young mother, from teaching April to drive to walking a grandson to sleep. Kelly thought Paul should be the one to read the poem, and Jan thought everything should be kept short. He'd overheard them in the kitchen talking it through, and then they came to him with their decisions. And he'd said fine. All of which is going to make the service exactly like the rest of their lives with these kids. You take your stand and then you back down as you need to, in consideration, because you love them. You love your kids. And at the end of the day there is not one thing that can match your perfect, solitary dreams.

But none of this matters because, like him, they are only getting through it, finding a pathway. And whatever happens, the funeral will take the day.

He wonders how long he'll be able to sit in this den alone. He is only sixty-seven and they keep saying that his heart is good again, so it could be twenty years, easy. Easy. The kids will keep coming, they will certainly make every effort, but without their mother they will be changed. And he will be a different father. Because of his situation. Because of his life going on.

He aches. His skin and his muscles and his bones are done. If anyone touched him now, he would disintegrate. That's what people mean when they say fall apart. They mean fall apart.

He is going to try to remember what he has been told to remember. That it could have been so much worse. That she was not, was never, scorched with pain. That she was saved from anguish, protected by medical science and by you, Jack. And by her grown kids and by her good friends. That her mind was clear right to the end, or nearly. That she had you, Jack.

Maybe a different man would call out to wake the house, to wake the dead, the long and recent dead.

"But I am not a different man," he says.

He studies his feet, which are not so bloated now, and then he hears Michael on the stairs. Michael is coming down in his pyjamas to turn out the last of the lights and maybe to check that the doors are locked. To tell his father that it is very late and that he should try to get some sleep, that he should call it a night. Decades gone and a son's soft footfalls on the stairs can still be identified. So it was never just their mother, listening?

The water in the roaster has cooled to lukewarm but his feet are Easter pink.

She Loves You

The United Church minister waits until everyone is seated in the funeral home, and after he leads them in the Lord's Prayer, he acknowledges both the storm and just how much Sandra must have meant to them all, to cause them to come out in such miserable weather, in such numbers. He uses a few recently collected anecdotes to try to bring her particular charm, as he calls it, to life, and then he asks everyone to think not only about the celebration of a life but also about something he calls "grievous acceptance." He names the people she has left behind, Jack and April and Michael and Jan and Paul, and their families, and prays again.

When he's finished there is music and then Paul goes to the lectern to read the poem Sandra wanted, "In Blackwater Woods," written by a woman named Mary Oliver. It's about trees and cattails and ponds, and love and unknown salvation. The poem leaves everyone with the caution, after they have loved, to let life, or to let love, go. It is followed by more music. Jack can hear Annie behind him, struggling and fussing in Kelly's arms, but when Kelly stands up to take her out he turns in his chair to push her down. Paul has made some good choices, Gordon Lightfoot's "Canadian Railroad Trilogy" because Sandra had been behind their countrywide trips, and those sisters she liked, the McGarrigles, for their harmony. But he has also picked the Beatles' "She Loves You," which just seems strange.

Then after the final prayer, Reg steps forward to remind people to sign the book of condolences and to announce that there will be a gathering at Jude and Gus's home, for people who want a chance to visit with the family. He tells them that the ground is pretty slick out at the cemetery so perhaps some will want to go straight over to the house.

Reg had not run this last suggestion past anyone and Jack isn't happy with the presumption. Can people withstand nothing any more? Unless it was a private interment, he and Sandra always went to the cemetery, rain or sleet or shine. He'd been trained to this as a boy, by his father. If you had to, you just took along an umbrella and an old pair of shoes to change into, or your boots. You saw people into the ground. The old stayed put in the warm cars. It was all understood.

The doors open and the mourners stand in their clusters on the sidewalk as the pallbearers carry the casket out to the hearse. Reg had the six names in his file, a straightforward, predictable list, Michael and Paul, Cliff and Jason, and Liam and Kate.

The sky is all low grey cloud and the snow continues. The cars with their little flags have been lined up behind the hearse, and while no one has to be told to put their lights on, Reg's assistant walks back and forth like a traffic cop, double-checking. Then Reg gets into the hearse and pulls away.

They don't move as slowly as Jack remembers, although they are hesitant at the intersections because you can't count on everyone to wait at a green light. It wasn't that long ago that a car would pull over in a full stop, and once he saw a tractor idling respectfully in the middle of a field, but now people stop only for ambulances and fire trucks, and even then not always. Sometimes he's glad that his father is gone.

As they drive through the cemetery gates he can see that Reg was right, the ground is slick. At the plot, the smart people have put on their boots, and the pallbearers stand behind the open door of the hearse, waiting to take their respective handles. How much better, he thinks, if they could lift her high, as bearers did when caskets were not so heavy.

His daughters and daughters-in-law stand close to him with the grandchildren, and after the casket has been set on its cradle above the grave, and the two arrangements have been placed, his sons' and his daughters' partners leave the graveside to join them. Liam and Kate walk over to stand with Jude and Gus and Richard and Colleen, and everyone else stays back, behind him. The flowers have already begun to seize with the cold.

"The Beatles?" he asks. He wonders if April or Jan might reach for his hand, to stop what they could take to be a threat. The threat of a joking, distraught, about-to-lose-it or already lost father.

The minister reads the traditional verses, ashes and dust and life everlasting, from his King James. And then that too is done. He can hear people behind him moving away to their cars, leaving them, the primary mourners, alone. No one except Gus has any new tears, and he has covered his face with his hands, like a child who believes this will make him invisible.

People have been invited to Gus and Jude's because he is tired of his own house. On the sidewalk after the service he heard Liam's Julie volunteer to go ahead, to be at the door to welcome people, and by the time they get there both sides of the street are lined with cars. He lets the others go ahead and when he gets inside he sees that someone has shifted Jude's living room chairs around to make a kind of central throne, for him, so people can approach him. Then he notices the absence of a Christmas tree, just like at home. He walks back to the kitchen to sit on the breakfast nook bench.

And not sure what to do, he turns around to look out the window at the backyard. The sun is out again and the snow has stopped. Gus's raised vegetable garden has almost disappeared into the wind-levelled lawn, but the branches of the big maple are absolutely still, their brittle shadows like cracks in the snow. As if the winter lawn might break into pieces.

One of Jude's neighbours gives him a plate of sandwiches and pickles and then Jan brings some of her old friends into the kitchen. Behind them, he sees Mrs. Granger in the dining room. She is still in her coat, which means that she has not yet been coaxed to stay, although that will happen. He can hear April introducing her to someone, trying to hand her off. "This is a neighbour friend of my mother's."

Richard walks through the kitchen in a hurry, maybe looking for someone, and then one of Jan's friends from high school reaches to touch his head, as if he's a widowed boy. "Just give it time," she says.

He shivers and looks up at Jan. "Paul did a good job with the poem," he says.

"He did," Jan says.

Her friends leave them and he can see in Jan's lowered head that she is sorry for her friend's condescension.

"Where did 'She Loves You' come from?" he asks. He can hear Sandra's voice, yeah, yeah, yeah.

"That was April," Jan says, ducking the blame.

Jan probably can't get a read on his mood, and it will not have occurred to her that there was a time in his life, all right, a short time, when he loved everything about the Beatles.

"Mom told April when she was a kid that it would make a great funeral song," Jan says. "April remembered so she told Paul."

"I'm not sure your mother intended that every single one of her words should be remembered," he says.

Jan leaves to mix with the crowd, as she's been taught to do. He realizes that he should get up and start moving through the rooms, because if he doesn't want to be touched like that again, and he doesn't, he is going to have to take some kind of control. The kitchen door is blocked with the Boston and Vancouver grandchildren, the dressed-up teenagers he hardly knows. And then Jing comes to talk to them, to lead them off.

"Oh, Babe," he says. "You should be here for those kids."

At home, before the service, the older grandchildren had come down the stairs transformed. The boys were quieter in their suits, more self-contained and a little hunched, but the two girls were as fine and graceful as they would ever in their lifetimes be. He walked over to shake his grandsons' awkward hands and to tell them, tall as soldiers now, but there was nothing he could say to the girls, because they knew. He just smiled an overwhelmed smile, with April and Jing, their proud mothers, standing watch. And then, to spoil everything, there were coats and boots to put on.

Now Paul is coming toward him with a nice stiff scotch. "Dad," he says. "You must be thirsty."

"My sensible boy," he says.

Paul hands him the drink. "We're in the sunroom," he says. "If you want to join us."

So the kids are sitting together, taking this chance to recall and repeat some of the things their mother said, and didn't say. This rare chance.

The window is so cold on his back now it's like sitting at a fire. In a few minutes he will stand up and go to the sunroom and then maybe he'll find Richard and Gus, who might be getting tired of carrying their share of his absence.

But Gus and Richard have also removed themselves. Gus has gone to sit high on the stairs and, seeing him there, Richard grabbed two drinks and joined him. And then Kate perched herself a few steps down with a piled-high plate of sandwiches, enough for all of them. People have been crossing the hall to get from one room to another, but no one has stopped.

Gus is telling Richard about his mother in Sweden, who lived a long and interesting life, and who is dead now. He explains that she was a chemist and that she looked like Kate. Or rather that Kate looks so much like her.

"The same way you remind everyone of Sandra," he says. "With the similarity mostly in the bone structure. In those family face bones."

"I like reminding people," Richard says. "Although I've been wondering if it's my face that's feminine or hers that was hard."

"I should have gone home more often," Gus says. "I should have taken Kate with me."

"You made a mistake," Kate says.

Richard is not going to argue with Gus to try to lift his spirits, because what Gus said is both true and past repair, which means it has to stand. And the amnesty, if it ever comes, will have to come from Gus himself. There is no point in forcing it now with cheerful, kindly words. He looks down at Kate on the step below him. "I suppose I could cry for a long time," he says. "But that might change my face and I want to keep it as it is."

"You *should* keep it," Kate says.

The women who are managing the food in the kitchen have left Jack to pass around their silver trays of tarts and squares. Someone turns on the living room lamps and then a hand that knows the house reaches around the kitchen doorway to switch on the dining room chandelier. Jack can hear Colleen and Jude in the living room, floating around. He knows their distinct voices and he can follow their self-control as it moves from one group to the next.

They apparently had words last night, a very loud disagreement, according to Gus. You should be here, he thinks, to fight with your friends.

Colleen and Jude don't mind doing the lion's share of the work. Some of the mourners have already begun to mention trivial things, things that have no meaning or relevance this afternoon. But they don't turn away from it. They are all performance now, pretending interest and moving on, connecting with each guest as they would at any gathering, in appreciation for people's trouble. They can do this because they are not young, because they believe that most people who do take the trouble, no matter what comes out of their pitiful mouths, probably intend to leave some good behind them.

Someone watching Colleen and Jude might say that they are moving through the crowd in easy tandem, with the complacent, second nature of long-time friends, the one woman as unaware of the other as it is possible to be. But Sandra would say that she has never seen them more alert, or so careful with each other.

Behind Jack's back the sagging winter sun will be dropping beyond the houses. He thinks about his kids waiting for him in the sunroom, about Paul's kind invitation, and how their mother would have got him up to his feet. And then, as if it's been waiting to catch him alone, the harder thought comes.

This is the afterlife.

But Sandra has heard and right away she tells him, "No, it is not."

2006

The Party

IF THEY'D ASKED JUDE if she wanted a big sixty-fifth birthday party, she would have said no. The kibosh would have been easy. She could have said that this birthday didn't mean that much to her, or that people are usually partied out by January. She would have stopped it not because life doesn't go on but because such a compulsory invitation would leave Jack with only two bad choices: to come to a celebratory party or to decline. It's been more than a year, and although they did stay pretty close to him for a while, they haven't seen much of him in the last few months. It feels all wrong, but Richard insists that only Jack can know what he needs.

And here it is. A party.

In the living room, a hired woman in a black dress and copper earrings with a tight sixties chignon and a severe set of thin dark eyebrows sits at the piano playing a mid-life birthday selection, from Billie Holiday through to Dylan and Joni Mitchell and Neil Young and even some Peggy Lee. That posture is so disciplined, Jude thinks, and she's put together the right mix. There have to be more than sixty people in the house and many of them will remember some of the words, they will know where the music is going. Maybe none of it is timeless but it isn't easy listening either. You couldn't say that. Or, you could, but you would be wrong.

Liam and Julie were able to orchestrate the party from Ottawa and it looks like they have stopped at nothing. She knows they were behind the party because Gus suggested Italy as a birthday gift, their first big trip in a long time, maybe the last, he'd told her. Besides, while he's a good enough partner, Gus is no one's idea of a party organizer. And Colleen would have known not to do it. Liam and Gus are in the front hall now, greeting stragglers, people who had earlier commitments. If Jack has decided to stay home, fair enough.

Gus is wearing his grey slacks and a dark red shirt that he's already rolled up at the cuffs, and Liam is in jeans. Kate is wearing jeans too, with a black tank top and a washed-out, inadequate bra. She has borrowed Sandra's rope of chunky stone beads, and it's good to see them from a distance again. Julie is pregnant, she and Liam made their announcement this morning. She isn't showing and she has not yet begun to relax around the edges, but she probably won't. After lunch, explaining that she has never been to this kind of middle-aged party, Julie asked what she should wear, and when she didn't get a useful answer, or any answer, Gus told her no one would care, thinking this should help. Jude watches Julie going toward the kitchen in her snow-white cashmere sweater and short, brown suede skirt and her red spikes, at least they used to be called spikes. She'd decided on her red silk cardigan, buttoned, with the winter-white pants and her comfortable, broken-in, brown leather flats.

After she and Gus finished dressing they'd stood tight together in front of the full-length mirror in the upstairs hall and she'd asked him her party question. "Would Kim Novak wear this?"

She was fifteen in tartan shorts when a friend's weird father whistled at her and told her that she was a ringer for Kim Novak, the actress who always looked half asleep and vampy, who was not her idol. "No," Gus promised her. "Ms. Novak would never wear that."

With her party confidence, such as it was, established, they'd started down the stairs. And then Julie came out of Liam's old bedroom and stopped dead in her tracks to shake her pretty head. "That's really funny," she said. "We could be twins, in a perverse kind of way." And met with two blank faces, she explained the obvious. "Because our colours are the same."

And, "Yes," Gus said. "That is funny."

Now the caterers are floating around the rooms, carrying silver trays of good wine or carefully placed canapés, standard-issue mushroom and onion tarts and recently shipped smoked salmon and trout, because the men will eat those, but there are more exotic, more recently concocted things too. The concocted canapés are taken mostly by the women, who can appreciate what they are looking at, who can estimate the time it took to assemble and chop and cut and shape and then reassemble every little portion. There are just a few canapés to a tray, which is the thing again, because someone somewhere has decided that the flat-out display of excess would be tasteless. This, their own little world, this precisely controlled release of choice, out-of-season, exorbitantly priced food served in humble, purchased silence and eaten fast as you stand on swollen feet is called . . . what? Style? So style is just middle-aged money? Aggressively accumulated, bored money looking for something to do with itself?

Of course you wouldn't want to tell that to someone like Julie, who had argued successfully for the high-end caterers, talking Gus into it. You wouldn't want to say it to Julie because hearing it she could turn on you, and in turning take Liam with her.

January or not, it must be a perfect night for a party because all the rooms are overflowing. Rooms, she thinks. She stands against the wall for a minute, smiling out, to let the word become a question. It's something she has asked herself before. How did she get to the rooms in this fine house, for instance, and to Sandra's bedroom, from that old farmhouse with Tommy? How, in fact, had she got anywhere? There have been no bridges between the places she's lived, no connections, no way for a woman to believe that one place might follow another. How did her relatively safe girlhood bedroom lead her to a crowded, overrun farmhouse kitchen? And how did her brother's cramped basement lead her through a worse basement and then through a city high-rise to this century-old and beautiful and paid-for house? A house in her name and, someday, in Liam's? It was money of course. But work, too. And risk. And love of one kind or another, tempting you on.

She leaves the wall to join her guests and maybe laugh at some set-piece story, but then she hears a boisterous, twangy voice at the front door, and it can only be Tommy's. Tommy the ex-husband showing his face at her birthday party, probably at Gus's generous, last-minute invitation. Because it was Gus who talked to him when he called, surprising them, to say that he was in the city. He has flown up from Houston, on leave from his third besotted wife, to tend, for maybe the last time, he told Gus, to Travis, his draft-dodging but accomplished, emphysemic brother.

She makes her way to the front hall.

Tommy doesn't seem to be aging, not at an acceptable rate. He is still long-limbed and gangly and there is no sign of a paunch, no jowls, or glasses with progressive lenses. The only difference since the last visit is a new and exquisite, high-gloss pewter, or maybe steel, cane. Immediately after his coat is off, after he has given Liam his fatherly hug and taken Gus's outstretched hand, before anything else can get said, he starts to express his condolences for the loss of Sandra. And although she's been gone for over a year, the condolences are still welcome, even from Tommy. He didn't know Sandra well, this evidenced by the fact that he'd enjoyed calling her a *feminista,* but Tommy always said he liked her, that was true. And after she sent him the clipped-out copy of Sandra's obituary, he did send a heavily embossed sympathy card.

"Happy birthday, sweetheart," he says, with the condolences taken care of, with his dandy, Southern smile. "To a woman I briefly loved."

Was that *briefly* supposed to be a concession to Gus? Had her front hall become some wild, vast plain, where the lesser male beast is smart enough to back away, easy now, easy, from the dominant? Since she made her vow, years before, to try to shield Liam from any hurt he was too young to bear, she has allowed Tommy no more than a half-life.

He bends down to kiss her lightly on the lips and then he looks at her in a way that brings to mind the old way, but in fun, of course. So an undaunted Tommy has come to mark the sixty-fifth birthday of a woman he didn't love for long. Back when the crust of the earth was cooling.

She doesn't much care about the crust of the earth, they are all of an age, but she did not appreciate the way he sang out the word *briefly,* the implication being that the two of them, or the three of them, have long since come to some sensible understanding. As if it's a kindness to Gus or maybe just smart middle-aged strategy to declare love stone-cold dead when it has been only transformed to a courteous, disciplined, lifetime non-love. As if they are all grown up, beyond it. Beyond sorrow. She might find a way to tell Tommy that she has discovered, since Sandra's death, that she herself is not beyond much of anything.

When Colleen comes into the hall, a grateful Tommy turns to reach for the distraction. She is exactly his height, which makes it easy for him to kiss first one cheek and then the other, bobbing. "Yummy," he says.

Colleen is head to toe in pale green silk to show off Sandra's pearl choker, and *yummy* is the last word she thought she'd hear tonight. But she always looks forward to getting a look at Tommy, to see if he's changed, to hear what he might have to say for himself. And now, as she hoped, three couples are leaving the party, crowding the door with their regrets and their phony best wishes to Jude.

Colleen has come to the front-hall commotion from the basement stairs, where she'd gone to sit with a glass of Glenlivet. She wanted a few minutes alone because Jack had turned up at the house that morning with Sandra's journals, bags of them. And she'd taken them off his hands. She had promised him that she and Jude would give the journals a precautionary read and then decide if April and Jan should have them. It seemed that he hadn't given any thought at all to what she and Jude might discover about themselves. To the praise or affection or annoyance or regret. And even if the journals can be declared completely safe, which is doubtful, what counsel are they supposed to offer April and Jan? Give yourselves some time, then go ahead, and maybe let Michael and Paul have a chance too? Or, don't? Just take an afternoon and feed them into the fireplace? Because private is private? It will all depend. And who are they to say what it should depend on?

No one except the caterers should have been in Jude's kitchen, but sitting on the basement stairs, thinking about Sandra's journals, about the obligation and the risk and about telling Jude that they've got them, she overheard some women talking on the other side of the basement door, voices she didn't recognize, guests she couldn't place. They were talking about the pianist, how miserably bad she was, and then one of them, who was maybe the wife of one of Gus's old construction friends, invited only to make the party bigger, announced that Jack was putting the house on the market, that it was a reno waiting to happen, and another woman said she was not surprised. And then the third thought that Sandra wouldn't much like what Jack was up to now, which prompted a group snort and a round of laughter. She was thinking about standing up to throw the door open when she heard one of them mutter that Sandra had been so damned pleased with that house, with herself in that barn of a house, and then she heard the first woman again, extremely pleased with her own self, spit out the word *oblivious.*

She got to her feet quietly. She could have charged through the door and knocked wine and disintegrating canapés everywhere but she didn't. She opened the door slowly and looked at each of them, and getting back nothing, which was pretty much what she'd wanted, she told them to leave the house, to get the hell out, to collect their poor, dumb boyfriends or their poor, dumb husbands and leave the party. But then one of them, apparently believing herself to be a lady you didn't mess with, stood a little taller and locked her smile. "It's Colleen, isn't it?" she said. "Nice party."

And yes, she thought, it is a nice party. For my friend.

Holding her inch of scotch with its pellets of ice, she was happier than she'd been in a year, no, in more years, and with a quick jerk of her hand she doused the woman's face, and after the gasp and the routine obscenities, it was over. And although none of the catering staff turned to look, they had certainly heard, and she could see that some of them were smiling over their work. One of them, a young man in a hairnet at the stove, gave a silent cheer. Yes, he mouthed, pulling his fist down through the air. But yes to justice or to the pleasure of a catfight, she couldn't begin to guess.

Now, with Tommy welcomed and left to Gus and Liam, she walks with Jude among the guests. When Jude sits down on the bench beside the pianist, she wanders off to find a fresh glass of Glenlivet, and to find Richard, to tell him her basement-stairs story. In the last few months, although Jude still gets most of it first, she has begun to tell Richard things, something she has seen or heard or dreamt up. Because she wants him to know her better. It's an experiment, like a family cat at the door with a bird.

Richard is in the dining room talking to a young woman with good teeth and limp hair and some small silver thing, maybe a baby bootie, wired into her exposed navel. She looks like someone's granddaughter.

"Goodbye," she tells her.

After the young woman turns away, confused or not, Richard says, "That was a new mother. She was describing for me the art of childbirth."

"Bully for her," she says. And then, "Have you talked to Jack lately? Has he said anything about selling the house?"

"Why?" he asks.

She tells him her story about the three women, about the presumption and the contempt and the fact that she encouraged them to leave and to take their dumb men with them. And about the kid at the stove with the hairnet, with his congratulatory, descending fist.

She sees her mistake only after she's told it, when he eyes her drink and slowly shakes his head. He is getting ready to ask why she is surprised by these people. And if he does, she'll leave him. She will wander off as she would at any party, in search of better company, maybe some friend of a friend with tales from a big trip, or a worthy anecdote. Some polished routine.

"Well done," he says. "My long-legged love. Maybe you've been as bad as I am all along."

"Do you think?" she asks.

"I think," he says.

"As bad as you?" she asks.

"Sure," he says. He reaches up to run a finger along Sandra's pearl choker. "In your way. With all your easy beauty."

"Easy?" she asks. So maybe there's going to be something new to talk about in their old age? "I'm going to check on the food," she says.

But she can't because the kitchen doorway is plugged with self-effacing, distracted wait staff. So she goes to the family room instead.

Someone has got a fire going in the fireplace, someone, maybe one of Liam's high school friends, who knew he'd find the wood stacked in the garage. This will please Jude, and the room is a bit cold anyway because the sunroom door to the patio has been opened by the smokers. The smokers are furtive and thinning out now, some of them the hard way. Gus likes the smell and sound of a wood fire even more than Jude does, he's the one who argued against conversion to gas, and she watches Jude, who has come in because she smelled the fire, watch her husband, waiting for the moment when he will find her with his glance and give her his look of immense satisfaction. Gus will be immensely satisfied because someone has done precisely what he wanted done, without being asked. Because Gus does insist on being understood without spelling things out.

Jude approaches the young man at the fire to thank him and then she turns to go back to the piano bench. And careful to leave the pianist all the elbow room she needs, she begins to hum along, getting no reaction whatsoever. She realizes that she will be swaying, keeping time, and that her face might be taking on the look that Gus used to call threatening, the look that says, I want to sing, why don't we all sing.

And why can't Sandra, she wants to know, be standing behind her? With her hands resting loose on her shoulders and swaying to the music to say, yes, we *should* sing? And maybe even drink one drink too many, to see what happens? Because Julie is standing where Sandra stood, and she is not swaying or resting her hands. She has probably wrapped her pale arms tight around her own small midriff, as she does when she's uneasy. She will be holding her small back in her own hands, like the kissing joke. But to be fair, how can Julie, still the half-stranger, understand that she's taken an occupied space?

In the long months after Sandra died, when Gus was encouraging Jude to name the ways she missed her, she told him that she might have to find herself another friend to drink with. This bothered him, certainly, and he was entitled to his bother, having been so careful with her, before. But she has slowed it down, almost to a stop. And Gus should have understood that Sandra's enthusiasm for drink was mock enthusiasm, that she was only a rare-occasion, sentimental, foolhardy drinker, needing only two glasses of whatever and either fatigue or a peculiar state of mind to set her off. They probably drank too much and laughed so hard doing it because it was so self-absorbed, so exclusive, so sentimental, no one dared to put a stop to it.

And what remains now of her perfect friend? Only the good times? That slippery slide down to the sentimental? "Sentimental Journey"? She wonders if the pianist might know that one. She certainly looks old enough, this close.

All along and likely used to worse, the pianist has been entirely professional, even through the humming. Maybe Jude will tell the woman how much she appreciates her choices, but what will that get her but the indulgence of a hired smile?

She should get up and mingle. She could make herself find Tommy, who can be found in any crowd because faces and attention usually follow in his wake. Then turning around to look, she does see him making his way through her party, busy shaking all the extended Canadian hands, withstanding all the short conversations. She is watching him the way she first watched him forty years ago, from a safe distance, across a crowded room. On one enchanted evening.

Oh, thank you, sweet brain, she thinks, for these bloated songs. As soon as the party is over, sooner if she can, she will tell Colleen what has dropped into her head. But from where? *Camelot*? *South Pacific*? *The King and I*? They did stay with you, those exotic locales, those studs with their deep, strong voices and their tight-as-paint pants, that choreographed longing. The thighs like parts of a big machine.

She leaves the pianist to carry on without her and as she gets closer to Tommy she can hear him accepting the sympathy of the guests who watched the towers go, people who don't know him, who know only that he's the American, the first husband, the old hippie, the soldier, Liam's father. She guesses that he has already said, several times but no less graciously, No, I didn't lose anyone, except my countrymen. And, God, yes, deranged.

And then she hears Gus.

"So you've got yourselves a new war," he is telling Tommy. Mocking, taunting, and plainly regretting his invitation, as she could have told him he might. But because this is a crowded, jubilant party for his beloved wife, Gus pushes it no further. And Tommy, looking up for it, lets it go. Everyone here will have been trying to wrap their heads around the younger Bush's obstinate war, just as they followed his father's Desert Storm, huddled in their safe Canadian houses listening to Scud talk, captivated by the light show, by those streams of stuttering, flying stars, like burning arrows in an older war. In better circumstances, she thought, sitting watching the news with Gus, in impossible circumstances, it could have been beautiful.

And now Tommy is with Liam. He's leaning against the dining room wall, talking to him not like a natural father but in evident complicity, like some older, trusted friend. They are both holding a tall glass of Gus's imported beer and leaning one into the other, protective of the space they've made and sharing as they more than ever do not only a face but a surprisingly deep laugh. And sharing too, she would guess, the undisclosed cost of an almost non-existent but never-ending, and here is proof of it again, connection. Although encouraged by many to do so, in her experience young boys did not write newsy letters to remarried veteran fathers who lived at the far edge of another country with a second family, and, eventually, they didn't waste much time sitting on the stairs watching the mail slot either. All that time they were waiting, as only boys can wait, for something else. An offhand conversation against a wall?

She believes that a daughter would not have waited so well and she sometimes wishes that her first short pregnancy had not been lost, that a first child had been born a girl. She likes to think that a girl would have exacted an interesting price from Tommy. She knew she would have, if she'd been the child.

Some of Liam's old beer-drinking friends have approached him, so Tommy excuses himself. She should stop watching. She should be more like Gus, who pretends not to notice things. What? he'll ask. What do you mean when you say that?

Gus is the best kind of priest, she thinks, looking around for him. But she is met with other faces, near the fireplace, Paul's and Kelly's, and protected between them, Kate's. Paul lifts his glass high in her direction and Kate is smiling, amused at something. Gus's ex-wife has remarried and moved to Victoria so he's just found Kate a better place, in London, with younger housemates.

She has now drunk just enough scotch to unleash her party loneliness, a low-grade discomfort that took her by surprise at twenty but shouldn't any more. She is crying. Very close to perfectly fine, but crying.

"Good turnout," Liam says.

He is leaning into her, butting her shoulder with his arm. From the time he could walk toward her of his own volition he has approached her without extended hands, like a domesticated animal, without the gift of precision. Butting himself first against her knees, then her hips, and now and forevermore her shoulders. But this, for Liam, is touch. She braces herself against his casual weight. She supposes she was looking weepy, but she has long been able to mock that look with another more-considered face, and mockery is a skill Liam can applaud. And anyway, he doesn't have to be told what's wrong with her.

Colleen is right behind him. "Lots of loot," she says. "I just spent a few minutes in the sunroom." The sunroom is where Julie wanted the birthday presents stacked, and she too had thought about going there, or somewhere, to remove her weepy self. In the sunroom she could have studied the piles of gifts and cards and wondered what Sandra might have given her.

She hasn't seen much of Colleen tonight but she didn't really expect to. Colleen will have been walking around introducing people, laughing at a story or throwing one in, working to make it a successful party. She buried her mother six weeks ago, but the death was neither horrible nor unanticipated, so neither is Colleen's grief. She seems all right, or at least herself.

She wants another drink but she's likely had enough because she is imagining the guests, who were for the most part sincerely welcomed, gone. What she really wants is a short breakdown cry in the shower and then one of her old nighties and bed. She wants to be good to Gus, then to pull the cool duvet up and to fall into a sound sleep, taking nothing with her but grief. With all of her other thoughts drowned out by Gus, who will be wide awake talking, replaying the party, his version, and laughing on her behalf whenever he can find a reason. Because this is the other thing he's been doing, looking around for something to laugh at.

Gus and Richard have come over.

"Is it time for presents?" Gus asks.

"I should start," she says. When she is sure of equilibrium she turns to go back into the living room. "Give me a hand, will you?" she asks. "All of you?"

Earlier, she was worried about the champagne toast, wondering who might get the assignment, hoping, God help us, that it wasn't Tommy, who would just charm everyone with some well-told, paltry joke.

Colleen is ready to follow Jude, to help her with the gifts, and she knows it won't be her who gives the toast. When Gus moved in with Jude, when instead of a legitimate wedding they had their intimate November party, she told Richard that she wasn't crazy about toasts because they could be so risky. She argued that the only thing toasts proved was that people didn't know each other as well as they thought they did, and that a person's true nature was, at the end of any day, a complete unknown. Toasts, she told him, too often sounded like inept, preliminary eulogies, a custom she had then, being younger, disliked. But it was Richard's position that after you were dead, people thought they could say whatever garbage came into their heads, because they were protected, because you couldn't rectify it or maybe hold to a good-sized, lifelong grudge. It was after you were dead, he told her, that free speech reigned supreme, and toasts and eulogies were meant to counter that. He said that praise spoken aloud was too damned rare and that the only good end to a life was knowing you had a few defenders.

Now she is thinking that it might be all right if someone does try to capture Jude's nature. No one but the United Church minister, who had known next to nothing, had done it for Sandra. But she has heard other natures captured, or nearly. She has listened to more than one eloquent eulogy from an honest, despondent friend who has not stood at a podium since the memorized speeches of grade school, who stood stiff and stared straight ahead, determined to say some honest thing. She has seen the tight podium grip of proud, defensive friends as they prevailed over more hateful mourners, who can just as easily fill a funeral home. But no one wants that kind of thing, that risk of sincerity, at parties. And parties shouldn't change.

Seeing Jude move toward the sofa has apparently given Julie the cue she's been waiting for. With Liam in tow, she goes into the sunroom and emerges with a handful of envelopes, many of which will be cards indicating donations to the fight against breast cancer, a gift for Sandra, so a gift for Jude. Liam follows Julie out with a big armful of presents and the people on the sofa get up to make room for Jude and Gus to sit down. She and Richard stand close and the other guests turn to watch.

Glasses of champagne are passed and Liam comes forward to give the toast. He starts by mentioning his mother's gift for digging up friends for herself, and how much she misses Sandra, every day, and then he mentions Gus, calling him of all things a blessing, and then he names Jack, and Richard and her, the people he says he can't remember not knowing. Then he waits, to collect his nerve.

"So here's to my mother," he says. "To might."

And they raise their glasses.

Colleen has no intention of crying but she understands what Liam intended to say. That Jude was a woman on her own with a kid who survived it, and that he knows himself to be the beneficiary. But she also understands that Liam doesn't know the half of it, because that's what women like Sandra and Jude hold back from their kids, to shield them. The half of it. She is proud of Liam. He has expressed sentiment without a lot of sentiment and this has obviously impressed many of the guests, although when she catches the pianist's eye it's clear the woman is bored stiff. Liam's toast did not exactly capture Jude's nature, but it was one version, and true.

Tommy, probably imagining that he has heard himself finally and publicly excused, because wasn't that toast his deliverance, wasn't it testimony that whatever he did, he had done to one tough woman, yells out, "Hear, hear." And then everyone shouts it. "Hear, hear." There seems to be not one doubt in the room.

Jude listens to them shout, and liking it, thinks, yes, here is right where we are. She realizes that she will have to say something because people are expected to respond when they are honoured, or cornered, and she wonders if she might get away with saying just that. Here, my friends, is exactly where we are. Every single one of us.

Now that she's been distracted, jolted from her party blues, she decides to give herself over to the fun of presents, like a birthday party kid. Because you can discipline yourself to anything, even to pleasure.

Colleen sits down on the arm of the sofa to help, to take care of the opened gifts. People have been thoughtful. There are athletic socks and gadgets for Jude's kitchen and a couple of small, unusual mirrors for her collection, and because she can lose a pair a week, mint-green, huge and ridiculous sunglasses, like Cher in her prime might have worn. Tommy has given her a badly wrapped white hat, a soft angora tam, and unable to stop himself he steps closer to insist that she put it on, so everyone can admire it. Which Jude reluctantly then boldly does.

"Does this mean I'm finally a figure skater?" Jude asks.

And she is right. The tam is exactly the kind of thing a pretty, innocent girl might have worn ice-skating and, looking at her, you can almost if not quite see her in a short, twirly skirt and those flesh-coloured, saggy tights. Up on her picks, ready, and then pushing off, cutting her figure-eight.

She and Richard have given Jude a two-cup teapot painted with a Hopper lake house, and Liam and Julie and Kate together have given her an elegant thin belt, because Julie has guessed that her mother-in-law is still vain about her not-yet-gone-to-rack-and-ruin waist. The waist that was always in unspoken competition with Sandra's, that Gus can still wrap his hands around. Jude holds the belt high to show it off and then she takes it and curls it up again in its box.

The last gift is a leather journal with a black satin bookmark. It's from Jude's neighbour, a woman who has lived on her street longer than anyone, a soft-spoken widow who is a champion of introspection, who, knowing Jude had lost Sandra, came to visit her once, to recommend introspection, and patience.

Jude confessed soon after she and Sandra met her that she had once kept an early adolescent diary, for the usual reasons, because she was hopeful and gullible and frantic. She said she could remember a pink plastic book held open to a crucial page, and prim handwriting and arrows connecting one important thought to another and stars and double stars for emphasis, things rubbed out, whole paragraphs scratched away, and then the immediacy, the sting of lonely complaint, which used to be called, whenever someone was telling her what she felt, hurt feelings.

Holding her new journal and standing up to embrace her neighbour, Jude thinks now that she might follow Sandra's example, that she might even enjoy trying to account for things in writing. For herself, for instance. Confiding to a journal you could compose yourself. Because whether or not you liked it, at this age you had the benefit of hindsight and, looking in that direction, it should be possible to call up distance and sifting and deliberation. Restraint and comprehension. Thankfulness? A touch of mercy? And from these maybe you can get your life back?

As she'd opened each of the gifts, she had handed the wrapping paper, tissue, ribbons, sprigs of dried flowers and all, to Gus, who'd crushed it in his builder's hands and then made a game of tossing it overhand into the open mouth of the garbage bag Julie was holding, all of which kept him entertained but evidently made Julie angry. It would be Gus's determined informality that upset her, the length and breadth of his blunt-fingered hands, his veto on the pretty tableau.

When she stands up to say her thank-yous, she turns to let everyone get a good look at her pleasure, because, why not, why should she hold it back? She decides to echo Liam's toast, to name Gus and Sandra and Jack and Colleen and Richard and then last but not least, Liam. And Julie. But before she can start, Julie calls from the kitchen that it's time to cut the birthday cake, and Gus deserts her to go to his bank of central switches to dim the lights, in waves, so very proud to show off his complicated, party-ambience wiring.

Colleen is watching Julie carry the cake in through the dark, through the guests, the sixty-five parts of the candlelight wavering with each high-heeled step, but burning on. Julie made the cake herself, from scratch. She came over that morning for a little help, and Colleen had made sure of the icing, finding Sandra's recipe among her own and holding the sticky page flat for Julie to follow. Julie had said those words, from scratch, the same way she might have bragged that she'd tanned the leather for her red spikes. The cake is rectangular and big, really a couple of cakes stuck together with seafoam icing, which is sometimes hard to get right because of the temperamental nature of egg whites, and which has been Jude's favourite since Sandra first made it for her. Colleen makes her way to the buffet to get Jude's mother's big-occasion sterling-silver cake knife in its velvet bag. Luckily, although Julie's cake might be called grand, it is not pristine, it is not too perfect to spoil.

And now Jude has blown out her candles, with her eyes shut tight and just the one silent wish. Because in the last year she has taken charge of her wayward wishes. I've boiled them down, she would have told Sandra.

Gus brings his lights back up, but then when Colleen tries to slip her the silver knife, it falls heavily to the carpet. Gus retrieves it and after he wipes it on his rolled-up shirt sleeve he puts it carefully into her hand, wrapping her fingers tight around the shaft in case she might have lost the reflex. It's a gesture he will expect to enjoy again later.

She watches the faces lift as they start to sing their song to her. The hired woman at the piano pounds it out, "Happy birthday to you, happy birthday to you." She thinks she can hear Gus and Liam and Richard and Tommy, each of them loud and low and unabashed but nevertheless clear, distinct from each other and from all the other men in the room. She hears Julie's high soprano, a trained, powerful, insolent voice but no less beautiful, and close at her side she can hear Colleen, who can't sing a note.

When it's over she bends to cut the first messy, ceremonial piece and then she stands up straight again, running a finger along the blade of the knife to get some of the icing. "Seafoam," she announces. The solid sterling knife is heavy, she has forgotten its weight. It's time, she thinks. Everyone is waiting for her to say the right thing. Now she will echo Liam's toast.

But she doesn't. She can't. Because Richard is standing in front of her answering his cellphone, and seeing this, the guests start to fall back into their smaller clusters.

Then Richard says, "Jack's coming. He just called from the restaurant."

"Good," Gus says. "Good for him." He turns to smile at Jude and Colleen.

"He's bringing a friend," Richard says. "He hopes that's all right."

"A friend?" Colleen asks.

"A woman?" Jude asks.

"You knew?" Colleen says to Richard. "And you didn't warn me? So the rumour is true? He's selling?" She thinks about Jack's visit that morning with the journals, which are piled in her spare bedroom. So having got himself a friend, Jack has run short of room? "Does she have a name?" she asks. Willing it to be a woman none of them know.

"Penny," Richard says.

Penny the unknown.

"She's young?" Jude asks.

"No," Gus says. "She's as old as you are."

"Oh, good," she says. "Then she'll be harmless."

Liam and Julie lift the cake to take it to the buffet, where Julie will serve it, but no one else approaches them.

"This is too damned soon for me," Colleen says. She looks at Jude but Jude has decided to put on her strictly disciplined let's-leave-this-for-later smile.

"Don't," Richard says.

"And don't you," Gus says to Jude, for insurance.

"Don't?" Jude asks, her smile gone now. "You're telling me, *don't*?"

Colleen wants the party to be over before Jack and his friend get there, because then there won't be any crowd to ease his entrance, to deaden its impact. But no one looks ready to leave. The coffee has been set up with the cake on the buffet in the dining room and the servers are bringing in trays filled with small glasses of liqueurs and pyramids of dark chocolates. And people are coming over to admire Jude's gifts.

When the doorbell rings, Liam hurries to welcome Jack and his friend into the party. Standing under the living room arch, Penny is grey and slight and hesitant and she's wearing big silver earrings that look like something you'd find in another country. She is also wearing tights and a deep purple tunic, which is a combination that neither Jude nor Colleen has worn or even seen in decades, except perhaps on some little girl. Richard crosses the room to take Penny's quickly offered hand and then he leans down to kiss her cheek and Gus is soon there to kiss it again, and then they both stand back and point her, as if she's lost, to them.

They turn together.

"Be nice," Jude says. "Nice as can be." These are Sandra words, used only when necessary, to stop something awful.

"She won't care about us," Colleen says. "Not if she's smart. And she looks pretty smart to me."

"But Jack might care," Jude says.

And now Penny is in front of them with Jack beside her, with his protective arm around another small waist. Standing this close they can see that she is delicately pretty, with small pretty eyes, and they can see a wedding band, thin with wear. Jack is working hard to hold a neutral expression, and failing, because if he isn't jubilant, he is happy. Neither one of them is jubilant, but only happy. And wanting, needing, looking for absolutely nothing here.

Jack takes a surprising step closer to wrap Colleen in his arms, to give her not a simple hug but a full embrace. And she lets herself absorb it. Someone watching might think they are looking at the embrace of a common history, or a depth of friendship, but what she feels in Jack's arms is the weight of an end. The suggestion that they have been wrong, all of them, to believe that anything, that any of it, could win the day.

Jude watches and waits for her own embrace. All she wants now is equality, and that's what Jack gives her. "Happy birthday, love," he says.

Jack does realize, stepping back, that Penny will have no reason to want to connect with Colleen and Jude. They won't have enough time now anyway, to work her into their old stories or their stances or their grief. When he gets his chance he will tell them the only thing they need to know. She is kind, he'll say. And she's fun. And, you have to let me be what I've had to become. He has already told the kids some of it, and then a bit more. Including their mother's suggestion. And then he left it with them.

There is no easy way to explain to any of them that he doesn't want to live his life without this kind, private woman, this chance to maybe use what he's learned. Or that there will always be costs and benefits, which will be his and his alone.

Gus and Richard come over to join them but not much is said. "Nice to finally meet all of you," Penny offers. "Terrific house . . . Oh, sixty-five isn't old, not any more." She is a retired teacher and Jack met her in the market downtown, when both of them were splitting off a couple of bananas from a useless, family-sized clump, as in some smarmy commercial. How funny. "And she has something in common with April," Jack says. "Because she's been active, she has been committed to the environment for a long time." They all know it's coming, certainly, that there are choices to make and habits to drop. The bottled tap water at the gym and the endless plastic, the still-mad packaging and the toxic kitchen cleansers. The status cars and the flying around. Never the cottages but probably the half-empty houses.

Penny is not divorced but a long-time widow who also lost her one child, and Colleen and Jude both know that this entitles her to their profound sympathy, or at least to something a few paces back from their cold, unexpressed curiosity. Their wintry curiosity. But moving toward that sympathy, they both think they might have caught a wave of satisfaction on the small, pretty face: I am not what you two have feared. Not even close.

Colleen would say that she hasn't been fearing anything. And Jude, even if she's begun to wonder if Jack can continue alone, has never imagined anything like the tights and tunic, which she assumed to be gone from the world, and certainly not the return of Sandra's naturally small waist, either. But here it is in front of them. A smart little soon-to-be-naked woman. A possibly smart little soon-to-be-second wife.

Jack takes Penny across the room to introduce her to Julie and Kate, and to Tommy, and to say hello to Paul and Kelly. And then he leads her around to a few of the guests, most of whom seem only mildly, politely interested. But they don't stay long, and when they go to the hall with Gus for their coats, everyone else is finally ready to follow, to offer their good-nights. Tommy is the last to leave and, as always, in character, he kisses them all, men and women alike. Except Julie, who quickly steps away and then, to cover for this, lifts her camera and invites them, Gus and Jude and Tommy and Liam and Kate, to line up for her. To smile into the future at grandchildren not yet born. Which makes Jude wonder about the questions those grandchildren might have, one day, about the names put to this picture. Liam and Tommy Davis. Gus and Kate Bjornson. Jude Tait.

The pianist asks if they want her to stay through their nightcaps but Gus tells her no and slips her an envelope and Liam walks her to her car. The caterers box everything up and carry it out to the van, their quiet servitude dissolved and replaced with exhaustion and a lot of banging around. The young man in the hairnet who cheered for Colleen in the catfight winks at her and one of the older women calls out, "Happy birthday," as she closes the door behind her, looking at Colleen by mistake.

With the house emptied, Jude sits down in her red swivel chair with her back to the window on the yard, and Colleen takes the chair beside it. Gus and Richard go into the kitchen for a promised mug of Julie's green tea and, with the kettle on its way to the boil, Julie and Kate join the older women, sitting on the floor. But Liam comes out of the kitchen and pulls them up to his side.

"I think we'll say good-night," he says. "We are beat."

"I loved it," Jude says. "Loved it. And the belt."

"Good production, guys," Colleen says.

"Yes," Julie says. "It was a good production."

Kate hits Julie on the side of the head as if she doesn't mean it and Jude half stands to say good-night, but the three of them lean down to her in her red chair, and then they leave to climb the stairs to bed. The kettle sings and Gus brings in two mugs of green tea and then he goes back to Richard at the kitchen table.

Jude rests her warm mug on her stomach. Nothing has ever been said about their fight after Sandra's visitation, or about Spain, or the upstairs bottle of Cutty Sark. Or about Colleen's on-the-face-of-it normal phone call a few weeks after the funeral, when Jude's prepared response was silenced. And maybe because they have had to find their own way back, there hasn't been a fight since.

Jane Fonda be damned, she thinks, sixty-five is old. Old as the bleedin' hills. People die every day of the week at sixty-five, surprising no one. Certainly you can say that forty isn't old, you can even say now that fifty isn't old, but, like so many fine things, it has to end somewhere. And this living room is somewhere.

Colleen is not going to tell Jude her story about the women in the kitchen because it would be wrong to dump such an ugly episode into her temporarily happy, party-loving, belt-loving head. She will suggest to Richard on the way home that they are going to keep this one to themselves, and if he has already shared it with Gus, well, Gus is safe enough. For all his scattershot indignation, Gus does understand the difference between one kind of story and another.

She will, however, tell her about this morning's delivery of Sandra's journals. That Jack is clearing things out. She will tell her tomorrow.

Jude is staring down into her tea. "No bubbles for me," she says. She leans over to check Colleen's mug. "Bubbles are money or friends?"

"Can't remember," Colleen says. "Do not care."

"We should have hired a fortune teller," Jude says. "Next time, for your party."

"I've just seen enough future to last me for a while," Colleen says.

Jude takes a drink. "We should likely ease off," she says. "One woman follows another. My good man followed another, and what's the difference? And anyway, who the hell are we?"

"So love is serial," Colleen says, making a gun of her hand. "Bang. Bang. Bang."

"And Gus?" Jude asks.

"But with Gus, you were replacing something you regretted," Colleen says. "Someone better forgotten."

"And have I forgotten Tommy?" Jude asks, ready to laugh. "God, is there some way I could get to do that?"

They can hear Richard and Gus at the kitchen table, talking and then quiet, talking again, waiting for them, hoping that nothing will have to be said about Jack and Penny, not tonight. A room away, a day away, they can both still feel that kind of hope in their men.

"Did you see her talking to Paul and Kelly?" Colleen asks.

"Yes," Jude says. She has forgotten Sandra's kids in all this. "If they're wise, they will approve of her," she says. "Because they might have less to worry about if Jack is, well, loved."

"Might," Colleen says.

"At least she's not half his age," Jude says, stupidly. Forgetting Richard's mistakes. "So he's spared us the usual drill."

"There's that, I suppose," Colleen says.

"No one gets lost here," Jude says. "Jack wants to fill the time he's got left. End of story."

"And loyalty?" Colleen asks. She swivels her chair to face the backyard, because even with more than fifteen years between tonight and Spain, there is no guarantee that Jude will be ready to allow that word.

"Loyalty?" Jude asks, turning her own chair. "Before we left Spain, to back me off, you told me a little something. I think you might remember. You told me that loyalty is not as pretty as it looks."

They study their flat reflections in the glass. Beyond the window, in the black night above the empty January trees, they can see the moon, which is misty, and attentive, as if it could stay exactly where it is. The stars are shrouded but Gus has strung his old constellation of tiny, tawdry, Christmas lights on a small Wichita blue juniper. His winter sky brought down to earth.

Soon after Sandra's death, Jude decided that Colleen had got it not quite right in Spain, that loyalty might be just pretty enough, and she decided too that she would be willing to live with its steadfast pull, even in the absence. Because that's what she has been left, Sandra's rope of stone beads and an absence that is ready to take its part of every one of her days. From the way people talk, she sometimes half expects something different, after a year. Gratitude, as you often hear, for the life lived. Or consolation. From some high storehouse of distracting memory. But none of this has come.

"Did you ever ask her if she was afraid?" Colleen asks.

"No," Jude says. "Although I don't think she was." She watches their reflection in the window, but no brave ghost comes to stand behind them. "A posed glass portrait," she says. "*Two Women.*"

"Only two," Colleen says. "But almost convincing. Close."

Their glass portrait is only and almost because Colleen has begun to believe that it was Sandra alone who made them three-dimensional, who pulled them up out of themselves. But the other thing she believes is that you have to protect yourself against grief's ambush. She thinks about their three unlikely lives, told and retold. Three temperaments made complementary, somehow, in the telling.

In giving their glass pose a name, Jude has reminded her of all the galleries they walked through, the grand foreign rooms filled with grand formal portraits, with Sandra often a room ahead but then slowed down by some distended royal family or by lovers or ascending angels or a field of slaughtered soldiers or a study of bridge builders or of peasants, bent over a crippling crop. As far as she remembers there were never any portraits of exhausted, faithful friends.

There is activity in the kitchen, the sound of a tap, and then Richard comes to stand behind Colleen and Gus behind Jude. Which means that their reflection is doubled and doubled and doubled again, with the coupling not just between them but from Gus to Jude and to her good friend, and from Richard to Colleen and to her good friend, and from the one man to the other, neither of whom is ever going to leave anyone.

The four of them wait with their separate, commonplace thoughts, about what has been taken from them and what's been left. About a perfected, dying Sandra and, now, tonight, this brand new Jack, and about six kids who for better or worse have been set loose in the world, and about the brutal, double slap of infidelity and the annoying if cheerful constancy of an ex-husband, about food and wine and pianists and toasts and hats and journals and belts.

And then Jude, looking at all of the faces reflected at once, asks, "Are we more convincing now?"

And, "Yes," Colleen says. "I would have to say yes."

Neither of the men is going to ask the question or any other question, because they are so used to it, the thoughts from nowhere, the qualified encouragement, the strange eruptions of laughter. And they've had enough. They are tired and not young. They want their beds and the women in them.

So their hands come down on their wives' shoulders to coax them up out of their red chairs, back into a late night, into an undone house that will hold until morning the remains of another successful party. The two wineglasses left carelessly on the dark piano, the chairs brought in from the dining room, the overstuffed garbage bag, the pile of gifts, the cards. The half-gone cake with the big-occasion sterling-silver knife still in it.

And, warm in his car with Penny, and close to her home now, asking his question and waiting, Jack can almost imagine this. What he's doing, though, is watching the street lights ahead. They seem to be farther apart on the outskirts of the city, and the wires that connect them are heavy with Lake Huron snow. But still, that light.